“All I can think about is kissing you.”

He paused, his forehead damp and his hands clammy. In desperation, he said, “You’re in my head, damn it. And in my gut. I can’t sleep. Tell me I’m not alone in this delusion. Or tell me I’m an ass, and I’ll go away.”

Almost in slow motion, he reached out and took her hand in his. “I need you, Dani. Badly.”

She looked at him with an expression that was partly fear and partly the same burning curiosity tearing him apart. She took a step toward him. “Nathaniel.”

The way she said his name, husky and sweet, was his undoing.

* * *

Billionaire Boss, Holiday Baby
is part of Mills & Boon Desire’s No. 1
bestselling series, Billionaires and Babies:
Powerful men…wrapped around
their babies’ little fingers

BILLIONAIRE BOSS, HOLIDAY BABY

BY
JANICE MAYNARD

First Published in Great Britain 2017
By Mills & Boon, an imprint of HarperCollins*Publishers*
1 London Bridge Street, London, SE1 9GF

ISBN: 978-0-263-92838-9

51-1017

Our policy is to use papers that are natural, renewable and recyclable products and made from wood grown in sustainable forests. The logging and manufacturing processes conform to the legal environmental regulations of the country of origin.

Printed and bound in Spain
by CPI, Barcelona

USA TODAY bestselling author **Janice Maynard** loved books and writing even as a child. But it took multiple rejections before she sold her first manuscript. Since 2002, she has written over forty-five books and novellas. Janice lives in east Tennessee with her husband, Charles. They love hiking, traveling and spending time with family.

You can connect with Janice at:
www.janicemaynard.com
Twitter.com/janicemaynard
Facebook.com/janicemaynardreaderpage
Facebook.com/janicesmaynard
and Instagram.com/janicemaynard.

For Charles,
who makes every Christmas special…

One

December 23

The calendar might say otherwise, but for Dani Meadows, *today* had been the longest day of the year. The morning started out okay. Business as usual. Her taciturn but oh-so-handsome boss had not by any stretch of the imagination been exhibiting a holiday mood.

She'd spent several hours locating hard-to-reach suppliers who were already in vacation mode. While most of the country was shutting down for a long end-of-the-year break, Nathaniel Winston, president and owner of New Century Tech, was looking for ways to increase the bottom line in the upcoming months. He worked hard. Dani, his executive assistant, matched him email for email, working lunch for working lunch.

The only place their schedules differed was in the fact that Dani left for home at five every day, while Nathaniel sometimes worked well into the evening.

He didn't expect that of her. In fact, he was an extremely fair boss who never asked anything of his employees that was out of line. If there were occasionally situations where the company needed an extra measure of devotion, Nathaniel never demanded it. Such assignments were strictly voluntary. The employees who participated were compensated well.

Dani glanced at her computer screen and sighed. She'd just received another out-of-office reply. That made a dozen in the last two hours.

Nathaniel should give up and go home himself. That, however, was as likely to happen as the snow-pocalypse forecast to hit Atlanta tonight. The capital of the Peach State got ice occasionally. Sometimes a dollop of snow. But never in December.

Yesterday had been a balmy fifty-five degrees. Today, though, a cold front was predicted to move through. In Dani's experience, that meant a miserable rain event and temps in the upper thirties. No worries. She kept her rain boots in a tote under her desk. A sprint to the MARTA station during a downpour wouldn't hurt her.

She raised her voice to be heard above the whoosh of the heat kicking on through the vents. "Nathaniel? I'm not having any luck. Do you want me to keep a record of these calls and emails and try again the first week in January?"

A tall, dark-haired man appeared without warning in the doorway to her office. He was overdue for a haircut, but his tailored suit was pristine. Intense brown eyes and a strong jaw shadowed with the beginnings of late-day stubble contributed to an appearance that was unequivocally male.

He raked a hand through his hair, for a brief moment appearing frazzled. The show of emotion was so unlike him, she blinked. "Um, you okay, boss? Is there anything else you want me to do before I leave?"

He leaned a shoulder against the door frame and frowned. "You've worked as my assistant for almost two years, right?"

She gulped inwardly. "Yes." Customarily, she went to his office and not the other way around.

Instead of answering, he glanced around her cramped quarters and frowned. "We need to do something in here. New carpet maybe. And furniture. Make that a priority when you get back."

"Yes, sir."

When he scowled, she backtracked quickly. "Yes, Nathaniel." His name threatened to stick in her throat.

In the privacy of her own thoughts she often referred to him as Nathaniel, but it was another thing entirely to say it aloud, even though he insisted that all his employees call him by his first name.

She noted he had said when *you* get back, not *we*. Which probably meant he would be working in this building all alone during the holidays. He didn't have any family that she knew of, though anything was possible. He was a private man.

It was ridiculous to feel sorry for him. The guy was a gazillionaire. If he wanted a homey, cozy Christmas, he could buy himself one.

After a long, awkward silence, Nathaniel glanced at his watch and grimaced. "I suppose I have to make an appearance downstairs?" The tone of his voice made it a question.

Dani nodded. "They'll be expecting you." She indicated a manila envelope on the corner of her desk. "I have the bonus checks right there."

"You could give them out."

She sensed he was only half joking. Just in case, she

answered seriously, "Your employees like hearing from you, Nathaniel. Getting a perk from the boss himself is a nice way to start the holidays."

"What about you?"

This conversation was taking a turn that made her palms sweat. "Payroll put a check in there for me, too," she said.

He grimaced. "You deserve more. This place wouldn't run half as well without you."

"I appreciate the sentiment, but the usual bonus check is fine. Let me shut down my computer, and I'll be right behind you."

"I'll wait."

She took that terse statement to mean *in the reception area.* But no. Nathaniel watched her every move for the next five minutes as she took care of the brief routine she repeated at the end of every workday. She decided not to take her purse and tote to the party. It would be easier to pop back up here before she went home. Because the office contained sensitive information as well as her valuables, she slipped a key card that opened the executive suite into her pocket. If the boss got trapped at the party, she didn't want to have to wait.

At last, she stood and smoothed the skirt of her simple black dress. She'd chosen sophistication over traditional holiday colors. At five feet four inches and with plenty of curves, she tended to look like a perky tomato when she wore all red.

Nathaniel studied her in silence. There was nothing insulting or offensive about his regard. Still, she knew without a doubt that in this moment he saw her as a woman and not simply a piece of office equipment.

She picked up the envelope with the checks and handed it to him. "Shall we go?" Her heart beat far faster than it should. It was becoming more and more difficult to act normally. Feeling so aware of him rattled her. Something had to change, or she was going to end up embarrassing herself.

No one would blink an eye if she and her boss entered the large conference room downstairs together. Nathaniel Winston might as well be a monk. His reputation with the opposite sex was not only squeaky clean, it was nonexistent.

That fact shouldn't have pleased her. But she was attracted to him, and in some tiny corner of her psyche, a fantasy flourished. It wasn't as if she had any real shot at a relationship with him. Even so, his single status kept her reluctant fascination alive. It was impossible to be near him day after day without wondering what it would be like to share his bed.

Dani felt on edge as they walked toward the elevator and then headed twelve floors down in silence. Nathaniel had his hands jammed in his pockets. More than once she had wished she could read his mind. In the beginning, it was only because she wanted to know if he thought she was doing a good job. Now that she had a serious crush on him, her curiosity was far more personal.

Why didn't he date? Or maybe he did go out but in secret. Not likely. What woman would put up with his workaholic schedule?

On impulse, she blurted out a clumsy conversational gambit. "Will you be traveling for the holidays?"

He shot her a sideways glance tinged with incredulity. "No."

Poor man. She had probably shocked him. No one asked the boss about his personal life. Dani was the closest employee to him, yet she managed to be remarkably circumspect despite the many questions she had. At this point, the deliberate choice to avoid any hint of intimacy, even conversationally, was the smart thing to do.

She wanted to learn everything there was to know about Nathaniel—of course she did. Keeping a professional distance was a matter of self-preservation. By relegating the man at her side to a box labeled *boss*, she told herself she could keep from getting hurt.

The elevator dinged as the door opened. The unmistakable sounds of merrymaking drifted down the carpeted hallway. “Well,” Nathaniel muttered. “Here goes.”

As bizarre as it sounded, Dani thought he was nervous. Surely not. Her boss was well educated, well traveled and wildly successful at a young age. There was no reason at all for him to dread this momentary formality.

Just inside the doorway of the crowded room, Dani abandoned the man who drew attention with no more than a quick, guarded smile.

As people greeted him, she found a group of women she had known from the beginning of her employment at NCT. Several of them shared a Pilates class. A couple of others had bonded over their young children. Ever since Dani became Nathaniel’s assistant, though, her coworkers treated her with a certain deference.

She didn’t particularly like it, but she understood it.

As she sipped a glass of punch and nibbled on a cheese straw, she noted the men and women who had already imbibed to the peril of their careers. Dani had nothing against alcohol. Sadly, though, some employees lost all circumspection when they enjoyed the office party a little too much.

Nathaniel was socializing, though his posture betrayed his lack of ease. At least it did to Dani. He was playing the genial host, but he would rather be most anywhere else. She’d bet her last dollar on it.

Nathaniel was never too excited about the office Christmas party. He wasn't a warm, fuzzy kind of guy. On the other hand, he was no Scrooge, either. At his urging, Dani had planned this lavish, catered affair complete with an open bar. The festivities had begun at four o'clock and were still going strong two hours later.

At last, Nathaniel made his holiday toast and passed out bonuses to key players of the various divisions. His speech was wry and funny and remarkably charming. Dani had to step forward when he called her name. "Thanks," she muttered.

Their fingers brushed briefly. "Merry Christmas, Dani," he said gruffly.

"Thank you." Her throat tightened inexplicably. Boyfriends were a dime a dozen. She needed a good job more than she needed a fling with her boss. But for the last year and a half—the length of time she had been fantasizing about Nathaniel—the idea of a physical relationship, no matter how unlikely, had made it increasingly uncomfortable for her to work with him. So much so that she had actually polished up her résumé and sent out half a dozen applications already.

During her five years working at New Century Tech, she had completed an MBA at Emory. She was definitely overqualified for the job she now occupied, however working as Nathaniel's executive assistant paid extremely well. Not only that, but watching him operate in the business world, learning from him, was invaluable experience.

Time moved on. People did, too, or they stagnated. It made perfect sense to extract herself from the temptation of a possible affair with the boss, and even more sense to pursue opportunities that would advance her career.

Unfortunately, all the pep talks in the world didn't make it any easier to do what she *knew* she had to do.

A couple of weeks ago—as soon as she emailed the first batch of job applications—the guilt began. NCT was a great place to work. Nathaniel had been a phenomenal boss from day one. Maybe she was jumping too soon.

Still, something was beginning to change, ever so slightly. She didn't think she had betrayed her intense fascination. Even so, she was getting a vibe from Nathaniel recently that was more personal than business.

Or maybe it was the mistletoe and her overactive imagination. If those feelings were real, she was in trouble.

A commotion on the far side of the room derailed her wistful thoughts. The maroon and navy drapes had been drawn before the party to shut out the gray December day. The heavy cloth panels, festooned with lighted garlands, gave the room a festive feel. Just now, someone had peeked out and received a big surprise.

A rain/snow mix had already begun to fall. The usually crowded thoroughfare in front of the building was alarmingly empty. Though local snowstorm forecasts were often disregarded because of one too many near misses, apparently this one might be the real deal.

Nathaniel assessed the situation in a glance and acted with his customary confidence.

"Let's wrap this up, folks. Unless some of you want to spend the holidays sleeping at your desks, I'd suggest you head for home ASAP."

He didn't have to tell them twice. It was Friday on a holiday weekend. A number of the staff had saved vacation days so they could be off until after the New Year. Suddenly, there was a mass exodus.

As Dani watched, Nathaniel said a quiet word here and there, making sure that anyone who was impaired ended up in the charge of a designated driver.

In half an hour, the room was empty except for Dani

and the boss, who stood in the doorway saying a few last goodbyes. Without thinking about it, she began to tidy the tables. Fortunately, there was not much food left. She chucked it all in a large trash container and stacked the trays. New Century Tech used a nearby catering company for all their events.

As she began folding the soiled tablecloths into a neat stack, Nathaniel startled her by speaking from behind her shoulder.

"Leave that alone," he said abruptly. "That's not your job. The janitorial staff will take care of it in the morning."

Dani turned slowly and lifted an eyebrow. "If the snow does what they're saying it will, I doubt anyone is going to go anywhere anytime soon."

"That's a lot of *anys*," he teased.

"Well, I'm right," she grumbled. "Besides, nobody wants to look at this mess when it's three or four days old."

"Do you honestly believe the storm is going to be that bad?"

The Weather Channel was headquartered in Atlanta. Dani knew the forecasters by name. At one time in high school, she had actually thought about going into meteorology as a career.

"They say it's possible. Moisture is riding up from the Gulf of Mexico and colliding with the cold air. Even when the snow tapers off, we may get ice on top."

Nathaniel grimaced. "That sounds lovely."

His sarcasm made her grin. "Look at it this way. We only get hammered a few times a decade. Apparently, we're overdue."

"Well, in that case, shouldn't you be getting out of here?"

"I'll catch the six-thirty train. I'll be fine."

"What if they shut down the system?"

For the first time, a trickle of unease slid through her veins. That thought had never occurred to her. Her car was parked at a commuter lot four stops north. What was the likelihood she'd be able to drive home even if MARTA took her where she needed to go?

This time, riding the elevator up and back down was more about expediency than anything intimate. While Nathaniel grabbed what he needed from his office, Dani shrugged into her coat, tugged on her boots and adjusted the strap on her purse so she could use it as a cross-body bag. She wanted her hands free to hang on to stair rails if necessary.

Outside, the city was eerily quiet. The snow was heavier now, blanketing buildings and muffling sound. Nathaniel cursed quietly beneath his breath when he saw the conditions. "I'll drive you to the train station," he said, his tone brooking no opposition.

"Thanks," Dani replied, not even bothering with a token protest. On a normal day, the half-mile walk was pleasant exercise. Under these conditions, she'd never make it in time, not to mention the fact that she'd be a frozen mess.

New Century Tech's main parking facility was a three-level garage attached to the back of the building. For VIPs, a private side-street lot big enough for a dozen spaces provided easy access and the assurance that no clumsy drivers would back into a high-end vehicle.

Nathaniel drove a shiny black Mercedes with all the bells and whistles. Dani had been inside it only once, when she and the boss had gone together across town to present a proposal to a clothing firm seeking to update their online presence and ordering capabilities. Today, when they rounded the corner of the building and spotted Nathaniel's car—the only one in the lot—she had a sinking feeling that Nathaniel's offer of a ride had been premature.

The Mercedes was coated with snow, and there were no marks on the ground. Either the various vice presidents had parked in the garage today, or they had left long enough ago for the storm to cover their tracks. Something about the solitary car looked odd.

Nathaniel was the first to respond. "What the hell?"

He jogged the last few feet, Dani close on his heels. They stopped abruptly in tandem. Dani blinked. "Is that a car seat?" she asked, her voice rising an octave in disbelief.

Nathaniel lifted the wooly blanket covering the oddly shaped lump. "Good God. It's a baby." His head snapped around, his gaze scanning the immediate area. The blanket was peppered with tiny bits of snow, certainly not enough to indicate the child had been there more than a few minutes.

Dani, too, peeked under the blanket and gasped. An infant, maybe six months old, slept peacefully in a baby carrier. The child was covered from head to toe in a fleecy one-piece snowsuit, but even so, the temperatures were dangerously cold.

"Call 911," Nathaniel said, his voice as icy as their surroundings. "I'm going to look around. Whoever did this must be close. My guess is they're watching us to make sure we retrieve the kid."

Dani was afraid to unfasten the straps and take the baby out. The heavy carrier was offering at least some protection from the elements.. As long as the baby slept, he or she must not be terribly uncomfortable. The snowsuit was pink. Dani took a wild shot that the child was a girl. The baby's cheeks were a healthy color. Her chest rose and fell at reassuring intervals.

Hoping she was doing the right thing, Dani removed her gloves and dialed the authorities.

* * *

Nathaniel was pissed. He'd received several texts in the last few days from a number he recognized all too well, offering veiled threats. Never in his wildest imagination had he imagined something like this happening to him. The escapade had his ex written all over it.

Ophelia wasn't actually an "ex" anything. Nathaniel had met her at an in-town conference over a year ago and spent two nights in her hotel bed. That had been the end of it. Or so he thought.

He'd used protection. No way in hell was this baby his, despite what Ophelia's rambling emails had insinuated. If she had ever come right out and accused him of fathering her child, Nathaniel would have secured a lawyer and taken the necessary steps to pinpoint the baby's paternity.

He stood in the shadow of his own building, covered his eyes to keep the snow out of them and scanned windows near and far. Damn it. Ophelia could be anywhere. What was she trying to pull?

At last, he gave up his futile search. Dani stood where he had left her, one hand resting protectively on the edge of the car seat. "I found a note," she said, holding it out to him. "I read it. I'm sorry. I guess I shouldn't have."

Nathaniel unfolded the elegant card with a sick feeling in the pit of his stomach. The contents were much as he had expected:

Dear Nathaniel:
I cannot care for our baby right now. You're my only hope. When I get my life back together, we'll talk.
Yours always,
Ophelia

He closed his eyes and took deep breaths, trying not to overreact. Women had tried to trap men with this ruse since the beginning of time. He'd done nothing wrong. He had nothing to fear.

Crushing the note in his fist, he shoved it in his pocket and opened his eyes to find Dani staring at him with a stricken expression.

"It's not mine," he insisted. "I went out with a crazy woman a time or two. She's trying to blackmail me or something. I don't know. What did the police say? How soon can they get here?"

Dani hunched her shoulders against the wind. "They weren't very encouraging. The snow is causing pileups all over the city."

His heart pounded in his chest. "What about the foster care system? Surely they can send someone."

"Do you really want to entrust a baby to a stranger on the Friday afternoon of a long holiday weekend? Most foster families are wonderful, but you hear horror stories..." Dani trailed off, her expression indicating that she was upset. Maybe with the situation. Maybe with him.

"Fine." He sighed. "What exactly do you think we should do?"

"We?" She stared at him as if he had grown two heads. "I'm walking to the MARTA station. If I'm lucky, my route will still be open."

Atlanta's transit system was only partially underground. Unlike other major cities, Atlanta did not have enough snow-removal equipment to deal with a weather event of this size. Blizzards were so rare the expenditure would be wildly extravagant.

Nathaniel's palms started to sweat inside his gloves. "You can't go yet," he said. "I need help." The words threatened to stick in his throat. He wasn't a man accustomed to needing *anyone*. Dani wasn't just anyone, though. He was counting on her soft heart and her overdeveloped sense of responsibility to sway her.

"What exactly do you think I can do?" she asked. Her eyes held a mix of dubious suspicion and the urge to run.

Nathaniel recognized the urge. He felt it in spades. "You're a woman. Help me get the kid to my condo. Let's get her settled. After that, I'll call a car service to take you home." Without waiting for an answer, he unlocked the car and leaned in to toss his briefcase on the back seat.

Dani thumped him on the shoulder, hard enough that he jerked and hit his head on the door frame. "Ouch, damn it. What was that for?" he asked, whirling around.

"Are you crazy?" Dani asked. "You can't drive around with an unsecured infant carrier, especially with snow on the ground."

In all his emotional turmoil over realizing Ophelia had dumped a baby in his lap, Nathaniel had lost track of the weather. Now he blinked and focused on the world surrounding them. The snow was at least two inches deep already and showed no signs at all of letting up. "Good God," he said weakly. "This is a nightmare."

Had he said that last bit aloud? Maybe not. Dani wasn't giving him any more of those disapproving looks. Instead, she huddled miserably against the side of his car, using her body to keep the falling snow from reaching the baby.

"We're out of options," he said, his brain whirling like a hamster on a wheel. "I'll put the seat belt around the carrier. My condo isn't all that far. Three miles. Come on. The longer we stand here, the colder we'll be." Without waiting for his unflappable executive assistant to protest, he retrieved the infant carrier, covered it with the blanket and scooped it up.

Holy hell. How did new mothers do this? The thing felt like it weighed fifty pounds.

Strapping it into the back seat was an exercise in frustration and guilt. To be honest, he half expected Dani to turn around and trudge away in the opposite direction, heading for the train station and home. But she joined him in the car.

The wave of relief he experienced was alarming. Was he honestly that afraid to be stranded alone with a baby, or did the idea of spending time with Dani outside the office hold a certain appeal?

She was a very attractive woman always, but today—dressed up for the office party—she exuded a warm, sexy charm that made him want to forget every one of his self-imposed rules.

Though it probably wasn't wise, he took one hand off the wheel and loosened his tie. Having Dani sit so close to him tested his patience and his self-control.

New Century Tech was located in a trendy section of Atlanta known as Buckhead. Elegant glass office buildings stood amongst quirky restaurants and specialty shops selling everything from expensive watches to high-priced real estate. Nathaniel's penthouse condo offered him the privacy he demanded along with an unparalleled view of the city.

Unfortunately, today's drive was not going to be easy. Though he managed to back out of the parking space and exit onto the street, he felt the tires slip and slide beneath him. He barely managed to avoid sideswiping a fire hydrant.

With his eyes on the road and a firm grip on the steering wheel, he focused on the objective at hand. Reach his condo. Rest and regroup. What he hadn't expected was to have Dani tug at his arm several blocks before their destination. "Stop," she cried. "That one's open."

That what?

At her insistence, he eased the car off the road and parked beside a chain drugstore. She didn't pause to explain. Before he could protest, she was out of the car and headed inside. With a shrug, Nathaniel retrieved the baby and followed Dani into the store.

The kid still slept. Had it been too long? Was she unconscious? His stomach knotted. What the hell did he know about babies? Even a bad foster family might be better than what Nathaniel had to offer.

Every inch of the infant's body was covered except for her rosy cheeks. Still, she wasn't wearing high-tech fabric rated for low temperatures. The little girl might be cold. How would *he* know?

Just about the time he had worked himself into a frenzy of doubt and frustration, Dani reappeared, her triumphant smile a blow to his stomach that took his breath and squeezed his heart.

Was he simply damned glad to have her help, or was the prospect of spending time with Dani enticing him to do something stupid? Every logical cell in his brain shouted at him to send her away. He was fine. He could cope.

Besides, though it was true he wanted Dani, he didn't "want" to want her. As long as he kept that in mind, he'd be okay. Despite his confusion and the alarm in his gut, he didn't tell her to go. That was undoubtedly his first mistake.

Somewhere, she had found a shopping cart. It was loaded with diapers, wipes, formula and bottles. He stared at the bounty of baby supplies, incredulous. He'd been so focused on getting the kid to his condo, he'd never even thought about the fact that he had nothing—zero—with which to care for a child, especially one this small.

If this were a test to see what kind of father he would make, he was already failng miserably.

Two

Fortunately, Dani didn't appear to notice his turmoil. "I did a lot of babysitting in college," she said. "I've tried to remember everything you'll need, but I don't know if I have it all. It's hard when you're not used to taking care of an infant."

"Tell me about it," he muttered. He wasn't going to admit he would have forgotten half of the items in that cart. "We're lucky somebody's still open," he said. This was a hell of a time to feel arousal tighten his body. Dani was irresistible with her pointed chin and her flyaway hair.

She gave him a cute little half frown that said she thought he was an idiot. "You should unbutton your coat," she said. "Your face is all red. We need to hurry."

"I was hoping to be home before she wakes up. If she starts crying, I don't know what we'll do."

Dani looked better than any woman should while negotiating the beginnings of a blizzard with her brain-dead boss and an unknown baby. She was average height for a woman, though her snow boots lent a couple of extra inches. Her body was curvy and intensely feminine. The clothing she wore to work was always appropriate, but even so, in recent months, Nathaniel had found himself wondering if Dani was as prim and proper as her office persona would suggest.

Her wide-set blue eyes and high cheekbones reminded him of a princess he remembered from a childhood storybook. The princess's hair was blond. Dani's was more of a streaky caramel. She'd worn it up today in a sexy knot, presumably because of the Christmas party.

While he stood there, mute, with melting snow making the wool of his overcoat steam, Dani fussed over the contents of her cart. "If the baby wakes up," she said, "I'll hold her. It will be fine."

"I hate to be the voice of reason in the midst of your impressive knowledge of babies, but the Mercedes trunk is small. We'll never fit all that in."

Dani's tired grin was cheeky. "The guy back at the pharmacy said they'll be making deliveries until ten tonight in a four-wheel drive. Right now, you and I will take only the essentials. I stressed to him how important it is that we get our order. He swears he won't let me down."

It was no wonder. Dani's smiling charm would be hard to say no to under any circumstances. She was an appealing mix of girl-next-door and capable confidence. In that moment, Nathaniel realized he relied on her far more than he knew and for a variety of complex reasons he was loathe to analyze.

Clearing his throat, he fished out his wallet and handed the cashier his credit card.

Baby paraphernalia was remarkably expensive. Once the transaction was complete, the clerk gave Dani a large plastic bag. The two women ripped open packages and assembled an only-the-essentials collection that would hopefully suffice for the next few hours until the delivery arrived.

"I think that's it," Dani said with satisfaction. "Let's get this little angel home."

Unfortunately, their luck ran out. The baby woke up and let the world know she was hungry and pissed. Her screams threatened to peel paint off the walls.

Dani's smile faltered, but she unfastened the straps of the carrier and lifted the baby out carefully. "I'm so sorry, sweetheart. I know you want your mommy. Nathaniel and I will have to do for the moment. Do you have a wet diaper? Let's take care of that."

The clerk pointed out a unisex bathroom at the back of the store, complete with changing station. Nathaniel found himself following in Dani's wake. The tiny room was little bigger than a closet. They both pressed inside.

For the first time, Dani seemed frazzled. They were so close he could smell the faint, tantalizing scent of her perfume.

"You'll have to stand in the door and hand me things," she said. "We can't both fit in here."

"Sure," he said, feeling guilty for not offering to take charge of the diaper change. On the other hand, the baby's needs should be paramount. God knows Nathaniel was the last person on the planet qualified for the task.

Was it weird that being this close to Dani turned him on? Her warmth, her femininity. Hell, even the competent way she handled the baby made him want her.

That was the problem with blurring the lines between business and his personal life. He couldn't let himself be vulnerable. On the other hand, he would be lost without Dani's help, so he didn't really have a choice.

It was clear Dani hadn't overstated her experience with

children. She extracted the baby from the snowsuit, unfastened the romper and made quick work of replacing the baby's extremely wet diaper with a clean and dry one. Fortunately, no poop…at least not yet.

Then it was everything in reverse. When they were ready to go back out into the cold, Dani hesitated.

"What's wrong?" he asked.

Dani grimaced. "I'm wondering if we should try to feed her before we start walking again."

Nathaniel brushed the back of his hand over the baby's plump cheek. Her skin was warm against his chilled fingers. "I think she can make it. She's a trouper."

"Are you basing this on your personal DNA?" Dani asked wryly.

"I told you, she's not mine," he said sharply. "The only reason we're taking her home is because of the storm and Christmas and the fact that every emergency worker in the city is covered in snow…literally."

"Okay. Calm down."

He bit his tongue to keep from making a cutting remark. Dani was helping him. He couldn't afford to alienate her, and he definitely couldn't risk wondering what it would be like to kiss her.

Outside, they faced the next hurdle. Three cars had slammed into each other right in front of the drugstore, effectively blocking the only exit from the parking lot.

Nathaniel cursed beneath his breath. "Well, that's just great."

"We can't wait," Dani said. "Besides, aren't we close to your condo?"

"I don't like leaving my car."

She grinned. "Might be safer here than out on the road."

He squared his shoulders. "I suppose so. I'd forgotten how insane drivers can be when this happens."

To be fair, the streets were a mess. Road crews hadn't been able to salt anything more than the interstates, and the swift drop in temperature had added a layer of icy danger to the situation.

In the short time he and Dani had been inside the store, the situation had grown exponentially worse. People in other parts of the country couldn't understand, but Atlanta was particularly vulnerable to weather events like this one.

After retrieving their personal items from the car and consolidating their purchases, he and Dani struck out for the final leg of their journey.

They walked in silence, negotiating sidewalks they could no longer see and trying to move as quickly as possible.

Dani had the baby tucked inside her coat for extra warmth, which had to be a damned awkward way to walk. Nathaniel lugged the carrier and the supplies. When he offered to take the child after several minutes, Dani shook her head. "I'm fine."

It was a miserable, soul-crushing slog through ice and snow. He could barely feel his feet. Dani must have been equally miserable, but she didn't complain. Thank God they didn't have far to go.

When they finally arrived at Nathaniel's building, he had never in his life been so glad to see the doorman or the elaborately decorated lobby.

They dripped their way onto the elevator with Dani juggling an increasingly fractious baby. On the top floor, Nathaniel found his key, unlocked the door and ushered his unexpected guests inside. "Home sweet home," he said.

Dani was frozen to the bone. Her feet had long since gone numb. Though her coat and boots were nice, they were never meant to trek through deep snow for any length of time. She had struggled to keep up. Nathaniel, by all indications, was naturally athletic. He probably played multiple sports in high school and college.

They took turns holding the baby while shedding their outerwear. Dani's chic black dress was damp and rumpled. What she wouldn't give for a roaring fire and a cozy robe.

At the drugstore she had paid for a handful of personal items just in case. It seemed unlikely she was going to make it home tonight, though she still held out hope. Right now, all she wanted was her own bed, a warm nightie and something fun to binge-watch on Netflix.

Now that she had stripped off her black tights with the silver sparkles and was barelegged, she began to shiver. Nathaniel noticed immediately.

"If you're going to feed the baby, we've got to get you warmed up first. Come with me."

Clutching the little girl like a life preserver, Dani followed her boss down the hall.

The first thing she noticed was that Nathaniel's condo was three or four times the size of her own modest apartment. It was decorated in soothing shades of blue and gray with occasional pops of color. Coral cushions. An abstract painting that called to mind a Gauguin nude in the tropics. The space was silent and perfectly appointed in every way. Not a magazine out of place. No dirty socks.

Dani wanted to like Nathaniel's home, but she couldn't. It looked more like a magazine spread than a peaceful sanctuary at the end of a long day. She stopped in the doorway to his bedroom, unable to take another step.

Nathaniel, clearly unconcerned, rummaged in his dresser and came up with a pair of cream woolen socks and some faded gray sweatpants that looked ancient. He lifted one shoulder and lowered it with a sheepish grin. "I was smaller back in high school. These will still be too big for you, but at least they'll stay up. I think."

After that, he flung open his closet and found a soft cotton shirt in a pale blue. "Here we go," he said triumphantly. "Will this do?" She caught a brief glance of neatly pressed dark suits and crisp white dress shirts before he closed the closet door again.

She nodded. "Of course."

"Use my bathroom," he said. "I'll entertain the little one."

Dani frowned. "What should we call her? The note didn't say."

"How about Munchkin? That's generic enough, isn't it?"

"What kind of mother leaves her baby in a snowstorm?"

"I think Ophelia was probably watching us from somewhere nearby. She's a little weird, but not crazy enough to bring harm to a child."

"Why would you get involved with someone like that?" Dani wanted to snatch the words back as soon as they left her lips. It was none of her business.

Nathaniel's neck turned red. He avoided her gaze. "We weren't exactly involved. It was more of a physical thing."

"Casual sex." She said the words flatly, oddly hurt to know that Nathaniel was no better or worse than any other guy.

"I think we should change the subject," he said tersely. "Hand me the munchkin."

Dani passed off the baby and scuttled past man and child, already regretting that she didn't have the little girl for armor. Using Nathaniel's bathroom felt oddly decadent and personal. Everything was sybaritic and gorgeous. Marble. Brass. And mirrors. Those mirrors were her downfall. She looked as if she had been on an all-night bender at the North Pole.

Wincing at her reflection, she quickly took off her dress. At least her bra and panties were dry. The sweatpants were fleece-lined, and the socks were thick and warm. The shirt was miles too big, but she rolled up the sleeves. Though she was still chilled, the borrowed clothes made her feel more human.

Nathaniel smothered a grin when she reappeared in his bedroom. Wise man not to make any smart remarks. She was in no mood to be teased about her appearance, especially when it was Nathaniel's fault she was in this predicament.

"I bought a few bottles of premixed formula," she said. "It's expensive, but I didn't want Peaches to have to wait any longer than necessary?"

"Peaches? I thought we were calling her Munchkin."

"Well, we found her on Peachtree Street, so it seemed fitting."

"Fair enough. If you girls want to get settled in the den, I'll change and join you in a minute. Then it might be time for the grown-ups to eat. Are you hungry?"

"Starving," Dani said.

She made her way back down the hall and found the den. It was a more appealing room than anything she had seen so far. And hallelujah, there was a gas-log fireplace. One flip of a switch and the flames danced.

"Oh, Peaches," Dani said. "What kind of mess have we gotten ourselves into? These are pretty fancy digs, but you should be with your mama, and I'm supposed to be going home for Christmas tomorrow."

The baby whimpered while Dani shook the bottle and removed the protective cap. The formula was theoretically room temperature, but it might still be chilled from being outside. Fortunately, the child was too hungry to care.

Dani settled deeper into a cushioned armchair and propped her feet on the ottoman. The baby suckled eagerly. Was she old enough to take any other foods? This was a heck of a mess. Maybe they should try another call to the authorities. Or even to social services directly.

Then again, it was after nine o'clock, and tomorrow was Christmas Eve.

The child was a sweet weight in her arms. Enough to wonder what it would be like if this were really her child. Dani envied her sister at times. Angie and her husband were happily married and hoping to start a family soon. Then again, her sister was thirty-five. Dani was only twenty-eight. There was still plenty of time.

She didn't know what was taking Nathaniel so long, but did it really matter? She couldn't imagine leaving him in the lurch, even if this situation was his fault. Could the baby really be his? Contraceptives failed all the time. He acted like the kind of man who would live up to his responsibilities, but did she really know him that well? He seemed very sure he wasn't a father.

What alarmed her was how content she was to spend this time with him. Though the moment was fraught with emotional danger, she was happy to be here. Against all odds, Nathaniel had shown her his human side. Seeing him in this situation made her feel woozy inside. He was visibly shaken and yet so very determined to seize control.

His masculinity was in stark contrast to the baby's helpless vulnerability. Dani's regard for him grew, as did her need to explore what was sure to be a doomed attraction on her part.

She was almost asleep, her head resting against the back of the chair, when her boss finally appeared.

Nathaniel surveyed the sleeping child. "She seems like a pretty easy baby, doesn't she? If all she needs are food and diapers, maybe it won't be so bad to wait it out until someone shows up to claim her."

"I burped her a couple of times halfway through the bottle. She took it like a pro. I still feel bad, though. Peaches should be with her family at Christmas."

"Fortunately, she's too young to remember any of this," Nathaniel said.

"Maybe. But she has to know we're strangers."

"I called 911 again. They asked me if the baby was in any danger. I said no. They wanted to know if the mother was someone I knew. I had to say yes. The officer apologetically insisted that they're completely at the end of their resources and recommended I preserve the status quo until Tuesday."

"Tuesday?" Dani cried, startling the child. "That's four days."

"I don't know what else to do." Nathaniel ran a hand across the back of his neck as he prowled the confines of the den. "It's already the weekend now. Sunday is Christmas, which means everything will be closed Monday. If the snow has melted, we should be able to get some answers on Tuesday."

Dani stroked the little girl's back. "Poor Peaches. Grown-ups can be so stupid sometimes."

"Was that a dig at me?" Nathaniel asked. He slouched in the chair across from hers. He looked very different in jeans, a navy sweatshirt and leather moccasins. Different and so very moody and sexy.

"Not at all," she said.

"I'm innocent until proven guilty. Ophelia's note means nothing."

"Relax," Dani said. "I'm not judging you. Besides, it's Christmas. Everybody deserves a little miracle this weekend."

"It will be a miracle if I don't find Ophelia and wring her neck."

"Poor Nathaniel. Everyone at works thinks you have no social life at all. Now you may have a child."

"I'm *not* the father," he said. "Quit saying that."

"So you don't want children?"

He huffed in exasperation. "Not now. Not today. Certainly not with Ophelia. I have no idea why she thought palming a kid off on me was a good idea. I haven't a clue what to do with Peaches."

"It's not so hard," Dani said, yawning. "The worst part is the sleep deprivation, or so I've been told," she said hastily. "I'm not ready to be a parent, either."

The room fell silent after that. Nathaniel had clearly nodded off. With his eyes closed, she was free to explore him visually to her heart's content. For years, she had seen him in suits. He was a very handsome man who wore tailor-made attire well. But here in his home habitat, tired and discouraged in comfy clothes like any other American male, he seemed more real to her.

She didn't want to care about his well-being. She didn't want to worry about him. And she most assuredly did not want to get involved with him. Life was complicated enough without adding drama and heartbreak.

Time passed. She must have dozed off herself. The drowsiness was the aftermath of being so cold for so long and then getting dry and warm. Now, though, her stomach growled when she roused. If she stretched her leg, she could barely touch Nathaniel's toe. "Wake up," she whispered. "Nathaniel, wake up."

He yawned and stretched, revealing a few inches of tanned, taut abs. "What's wrong?" he grumbled, only half-awake.

"You promised to feed me."

His eyes shot open. A look of stupefaction flashed across his face before he got ahold of himself. "Right."

Dani rolled her neck to get the kinks out of it. "Sorry, it wasn't a dream. The kid and I are still here."

"Very funny." He rolled to his feet. "I usually order in, but somehow I don't think that's an option."

"I'd settle for peanut butter if you have any."

"That I can do."

After Nathaniel left the room, Dani stood carefully and cradled the sleeping baby against her shoulder. Her body ached from sitting in one position. More than that, she needed to walk around, anything to break the spell of intimacy that came from napping in her boss's den. Too cozy. Too weird. Too everything.

Built-in bookcases flanked the fireplace. Books of every genre were mixed in together with no apparent regard for organization. Interesting pieces of glass and pottery shone in the illumination from can lights overhead.

Nothing about the library or the art matched what she knew of Nathaniel. Curiouser and curiouser.

He returned silently, startling her badly. The baby whimpered when Dani jumped. Nathaniel didn't seem to notice. He set the food on the coffee table. "I have coffee or soft drinks. Which would you prefer?"

"Black coffee if it's decaf."

"It is."

The tension in the room increased exponentially along with the vivid awareness that Dani didn't belong here. Her presence was an accident of weather and timing. She bore no responsibility, either moral or otherwise, for Nathaniel and his surprise Christmas gift. Even if the little girl truly wasn't his, Dani was not involved in that fight.

Then why was it so painful to think about leaving this sexy man and adorable baby tomorrow?

As if he had picked up on her tumultuous thoughts,

Nathaniel shot her a look as he poured coffee. “Is there someone you need to call?”

“My family will be expecting me tomorrow afternoon, though with the weather, I’m not sure we’ll all be able to make it.”

“Where do they live?”

“My parents are in Gainesville. My sister and her husband settled in Chattanooga for work and because they love the area. My only brother, Jared, lives in Marietta. He’s probably the one who will have to come get me if I can’t drive my car. Mine’s a VW Beetle, so not really snow-worthy.”

“I see.”

It wasn’t much of a response. She gave up on chitchat and managed to eat one-handed. Either Nathaniel made a habit of buying gourmet peanut butter, or Dani was hungrier than she realized.

Her dinner companion prowled while he ate. The tension in his body broadcast itself across the room. Dani could understand his frustration.

When he pulled back the drapes and stared out into the night, Dani joined him at the window. All they could see in the beams from the streetlights was heavy, swirling snow. Nathaniel pulled out his phone and tapped the weather app. “Good Lord,” he said. “Look at the radar.”

The storm was far from finished. In fact, there was every indication it would still be snowing until the wee hours before dawn.

The scary situation had turned into an actual blizzard. It didn’t matter that by Tuesday the temps were supposed to be in the midfifties again. For now, they were well and truly stranded.

Nathaniel left her and began prowling again.

The silence built until Dani couldn’t bear it anymore.

"Are you Jewish?" she asked, blurting it out before realizing that was not the kind of question one asked a work colleague.

He paused in his pacing to stare at her. "No. Where did that come from?"

Dani shrugged. "No Christmas tree. No decorations." It was a logical conclusion.

"I live alone," he said, his tone indicating a desire to shut the door on this particular line of conversation.

"So do I," Dani pointed out. "But I have a tree and other stuff. It makes the season fun."

"That's a lot of work for only me to see. Can we change the subject?"

"Sure." Maybe Nathaniel was a certified Scrooge. The idea made her sad. But she couldn't very well persist in the face of his disinclination to explain. His lack of December frivolity was well documented and would remain a mystery. "I *am* worried about one thing," she said.

"What's that?"

Nathaniel had finished his sandwich and now cradled his coffee cup between his big, long-fingered hands. *Oops. No thinking about hands, Danielle.*

"Well," she said slowly, hoping she wasn't blushing. "I'm afraid this little one has slept so much during the evening she'll be up all night. I've heard about babies who get their days and nights mixed up."

"I can get by on a few hours of sleep. I'll take the night shift. You deserve some rest." He stood up. "Let me show you the guest room. I guess you'll need a different shirt to sleep in?"

Three

He made it a question. Having Dani wear his clothes and wear them so damned well made it hard for him to think about babies and responsibility. He'd been attracted to her for a long time, but he knew better than to get involved with an employee. He'd learned that lesson the hard way. It wasn't one he would soon forget.

It was imperative that he get rid of Dani before he did something stupid—imperative for two reasons. One, he didn't need the temptation of having his charming, cheerful, cute-as-the-proverbial-button assistant underfoot outside of office hours. And two, he felt guilty as hell for ruining her holiday plans. Maybe they were still salvageable. She said she hadn't planned to leave until tomorrow, and Gainesville was not even two hours away.

Unfortunately, the massive and almost unprecedented winter storm was the wild card in this scenario. And then there was the baby. If he did the right thing and sent Dani home for Christmas, he'd be stuck caring for an infant. The notion was more than a little terrifying.

"Another shirt would be helpful," Dani said quietly, not meeting his gaze.

"Follow me," he said gruffly. The condo had two guest rooms. One he used as a home office. The other was furnished simply and elegantly in shades of amber, chocolate and ivory.

He'd hired a professional to do the whole condo when he bought it. Everything but the den. That was his and his alone. The huge comfy couch, big-screen TV and gas fireplace were things he had purchased on his own. Except for sleeping, he spent most of his leisure hours in the den. Ah, who was he kidding? He worked in there, as well. Creating boundaries had never been his strong suit.

In the guest room, Dani explored, the baby still in her arms. But the little girl was waking up.

Dani grinned and kissed the baby's head. "Hey there, Peaches. Mr. Nathaniel is showing me around. You want to sleep in here with me?"

It was tempting, very tempting, to let Dani rescue him. But such cowardice would be wrong on several levels. He took the baby from her and shook his head. "Take a shower if you want to. Get ready for bed. Then you can help me get everything set up in my bedroom for the night."

"Okay." Dani's eyes were big as saucers. Maybe she was worried about the innocent baby.

"I won't let anything happen to her," he said. The defensive note in his voice was unavoidable. As unpalatable as it seemed, he had to at least acknowledge the possibility, however slim, that Peaches was his. "We'll give you some privacy," he said. "When you're ready, come find us."

* * *

Dani returned to the foyer and gathered all her things. If she hung the dress and tights carefully, they might be wearable again. At the drugstore, she had bought toothpaste, a toothbrush and some facial cleanser. Fortunately—because of the Christmas party—she had made sure that morning to put mascara and other makeup in her purse for touch-ups.

After a quick shower, she rinsed out her bra and panties and hung them on the towel bar. Then she put on the sweatpants sans undies and spent a few minutes blow-drying her hair. It was thick and shoulder length, maybe her best feature. Because it was still a little damp when she was done, she left it loose. Whenever Nathaniel remembered to give her a second shirt, she would change into that for the night.

Barely half an hour had elapsed by the time she went in search of her host, forty-five minutes at the most. It wasn't hard to locate him. All she had to do was follow the sound of screaming. Little Peaches had a great set of lungs.

Dani stopped dead in the doorway of Nathaniel's bedroom, taking in the scene with openmouthed awe.

Nathaniel's head shot up and he glared at her, his expression hot enough to melt steel. "If you dare laugh, you're fired."

She swallowed hard, schooling her face to show nothing more than calm interest. "I wouldn't dream of laughing." It was maybe the biggest lie she had ever uttered. Poor Nathaniel.

Peaches had experienced what those in the parenting world not-so-fondly call a *blowout.* A poop so big and messy it squirts out the sides of the diaper and into every crevice imaginable. It was clear Nathaniel had made a heroic effort to remove the dirty diaper and replace it with a clean one, but he was taking too long, and poor Peaches was mad.

Dani grabbed several wipes out of the container and began cleaning the spots Nathaniel had either missed or hadn't gotten to yet. The baby was stark naked. Nathaniel had poop on his hands, his sweatshirt and if she weren't mistaken, a smudge on his chin. He was wild-eyed and flushed.

Her heart squeezed in sympathy. Most parents had nine months to get used to the idea of a baby. Nathaniel had been tossed in the deep end. If Peaches weren't his at all, this whole experience was even more unfair.

"I'll pick her up," Dani said. "You start getting rid of all the nasty stuff and throw your comforter in the washer." She was afraid the bed covering was beyond redemption.

Carrying the baby into the bathroom and using the sink as a miniature bathtub was her next step. Fortunately, the little one stopped crying when she saw herself in the mirror. Dani adjusted the water temperature and grabbed a washcloth.

The bottle of liquid hand soap on the counter would have to do for now. Moments later, she wrapped the sweet-smelling infant in one of Nathaniel's big, fluffy towels and returned to the bedroom.

Nathaniel had just finished cleaning up the mess that was his mattress. He held out a fresh diaper. "You can do the honors."

"Of course. I can't believe this Ophelia person left you with nothing. We don't even have another outfit for the baby."

"I turned up the thermostat. And I put her sleeper in the wash with all the rest. It will be ready in a couple of hours."

"I guess that will have to do." Since Peaches was sucking on her fist, it seemed another bottle was in order. "I'll feed her again. Your turn in the bathroom."

When she turned to walk away, Nathaniel put his hand on her shoulder lightly. "Thank you, Dani. I know my thanks is not enough, but I want you to know I'm grateful."

They were standing so close together she could see the dark stubble on his chin. It was the end of the day. That made sense. His brown eyes were deep pools of melted chocolate. He smelled of soap and a tiny hint of aftershave and maybe even a whiff of baby poop. Dani bit her bottom lip. Why had the baby chosen now to be docile? A diversion would be helpful.

"You're welcome," she said quietly. "I know this isn't easy. You're doing the right thing."

He shrugged. "It's not as if I had a choice."

"Even without the snowstorm, I think you would have taken the child. Because you have to know…one way or another."

"Who made you so smart?"

"Not smart. Just realistic. You're not the kind of man to walk away from a responsibility, unpleasant or otherwise."

"It's more that that," he said.

His hand was still on her shoulder, fingers splayed, though she wasn't sure he noticed. "How so?"

"What if Peaches *is* mine? Birth control is never a hundred percent. What if this little girl is my only shot at having a child?"

"You don't think you'll get married one day?"

The hour was late. It had been a very strange day. Nathaniel was practically embracing Dani and the baby. She wanted to lean into him and rest her head. She was tired and confused and very afraid of doing something she would regret.

It took everything she had to step back and break the

spell. "I shouldn't have asked you that," she said hastily. "I'm sorry, Mr. Winston." She used his last name as a shield, but it was flimsy armor at best.

You can't put a genie back in the bottle, though. Nathaniel gave her a pointed look as if he saw right through her attempt to be businesslike. "I think we have to concentrate on what's important here. If you and Peaches are really okay for the moment, I'll jump in the shower. I still smell like a diaper pail."

"No, you don't," Dani protested, laughing. "But yeah, we're fine. Take your time."

On her way to the den, the doorbell rang. No one could come up without going through the reception desk downstairs, so this must be the delivery from the drugstore. She pressed the intercom button and waited for confirmation just to be sure.

After the young teenager unloaded all the baby paraphernalia in the foyer, Dani tipped him well and sent him on his way.

"This is it, Peaches," she said, bending down to pick up the smallest package of diapers. "I hope I did the math right. This has to last us until the snow melts or your mama shows up, whichever comes first."

Of course, it didn't take a genius to guess that Ophelia was probably snowed in wherever she was hiding out. It was creepy to think a woman like that had been watching as Nathaniel and Dani spotted the infant carrier for the first time. What would she have done if the two of them had walked away? She must have been relying on the decency of human nature. Even so, Dani would never have left her own baby in such circumstances. It was too risky.

She wandered back to the den and spread an afghan on the thick carpet so the baby could have tummy time. Peaches was very mobile already and trying her best to sit up. No signs of any bottom teeth poking through. Dani guessed the little girl was about five months old, maybe six.

As the baby played with a rattle from the drugstore, Dani stretched out beside her and leaned back on her elbows. It was a strange feeling to be a guest in her boss's home. Definitely outside the parameters of their usual interactions. Up until today, she'd had no clue where he lived.

Now, suddenly, everything was different.

When Nathaniel reappeared, his hair was damp and he had ditched the clothes the baby had desecrated.

"Much better," Dani teased, telling herself her heart wasn't beating faster.

He grinned, the sudden smile taking her by surprise. Her boss was more serious than playful as a rule. "Is it still Friday?" he asked, leaning a hip against the arm of the sofa. "I feel like we've fallen through the rabbit hole."

"Still Friday. I'm guessing your life isn't usually so tumultuous?"

"You could say that." He raked both hands through this hair. "I shouldn't have dragged you into this."

"Look at it this way. You probably saved me from being stranded on the side of the road. At least I'm safe and warm and dry."

"What a testimonial. Have you called your family yet?"

"Yes. I told them I was staying with a friend and that I would check in again tomorrow."

"Let's hope we don't lose power."

"Bite your tongue. That's not even funny."

"I wasn't joking. If we do get ice on the back end of this thing, the situation could get dicey."

"Oh, goody. Something to look forward to."

He cocked his head, his lips twitching. "How have I never noticed what a smart mouth you have?"

"I'm always deferential in our work environment." She smiled demurely, astonished to realize they were flirting. Of course, with a baby between them nothing could happen. But still…

Nathaniel stood up to pace. She was beginning to recognize his signature mood when he was agitated. He did it occasionally at work, but it was more pronounced on his home turf. "Is she getting sleepy?" he asked. "When should we put her to bed?"

"How should I know? Do you have work you need to do? You might as well let me take care of her for the moment. It's not like I can go anywhere."

"I know, I know. And I'm sorry."

"Quit apologizing, Nathaniel. Humility doesn't become you."

"Ouch." He squatted and rubbed the baby's tummy, his gaze pensive. "She doesn't look like me, not even a little bit."

The non sequitur betrayed his inner turmoil. Dani felt her heart squeeze. "In my experience, babies this age rarely look like anybody but themselves, Nathaniel. Don't torment yourself. Until you know for sure, she's just a baby."

"I suppose." He glanced sideways at her. "Go on to bed, Dani. I'll come get you if I get in trouble."

"You promise?"

"I do."

Nathaniel sighed beneath his breath. Hopefully Dani didn't realize how completely out of his element he was. He had learned long ago—while earning his stripes in the business world—never to show fear. He could negotiate with the baddest of the badasses. What he didn't know how to do was take care of a helpless human. Little Peaches was so damned fragile.

He scooped her up. "Here's the thing, kiddo. I need you to cut me a break tonight. I'll feed you and change your diaper, but you need to sleep. That's what babies do."

The little girl stuck a thumb in her mouth and stared up at him, unblinking. What was she thinking? Did babies think about anything?

After turning out the lights, he carried Peaches to his bedroom and surveyed the furnishings. As far as he could tell, the most important thing was to keep the kid confined. He knew it was dangerous to put her in his own bed. After getting out of the shower earlier, he had spread a sheet on the soft carpet and surrounded it with several wooden chairs. He'd probably be awake all night worrying about the kid, but he'd survive.

Fortunately, the baby had worn herself out playing with Dani. All it took was a few circuits around the bedroom with Peaches on his shoulder, and gradually her little body went limp. He crouched and laid her in the makeshift bed. Poor kid. She should be with her mother right now. It was impossible not to think about the marked differences between Ophelia and Dani. One woman was self-centered and flighty…the other generous and dependable.

At one time in his life, he had assumed all women were self-centered. His mother had taught him to believe that. It wasn't true, though. God willing, this little sweetheart would grow up with kindness in her heart.

On a normal evening, he was awake until after one. Tonight, that was a luxury he couldn't afford. Stripping down to his boxers, he climbed into bed, stretched out on his back and exhaled. What a hell of a day.

It was impossible not to think about the fact that Dani was sleeping in his guest room just down the hall. He liked and respected her. In recent months, he'd stumbled upon another feeling he couldn't, or wouldn't, acknowledge.

Dani deserved to find a man who would put her first, a man who would be happy to settle down with her and create a normal family life. That man wasn't Nathaniel. He'd certainly never experienced such a thing as *normal* in his formative years. All he knew was work and more work. That focus had propelled him to the top of his career. Given his long hours and his absolute refusal to date anyone remotely connected to New Century Tech, his options for meeting women were limited.

Loneliness and sexual hunger had been to blame for his hookup with Ophelia when they met at a conference. It had taken less than forty-eight hours for him to figure out that she was a narcissist and incredibly high maintenance. He'd broken off the relationship before it started, but perhaps the damage had been done.

The prospect of co-parenting with Ophelia for the next twenty years was daunting. Depressing, even. But if Peaches were his daughter, he would suck it up and be the best damned dad he could be. Never would he make that sweet little girl endure the kind of childhood he had experienced.

Unbidden, his thoughts returned to Dani. After seeing his father's life ruined years ago, Nathaniel had forged ironclad rules for his own business relationships.

That line in the sand had never been difficult to preserve until Dani walked into his life. She had become necessary to him. He told himself it was nothing more than a good working partnership.

Now, in the darkness and privacy of his bedroom, he acknowledged the possibility that he had been lying to himself. She was here. Now. Sleeping under his roof and making him think about things that were definitely not conducive to relaxation.

Arousal tightened his body and fractured his breathing. *Damn it.* He rolled onto his side and told himself he wasn't a slave to his urges.

Yawning, he tried converting foreign currencies in his head. It was better than counting sheep. Eventually, exhaustion claimed him…

The waning hours of the night turned into a long, wretched dream. The baby woke him every forty-five to ninety minutes. He knew she was disoriented and unsettled. Thankfully, each time he picked her up and cuddled her, he was able to coax her back to sleep.

At 5:00 a.m., though, the volume of her cries told him she was hungry again. Carrying her into the kitchen, he found one of the premixed formula bottles and uncapped it. He would have to learn how to mix the powder, but not while it was still dark outside.

Earlier, he had thrown on a robe with his boxers. Now he and Peaches settled on the sofa in the den. Pulling an afghan over both of them, he leaned back and watched as the baby gobbled down her meal. He remembered Dani mentioning the need for burping. When the bottle was half-empty, he hefted the baby onto his shoulder and patted her back. Peaches didn't like being interrupted, but her loud belch told him he'd done the right thing.

While the infant finished her formula, he reached for the remote and turned the TV on with the volume muted. He had a million channels to choose from, but nothing interested him. He wanted a distraction…some assurance that the world still spun in its normal orbit. Skipping over infomercials and weird sports channels, he landed on an old movie, a Christmas film.

He had never seen it all the way through, but he knew the general premise. A man unhappy with his life wished he had never been born and then had a chance to see what the world would have been like without him.

The scenario hit uncomfortably near home for Nathaniel. He had no close friends by design. As head of the company, he knew better than to build relationships that might backfire on him. Because he worked all the time, there was no opportunity for socializing even if he had wanted to. Other than a couple of guys he occasionally played racquetball with at the gym, he was a loner, and he liked it. Mostly.

By following a rigid set of rules for his personal life, he kept his days running smoothly. This blip with Ophelia only proved what it cost to deviate from his usual behavior.

Again and again, he wondered what he would do if Peaches were his. Again and again, he shut down that line of thinking. Until the truth came out, speculation served no purpose.

Too late, he realized he should have changed the kid's diaper *before* giving her a bottle. Now she had sucked down the last ounce of formula and was out cold. Fortunately, Dani had already stocked most rooms in the house with diapers and wipes. Thank God for her babysitting experience. At least one of them had some exposure to infants. Otherwise, the situation would have been far worse.

Luckily for him, Peaches slept through the diaper change, even though he fumbled and cursed and struggled with the seemingly simple task. He was able to return to his room, tuck her back into the little protected corner and fall into his own bed, facedown, unconscious in seconds.

The next time he surfaced, the clock said seven. He had a hangover headache, and he hadn't even had a beer last night. Stumbling to his feet, he visited the bathroom and then moved stealthily toward Peaches's corner on the floor to check on her.

The nest was empty. Panic flooded his chest for half a second before common sense intruded. The chairs were intact. Dani must have the child.

He found them both in the kitchen. Dani had fixed a pot of coffee, God bless her, and she was sitting at the window, baby in arms, drawing pictures in the condensation on the glass.

She looked up when Nathaniel entered the room. "Good morning. It sounded like this little stinker gave you a rough night."

He winced. "You heard us?"

"I'm a light sleeper." She shrugged, her expression guarded. "I decided that if you wanted help, you would ask, so I didn't disturb you. You're a very capable man."

Pouring himself a cup of coffee and gulping it with no thought for scalding his tongue, he snorted. "Didn't feel like it last night."

"Poor Peaches. I guess she knew she was in a strange place."

"Getting stranger by the minute. Have you heard a forecast?"

She nodded glumly. "The official totals are twelve to fourteen inches so far, with more, north of the city. It's supposed to change over to freezing rain in the next couple of hours. The governor has declared a state of emergency. All roads are virtually impassable because of abandoned cars, including major interstates."

"So you're stuck with me?" He tried to smile, but the knot in his chest made it hard to breathe.

"It looks that way. But on an up note, I've already talked to my family. They're all stuck, too, except my Chattanooga sister. The storm stayed south of them. My parents have decided we'll simply postpone Christmas until at least the twenty-seventh. It's supposed to be sixty-two and sunny then."

"Welcome to winter in the South."

"Exactly."

He had no clue how to act, what to say or do. This bizarre scenario was unprecedented. Nausea swirled in his belly, and he felt light-headed.

Blaming it on the lack of sleep was less worrisome than admitting he was afraid to be trapped with Dani. Sitting there with a warm smile on her face, wearing his shirt and holding a child who was possibly his baby, she personified everything he feared, everything he had avoided for so long and so well.

He hoped like hell his unease wasn't visible. He didn't want to give in to temptation, but he sure as hell didn't want to hurt her, either.

Four

Dani cocked her head, her smile dimming as a knot of *something* settled like a rock in her stomach. Nathaniel was acting very strangely. Despite her misgivings, she forged ahead with the idea that had come to her while she waited for him to wake up. "I have a question, Nathaniel. You can say no if you want to."

As she watched, he took two steps backward, set his empty cup on the counter and shoved his hands in his pockets.

"Ask away," he said. But his gaze didn't meet hers. His body language was one big keep-off-the-grass sign.

Sighing inwardly, she nuzzled the top of the baby's head. "It's Christmas Eve," she said flatly, as if he didn't know. "And tomorrow is Christmas Day. Your condo is virtually empty of any sustenance, holiday or otherwise. I checked around online and found a small market about a mile from here that's opening up from ten to four today. If I make a grocery list, will you go shopping for us?"

His lips quirked in a reluctant smile. "That's doable."

"I'm not the greatest cook," Dani admitted. "I don't think I'd be confident preparing a turkey, even if they have any. But I could do a pot roast with all the trimmings and some kind of fancy dessert. Are you allergic to anything?"

"No." He didn't look happy.

She was even tempered as a rule, but his silence grated. "Do you have an objection to observing the holiday with good food?" The words came out more sharply than she had intended. Still, she didn't regret them.

Nathaniel sat down on a bar stool at the counter and grimaced. "My family was not as warm and fuzzy as yours, Dani. My mother was diagnosed with schizophrenia, but not until I was in high school. I don't know if you can imagine what my childhood was like."

Suddenly Dani felt small and mean. "What about your father?"

"He loved my mother in spite of everything—and he loved me, I'm sure. But he wasn't the kind of man who could keep gluing bits of our life back together and making things work. His solution was to spend all his time at the office."

"I see." In fact, she saw more than she ever had before. Nathaniel had layers upon layers, it seemed. The more she learned about him, the more it became apparent he was destined to hurt her if she let herself get too close. The man didn't want a girlfriend or a wife. In fact, he seemed to be rabidly opposed to human emotion in general.

Squashing her disappointment, she managed a light tone. "So is that yes or no to the dessert?"

Finally, she coaxed a smile from him. "I may not know how to properly observe Christmas, but I do like to eat."

"Well, there you go." For no apparent reason, Dani felt like crying. She didn't want to see Nathaniel as a person, a man with hidden vulnerabilities. She didn't want to like or understand him anymore than she already did. Liking him led to fantasizing about a future that would never be hers. Fortunately, Nathaniel was oblivious to her turmoil.

"Your grocery store plan still doesn't help us with the baby's clothing situation, or lack thereof," he said.

Dani nodded. "I have a lead there, as well. Your poor doorman made it into work this morning, but he's bored, because clearly there's not much action in the lobby. I phoned down to him earlier with a question or two. In the process, he told me his daughter has a little girl who's a year old. He thinks they might have some hand-me-downs we can use for Peaches. And they live close enough he can walk to their apartment tonight after work."

"Do you make friends with anyone and everyone?"

His tone didn't sound as if the question was a compliment. Dani chose her words carefully. "The world can be a difficult place. We're all interconnected. I see no harm in being open to other people and experiences."

"Maybe you were a hippie flower child in another life," he muttered.

"I can go, Nathaniel," she said sharply. "You asked for my help. But if you're going to act like a horse's ass all weekend, I'd just as soon leave."

Her accusation found its mark. For a moment, Nathaniel turned icy and distant. She wanted to run from his disdain, but she held her ground. The standoff felt interminable.

Gradually, his posture softened. His chest lifted and fell in a huge sigh. "I apologize," he said. "Apparently, I'm not as good at sleep deprivation as I thought."

"You're forgiven. I know you're exhausted." Dani didn't hold grudges. Life was too short. A change of subject was in order. "I'm worried that if you get everything we need at the market, it will be too heavy to carry."

"I have an old army-surplus duffel bag. It's practically indestructible. I can load it up, cinch the top and drag it back, if necessary."

"That could work." The thought of filling Nathaniel's somewhat-sterile condo with the appealing scents of Christmas excited her.

"Is there anything else Peaches might need that I could get at the store?"

"We covered the basics last night. She's old enough to begin sampling simple foods, but since we don't know if Ophelia has given her anything yet, I'd be afraid to try. The formula will be enough for now."

"You're the expert."

"Hardly. I'm just grateful Peaches is an easy baby. I've heard stories about colic and other stuff. This situation could have been much worse."

"It *would* have been," Nathaniel said bluntly. "Without you."

She flushed. "I was an extra pair of hands, that's all."

"No," he said carefully. "It's more than that. I see it at NCT all the time. People come to you with problems and questions. You triage. You offer solutions. You give support. You're an extraordinary woman, Dani. Don't ever underestimate yourself."

With that, he turned on his heel and walked out of the room.

Dani put a hand to her hot cheek. *Wow.* That was the warmest and most personal testimonial she had ever received from her boss. And it told her he actually noticed what she did for the company. Sometimes she wondered. He became so absorbed in his work, she'd been convinced at times that he saw her as no different from a computer or the copy machine.

It was disarming to know he was watching.

Peaches had drooled all over the shoulder of Dani's shirt, which was, of course, Nathaniel's shirt. At this rate, she would have to borrow half a dozen to keep up with the baby's tendency to destroy clothing.

This was the strangest Christmas Eve Dani had ever experienced. Over the last decade, she had dated a number of men, but none of them long enough to warrant spending the holidays with their families or vice versa. The only Christmases Dani had ever known were celebrated in the bosom of her family.

Though Nathaniel's condo was a far cry from her parents' warm and welcoming home, Dani was determined to make this day memorable. For Peaches. For Nathaniel. Heck, for herself.

Someday, God willing, she would be marking the holidays in a house of her own with a husband, two as-yet-to-be-named kids and maybe a dog. *She* would be in charge of the meals and the decorations and the Santa gifts.

Maybe this odd Christmas was a testing ground. Did she have it in her to make the holiday special under these circumstances? Would Nathaniel even care?

One glance at the clock on the stove told her she had no time to spare. Presumably Nathaniel had disappeared to suit up for his foray into the winter wonderland. Dani loved playing in snow as a rule, but she didn't have the appropriate clothing, and it was too cold for the baby even if Dani had wanted to go along.

With Peaches in one arm, she quickly scanned the contents of the cabinets. They were mostly empty. One set of salt and pepper shakers. An out-of-date container of cinnamon. Half a bag of questionable flour. But at least the basics of cookware were represented. Maybe a woman had furnished the kitchen.

She found a pen and started writing. By the time Nathaniel returned carrying the big empty duffel bag, Dani had filled three pages of a notepad advertising a well-known realty company. "I hope you can read my writing," she fretted. "I'm not good at one-handed penmanship."

Nathaniel grinned. "We have these things called cell phones..."

"Well, that's true. But what if I'm changing a diaper at the exact moment you need to call me?"

He shrugged. "Then I'll wait." Even bundled from head to toe, he managed to look ruggedly handsome.

"What about eggs and bread?"

"I'll put them on top. It will be fine. Quit worrying. You should know, though, that walking a mile and back in a foot of snow won't be quick. Not to mention how long it's going to take me to find all this stuff." He waved the list in the air.

"Sorry," Dani said. "I guess I got carried away. Maybe I was making sure you didn't have to make a second trip."

"Maybe," he chuckled. He kissed the baby's cheek, his lips dangerously close to Dani's, close enough to give a woman ideas. "You girls stay out of trouble while I'm gone."

On the elevator ride down to the lobby, Nathaniel started to sweat. He'd put on clothes from his last Colorado ski trip. When he stepped outside, he was glad he had kept the heavy winter gear. As useless as it normally was in Atlanta, today it was going to come in handy.

The snow had turned into a nasty drizzle that froze on contact. Soon, he couldn't feel his cheeks. He wrapped his fleece scarf around all of his face but his eyes, and picked up the pace. It wasn't easy. Snowshoes might have been a good idea if he had owned any.

He relished the physical exertion. Despite his lack of

sleep the night before, he *wanted* to push himself to the limits, anything to keep from thinking about Dani. She was his very valuable assistant, not a lover. He had to remember that, no matter how great the temptation.

He'd never seen Atlanta like this. It was a ghost town, a frozen ghost town. Occasionally, an official vehicle passed. There were a few intrepid explorers out, like himself. For the most part, though, his fellow citizens had hunkered down to wait for the snow to melt.

What did normal people do on December 24? There would be no last-minute shopping today, that's for sure. Even Amazon couldn't fulfill impulsive wishes in the midst of a blizzard. Fortunately, Nathaniel had resources Amazon didn't possess. Early this morning, he had made a couple of phone calls and arranged to get a gift for Dani. She deserved at least that much for putting up with his bizarre situation.

The small neighborhood market shone like a beacon at the end of his journey, bringing cheer to the gray, icy day. In addition to the store's normal illumination, swags of colored lights festooned the entrance.

Inside, Nathaniel grabbed a shopping cart and stripped off his outer garments. Christmas music played from overhead speakers. Oddly, it didn't irritate him as it sometimes did. When he found himself humming along with a familiar tune, he frowned and concentrated on Dani's list.

The store was mostly empty. He was able to go as slowly as he wanted, one aisle at a time, until he was confident he had fulfilled his mission.

At the checkout stand, he began to have a few tiny doubts about getting all this stuff back to the condo. No matter. He'd told Dani it might take a while.

The store manager rang up the purchases. "You're a

brave man," he said. "Must have a woman at home ready to cook."

"Something like that."

When the last item was scanned, Nathaniel handed over his credit card and began loading the canvas duffel, putting the canned goods on the bottom. The manager looked to be in his late forties and bore a passing resemblance to Santa Claus. He was dressed in overalls and a red flannel shirt, probably not his usual work attire.

The older man began grouping smaller items and tying them into plastic bags to make them easier to stuff in the duffel. "You got a tree already?" he asked.

Nathaniel shook his head. "No. I don't usually decorate. It's a lot of trouble."

The Santa look-alike frowned. "Then you should take one of those small live trees. On the house. They'll be useless to me by Monday. For that matter, I'll throw in a stand and several strands of lights. Might as well. I'll be stuck with that whole display seventy-five percent off. I'd rather you and your lady friend enjoy them."

"Oh, but I—"

The manager interrupted, "I know, I know. You're walking. I get it. My son, Toby, is in the back unloading pallets. Do you know how hard it is for a seventeen-year-old boy to be snowed in the day before Christmas? The kid needs some exercise. He's driving me and his mom crazy. Let him walk back and carry the tree for you."

"It's a long way," Nathaniel protested.

"Won't matter." The man punched in a message on his cell phone. "He's on his way."

Moments later the kid appeared. Six foot four at least, with shoulders that told Nathaniel he probably played football. The teenager was visibly eager, chomping at the bit to get outside. "Happy to help, sir," he said, beaming at Nathaniel. "Which tree would you like?"

Nathaniel wanted to say *forget it*, but in his gut he knew Dani would love having a tree. "Any of them." Good grief.

The manager grimaced. "Sorry we don't have ornaments."

"Believe me," Nathaniel said, "it's okay."

The trip back to the condo was surprisingly entertaining. Nathaniel dragged the heavy duffel bag along behind him, occasionally changing arms when his shoulder protested. "So tell me, Toby, do you work at the store on a regular basis?"

"When I'm not practicing football or basketball or out with my girl."

Toby had the four-foot, live tree—in a plastic stand—balanced on one shoulder. In his other hand, he carried Dani's precious eggs, a loaf of bread and the strands of lights. The teenager wasn't even breathing hard, nor was he wearing gloves. Nathaniel, probably only fifteen years his senior, felt like an old man trying to keep up.

"Have you been dating this girl for a while?"

"A year and a half, sir. We have plans to go to college together and get married when we graduate."

"Your parents are okay with that?"

"Oh, yeah. They adore Kimberly. Her parents have been married almost as long as mine. Mom always told me to look at a girl's family. That way you know what's important to her, and you can decide if you're compatible."

The young man's casual confidence rattled Nathaniel. Was this what happened when you grew up with actual parental guidance? Surely this kid was far too young to know what he wanted out of life. Then again, Nathaniel wasn't qualified to weigh in on interpersonal relationships, not by a long shot.

Toby used the next twenty minutes to bend Nathaniel's ear about everything from his interest in NASCAR racing to his amazing girlfriend to the Central America trip he and his youth group were going to make during the summer.

Nathaniel listened with half an ear, wondering if he himself had ever been as passionate and excited about life as this young man. For Nathaniel, every goal had been about getting out on his own and proving himself *without* his parents. Yet here was an all-American kid who actually enjoyed his life.

Even Toby tired after the first half mile. When they stopped to catch their breath, Toby set the tree and his packages carefully on the ground and rolled his shoulders. He even put on a pair of gloves.

Nathaniel hid a grin. He did remember what it was like to be seventeen and driven by testosterone. Of course, with Dani in his home, those feelings were pretty much the same right now. He didn't feel the need to flex his muscles, but on the other hand, he *had* made a long trek through knee-deep ice and snow to bring home provisions. Maybe this was the twenty-first-century equivalent of slaying a wild animal and dragging it back to the cave.

Toby blew on his hands and bounced from one foot to the other. "What about you, Mr. Winston. Do you have any kids?"

For some reason, the question caught Nathaniel completely off guard. "Um, no…"

Toby grinned. "You don't sound too sure."

"I'm sure," Nathaniel said firmly. "Come on. Let's get going before we freeze to death."

At the condo, Dani buzzed them in and welcomed them at the door. The way her face lit up when she saw the scrawny little tree gave Nathaniel a warm fuzzy feeling that was scary as hell.

"This is Toby," Nathaniel said. "His dad manages the market. Toby got drafted to help me get back with all of this."

Dani beamed at the teenager, baby Peaches on her hip. "Thank you *so* much, Toby. Here, wait." She reached into her purse on the table in the foyer and pulled out a twenty-dollar bill. "Merry Christmas."

The boy's cheeks reddened even more than they had from the cold. Dani's smile could melt a snowman at fifty paces. "Merry Christmas, ma'am. Happy to do it."

"Will you stay long enough for me to make some hot chocolate?" Dani asked.

Toby grimaced. "Wish I could, but I'd better get back to the store. Your baby is cute." Peaches flirted with him unashamedly.

Dani blinked. "Oh, well, she's not mine, but thanks."

Toby shot Nathaniel a raised-eyebrow look. The baby wasn't Dani's, and Nathaniel had said he didn't have kids. No wonder the boy was confused.

Nathaniel decided to hurry the goodbyes along. "Too bad you can't stay. Thanks for your help. Tell your father thanks, too. Merry Christmas."

When the door closed behind the teenager, an awkward silence fell, one that weighed a thousand pounds. Nathaniel cleared his throat. "I got a tree," he said.

Dani nodded, eyes wide, cheeks flushed. "I see that."

"I thought you'd like it, it being Christmas Eve and all." He didn't tell her it wasn't his idea.

"I think it's wonderful," Dani said softly. She went up on tiptoe and kissed his cheek, so quickly he barely felt it. "Thank you, Nathaniel." She paused. "If you don't mind taking the baby, I'll start putting the groceries away. Would you like something warm to drink? I have a fresh pot of coffee brewing."

"Give me a minute first," he said gruffly. "I need a shower and different clothes."

Dani regretted the kiss as soon as she did it. She wasn't sure what had come over her except that she had been so darned touched by Nathaniel's effort. Toby had helped significantly, but still…

She suspected she had either shocked her boss or made him extremely uncomfortable or both. She came from a very affectionate family. For a moment, she had forgotten where she was. It was a mistake she wouldn't repeat. Nathaniel had disappeared so fast, he probably left a trail of steam.

Before Toby departed, the two men had hefted the full-to-the-brim canvas duffel onto the granite-topped kitchen island. Even with Peaches on one hip, Dani was able to begin putting cans and dry goods into the cupboard. She often enjoyed watching cooking shows on cable, but she didn't consider herself a pro. Something about Christmas Eve, though, gave her a tingling sense of anticipation for the dinner to come.

"Here's the thing," she whispered to Peaches. "It would be super helpful if you would take a nice long nap. Nathaniel needs one, too, and I have a ton of cooking to do." The little girl gazed up at her, fist in mouth. She didn't look at all sleepy.

"Okay, fine. Stay awake. But Santa doesn't visit cranky children, now does he?"

After half an hour, Nathaniel still hadn't appeared. Was he avoiding her? If they were to eat at a decent hour, she needed to get the roast in the oven and start on the pecan pie. For Christmas morning, she had planned a coffee cake with streusel topping and mimosas. Christmas lunch would consist of open-faced beef sandwiches with a cranberry salad.

Without the internet, she would have been lost. Her phone was her lifeline. It helped that Nathaniel kept a drawer full of extra charging cords. Impromptu travel with literally nothing except her purse was not the easiest thing in the world.

When four thirty rolled around, she decided to go in search of her missing boss. She found him facedown on his mattress, sound asleep. Poor man. She knew he wouldn't have left her to handle everything on purpose.

He was bare from the waist up, his tan evidence of holidays spent in tropical climates. His shoulders and back were smoothly muscled. The pair of navy knit pants he had pulled on rode low on his narrow hips.

This was what Nathaniel Winston would look like on lazy Saturday mornings before he climbed out of bed. *Or maybe he sleeps in the nude, Dani. He can't very well do that with his executive assistant and a baby in the house.*

Her cheeks hot, she debated her course of action. Peaches took it out of her hands. The little girl chortled loudly. Nathaniel shot straight up in bed, wild-eyed. "What's wrong?" He scraped his hands through his hair.

"Nothing," Dani said quickly. "Sorry to wake you. But I need to start dinner, and I can only do so much one-handed. I thought Peaches would be asleep by now, but she obviously knows it's Christmas Eve, and she's too excited to close her eyes."

Nathaniel didn't seem amused by her whimsy. "Let me have her. We'll play in the den and stay out of your way."

"How thoughtful," she said, deadpan.

His sharp look questioned her sincerity, and rightly so. It didn't take a genius to see that Nathaniel wanted to avoid

Dani as much as possible. Fine. She didn't need him in the kitchen getting underfoot anyway.

Fortunately, her ambitious Christmas Eve dinner menu consumed her attention for most of the subsequent hour. Once she had seared the roast and tucked it in a deep pan flanked with carrots and potatoes, she put the pie together and popped the sweet treat in the oven with the meat, very glad both dishes cooked at the same temperature.

The condo had a small dining room just off the kitchen. Inside a modern-looking buffet, Dani found navy placemats that matched the navy-and-cream stoneware in the kitchen cabinets. It frustrated her not to have the trappings of holiday colors or even a store-bought poinsettia. Even a couple of red candles would have been nice.

That was the problem with bachelors. They didn't know how to set a scene anywhere but in the bedroom.

Oops. Thinking about Nathaniel and bedrooms was bad mojo. She was already in trouble for her innocent thank-you kiss. Best not to let him see that she was curious enough and attracted enough to be fascinated by thoughts of his private life.

Which brought her directly back to Peaches and Ophelia. Damn Nathaniel's mystery woman. How had she found the chutzpah to pull off such an outrageous stunt?

Brooding over the baby's lack of a proper Christmas didn't help matters. Best to concentrate on what she could control. The only thing left was to put together a spinach-and-almond salad and prepare a light dressing. Serving pieces were ready. She and Nathaniel could take turns holding the baby during dinner, if necessary.

The roast and pecan pie had to cook for thirty more minutes. Plenty of time to put the Christmas tree in the den and decorate it. That meant running into Nathaniel again, but at least he had put on a shirt before he left his bedroom.

She knew that only because he had made a quick appearance in the kitchen earlier to grab coffee. Neither of them was dressed for a formal Christmas Eve meal. She supposed he had kept his appearance very casual in light of her predicament.

Wistfully, she imagined what it would be like if they were actually dating. She might find herself wearing a very special, sexy dress, knowing, or at least hoping, that Nathaniel would remove it at the end of the evening.

After her boss's chilly reception earlier, it took a measure of courage to intrude on his privacy. But the den was arguably the best place for the tree, and this designer condo needed a punch of color and light, tonight of all nights.

Nathaniel didn't look up when she entered the den dragging the tree along behind her. The fir had lost a significant percentage of its needles en route from the store, but it was still presentable. With the heavy plastic base already attached, all Dani would have to do was add some water tonight before going to bed. After all, the tree would stand guard beside the fireplace barely twenty-four hours before the lord of the manor tossed it out. She was pretty sure she knew Nathaniel that well.

Without speaking, she unboxed the tiny lights and began twining them around the tree, attaching one strand to the next. Still, Nathaniel didn't acknowledge her presence. Peaches sat on his knee, trying to get one of his shirt buttons in her mouth. Nathaniel held her firmly, but his attention was on the television. He flipped channels rapidly, presumably checking the football scores.

When she finished the tree and plugged it in, she expected at least a token comment. Her boss was mute. He had to have noticed the cheerful Christmas tree. It upped the cozy factor of the den tenfold. But maybe Nathaniel just didn't care. Stubborn, gorgeous man. She didn't know whether she wanted to kiss him or smack him.

Subdued and disappointed, she tweaked a branch and turned to walk out of the room. "Dinner in twenty minutes," she said over her shoulder.

"Wait, Dani," he said.

She turned around, bracing herself for criticism. "What?"

He lifted a shoulder and let it fall. "I don't mind the tree. But don't expect too much from me. This holiday stuff isn't my thing."

Five

A man knew when he was being an ass. Dani walked out on him without another word. Nathaniel was fully cognizant that he was exhibiting every characteristic of a bad host. The stupid Christmas tree was charming. And festive. Even Peaches cooed when she saw it. So why had he deliberately downplayed Dani's efforts?

Why were the aromas wafting from the kitchen both tantalizing and unsettling? He didn't want his condo to smell like Christmas. He didn't want a tree. He didn't want Dani.

What a liar you are. His libido was more honest than he.

In barely twenty-four hours, Dani had transformed Nathaniel's hideout from the world into a warm, holiday-scented, incredibly appealing home. How she had done it so quickly and so well, he couldn't exactly say. It was more than the groceries and the tree, though he couldn't put his finger on what was so different with her here.

Maybe it was the baby. Everyone knew that babies were precious and cute. Perhaps little Peaches was bachelor kryptonite. He sniffed her hair, wondering for the millionth time if he was her biological father. Shouldn't he be able to tell instinctively? Wasn't there some sort of parental bonding moment when all became clear?

If there was, he hadn't experienced it yet.

Dani didn't bother calling him to dinner. His phone dinged with a blunt, unemotional text. It's ready…

Standing up with a sigh, he took the baby to the tree. "Do you like it?" he asked softly. "It's supposed to have ornaments, but I don't have a single one."

The baby reached out to grab the lights. She'd probably chew the cord in two if he let her. Those bottom teeth had to be poking through soon. "No touching," he warned, nuzzling the top of her head with his chin. "We'd better go wash up for dinner before Dani loses patience with us."

The kitchen was filled with steam, delightful smells and a woman who resembled his efficient executive assistant, but in this setting looked more like a wife. The knot in his stomach grew.

Dani glared at him, clearly upset that he hadn't appreciated her efforts with the tree.

"Smells wonderful," he said, hoping to win a few points with genuine appreciation for her culinary efforts.

"We're eating in the dining room," she said, her tone frosty. "We may as well serve our plates in here. That way things won't get cold. I took the liberty of opening a bottle of wine. Let me have the baby. After you fix your plate, I'll do mine. There's plenty, but save room for dessert."

The solid meat-and-potatoes meal reminded him of something his grandmother might have prepared. His mother had grown up in her aunt's home, an orphan by the age of eight. But Nathaniel had substantial memories of his paternal grandmother. She had come over from Italy and spoke heavily accented English. Her cooking had been sublime.

He piled food onto his plate unapologetically. After his marathon trip in the snow today, a few extra calories were neither here nor there. Once he had set his plate in the dining room, he took the baby back. "Your turn, Madam Chef," he said lightly. To his surprise, Dani disappeared and came back lugging the Fraser fir—stand, lights and all.

"That's the advantage of a small tree," she said smugly. "They're sort of portable."

She plugged in the lights and sat down. At the last moment, she took her phone from her pocket and cued up Christmas music. Soon, they were eating in silence, save for the holiday tunes playing softly in the background.

With every bite Nathaniel took, his stomach tightened. The food was spectacular. The baby behaved. It was something else, something powerful and dangerous that stole his appetite and tightened his throat.

In this room, here and now, was everything he had never had, everything he told himself he didn't need. Family time. Cozy holidays. A beautiful, capable woman willing to work at his side to create a home.

He forced himself to clear his plate in deference to Dani's efforts on his behalf. Two glasses of wine didn't still his unease. They chatted lazily during the meal about the weather and the bowl games and whether the thaw would start Monday or wait until Tuesday.

Eventually, the baby fell asleep in Dani's arms. The two females were flushed and beautiful, Madonna and child.

"I feel terrible about this," Dani said suddenly, her expression troubled.

"About what?" There was no way she could have read his mind.

"About Peaches's first Christmas. She should have a stocking and leave cookies for Santa. That's how it's done, or so I'm told. Her mother's selfish behavior is robbing her of a special occasion."

Nathaniel shook his head. "As far as that baby's concerned, today might as well be April Fools'. The kid doesn't know the difference."

"*I* know," Dani said stubbornly.

"There's nothing we can do about it."

"If this was *Little House on the Prairie*, I'd make her a pinafore out of a flour sack, and you'd carve her a toy train with your pocketknife."

Even in the midst of his turmoil, he was amused. "I don't own a pocketknife."

"Well, I should have bought you one for Christmas."

An awkward silence fell. Nathaniel wished he was holding the baby. Peaches was a helpful decoy and a place to focus his attention.

In a few hours, it would be Christmas Day. If this was how Dani did Christmas Eve, what did she have up her sleeve for the following morning?

For the briefest of moments, he caught a flash of the two of them in bed, laughing, the baby between them. At the table eating breakfast. In front of the tree, opening presents. Panic shot through him with the force of an erupting geyser.

"This isn't real," he said, concealing his desperation beneath a veneer of calm.

Dani looked at him with a frown. "What's not real? The food? The baby? The tree? I'm confused."

He stood up to pace, tossing his napkin on the table. "We need to talk, Dani."

Her face went white, and she clutched the baby closer. "Go right ahead. Say what you have to say."

"*None* of this is real," he said doggedly. "We're not a family. This isn't a Norman Rockwell Christmas Eve. You and I are business associates. Peaches being with me is a big misunderstanding."

"I don't understand why you're so upset," Dani said quietly. She watched him with big blue eyes that saw far more than he wanted her to see.

Seeking to temper his anxiety and his distress, he sucked in a huge breath and turned his back for a moment on the sight of Dani and the baby sitting at his elegant mahogany table. The blizzard was to blame for all of this. All he had to do was remember that life would get back to normal soon.

He swung back around and sighed. "My father lost his company in his midfifties."

Dani blinked. "He did?"

Nathaniel nodded jerkily. "I told you my mother was not diagnosed until I was in high school. The episode that triggered her hospitalization was so severe she suffered a massive break from reality."

"That must have been terrifying for you and your dad."

"My father protected her as best he could all those years, but now she was institutionalized with little hope of returning home. It crushed him. He couldn't or wouldn't confide in me. Maybe he thought I was too young. The stress affected his health. Eventually, he found solace in the arms of a woman who worked for him. It didn't last long. Still, the damage was done. The employee filed a sexual harassment lawsuit, including charges for mental pain and anguish. A court awarded her a huge settlement, and my father had to liquidate the company to meet his obligations."

Nathaniel expected some response from Dani, any response. She stared at him blankly, as if nothing he had said made sense.

The silence grew—with it, the certainty he had ripped apart something fragile and wonderful. Dani's long-lashed blue eyes shone with tears. To her credit, she blinked them back successfully.

She bit her lip, her pallor marked. "Let me be sure I understand. This lecture you're giving me is because I cooked dinner and dared to acknowledge that tonight is Christmas Eve? Based on that, you're afraid I'm going to sue you and take away your livelihood? Have I got it, Nathaniel? Is that what you're telling me?"

"You're making me sound like a lunatic," he said sullenly.

Dani jumped to her feet, glaring at him, and headed for the door. Her chin wobbled ever so slightly. "No," she said, her voice tight with hurt. "You're doing a fine job of that all on your own. The thing is, Nathaniel, you're not a Scrooge at all. You're something far worse. Scrooge had a change of heart in his life. You don't have a heart at all. You're a machine. A cardboard figure of a man, a coward. I hope you choke on your pie."

If she had stormed out of the room, he might have found the energy to fight back. Instead, her icy, dignified departure warned him to let her go. It was Christmas Eve. The woman who had helped him with his baby crisis and done her best to create a bit of holiday joy in the midst of a snowstorm was insulted and pained beyond words, and it was his fault.

He should have handled things better. Nothing he said was a lie. But what he had failed to mention was how much it hurt to see what his life might have been like if he hadn't learned from his father's weakness.

Nathaniel didn't want to be weak. He didn't want the

responsibility of a spouse and children. His life had been rumbling along just fine. Why in the devil had he let himself fall prey to feelings that were nothing more than syrupy commercialism?

Holiday music and Christmas lights and good food were nothing more than a Band-Aid covering the world's ills. Come Monday, everyone's life would be as good or as bad as it ever was. Nathaniel was guided by reason and pragmatism. Those qualities in his leadership style had helped make New Century Tech prosper.

Doggedly, he ignored the sick lump of dread in his stomach. He went to the kitchen, cut a piece of the beautiful pecan pie, topped it with a swirl of whipped cream and returned to the dining room to eat his dessert in solitary splendor. After several minutes, he placed his fork on the empty plate and rested his elbows on the table, head in his hands.

Damn it, the pie was good. Downright amazing. The pecans had a crunchy glaze and the filling was sweet but not too sweet. If you wanted to know what happiness and love tasted like, this was it.

The condo was as quiet as a winter snowfall. Nathaniel had spent at least half a dozen December 24ths alone during his adult life, maybe a few more. But tonight—this very moment—was the first time he had ever *noticed* something was missing on Christmas Eve.

His outburst drained him. Dani's stricken response excoriated him. He felt raw, his emotions exposed for all the world to see. It wouldn't have mattered so much except that he valued Dani's good opinion.

Moving quietly, he cleared the table and set about cleaning up the kitchen. It was only fair. He hadn't helped with meal preparations. Truthfully, though, the reason for his efforts was more about delaying consequences than it was having a tidy home.

His brain whirred, jumping from thought to thought like a hound dog chasing butterflies in a meadow. What had he done? For that matter, what was he doing now? If Peaches were really his daughter, what did the future hold for him?

In forty-five minutes, every pot and pan and plate and bowl was out of sight. Countertops gleamed. It was easy enough to restore a kitchen to its original state. Unfortunately, the harsh words he had served Dani were far more difficult to put back in the box.

First things first. He picked up his phone and sent a text.

It's late. I'm coming to your room to get Peaches.

Dani's response was quick and terse.

No. She's asleep. You had her last night. My turn.

Nathaniel sent two more texts insisting that he be the one to deal with the baby, but there was no response at all. Either Dani had turned off her phone, or she was ignoring him. He couldn't bring himself to knock on her door. She deserved her privacy.

After half-heartedly watching TV for a couple of hours, he headed to his own room, intending to read. He'd bought the latest medical thriller by an author he admired. That should distract him from his jumbled thoughts.

Unfortunately, all he could focus on was the image of Dani. By now he had memorized everything about her. The low, husky music of her laugh. The way her blue eyes changed from light and sparkly to navy and mysterious. The graceful way she moved.

As the night waned, he dozed only in snatches. The silence in the house became oppressive. Was Dani okay? Was Peaches? Were both females sound asleep? He'd never experienced the wakefulness of being responsible for another human being.

Actually, that wasn't true. Long ago, during a time he tried to forget, this same stomach-curling worry had been his from time to time. Whenever his father had gone out of town on business, he always reminded Nathaniel to *keep an eye on your mother.*

Nathaniel had never really understood what he was watching out for. He only knew that his mother was not like his friends' moms. Those women baked cookies and sat on the bleachers at T-ball games. Nathaniel's mother mostly ignored him. When she did focus on his hapless self, her tendency was to smother him with adoration that held a marked tinge of frantic desperation and mania.

As much as he had craved her attention as a boy, he learned early on that it was better for the family dynamic when she didn't notice him.

His thoughts drifted back to Dani. She was warm and nurturing and so completely natural with Peaches. Not one echo of disapproval or reluctance marked the way she related to the baby. Even if she thought Nathaniel was a cold bastard for ignoring his own child up until now, she never voiced her concern. He had no idea if she believed him or not when he said the infant wasn't his.

What if he were wrong?

The mental struggles kept on coming. In the wee hours of Christmas morning, Nathaniel faced an unpalatable truth—the real reason he had created such an unfortunate scene at dinner.

For months now, he had been deeply attracted to his executive assistant. The only way he had been able to manage his unfortunate response to her was to pretend she was part of the office furnishings. Maintaining the status quo meant he was the boss and Dani an extremely valued employee.

The blizzard, along with Ophelia's dramatic stunt, had upset the balance in Nathaniel's life. At this point, he doubted whether the tide could be turned again. Dani was funny, compassionate…a *real*, breathing woman living beneath his roof. He liked her scent and the messy knot she fashioned to keep her hair out of her face. He loved the way her generous curves filled out his boring dress shirts.

Seeing her in his clothes was gut-level sexy. Like a film star in a magazine caught on camera in her own backyard, Dani was just Dani. No artifice. No mask to hide behind. No attempt to impress.

Nathaniel was very much afraid he was infatuated with her, maybe worse.

As he lay there in the dark, battling emotions he had kept locked away for so long, his chest ached and his eyes burned. Damn Ophelia. Damn the storm. If things hadn't gotten all jacked up, perhaps he could gradually have tested the waters with Dani.

Instead, here they were, thrust together in a faux environment. His sex hardened and his breathing grew ragged. What would it be like to take her here in his bed? Did she even have a boyfriend?

It stunned him to realize he didn't know the answer to that question. In the midst of his fantasies lay the grim realization he was probably the last person on the planet to whom Dani Meadows would turn for a relationship.

In little more than a week, they would both be back at New Century Tech, hard at work, each easing into familiar roles. Could he bear it? After having her here, just down the hall, would he be able to treat her like an employee again?

At 3:00 a.m., he climbed out of bed. He was only torturing himself by trying to sleep. In his sock feet, he tiptoed down the hall and listened at the guest room door. Not a sound emanated from within, though a tiny strip of light showed underneath the door.

He tapped quietly. "Dani. Are you awake?"

No answer. Any one of a number of possibilities came to mind. Dani might have fallen asleep exhausted and left a light on unintentionally. Or perhaps it was on so she could check the baby easily.

He shouldn't open the door. Every rule or law of hospitality expressly forbade it. Not to mention the fact that he and Dani had parted on angry terms.

Nathaniel turned the knob anyway.

The room was empty.

He stood there in the middle of the expensive plush carpet with his mouth agape. The bathroom door was open. No sense peering in there. Dani would have been talking to the baby if they were in residence. He liked how she communicated with the kid as if Peaches could understand every word.

Clearly, Dani had managed to slip quietly past Nathaniel's bedroom without him hearing a single thing.

Undaunted in his quest, he did an about-face and headed for the den. There he found a scene that gripped his heart and wouldn't let go.

Somehow, maybe while the baby slept, Dani had retrieved the small tree from the dining room and returned it to the place of honor beside the dancing orange and yellow flames. A simple cotton afghan was spread at the base of the tree. The baby slept peacefully on her tummy, one fist curled against her cheek.

Dani wasn't asleep at all. She sat on the stone hearth, elbows on her knees, fingers steepled beneath her chin. Wearing only his shirt that reached almost to her knees, she was barelegged and gorgeous. The misery on her face made his chest hurt.

He took the end of the sofa nearest the fireplace and leaned forward to face her. "I'm sorry," he said.

"No, you're not." Dani's cold certainty was worse than her anger. "You meant every word you said. The only reason you have any regrets now is because we're stuck with each other for at least another thirty-six hours, maybe more."

"Will you cut me some slack?" he pleaded.

"Why? Why should I?"

Who knew that blue eyes could freeze a man? He swallowed. "I don't know if I can explain."

"Try me." Perhaps she wasn't completely calm. She jumped to her feet and wrapped her arms around her waist, standing beside their small, fragrant Christmas tree and staring at it intently as if it had the power to provide answers to difficult questions.

She was so beautiful and yet so far away. *He* had put that emotional distance between them. Because he was scared. "Look at me, Dani." He stood as well, but he didn't pace. This was too important.

Slowly, she turned to face him. He couldn't read her expression. The woman who was usually open and without artifice had locked her emotions in a deep freeze. "You're the boss," she quipped, her tone deliberately inflammatory.

"This isn't easy for me," he said. The words felt like sand in his throat.

That chin wobble thing happened again. Dani's jaw worked as if she were trying not to cry. "Today is the worst Christmas I've ever had," she whispered. "And that's counting the one when my mom was in the hospital with pneumonia and my father burned the turkey. So don't talk to me about easy."

He bowed his head, tormented by guilt, wracked by indecision. No bolt of divine intervention came to save him. With a deep ragged breath, he managed to look at her straight on without flinching. "I'm becoming obsessed with you, Dani…and that scares the hell out of me. I don't know what to do."

"You probably ate too much," she taunted. "Indigestion passes. Grab an antacid. You'll be fine."

"Don't be flip," he growled. "I'm serious. All I can think about is kissing you to see where it takes us."

As it had earlier in the dining room, every scrap of color drained from Dani's face, leaving her pale. "You don't want to kiss me, not really. You think I'll ruin your life."

"Of course I want to kiss you, but that *won't* be the end of it. You're in my head, damn it. And in my gut. I can't sleep." He paused, his forehead damp and his hands clammy. In desperation, he said the one thing that a woman like Dani might respond to favorably. "I need you, Dani. Badly."

Almost in slow motion, he reached out and took her hand in his. She looked at him with an expression that was three parts fear and one part the same burning curiosity tearing him apart. If she had shown the slightest resistance, he would have stopped instantly.

Instead, she took a step toward him. "Nathaniel." The way she said his name, husky and sweet, was his undoing. He dragged her against his chest and held her so tightly she laughed softly.

"I have to breathe," she said.

Releasing her a millimeter, he sighed. "I'll breathe for both of us." He rested his chin on top of her head, feeling the silky, caramel-taffy waves tickle his middle-of-the-night beard. "Tell me to stop," he pleaded hoarsely.

"I won't." She licked the pulse beating at the base of his

throat. "But I won't be accused of seduction, though. If we do this, it's all on you, *Mr.* Winston. Maybe you should think long and hard before you do something you'll regret."

Her schoolmarmish admonishment only made him more desperate. How could she stand there and be so cool? "I'm already long and hard," he complained. "That's what I'm trying to tell you."

Dani felt ill. For months and months, she had wondered what it would be like to have Nathaniel look at her the way a man looks at a woman he desires. Well, now she knew. And it wasn't good.

Her boss didn't *want* to want her. Somehow that was a thousand times worse than the strict professionalism he showed her in their working relationship.

It took everything she had to pull away from him and back up when all she wanted to do was rip off his clothes. "I'm serious, Nathaniel. Do we have a physical spark—yes, but you're giving me mixed signals. Heaven knows that might be the understatement of the year. I'm a grown woman. I have needs, too. We're snowed in together with nothing to distract us. It stands to reason we might feel *something*. That doesn't mean we have to act on it."

"I said I was sorry for earlier." His gaze was stormy and hot with male intent.

"Sorry, maybe. But you spoke the truth. What could possibly induce me to do something so reckless and self-destructive?"

Reeling her in for a second time, he smoothed stray hairs from her cheek and tucked them behind her ear, his smile lopsided. The touch of his fingertips on her hot skin undid her. Like a foolish Victorian maiden made to swoon by pretty words and innocent caresses, she melted into his embrace.

As kisses went, it was world-class. Despite his professed conflicted emotions, Nathaniel was now totally in control, completely confident. He held her without a sign of awkwardness, as though the two of them had been intimate for weeks and months.

To his credit, he coaxed rather than insisted. The first kiss was soft and warm and exploratory. His taste was sinful and decadent. Dani's hands clung to his shoulders as if she were about to go down with the *Titanic*. Her heart beat so loudly in her ears, she wondered if he noticed.

One of his arms held her firmly against his chest. The other hand tangled in her hair and loosened the rubber band that was her only claim to style. Now her hair tumbled onto her shoulders. She had washed it at bedtime. It was still damp.

Nathaniel shuddered and buried his face in the curve of her neck. "You smell like apple pie," he muttered.

"It's the shampoo in your guest bathroom," she said primly. One part of her brain couldn't believe this was actually happening.

"Please tell me I'm not making a fool of myself, Dani."

She shook her head, finally brave enough to stroke the silky hair at the back of his neck. "You're a lot of things, Nathaniel Winston. But never a fool."

He pulled back and stared into her eyes. "Do you want me? Do you want this? Be honest, please."

Taking his face between her hands, she managed a smile. "I've never wanted anything more." She paused, biting her lip.

"What?" he asked sharply.

His frown alarmed her. "I'm on the Pill, but I need you to wear protection."

"Of course."

A dark red flush spread from his throat to his hairline.

She had either embarrassed him or angered him. "I'm not the kind of woman who takes chances," she said, "all evidence to the contrary."

"Of course not," he said. "But you need to believe me when I say I took no chances with Ophelia. It might have been a one-night stand, but I'm not suicidal. I used condoms. If Peaches is mine, it was conception that defied the odds."

The baby in question slept peacefully at their feet, the lights on the little tree casting colored shadows on her small body.

Dani sighed. "I believe you. Accidents happen, though."

He gripped her wrist, forcing her attention away from the child and back to him. "I'll get condoms," he said. "Don't move."

Nodding jerkily, she forced a smile. "Hurry."

When she was alone again, Dani blinked and sank to her knees on the rug. "Oh, Peaches. What have I done?"

Six

For one wild moment, Dani started to scoop up the baby. It wouldn't be hard to prevent herself from crossing a monumental line in the sand. All she had to do was pretend Peaches had awakened on her own. Babies did that all the time.

Her hand hovered over the downy head for what seemed like forever. Nerves sent her stomach into a free fall and then whooshed it back up again. *Oh, God, am I insane?* Nathaniel Winston was going to break her heart.

"Having second thoughts?"

The masculine voice startled her so badly, she lost her balance and sat down hard on her butt. "I didn't expect you back so soon."

He stared at her strangely. "My bedroom is two doors away. How long did you think it would take?"

"Oh." Suddenly, her nerves returned full force. Nathaniel was a sophisticated, highly sexual man. Dani was completely out of her depth. She swallowed hard. "When I fantasized about this, I was wearing my best panties and a sexy negligee."

His jaw dropped. "You fantasized about me?"

"Well, of course. You're you. Don't you ever look in a mirror?"

"That's ridiculous."

Against all odds, she had gained a temporary advantage. She stuck out her hand. "Help me up, please." When his hard, warm palm took hers, male fingers clasping smaller female ones, she exhaled shakily. "I didn't change my mind."

"Thank God."

Nathaniel scooped her up in his arms and carried her the few steps to the sofa. He deposited her on her back and began unbuttoning the borrowed shirt she wore. Dani had already rinsed out her only set of underwear in preparation for wearing it again the following day. Consequently, she was completely naked underneath.

When Nathaniel realized that pertinent fact, he froze for several seconds. Then he laid back the two sides of the shirt and studied her raptly. "Merry Christmas to me," he muttered, his eyes glazed with unmistakable hunger.

Dani had the strongest urge to reach for the afghan and cover herself. Her breasts were on the large side. Her tummy wasn't completely flat. The women in her family loved to cook and it showed. "Turn off the lamp," she begged. "We'll still have the tree."

Nathaniel shook his head slowly. "No. I want to see everything."

Reverently, he put a hand on one breast, cupping her fullness with his fingers.

Dani flinched instinctively. She wanted to dive into sex

without thinking, letting madness take control. Instead, Nathaniel seemed prepared to savor the moment.

She reached for the hem of his shirt, trying to lift it over his head. "We should hurry," she said. "Before the baby wakes up."

Nathaniel grabbed her wrist. "Not so fast. I want to look at you."

Apparently, he meant that quite literally. For the longest time, he simply stared. Beneath his intense regard, the tips of her breasts pebbled and ached. Gooseflesh broke out all over her body, though the room was plenty warm.

"Nathaniel..." She trailed off, not sure what she wanted to say.

His gaze met hers. "What?" His pupils were dilated.

"You're embarrassing me."

A tiny frown creased the real estate between his eyebrows. "Why? You're exquisite. A man could lose himself for hours doing nothing more than this." But at last, he released her breast and placed his hand, palm flat, on her abdomen. "I want to spend all night learning what you like...what you want."

"We don't have all night." It was true. They'd be lucky to have half an hour. Why was Nathaniel wasting time? She rested her fingertips on his taut thigh. "I want you naked. That's my Christmas wish right now. Come to me, Nathaniel."

Her urgent plea got through to him. With one rueful glance at the sleeping baby, he stood and ripped his shirt over his head.

The man was beautiful. There was no other way to describe it. Broad shoulders, a dusting of dark hair on his tautly muscled chest, bronzed skin. When he dragged the soft cotton pants down his legs and kicked them away, his erection sprang free, tall and thick and ready for action.

Oh, my.

He knelt beside the sofa and touched her upper thigh. "Let me pleasure you, sweet Dani. I want to hear you scream my name."

What followed next was an erotic assault on her senses. He caressed and teased and aroused her until she was half-mad with wanting him and completely blind to all the reasons she shouldn't. Dani had been with only two men. One was a long-term relationship in her early twenties, one that didn't work out. The second was a mistake born of loneliness and the conviction that life was passing her by.

Now here was Nathaniel. Not long-term. Definitely a mistake.

How could a woman leap into disaster and not even care? Turned out, it was easy. Too easy. All she had to do was close her eyes and pretend that Nathaniel was her happily-ever-after. That's what women did, right? Weave fantasies?

Unfortunately, Nathaniel wasn't in a mood to appease her fairy tales. At last, he stood again, this time coming down on top of her and moving between her thighs. "Open your eyes, Dani. This is me you're hiding from. I won't have it. Open your eyes."

Holding Nathaniel's gaze while he slid deep into her body shattered her. He witnessed every nuance of her reaction, including the slight wince when he pressed as far as he could go, thrust irrevocably at the mouth of her womb.

Dani shuddered and panted. It was too much and not enough. He filled her almost uncomfortably. She was tense and frightened—not of Nathaniel, but of her own wildly careening emotions.

She turned her head, watching the dancing flames that somehow had found their way into her body and were roasting her alive.

Her lover grasped her chin and turned her head to face him. His gaze was fierce. "If you wanted to change your mind, all you had to do was say so."

Shocked to the tips of her bare toes, she saw that she had hurt him. "Oh, Nathaniel, no. It's not that. I want you, I do." She linked her arms around his neck and canted her hips, allowing him to steal one more millimeter.

He kissed her roughly, his tongue tangling with hers. "Then why do you keep escaping in your head?" He nibbled the sensitive flesh below her ear and raked her collarbone with sharp teeth.

Dani moaned. "I'm scared. You make me crazy." She was afraid to come, terrified that she would shatter into a million jagged pieces and never be the same again.

His kisses gentled, even as his big frame shuddered. Much of his weight rested on his forearms, protecting her. But his lower body held her fast. "We're on even ground then, because I don't know what the hell we're doing. Don't be frightened of me, my brave, bighearted Dani. I won't let anything happen to you, I swear."

She kissed him then. Some might have called it a kiss of surrender. Dani knew it was more. It was taking what she wanted despite the inevitable consequences. "Make love to me, Nathaniel."

Whatever gentleness he had shown her in the beginning burned up in the fire of simple, undeniable, lustful pleasure. He pumped hard, rapidly. Her first climax hit sharp and sudden. She cried out and moaned as he carried her through it. But Nathaniel was far from done. They tumbled to the soft carpet with Dani on top. His fingers dug into her hips with bruising strength.

His chest heaved. His eyes blazed. "Ride me, honey. Find what you need. I can wait…maybe."

She took him at his word. It was exhilarating and frantic

and more wildly pleasurable than she had ever imagined. Twice more, she climaxed. With the last one, Nathaniel came as well, dragging her down to his chest and holding her in arms of steel as he groaned and thrust his way to the finish line.

When it was over, the only sound in the room was their labored breathing and the gentle hum of the gas logs.

Dani's bottom, exposed to the air, started to get cold. She dared not move. If she did, she would have to face Nathaniel. How could she do that? How would she ever again be able to look him in the eye and pretend they were nothing more than boss and assistant?

Thank God she had already been sending out résumés. Perhaps tonight was her subconscious way of making sure she followed through on her decision to leave New Century. Nothing about Nathaniel had changed. He'd warned her as much at the dinner table. Dani would have to be the one to make smart decisions.

But how? How was a woman supposed to resist a man who combed his fingers through her hair and seemed not to notice that she had the beginnings of muffin top? He made love to her like she was a pool of life-giving water, and he'd been lost in the Sahara. She'd felt his desperation. His whole body shook, and not just with orgasm, but as he caressed her breasts and kissed her so sweetly.

Doggedly, she told herself that Nathaniel was right. *None* of this was real. They were playacting. Making the best of a bad situation, or two bad situations, if you counted Peaches. The snow and the child. Blizzards and babies and boners, oh, my.

The irreverent thought made her giggle.

Nathaniel noticed, of course. He opened one eye and glared up at her. "I hope you're not laughing at me. I might point out you're in a very vulnerable position."

She sobered rapidly. "No, sir, boss." Brushing her lips across his stubbly jaw, she played the aggressor. "Merely wondering how long I have to wait for round two."

Disengaging their bodies, he scrambled to his feet and pulled her up with two hands. "I have a great shower. Lots of settings on the showerhead. You'll love it."

"Um..."

He lifted her chin. "Talk to me, little Christmas elf. I'm having the damnedest time reading you right now."

She shrugged, trying to pretend she wasn't naked. "Showers are kind of personal. I'm not exactly a *sharing* kind of person when it comes to personal hygiene."

Nathaniel's lips quirked. "It's a good thing you're cute."

"Why is that?"

He kissed her nose. "Because you're a lot of work."

"I am *not*," she said, affronted. "Have I complained once about being kidnapped and forced to be your nanny?"

"You've been a saint," he said gravely. "But I was talking about your emotional state. I've seen pictures of a sphinx who's less inscrutable than you are. Two days ago we were in the office doing the usual, and now you tell me you've been fantasizing about me. Who knew?" He sounded aggrieved.

It was too perfect an opening not to ask. She stroked one of his biceps, loving the way her caress made him shiver. "I'm curious. Did you ever fantasize about *me* when we were at the office?"

Doors slammed shut in Nathaniel's brain. *Danger, danger.* He drew in a ragged breath. "Hell, yes. But that was very unprofessional on my part." He backed away. "I think you're right about the shower. If you don't mind, I'll go first. If Peaches wakes up in the meantime, I'll give her a bottle so you can get some sleep."

He didn't remember how he got to his bedroom. He must have released Dani. He must have grabbed his shirt and pants, because they were clutched in his hands.

Swallowing back the taste of dread and panic, he showered quickly and changed into jeans and an old college sweatshirt. Despite the hot water, he was cold through to the bone.

The expression in Dani's eyes when she looked up at him hadn't been inscrutable at all. It encompassed vulnerability and shy affection and probably a million questions. Simple questions any woman had the right to ask when she had just surrendered her body to a man she should be able to trust. A man who had vowed to protect her.

For ten minutes, he paced the confines of his bedroom, formulating a game plan, deciding what to say. If he and Dani continued to have sex, she would expect things from him. Things he likely couldn't or wouldn't give. But if he came right out and said he was only playing around, he would leave himself open to her recriminations, maybe even reprisals.

She was a decent woman. With a kind heart. Still, he and she together had crossed a line. A line that made him as vulnerable as his father had been all those years ago.

Dani wouldn't sue him. He wouldn't lose his company. The chances of that happening were infinitesimal.

Without warning, a distant memory flashed, one he had forgotten in the mists of time. A woman in a professional, powder blue suit occupied the witness stand, her face hard and cold as she listed Nathaniel's father's transgressions, demanding vengeance. Nathaniel, almost eighteen by that time, had been sitting in the back row of the courtroom.

His mother was hospitalized. His father was a broken man, forced to appear before judge and jury and have his life's work torn to shreds. Nathaniel hadn't known how to help either of his parents.

A sound from outside the sanctuary of his bedroom jerked him back to the present. He had to go back to the den and face Dani. Squaring his shoulders, he told himself not to overreact. All he had to do was tread carefully. As soon as the snow melted and Ophelia retrieved the baby, life would go back to normal.

When he found his two female houseguests, they were ensconced on the sofa, wrapped in an afghan, Dani was wearing his shirt again. Her eyes were closed, her head resting against the back of the seat. Peaches was awake, noisily downing a bottle of formula. The lights were off. Only the flames from the fire illuminated the room.

Carefully, Nathaniel sat down beside woman and child. He put a hand on Dani's knee. She was sitting cross-legged with the baby in her lap. "You okay?" he asked softly. "Do you want me to take her?"

Dani opened her eyes and stared at him. He bore her scrutiny stoically. His assistant was a smart woman. She had to know something was wrong. Thankfully, she let it slide. "We're fine, Nathaniel. Why don't you go back to bed? You have no idea how long Peaches will be staying with you, and unfortunately, I won't be around to help much longer. You should get sleep while you can."

He inhaled sharply. Apparently they weren't going to discuss his earlier behavior. Instead, Dani let it be known very plainly she was not going to linger in his home waiting for scraps of his attention and affection. There was a quiet dignity about her that shamed him. The open, joyful response he'd seen in her after their intimate encounter was gone.

Moving his hand from her knee, he tried to breathe naturally. The gaping hole in his chest made that difficult.

Had he crushed the only person in his life who actually cared about him?

Dani lifted the baby onto her shoulder and patted her back. "How will you go about finding Ophelia?"

"I've contacted a private investigator. Needless to say, he's not eager to leave his family on Christmas. He's promised to get to work on the case first thing Monday. I'm confident Ophelia's still in the city. After all, how far could she get? If we're trapped, so is she."

"Good point." Dani stood, holding the baby carefully. Peaches had nodded off. "I think she'll sleep a few more hours now. We'll see you in the morning."

Nathaniel jumped to his feet. "Wait," he said hoarsely.

Dani turned back, but her posture was defensive, and she held the child as a shield. "What, Nathaniel? What do you want?"

On the surface, it was almost a rhetorical question. As if she knew he didn't know why he had stopped her. But then again, maybe she was demanding more. Explanations. Assurances. Unfortunately, he had none to give.

"It's December 25 already," he said, feeling foolish and desperate. "Merry Christmas, Dani."

Her smile was wistful, perhaps even sad. "Merry Christmas, Nathaniel."

After that, he let her go, because it was the right thing to do. He had no right to coax her into lingering so he would have someone to talk to. He liked being alone. He enjoyed his own company. It was only the snow and the holiday and the baby throwing him off balance.

He prowled the condo, unable to contemplate sleep. If he hadn't been such an ass, Dani might have been in his bed this very moment, her cuddly, warm body pressed against his as they dozed in between bouts of hot, satisfying sex.

What would it take to win a woman like Dani? For one

thing, he would have to change virtually everything about himself. Dani would expect open communication and an honest exchange of feelings and emotions. The thought made him shudder. He'd perfected the art of walling himself off from the world. It was too late to change now.

Walking alone was the only way he knew.

Dani cried herself to sleep. When she awoke four hours later, her head ached and she faced the inescapable conviction she was her own worse enemy. She *knew* what the boss was like, perhaps better than anyone else in his life. Why on earth had she asked him such a stupid question? *Did you ever fantasize about me when we were at the office?*

The raw honesty of his answer had revealed the extent of his conflicted emotions. Nathaniel was a man. Men were creatures of the moment. They compartmentalized things in their brains. Work, sex, food, sleep. The only reason she and Nathaniel ended up being intimate was the result of an unlikely set of circumstances.

As she changed a wet diaper and blew raspberries on a soft baby tummy, she fretted. She needed to get out of this condo. The sooner, the better. If she had sex with her boss a second time, she'd never convince herself to leave. Even worse, she might ignore all common sense and be put in the ignominious position of being *asked* to leave.

That wasn't going to happen. Ever. She might not be able to eradicate her feelings for the man down the hall, but he didn't have to know he was breaking her heart into jagged shards that would never properly fit back together.

Moving to the window, she twitched aside the sheers and looked out. The thaw was supposed to begin today, in theory. High of thirty-eight. Peeks of sunshine. So far, the skies were gray. The coating of ice on top of fifteen inches of snow meant the city was still obliterated. Only the most intrepid would venture out on Christmas Day.

When she closed the curtains and turned around, Nathaniel was standing in the doorway of the guest room. He held out a shopping bag with a quizzical smile on his face. "Your new friend, Reggie, the doorman, came through for us. He dropped off all these baby things a few minutes ago. I thanked him."

"And gave him a big fat Christmas tip, I hope."

"Of course."

"Too bad he has to work the holiday."

Nathaniel nodded. "At least he's only here until two. Several of them are dividing shifts today so no one gets stuck the whole time."

"I'm glad." Dani clutched Peaches like a lifeline. She had worried about imagining Nathaniel naked. The reality was much worse. He was fully dressed in khakis and a white button-front shirt with the sleeves rolled up. His tanned arms, lightly dusted with dark hair, were very masculine, as was the high-end gold watch on his left wrist. But that wasn't the bad part. What made her stomach do sickening flips and flops was this new awareness between them. She couldn't explain it, but it was *there*.

While she stood by the bed trying not to blush, Nathaniel upended the shopping bag and dumped a pile of baby clothes on the bed. "Good news, kid," he said with a chuckle. "You finally get to wear something new."

"Now, if only Reggie had access to my size," Dani joked. The fact that she was modeling another of Nathaniel's soft cotton dress shirts over the same gray thermal pants put her at a distinct disadvantage.

Nathaniel shot her a grin, his expression smug. "It's still early," he said. "I'm sure Santa hasn't forgotten you, Dani."

She had no clue what that meant. But she wasn't in the

mood for flirty repartee. Today was going to be Christmas without the feels.

To keep things on an impersonal track, she propped Peaches on her hip and began sorting through the clothing. Like most baby things, the rompers and sleepers and adorable dresses were mostly in mint condition. At this age, infants grew so fast, it was almost impossible to wear an outfit enough times to do any damage.

Nathaniel stood beside her, making her clumsy and nervous. He picked up a tiny green dress with candy canes appliqued at the hem. "I vote for this one," he said. "Perfect for Peaches's first Christmas Day."

Casually, Dani moved aside, putting a few feet between herself and temptation. "I agree. Why don't you do the honors?"

He blanched. "Me? I have big hands. This stuff looks like doll clothes. You'd better do it. If you don't mind."

Dani hesitated. "Well…"

"What's the problem?"

"I'm leaving when the snow melts, Nathaniel," she said bluntly. "You'll have to do all this yourself."

His expression gave new meaning to the term poker face. "I'll worry about that when the time comes. Besides, Peaches would rather have you dress her right now. She's more comfortable with you."

Dani laid the baby on the bed and quickly switched out the sleeper for the green dress. "Oh, my gosh. Look how cute she is. Hold her, Nathaniel. Let me take a picture." She grabbed her smartphone while Nathaniel made silly faces at Peaches and scooped up the little girl who might or might not be his daughter.

The sight of the big, macho man holding the small, smiling baby made her heart squeeze. They looked right together.

Moments later, Dani tucked the phone in her pocket and managed a casual smile. “If you two are okay for the moment, I’ll put breakfast in the oven. Did I smell coffee brewing? Please say yes.”

“Plenty for both of us,” Nathaniel said. He rubbed noses with the baby. “This beauty and I will be in my office taking care of a little business. Come find us when it’s ready.”

She stared at him. Something in his voice gave her a little fillip of excitement. “Christmas secrets, Nathaniel?”

Seven

Nathaniel smiled, his expression deliberately bland. "Maybe yes, maybe no. I won't be long."

In his office, he spread a blanket on the floor. He'd grabbed it up from the pile on Dani's bed. "Play with your rattle, little one. I've got to wrap a package."

Reggie had proved to be quite accommodating when Nathaniel explained the situation. The overnight delivery had been signed for, and the doorman had sent up Christmas paper and tape. Unfortunately, turning out eye-catching packages was not in Nathaniel's skill set. He'd been a Boy Scout, but tying knots was a long way from handling thick, glossy paper and recalcitrant ribbon.

At last, he was satisfied. He held up the large rectangle and examined it. "What do you think, Peaches? I'm counting on this to win points with a certain prickly woman."

The baby gummed a pink-and-green teether from the drugstore enthusiastically, but didn't endorse Nathaniel's efforts. "I know," he said glumly. "It's probably too little, too late, but she deserves a merry Christmas, even if I *am* a Scrooge."

Since Peaches was in a mood to be cooperative, Nathaniel did a quick check of email, looking over his shoulder guiltily. There was more to life than work. He knew that. Trouble was, up until this particular odd Christmas, work was all he'd ever had on a day like today.

Half an hour later, Dani showed up, flushed and bright-eyed. "Everything's on the table," she said. "Come and eat."

Fortunately, he'd hidden the box behind a tall wooden file cabinet. Even when Dani crouched to pick up the baby, the gift was out of sight. Timing was everything.

In the kitchen, Dani had opted for casual, preparing two places at the granite counter island instead of in the dining room. The room smelled of cinnamon and yeast. "Wow," he said, inhaling with enjoyment. "You went to a lot of trouble." The mimosas were especially tempting, particularly since no one had to go anywhere.

On the other hand, he needed a clear head to negotiate a peace treaty with his beautiful houseguest. He took a stool and held out his hands. "I'll hold her while you eat."

Dani shook her head. "We can both eat. I think she'll be happy in her carrier for a little bit."

Either Dani was a gourmet cook or Nathaniel was starving or both. The streusel-topped coffee cake was warm and fragrant and tasted like heaven on a plate. He was on his third piece before he noticed Dani watching him with a grin.

He stopped dead, his fork halfway to his mouth. "Sorry," he mumbled. "I did leave some for you."

Her sunny smile was the first open, uncomplicated one he'd gotten from her since their encounter in the middle of the night. "It's quite all right. A cook likes to know her efforts are appreciated."

Deliberately finishing the last bite on his plate, he wiped the corner of his mouth with his napkin, drained his glass and reached across the small space separating them to stroke his thumb across her cheek. "I appreciate the hell out of you, my little Christmas elf."

Dani turned bright red and busied herself with the baby. "A simple thank-you will suffice," she muttered.

"What shall we do between now and lunch?" he asked in his most genial Christmas host voice. "When Peaches takes a nap, all sorts of things come to mind." He was treading a line between forcing Dani to remember the good parts of last night and hoping like hell she would overlook the bad ones.

"I really need to talk to my parents," she said, not taking the bait. "To see what the plans are for Tuesday. Perhaps you could entertain the baby while I do that. Afterward, I'll feed her and put her down."

"Of course."

To his disappointment and dismay, Dani handed off the kid and disappeared into her bedroom. Had Nathaniel spooked her, or was the excuse a genuine one?

He couldn't exactly listen at the door. Since he was too jumpy to sit down for any length of time, he cleared the breakfast dishes with one hand and loaded the dishwasher. Fortunately, there was no one around to reprimand him when he sneaked a few more bites of cake.

By the time Dani finally reappeared forty-five minutes later, the baby was getting fussy. Instead of handing her over, Nathaniel decided it was time for him to step up his game. "Let's go to the den," he said. "We don't want to waste that world-class tree. I'll feed the baby, and you can pick a movie. How's that?"

Dani seemed dubious, but she followed his lead. Nathaniel didn't bother with the sofa. He picked the recliner and got comfortable with Peaches in his lap. The baby, as always, guzzled her bottle and conked out.

Dani flipped through his Blu-ray collection and finally settled on one of the original Star Wars movies. He didn't have a single one of the romantic comedies that most women liked, so it was a good thing his guest seemed to share his taste in classic sci-fi/fantasy.

The opening credits had barely finished rolling before the second female in the room fell asleep. Nathaniel grinned wryly. So much for being a stimulating companion. He rubbed the baby's head. "Were you awake a lot during the night, little scamp? Or is Dani tired for another reason?"

His body tightened and his breath caught as lust roared in uninvited. His den was a far different place in the middle of the day than in the dark of night, but it was difficult not to remember holding a naked Dani in his arms and making love to her like a madman.

Hell. Why hadn't he stayed in the kitchen where the atmosphere was far less charged?

He watched the movie, but he'd seen it half a dozen times. It was far more satisfying to study the woman sleeping a few feet away. To a stranger, this scene would have seemed perfectly normal. Only Nathaniel and Dani knew how very abnormal it was.

She had made no bones about her plans to leave him. If memory served, Dani was using vacation days this week to spend time with her family. They certainly wouldn't understand if, at the last minute, New Century Tech demanded her attention.

No, work wasn't the answer. If he were going to keep Dani here, he'd have to try something risky. Maybe tell the truth. He didn't want to be alone this week. Not after he'd had a taste of what the holidays *could* be like.

In the meantime, he'd be content with the status quo.

Dani slept for half an hour and woke with a start. Her cheek was creased from the trim on the sofa arm, and her hair was mussed. "Sorry," she said, adorably flustered. "What did I miss?"

He laughed softly, careful not to wake Peaches. "Nothing you haven't seen before." He picked up the remote and hit Pause. He and Dani had known each other forever. They didn't need a movie for distraction, did they?

"Do you want me to take her?" Dani asked. "I've had a nap. It's your turn."

"I'm fine. Don't worry about me."

"If you say so."

An awkward silence fell. Maybe he was wrong about the movie.

He debated his options. The next move could make things better or worse. It surprised him that he couldn't predict the outcome. In a business negotiation, he would have known. But not now.

"Dani?"

"Hmm?" She stared at the fireplace, her expression pensive.

"Do you mind grabbing something from my office? I don't want to move and wake her."

"Of course." She hopped to her feet. "What am I looking for?"

"A large box on the far side of the wooden file cabinet."

"Got it. Back in a flash."

When she returned, she was carrying the package he had tried so hard to wrap artistically. The result looked even more amateurish now. "Thanks," he said.

"What did you do, Nathaniel? Buy her a four-foot teddy bear? This is heavy."

He shrugged. "It's for you. Merry Christmas, Dani."

She froze, her gaze panicked. "Oh, no. I have nothing for you. This is entirely inappropriate. I appreciate the gesture, but I can't accept."

"You don't even know what it is," he said, his tone mild. He knew if he pushed too hard, she might grow even more stubborn in her refusal.

Her hand smoothed the bright red paper, almost a caress. "It doesn't matter what it is," she said. "You gave me a Christmas bonus at the party Friday."

"It's not a present from your boss," he said, losing patience. "Open the box."

"So it's not from you?"

Was she deliberately misunderstanding him, or were they fighting some war he wasn't prepared to engage in? "Yes," he said, jaw clenched. "It *is* from me. To you. Man to woman. Not boss to assistant."

Dani set the box on the floor and curled her legs beneath her. "Did you get whatever this is before we had sex last night?"

"Well, of course, I did," he said unable to hide his irritation. "We've both been a little busy since then."

She studied his face, her expression earnest. What did she want from him?

"I don't think I can accept a present from you, Nathaniel." Her tone was apologetic. "It's a lovely thought, but under these circumstances, I think it would muddy the waters."

He counted to ten and then to fifteen. "Dani..."

"Yes?"

Why did she have to look at him like he was an ogre?

What did she think he was going to do to her? Lock her up in a harem?

"Open the damned box. Or you're fired."

"Fat chance," she muttered. "No one else would put up with you."

Apparently losing his temper had convinced her. Strange woman.

She picked at the paper like a Depression-era housewife planning to reuse every scrap of paper and tape and ribbon. The whole process was so slow, he wanted to bellow at her to hurry. It took a great deal of self-control to keep his mouth shut and let her finish.

When she finally removed the box lid and lifted the tissue, her mouth opened in a cute little O of surprise. "Nathaniel. What is all of this?"

Dani didn't know what she had expected. Truthfully, she had handled the gift with all the finesse of a bomb squad technician defusing a dangerous device. She didn't want gifts from Nathaniel. Not when their current situation was so remarkably out of control.

Once she had folded back the tissue, she simply stared at the contents, lifting one thing and the next in amazement. Nothing in the box raised any red flags. If anything, the individual items were extremely practical and thoughtful.

Nathaniel watched her, eagle-eyed, making her uneasy. "Well," he said gruffly. "What do you think? It's not the most exciting present in the world, but you strike me as a very practical woman. Who knows if you'll be able to get back to your apartment before you go to see your family. I tried to think of everything."

Everything was not an exaggeration. Inside the large, deep gift box was a collection of the most elegant clothing and toiletries Dani had ever owned. Dressy black pants in warm wool crepe. A red cashmere V-necked sweater. Two bras and several matching panties, more on the practical than sexy side, but very expensive.

Beneath that were designer jeans, casual tops, elegant sets of flats in black and taupe. Tennis shoes. Socks. A whisper-soft nightgown and matching robe in the palest ivory.

And then the cosmetics, glory be. Cleanser and lotion and mascara and everything else a woman might need to dress herself up for the holidays.

"How on earth did you manage this, Nathaniel?" She stared at him in amazement. "I know you work magic in the business world but this is incredible, even for you."

He shrugged, but she could tell her reaction pleased him. "I have a business associate whose wife works at Neiman Marcus. I called her first thing yesterday morning and told her what had happened with the blizzard and being stranded. I explained in general terms what I wanted to give you. She made it all happen."

"In the snow."

"Yep. I was very persuasive."

"This must have cost a fortune." She frowned slightly. "The snow was going to melt eventually. You know this wasn't necessary."

"It *was* necessary," he said forcefully. "Your holiday plans were wrecked. You've had to help care for a baby who is not yours. You've worked out grocery lists and prepared wonderful meals. This was the least I could do."

Dani set the heavy box aside and went to crouch beside his chair. "Thank you, Nathaniel," she whispered, her throat tight with emotion. Clearly he had gone to a great deal of trouble. The sizes were all correct, too. "For a man who bears a remarkable resemblance to Scrooge, you've done a lovely job with this Christmas surprise."

She kissed him softly on the cheek. "I don't know what to say. I'm touched."

He grumbled beneath his breath. "Babies sure as hell cramp a guy's style."

She grinned. "You were hoping my gratitude would translate to sex?"

"Nothing quite so crude." He winced. "But I did hope you wouldn't be mad at me anymore. I want you to be happy, Dani."

She noted that he didn't add the words *with me*. Maybe she was being too picky. "I am happy," she said quietly, brushing a lock of his hair from his forehead. He was holding the baby and couldn't respond physically, but his gaze seared her with its intensity. "Do you mind if I go take a shower and try on some of these things? I can't wait. Not that I don't appreciate the loan of your wardrobe," she said hastily.

He chuckled softly, caressing her visually, giving her goose bumps. "You look fine to me just like you are, but sure. Knock yourself out."

Dani practically danced down the hall. After two whole days of feeling grubby and unsophisticated, she was finally going to be able to meet Nathaniel on level ground. After a super quick shower during which she kept her hair dry, she put on the new undies and tried the red sweater and black pants. Everything fit perfectly.

Instead of twisting her hair up in a messy knot, she took the time to brush it over and over again until it swung thick and shiny at her shoulders. Too much makeup seemed like overkill at this point, but she used the mascara, and she added berry-red lip gloss to match her sweater. In the mirror, her reflection wasn't half-bad.

When she returned to the den, Peaches was awake and playing happily with a teething ring. Nathaniel's eyes widened when he saw Dani. "You look stunning," he said quietly. "Red is a great color on you."

"Nothing like new clothes to give a woman a boost. Thanks again."

"It was the least I could do."

"Are you getting hungry?"

"I could eat."

The stilted conversation was at odds with the almost palpable hunger coursing between them. Dani trembled. "I'll put Christmas dinner together. It will end up being a midafternoon meal, but we can snack later if we get hungry. Do you mind if I open a bottle of wine?"

"Mi casa es su casa," Nathaniel said. "Whatever you want." His words were warm, caressing.

In the kitchen, Dani was torn. Last night she had made use of the dining room for their dinner, and Nathaniel had freaked out. It didn't seem right, though, to have Christmas lunch at the kitchen counter. So no matter how skittish her boss was, she went right ahead with her holiday preparations the same way she would have if this were an ordinary situation.

She whisked together brown gravy. When it was warm and bubbling, she sliced the leftover roast beef in small pieces and added the meat to the pot. Peeling potatoes gave her too much time to think. Tonight the baby would fall asleep, and Dani would find herself alone with Nathaniel again. What was she going to do if he wanted sex? Could she hold him off? Did she want to say no?

Maybe she wanted to enjoy whatever time they had left in this odd and emotionally charged situation.

In less than an hour, she managed to put together a respectable meal—nothing too fancy, but far better than the peanut butter they had dined on the first night. Open-faced roast beef sandwiches on sourdough toast. Fluffy mashed potatoes. Cranberry salad and, of course, plenty of leftover pecan pie for dessert.

The end result was gratifying.

Nathaniel and Peaches appeared just as she was putting the finishing touches on the dinner table. Her boss frowned.

"What now?" Dani sighed. "I left the tree in the den. Nothing holidayish, I swear."

"It's not that," he said. "I just realized I'm going to owe you half a dozen fancy dinners at four-star restaurants to repay you for all you've done."

"Sit down and don't be ridiculous," she said. "I like eating as much as the next person. If I'd been at my parents' house, I would have worked even harder. My mom puts on quite a spread."

Nathaniel consumed most of his meal without speaking. It was impossible to read his mood. Once again, Dani was glad to have the baby as a diversion. Breaking bread together was actually a very intimate thing to do. This time, Nathaniel was the one holding the child and eating one-handed.

At last, Dani couldn't bear the silence any longer. "What are your plans for tomorrow?" she asked. "Assuming the weather does what they say it will."

He stood abruptly. "I'm going to grab some pie. You want yours now or later?"

"Later," she said. Was he in that much of a hurry for dessert, or did he not want to answer her question?

When Nathaniel returned, he held Peaches in one arm and a generous serving of gooey pie in the other hand.

Dani raised an eyebrow. "You'll make yourself sick," she warned.

His smile was wicked. "What a way to go."

While she appreciated the fact that her boss enjoyed her

cooking, bigger issues loomed on the horizon. Sex. The baby. Dani's imminent departure.

"I talked to my mom on speakerphone while I was cooking," she said.

Nathaniel swallowed a bite of pie. "Oh?"

"They thought about postponing our family Christmas until Wednesday, but my siblings can't be off work that day. So we're definitely celebrating Tuesday. I've promised to be there by ten in the morning."

"Sounds good."

Such a bullheaded, frustrating man. "Look at me, Nathaniel."

He lifted his head and eyed her with a deceptively mild expression. "What's wrong?"

"Nothing. Not exactly. But I'm worried about leaving you alone with the baby. Single parenting is hard for anybody."

"Especially a clueless male like me?"

"I didn't say that. Peaches is getting very comfortable with you and vice versa." She shook her head, wondering why she was obsessing about this. Peaches wasn't her problem. Still, it knotted her stomach to think about leaving man and baby to fend for themselves. "The trip from here to home is an hour and a half, give or take. Normally, I would simply drive up Tuesday morning. But first of all, we don't know how much snow and ice will melt tomorrow, and second of all, any standing water will probably refreeze tomorrow night."

"I'd say you're right."

"So I'll have to go tomorrow afternoon."

"Whatever you need to do."

"Do you even care that I'm leaving?" she cried.

He stood up abruptly, nearly knocking over his chair. Her statement echoed in the small dining room.

"This was never supposed to happen." He waved a hand. "I get it. You want to be with your family. I won't stand in your way. You have no obligation whatsoever to me or even to Peaches."

He was saying all the right words, but he was breaking her heart. He was so very much alone. Dani took a deep breath and gambled. "Come with me to visit my parents," she begged. "You and Peaches. I can't bear the thought of leaving you here alone."

Eight

Nathaniel blinked, feeling his anger and frustration winnow away to be replaced by something even more unsettling. He knew what it was like to have someone feel sorry for him, but it had been a very long time since he had been on the receiving end of that reaction. He didn't much care for it. There were any number of things he wanted from Dani. Pity wasn't one of them.

"I have to be at work on Tuesday," he said calmly, careful to reveal nothing of the confusion tearing him apart. "New Century Tech will be open for business. I have employees."

"What about the baby?"

Dani's dogged insistence on planning was commendable, but since he didn't have any of the answers she wanted, his only recourse was stonewalling. "I'll work something out. Besides, the baby will only be with me a day or two longer. I'm confident the investigator will find Ophelia quickly."

"I'm all in favor of positive thinking," Dani said wryly, "but that's not much of a strategy. Seriously, Nathaniel, come to Gainesville with me. It won't be odd if you show up. Mom and Dad often have stray guests at the dinner table, even at the holidays. We wouldn't sleep overnight at the house, of course. There are several nice hotels nearby."

"I appreciate what you're trying to do," he said, "but I'll be fine."

The combative subject was dropped by unspoken consent when Peaches decided she was hungry. Dani fed the baby while Nathaniel cleaned up the kitchen. Already, they had blown through most of the groceries he'd brought home on Saturday. Even the baby supplies were getting low.

When the kitchen was clean and the baby asleep on his bedroom floor, he realized he had to get out of the condo or risk making love to Dani. If they had sex again, she would make assumptions about the two of them. He wasn't ready for that.

The wonderful meal he had consumed sat like lead in his stomach. "I'm going to the store for round two," he said suddenly. "Make a list. I'll be back in a minute."

"Oh, but—"

He exited the warm, cozy kitchen before Dani could say anything else. When he had donned his parka and ski pants and gloves, he went back for the list. "Is it ready?" he asked, not looking at her. The cherry-red sweater he'd given her for Christmas clung to all the right places. Looking at her breasts was a bad idea.

"You can't go to the store, Nathaniel."

"Of course, I can."

"It's Christmas Day. I'm sure there might be some places open here and there, but probably not in walking distance. Quit worrying. I can stretch the food we have left until Monday afternoon. We can always do something simple tomorrow like bacon and eggs and pancakes."

He stripped off his outerwear a piece at a time, feeling ridiculous. "I keep forgetting it's Christmas," he muttered.

Dani shook her head in amusement. "First I've inundated you with too much Christmas, and now you say you forgot about it entirely. Make up your mind."

He shot her a glance, feeling his resolve wane. "I needed to get out of the house," he said bluntly. "Away from you. It wasn't really about the groceries."

"Oh." She looked stricken.

"I want you, Dani. Under the circumstances, it doesn't seem fair to you."

"Because?"

"Because you can't say no without causing tension between us." When she didn't say a word, he lifted his shoulders and rotated his neck. "Never mind. I'm going for a walk. Call me if there's an emergency."

Desperate to get away, he turned on his heel and strode out of the room. He made it to the front door before Dani intervened. The relief he experienced when he heard her voice call to him was overwhelming and inexplicable.

"Don't go out in the cold, Nathaniel. Stay with me."

He turned around slowly. She smiled faintly, but her eyes held secrets. Clearing his throat, he tossed his gloves on the console by the door and ran his hands through his hair. "If I stay, I'll make love to you. Sooner or later. You know that's true."

She swallowed visibly. "Yes."

"Things between us are complicated. You have to be sure."

Waiting for her answer was the longest five seconds of his life.

"I can't think of a better way to spend Christmas," she whispered.

The look on her face made him damned glad she had stopped him. "Now?" he asked hoarsely.

"Shouldn't we wait until tonight?" she said, her wide-eyed expression betrayed the struggle between madness and common sense.

"Maybe. But I can't." Deliberately, he began undressing, not only his cold-weather gear, but his socks and shoes and belt and everything down to his shirt and pants. Dani watched him intently, her cheeks flushed.

The door to his bedroom was open down the hall. They would hear the baby if she woke. "Say something," he demanded. "Tell me what you want."

"I'm not sure *what* I want," she said, wincing. He heard the truth in her words. "Maybe I just need you to know that *I* know."

His hands stilled on his shirt buttons. "Know what?"

"That we're taking a moment out of time. Period. That this ends when we walk out your front door tomorrow. I get it. You don't have to worry about me, Nathaniel. You're a sexy, interesting man. I want to be with you. But I won't make any uncomfortable demands. No awkward endings. You have my word."

Her ability to see right through to the deepest layers of his psyche alarmed him. The trouble was, he didn't have any pretty speeches to say in reply. Dani was one hundred percent correct. They had today and tonight and maybe tomorrow.

After that, the snow melted, the baby was reunited with her mother and Nathaniel went back to being top dog at New Century Tech. Business as usual.

He held out a hand. "Come here, little elf."

The choice on his part to remain still was deliberate.

He needed Dani's physical assurance that she wanted to take this step.

Instead of taking his hand, she flung herself at him, wrapped her arms around his neck and knocked the breath from his lungs. "Merry Christmas, Nathaniel."

He hugged her instinctively. Finding her mouth with his, he dove in for the taste that was his new addiction. "God, you're sweet."

She bit his neck, sharply enough to bruise. "I'm not particularly interested in *sweet* right now. Take me, Nathaniel. Show me the real you. I won't break, and I won't run away."

"God help us both," he muttered. He kissed her wildly, sliding his hands beneath her sweater and finding warm, soft breasts. "You didn't have to wear a bra," he complained.

"Your fault." Her voice was muffled against his collarbone. "New clothes. Didn't want to hurt your feelings."

Clumsily, he tugged the sweater over her head and unfastened the offending undergarment. When Dani was bare from the waist up, he put his hands on her hips and dragged her against him. "I'm too close to the edge," he groaned. "Embarrassingly so. Give me a minute."

Dani shook her head and leaned back to look up at him, her eyes bright with pleasure. "I like driving you mad," she said. "It gives me power."

She was joking. He knew that. He *knew* Dani. Still, the words sent a frisson of unease down his spine. Shaking off the sense of foreboding, he kissed her gently. "Take all the power you want, little elf. Tonight, you're mine."

Dani was under no illusions. She could only take what Nathaniel gave freely. There was a part of him that was off-limits to her, to everyone. She would have to be satisfied with the very appealing bits and pieces he offered. If the next twenty-four hours were to be their swan song, this unlikely pairing would be as special as she could make it.

Stuffing her doubts into a dark closet, she cupped his face in her hands. “You know how in movies the hero sometimes takes the heroine up against the front door, because he can’t make it any farther before he has sex with her?”

Nathaniel rolled his eyes, but he grinned. “I get the general idea.”

“Well…” She removed his shirt and pressed her naked breasts to his wonderfully hard, warm chest. “I was thinking we might try that.”

He shuddered when she linked her arms around his waist and slid her fingertips inside his jeans, caressing his lower back. “I *could* use some exercise,” he said soberly.

“Sex burns calories,” she muttered. Perhaps they might just stand here like this all afternoon. She felt safe and warm, as if nothing bad would ever happen.

Nathaniel took her idea and ran with it. Before she blinked twice, he had her pants and undies down her legs. “Step out of them,” he demanded.

There must have been a draft in the foyer. Goose-flesh broke out all over her body, and her nipples went on high alert. Stark naked, she wrapped her arms around her breasts. “Stop,” she said hastily. “Your pants have to go, too.”

He lifted an eyebrow, kneeling at her feet. “I’ve seen one or two of those movies. The guy keeps his pants on sometimes. You know…’cause he’s in such a hurry.”

She chuckled, despite her tendency to hyperventilate. “Now you’re mocking me.”

“A little bit.” He stood and shucked his trousers and boxers casually, removing a couple of condoms from his pocket along the way. "If my back goes out from these shenanigans, you'll have to carry me to bed."

The humor didn't really compute. A naked Nathaniel Winston was even more powerful and intimidating than the one in the tailored suits and pristine white dress shirts. He was a male animal in his prime.

If she hadn't been breathless with longing and terrified the baby was going to wake up at the most inopportune moment, Dani might have taken the time to study her lover's body in detail. As it was, urgency overtook any desire to savor the moment.

"How do we do this?" she asked, the words embarrassingly weak and shaky.

Nathaniel's smile took all the starch out of her knees. "You let me worry about the logistics, honey. Right now I'm going to kiss you until you forget your name." With a nonchalance Dani could never have managed in a million years, he took care of the condom and tossed aside the packet.

Dani sighed when he folded her in his arms and held her loosely, brushing her forehead with a tender kiss.

"My lips are down here," she pointed out, trying to speed things along.

"I never noticed how bossy you are."

"I never noticed how slow you are."

Without warning, he scooped her up and palmed her bottom. She buried her face in the crook of his neck and wrapped her legs around his waist. His thick erection pressed against her. He shuddered and panted, his entire body rigid. "More foreplay later, I swear."

"I believe you."

The muscles in his arms corded and bunched as he lifted her slowly and carefully lowered her onto his sex. The feeling was indescribable. Despite their pretense that

Dani was calling the shots, this particular position put Nathaniel irrevocably in charge.

Gravity worked in his favor. The fit was tight, almost uncomfortable. Dani started to shake as nerves and arousal duked it out in her stomach.

Nathaniel cursed and groaned. "Too much?" he asked, jaw clenched, the words barely audible.

"No, no, no…but don't forget the door."

He staggered and laughed and stumbled forward until Dani's bottom made contact with cold, hard wood. "You asked for this, elf." With purchase now to aid his mission, Nathaniel thrust forcefully.

Dani held on, fingernails scoring his shoulders. Eyes closed, lungs starved for oxygen, she let him take her savagely, recklessly. It was too much in one second and not enough the next. Laughing, sobbing, she clung to him until she felt her orgasm rise up from the depths of her soul. It flashed and burst and consumed her.

A heartbeat later, Nathaniel pummeled his way to his own reward. "God, Dani. Hold on…" His words faded as he shuddered for what seemed like an eternity and finally slumped against her, pinning her to the door that had been the vehicle for her fantasy.

Afterward, she was never sure how long they stood there. Or rather, Nathaniel stood. Dani was limp and exhausted and completely at his mercy. She wouldn't have changed a thing.

In the aftermath of insanity, one thing was clear. She was in love with her boss. If she weren't mistaken, she had been for a very long time.

The blinders came off painfully. For months, she'd been telling herself she had to find new employment. Now she knew why. This was more than a simple crush. She was deeply, irrevocably in lust and love with this virile, complicated man.

She started to tremble and couldn't stop.

Nathaniel read her response as being cold. Without speaking or changing their positions, he carried her down the hall to his bedroom. They scooted past the baby and into the opulent master bathroom. Carefully, he lifted her and set her on her feet. "Was that everything you wanted it to be?"

His teasing smile—along with the smug satisfaction he radiated—made her blush.

"It was lovely," she said primly. "I'll check that off my bucket list."

He kissed her nose. "Something tells me I'd like to see your list if those are the kind of things on it."

"Private," she said airily. "Need-to-know basis, only." *And you don't need to know, Nathaniel Winston, because you won't be around to help me check them off.*

Refusing to ruin their romantic moment with her grief, she twisted her hair into a towel and turned on the water in the shower. "I don't want to get my hair wet. Peaches will be awake soon. Why don't I go first?"

Nathaniel shook his head, his expression brooking no argument. "I'll keep your hair dry, Dani, but you're not getting in *my* shower without me."

"Okay. It's your call." But the shower took a turn she hadn't expected. By the time she reached for the faucet and adjusted the water temperature, her boss-now-lover was hard again, impressively so.

Pretending not to notice, she backed into a corner of the marble enclosure. Grabbing a washcloth, she soaped it and prepared to execute the quickest cleanup on record.

Nathaniel took matters—and the washcloth—out of

her hands. “Don’t be shy, Dani. Maybe this one is on *my* bucket list.”

It was depressing to think he had probably enjoyed shower sex with any number of strange women. But when he gently washed her breasts and then moved lower, her eyes closed and her body went lax with pleasure. After he completed his mission, fore and aft, he used the detachable shower sprayer to rinse her completely. As he had promised, the towel protecting her hair stayed perfectly dry.

“Thank you,” she muttered. She felt as if her entire body was covered in one big blush. She’d had sex with the man twice already. Yet still, his touch in this new context left her feeling vulnerable and uncertain.

“Will you do the honors?” He held out the washcloth with a challenging gleam in his eye. Not for the world would Dani let him see how very far out of her depth she was. Ocean deep. Wishing for a life raft. In imminent danger of drowning.

Nathaniel had been careful to point the showerhead away from her. Which meant that she could kneel at his feet and soap him up to her heart’s content.

It was a dangerous game they played. Nathaniel clenched his fists, his eyes closed. His head fell back to rest against the wall. The length of him was fascinating—alive, powerful and so very sensitive to her touch.

For a man to allow a woman this level of intimate attention required a level of trust. In one brief moment, Nathaniel had chosen to yield his power for the sweet pleasure a lover’s caress could bring. Dani held him in two hands, marveling at a creation that was at once so commonplace and yet so incredibly beautiful and life-giving.

The physical relationship between them was new and short-lived. Cleansing him was one thing. Other more intimate attentions were beyond her comfort level. She brushed a soft kiss across the head of his erection and rose to her feet. "Turn around, so I can finish."

His back was almost as compelling as other parts. Sleek muscles, male sinew and bone, all of it fascinated her. At last, she took the sprayer and removed every soapy bubble. "All done," she croaked.

Nathaniel spun around so quickly she gasped. He dragged her against him and kissed her hard, desperately. She felt the tang of blood in her mouth. "Dani," he groaned. "Dani, my sweet Dani." Maneuvering her like a rag doll, he turned her to the wall and placed her hands above her head, palms flat on the slick, wet surface. "Don't move."

One breathless heartbeat later she felt him enter her from behind. This time the theme was slow possession, so measured and deliberate she wanted to claw the wall. Her climax built in gentle swells and waves, one after the next. Nathaniel drew back and pushed in again, his size and force stimulating sensitive flesh already tender from their earlier lovemaking.

His big hands gripped her hips. "I won't let you forget this," he growled. "I'll take you again and again today until you beg me for more, and then we'll start all over again."

The provocative mental picture he painted sent her over the edge. She cried out and tried to stay still, but the end was too much for both of them, the shower floor too slick. Nathaniel scooped her up, took two steps out and deposited her on the thick, fluffy bathroom rug. He moved between her thighs with frantic haste. "Now," he moaned. "Come again, come with me."

Nathaniel slumped on top of Dani and tried to remember how to breathe. In the other room, the baby stirred. Damn it. How did couples with babies ever talk? No that he wanted to talk, not really. He was screwed and he knew it.

Dani would have to go to another division, another boss. The idea made his skin crawl. But he wasn't in denial. There was no way he could work with her now and not be constantly sidelined by lust. Already, he wanted her day and night.

The depth of that wanting scared him more than anything he had ever faced. No woman had ever mattered to him this way. He'd never allowed it. Now, though, he was torn between wanting to keep Dani at arm's length and being wildly jealous of any other man at NCT who might cross her path.

Incredulous that he had allowed himself to stray so far from his life's plan, he felt a lick of despair and panic.

He needed to think. He needed a plan. Unfortunately, this entire situation was spiraling madly out of control.

Dani shoved at his shoulders. "Let me go get her, please. She slept forever. I'm sure she's starving."

Rolling to one side, he slung an arm over his eyes and tried not to freak out. In his peripheral vision, he saw Dani take his terry robe from the back of the door and belt it twice around herself. The way her narrow waist flared into a curvy ass was an image he would never get out of his brain. His hands tingled with the need to touch her again.

He decided to let Dani tend to the kid for a few moments while he pulled himself together. Once he was dressed again, he felt marginally more normal. Unfortunately, he couldn't stay in the bathroom forever.

When he opened the door to the bedroom, woman and baby were gone. Made sense. The formula and bottles were in the kitchen. He found his missing houseguests there. Dani perched on a stool. Peaches was in her lap.

Dani didn't look at him, but she muttered a greeting. Her gaze was fixed on the baby. "I've seen how you look at her," she said. "You're already halfway in love with this baby. It's going to hurt like hell if she's not yours, isn't it?"

He poured himself a cup of coffee. "Sharing custody of a child with Ophelia would be a nightmare, so no."

"I wasn't talking about Ophelia. I was talking about you and Peaches. I've watched you with her. Deep down, you wouldn't be too upset if this baby carries your DNA."

"Quit trying to psychoanalyze me, Dani. I'm not a kid person. Never have been. Never will be. The baby is cute. I'll give you that. But believe me, I'll be happy to hand her back to her real parent. Hopefully sooner than later."

The inquisition should have bothered him far more than it did. But his body was relaxed and sated from really great sex, so it was almost impossible to get mad at Dani for weaving her naive theories.

"I do have a Christmas present for you after all," she said. Peaches finished the bottle. Dani put the baby on her shoulder and patted her back. "It's on my phone. Take a look."

The photograph Dani had captured at some point this weekend when he wasn't aware was beautiful. Even he had to admit that. He'd been in the den with the baby showing her the Christmas tree. The damned shot could have made the cover of a parenting magazine. *Man in Love with His New Child. Father Shares the Joys of Christmas with the Next Generation. Innocence and Trust. Daddy and Daughter.*

He clicked out of the photo app and laid the phone on the counter. "Thank you. Text it to me. It will be a good reminder to vet my future bed partners more carefully."

When Dani's face went blank, he cursed. "I'm sorry," he said stiffly. "That was a stupid thing to say. I'm sorry, Dani." He went to her and put his arms around her and the baby. "I'm not usually so clumsy. I was trying to be funny, but it wasn't funny at all. You're the only woman I want in my bed, I swear."

"For now. Not forever."

"I thought we both agreed this was a for-now kind of thing." Was she trying to make him feel guilty? It was working.

"We did. Of course." Dani wriggled free of his embrace and stood. "I think this would be a good time to finish that movie we started earlier."

Nathaniel released her reluctantly. Somehow they had segued from mind-blowing sex in his bedroom to acting like stilted strangers. He knew it was his fault. What he didn't know was how to fix it.

The remainder of Christmas Day passed slowly. Their snowed-in weekend was drawing to a close. Outside, a few of the main thoroughfares had been plowed and salted. Traffic was moving again, albeit slowly. The temperature had climbed above freezing for a few hours, but there was still plenty of snow cover. The side streets would be a mess.

Peaches was content to play on a blanket for long periods of time. She had napped a great deal of the day, so now she was awake and in a good mood.

Nathaniel was glad to have the child as a chaperone. Again and again, he revisited the invitation to accompany Dani to her parents' home. Was there a trap hidden in there, a trap he didn't see?

Dani was the least manipulative woman he knew. Then again, he had allowed her unprecedented access to his private life. Something had changed. Something more than the initiation of a physical relationship. He found himself wanting to lock the door and never let her leave. Here in his condo, he could control the outcome.

Once the real world intruded again, all bets were off.

Christmas supper was leftovers, but damned good leftovers. Afterward, Nathaniel entertained the baby while Dani spoke on the phone again to each of her siblings and her parents. It was clear to him that the Meadows clan was a tight-knit bunch. If Dani showed up with her boss and a baby in tow, wouldn't everyone think it was odd?

Again, he tried to sniff out danger. Finally, he asked Dani outright, "Won't your family think it strange if Peaches and I tag along with you?"

In her red sweater and black pants, Dani looked elegant and not nearly as approachable as the woman wearing his shirts. "Why? Are you thinking about changing your mind?"

"That's not an answer," he pointed out wryly.

Dani wrinkled her nose. "I'm the youngest. My parents have seen it all. Before my sister got married, she dated an insurance salesman with three boys under the age of seven. The man was looking for a built-in babysitter. Fortunately, Angie wised up before it was too late. He wasn't the only weirdo, though. There was a musician in an alternative rock band and a tax accountant turned street preacher."

"Wow."

"Yeah. Angie went through a rebellious stage before she settled down with my brother-in-law, who, by the way, is pretty much a saint."

Nathaniel grinned. "What about your brother?"

"He's not married yet. For the last couple of years, he's been dating a string of short-term partners. Nice women, but they haven't a clue what to do with Jared. He has an IQ in the hundred fifties. The man needs intellectual stimulation, even if he doesn't know it yet."

"I'm sure it will dawn on him eventually."

"We can only hope."

"I'm not sure where I fit in," Nathaniel drawled. "I'm

not a musician or much of a churchgoer. But I do temporarily have a baby to look after."

"I've been thinking about that," Dani said earnestly. "If you decide to come with me to Gainesville tomorrow, I'll simply introduce you as my boss. They know your name, of course, because I've spoken about you. I'll say you're caring for a friend's baby and that we got snowed in together. That's all they need to know."

"In their shoes, I might have a lot of questions."

"Even if that were true, they wouldn't make you uncomfortable. My parents are the consummate Southern hosts. They may feed you too much, and you might have to listen to my father's dumb jokes, but no one will put you on the spot."

"I'll think about it," he said.

Dani's pleased expression was its own reward.

At bedtime, they faced an awkward moment. Dani held Peaches, prepared to disappear into her room for the night. Nathaniel stopped her with a hand on her arm. He kissed her cheek. "Sleep in my bed tonight," he muttered.

"Are you sure?" Dani looked up at him searchingly as if she saw every one of his doubts.

"I'm sure."

Nine

An hour and a half later, he wasn't sure at all. Peaches was asleep in her little walled-off nest in the corner. Dani had chosen to get ready for bed in her own room and returned wearing the simple ivory silk gown and robe. She looked young and innocent and disturbingly bridal.

"I know I gave you those," he said gruffly. "But I'd rather have you naked."

Dani lifted an eyebrow. "Maybe if you dim the lights first?" she said, laughing.

"No. I don't think I will." He was counting on the fact that his feisty assistant never backed down from a challenge.

She shot him a glare promising retribution but seconds later stripped down to her bare skin, tossed the night clothes on the nearest chair and scuttled under the covers. "I'm cold," she complained.

The obvious ploy to reverse his command had no effect whatsoever. "I'll warm you up," he said.

Dani had the blanket pulled up to her chin. Her sultry smile promised all sorts of naughty delights.

With shaking hands, he unbuttoned his shirt and unfastened his pants. Having Dani watch him with rapt fascination did good things for a man's ego. When he was completely naked, he let her look her fill. His sex was rigid with anticipation, his body primed and hungry.

"Invite me to come to bed, little elf."

"It's your bed," she pointed out with inescapable logic. "I'm only visiting."

"You look good in there."

It was true. It had been a very long time since *any* woman had graced his condo with her presence. Now he had two females under his roof. No wonder he felt off balance.

Dani's dark, honey hair tumbled across the pillow. Her eyes were heavy-lidded with arousal. She couldn't hide from him. Not anymore.

"When I asked you to sleep with me tonight, I meant that literally," he confessed.

"I know." Her smile was equal parts wistful and wry. "But between the baby waking up at all hours and you waving *that* thing around, I can't imagine either of us will get much rest."

"It's called a penis," he chuckled, climbing underneath the covers and dragging her into his arms. She felt amazing tucked up against him. Feminine curves and soft, soft skin. "This was a very good idea."

"And you're so modest, too."

"Brat."

"Autocrat."

"Shrew."

She laughed softly, curling one arm around his neck and kissing his chin. "I like fighting with you."

"Is that what we're doing?" He rubbed his hands over her rounded butt, squeezing experimentally. "I thought we were negotiating."

She pulled back and stared at him, her expression wry. The lamp on the bedside table was still on, though the bulb was small and the light it cast not bright at all. "Everything I have is yours tonight, Nathaniel," she said softly. "No negotiating necessary. I'm here because I want to be."

Big blue eyes seemed to reflect the knowledge that he was incapable of giving her what she needed. He couldn't let this go too far. Not without risking his heart and his professional life. What did Dani expect from him?

His throat was so tight he had to swallow before he could speak. "I'm glad," he said gruffly.

Giving in to the greatest temptation he had ever known, he let himself wallow in her goodness, her welcome, her much-needed warmth. He had stocked the nearest drawer with a dozen condoms, and even that might not be enough. They came together in every way imaginable, hard and fast, lazy and slow. They dozed from time to time, and then he took her again.

He didn't know what love was. Surely not this desperate need to bind and irrevocably mark a woman. Love wasn't a sick feeling in the stomach, was it? Or the terrifying conviction that he had lost all control of his life? The notion that Dani was becoming *necessary* to him was scary as hell.

She was a decent woman and more honest than any other he had ever known. Her life was an open book. But if he told her even a fraction of what he was feeling, that would give her power over him, the power to destroy.

So he held his tongue, but he showed her with his body. Like a madman, he forced his way between smooth thighs and took her in an agony of longing, as if he would never get enough. As if filling her and finding release was the ultimate calling of his life.

Loving her gently was far easier when the first storm had passed. He stroked curves and valleys, feathering his fingertips across her most sensitive flesh and relishing her ragged cries when he gave her what she needed most.

Holding her afterward was almost as good. With her back pressed to his chest and her bottom cradled against his pelvis, he found peace. Burying his face in her hair, he inhaled her scent and tried to commit it to memory. Nothing this good could last. Nothing ever did.

In the middle of the night, Dani took a turn waking him. "Hold me," she whispered. "Make love to me again. Christmas is over, and I'm afraid of tomorrow."

He had no assurances to offer. They both knew the score. It added up to messy confusion and ultimately, change. A change he didn't want, but a change that was necessary. The best he could do right now was pretend.

Dani woke up just before 5:00 a.m. and went to the bathroom. Then, with her heart breaking, she stared into the mirror and tried to recognize the woman with the tousled hair and the tired eyes and the whisker burns on her neck.

How could they go forward from here? Nathaniel was never going to change. Dani had too much self-respect to settle for a relationship that was less than a hundred percent. She wanted a normal life.

Nathaniel Winston was not normal in any way. He was brilliant and driven. Generous, but at the same time distant. She knew he cared about her in an academic fashion. Just as he cared about Peaches. That wasn't enough. Dani wanted everything or nothing at all.

Maybe he felt something more for her than a primal, male need to possess. Maybe he could fall in love with her.

Was she willing to take that chance? Was she willing to wait for something that might never happen?

Yawning and desolate, she returned to the bedroom and climbed back under the covers. Nathaniel was dead asleep, but when she touched his chest, he mumbled and reached for her, dragging her against him. Dani closed her eyes and fell asleep, wrapped in the bittersweet comfort of ephemeral bliss.

The next time she awoke, the room was filled with light. Nathaniel lay on his side facing her, his head propped on his hand. He looked younger and happier than she had ever seen him. Peaches lay between them, contentedly gumming the edge of the sheet.

Dani rubbed her eyes with the heels of her hands and stretched with a yawn. "Sorry, I must have been out cold."

Nathaniel grinned. "You were indeed. I suppose someone kept you awake most of the night."

His smug, male satisfaction amused her despite the turmoil in her heart. She twirled one of the baby's curls around her finger. "Naughty baby."

"Very funny." He tangled his hand in Dani's hair and leaned over to kiss her. "I've decided to go to Gainesville with you. If the offer's still open."

"Of course it is. But what about work? What changed your mind?"

"NCT can do without me for one day. We've all three been cooped up since Friday. A road trip sounds like fun. You can tell your brother not to worry about picking you up."

"I hate to burst your bubble, but how exactly are we going to get there? Your Mercedes is in a drugstore parking lot under a mound of snow, and there's still the matter of the car seat."

"Out of curiosity, how did *you* envision us traveling when you first invited me to go with you?"

"Truthfully?" She grimaced. "I thought you would say no immediately, so it was a moot point."

Her answer bothered him. She could see it in his eyes, but he recovered quickly. "Well, I guess the joke is on you. I'm coming, and I've got the transportation problem solved. I've ordered a vehicle with a regulation car seat already installed."

"A car?"

"A vehicle."

"As in…?"

For a moment, he looked like a kid caught cheating on his homework. "I requested a Hummer. It will be delivered at four this afternoon."

Dani gaped. "A Hummer? Are you serious? Why would you do that?"

Nathaniel shrugged. "It's a virtually indestructible vehicle. Look out the window, woman. The melting has started, but it won't be gone in an hour. Nobody in Atlanta knows how to drive in the snow. It's dangerous to be out and about. Besides, all that water has to go somewhere, which means flooding. Peaches may not be mine, but I have a responsibility to keep her safe until the investigator gets some answers. I want to keep you safe, too."

"And you want to drive a Hummer."

His sheepish grin acknowledged the truth of her accusation. "Is that so bad?"

"My brother will go nuts. I hope you don't mind sharing. He'll have the two of you careening all over Hall County."

"There are worse ways to spend an afternoon."

"Good grief." She muttered the words beneath her breath as she got out of bed. At five this morning after visiting the bathroom, she had donned her nightgown before getting back under the covers. Her mental state required some kind of armor, even if it was flimsy silk and even if the silk had been purchased by the man on the other side of the bed. Now she added the robe and belted it. "Shall I fix us some breakfast?"

Every bit of humor left his face. His eyes darkened and his jaw tightened. "What I'd like is for Ophelia to reclaim her baby so I can spend a few more hours in bed with you. Last night was amazing."

"Hush," she said. "Not in front of Peaches."

He stared at her so intently her nipples beaded beneath two thin layers of silk. Nathaniel noticed, of course. "She doesn't understand a thing I'm saying. Nor does she know how badly I want her to take a long, morning nap."

"Stop it, please. You're embarrassing me." Her cheeks felt sunburned. Why did the man in the bed have to be so sexy, so charming, so funny, so *everything*?

"Fine," he said. "Go scramble a few eggs if it will make you happy. But don't expect me to forget about sex. Not after last night."

If Christmas Day had been long and lazy, Monday was anything but. Since the holiday fell on Sunday, most of Atlanta had Monday off, which meant traffic was lighter than usual on the interstates. That helped road crews who were trying desperately to restore order. Unfortunately, even that advantage was negated by the dozens of wrecks all over the city. Dani and Nathaniel took turns listening to the radio, scouring online news sites and occasionally, catching breaking-news updates on TV.

Peaches was inconsolable for most of the day. She did, in fact, have one tiny tooth poking through on the bottom with a second one soon on the way. "No wonder she's cranky," Dani said after lunch. "Poor thing is miserable."

Since they didn't want to get out twice, Dani made a list

and Nathaniel placed a phone order to the same pharmacy/discount store where they had first gathered supplies for the baby. This time Dani included infant acetaminophen and a fluid-filled teething ring that could be frozen. They needed something to comfort the poor child.

While the grown-ups took turns packing overnight bags, the baby slept for no more than ten minutes at a time. Dani, frazzled and exhausted, began to wonder if this trip to Gainesville was a good idea after all. On the other hand, her parents would be crushed if she cancelled at this late date.

Nathaniel loaned her a small suitcase. She managed to get all of the gifts he had given her folded neatly inside. The family lunch would be extremely casual, and she had told Nathaniel as much. The jeans she chose to wear from her new mini wardrobe, however, were superchic, as was the long-sleeve top in shades of purple and mauve and silver. Never had she spent this much money on items that were essentially a knock-around wardrobe.

The outfit must have been flattering, because Nathaniel's eyes narrowed and his neck flushed when he saw her. "You almost ready?" he asked.

Dani nodded, tucking her hair behind her ears. "I think we're just waiting for the drugstore order and we're good to go."

Nathaniel handed her the baby. "I'm going downstairs to sign for the car. I'll load the delivery straight into the back."

"You won't need all that for one night."

"Doesn't matter. I've got plenty of room in the Hummer."

She laughed. "You love saying that, don't you?"

His wicked smile made her stomach flip. "I don't know *what* you're talking about."

When the front door slammed behind him, Dani nuzzled Peaches's soft cheeks and tried to remember everything she needed to pick up at her apartment. Thanks to Nathaniel's largesse, it was mostly only the presents for her family.

Thirty minutes later, they were on the road. Dani had worried about Peaches's safety, but the car seat was top-of-the-line and installed correctly. The baby settled down once they were in the ridiculously large and noticeable vehicle, perhaps from the novelty of being outside.

The huge amounts of melting snow did indeed create a nightmare. Not only that, but Nathaniel was forced to dodge vehicles that had been abandoned Friday night. The side trip to Dani's apartment took far longer than it should have. She shared the top floor of an old Victorian house in the Piedmont Park area.

"This is nice," Nathaniel said, surveying the tree-lined streets and charming architecture.

"I won't be long at all."

"Don't you need help?"

"No. I'll be fine." She didn't want Nathaniel inside her home, even briefly. It was going to be hard enough to root him out of her life without the memory of his presence inside the one place that was her peaceful sanctuary at the end of a long day.

She was gone fifteen minutes, maybe twenty. "Sorry," she said as she carefully placed the sack of gifts in the back and climbed into the front of the vehicle. "I had to water a couple of plants."

"No worries."

As Nathaniel negotiated the newly created obstacle course to get out of town, Dani texted back and forth with her mother. Finally, she shut off her phone and tossed it in her purse. "I hope we make it to Gainesville and the hotel in one piece."

He shifted into a lower gear to tackle an icy hill. "We'll make it," he said. "And we'll celebrate in bed, little elf. Frankly, it's all I'm thinking about at the moment. That and trying not to smash up this tank I'm driving."

"I thought it wasn't smashable," she quipped, goading him for no good reason.

He scowled as the driver to their right ran a stop sign. "True. It would be more correct to say I'm worried about smashing up all the *other* vehicles on the road. Do me a favor and quit talking for now. I need to concentrate."

Normally the drive from Atlanta to Gainesville—northeast of the city—took an hour to an hour and half, depending upon time of day. Today, the traffic crawled. All lanes of the interstate were clear, but stranded vehicles on the side of the road created hazards. Not only that, but the people who hadn't been able to travel Saturday and Sunday were out in full force, clogging the roads.

When they finally made it to the outskirts of Dani's hometown, she had a tension headache and an empty stomach. Peaches had slept the first hour and cried on and off the rest of the trip. Nathaniel pointed out a popular steak house. "Do you want to stop for dinner before we check in?"

The thought of juggling a cranky baby was daunting. "Would you mind if we ordered pizza and had it delivered to the room?"

"Not at all. I should have thought of that."

The all-suite hotel Dani had chosen was part of a chain, but a nice one. A friendly bellman helped them wrangle all their stuff upstairs and beamed when Nathaniel tipped him generously. The young man wanted to linger and discuss the Hummer's unique features. Dani eased him out the door. "We need to feed the baby. Thanks again for all your help."

Nathaniel collapsed in an armchair and rubbed his temples. "I *never* want to make that drive again."

"Me, either," Dani said, feeling guilty. "I had no idea it would be so bad. I'm sorry I dragged you into this."

He gave her a tired smile that still had enough wattage to curl her toes. "I came along of my own free will. Besides, this may be the only time in my life I can justify the Hummer."

"Was it worth the price?"

"Every penny." He kicked off his shoes. "Let me have the baby, and you order our pizza. I'll eat anything but anchovies. And onions."

"Sounds good."

Often, when Nathaniel decided to work through lunch at NCT, Dani was the one who ordered meals brought in. It wasn't unusual for the two of them to sit together in Nathaniel's office and eat while he kept working and she took notes or sent emails at his request.

Never once in those situations had she ever felt self-conscious or weird. Tonight, every moment felt like new territory.

Fortunately, the local pizza place was close by. Delivery was prompt and efficient. While Dani handled the meal order, Nathaniel gave Peaches a bottle. He was an old pro at it already. Soon, Peaches was asleep. They spread a blanket on the rug near them and put the baby on her tummy. She scrunched her cute little face and drew her knees under her, her bottom tilted upward in her favorite sleep position.

While they consumed the hot, extra cheesy ham-and-pineapple pizza, silence reigned. Dani knew she should come right out and tell Nathaniel she was looking for another job. He would probably be pleased. It would be impossible for things to go back to the way they were at the office. After this bizarre Christmas weekend that was both wonderful and challenging in equal parts, life was going to be very different.

Dani wasn't scheduled to go back to work until January 3. She'd banked the last of her vacation time to give herself a nice, long holiday at the end of the year. Her plans for the remainder of this week were modest: clean out her closet, see a couple of movies she had missed and stock up on groceries to cook healthy, yummy meals for January.

She didn't always make New Year's resolutions, but this time around was different. In the spirit of being proactive, she would schedule herself an appointment on Nathaniel's calendar for that first day back, sit down with him and quit her job face-to-face.

Just thinking of it made her hands clammy and her stomach queasy. The boss was a holy terror when he was mad. Woe to the person who became the focus of his icy cold displeasure. Still, only a coward ended a job *or* a relationship with a note, online or otherwise.

Nathaniel tapped the edge of the box. "You want to share the last piece?"

"It's all yours," she said.

If Nathaniel had even once offered a single shred of evidence that he was thinking about a future for the two of them, she might have found the courage to tell him she loved him. After all, nothing dictated that the man had to be first to lay his heart on the line.

Unfortunately, Nathaniel had done nothing to indicate a desire for permanence.

Which meant that tonight and tomorrow were it.

Without saying a word, he gathered up the empty pizza box and the paper plates and napkins, and carried them out to the trash chute in the hall. When he returned, he lifted an eyebrow. "What's wrong, Christmas elf? I've never seen you bite your fingernails."

She jerked her hand away from her mouth. "Nothing's wrong," she lied. "I might be a tiny bit nervous about tomorrow, that's all."

They had been sitting on the floor with their backs against the sofa. He dropped down beside her and put a hand on her knee. "Peaches and I can always stay here. Your brother could pick you up and bring you back."

"I want you to come," she said slowly. "I just don't want anybody getting stupid ideas about you and me."

It was the perfect opening for him to make a suggestive remark, or even admit he wouldn't think that was a terrible idea if it happened.

Nathaniel did neither.

Instead, he picked up his phone and began looking at emails. "I thought I would hear something from the investigator by now."

Dani swallowed her disappointment and hurt. It wasn't Nathaniel's fault she'd been weaving fantasies. She stood and crossed the room to put some distance between them. "Did he say how he would start his search?"

"I imagine he'll follow the credit card trail. That seems to be the easiest route."

"Except if Ophelia got stuck in one place like we were, there might be no credit card activity to find."

"True. But even if that were so, I'm betting today is different. As soon as transactions start popping up, he'll find her."

"I hope so." She crouched beside the baby, already half in love with Peaches herself. "She's so sweet and good-natured. I hope that means Ophelia is a good mother most of the time."

Nathaniel's expression darkened. "I didn't have much of a mother at all, but I turned out okay, didn't I?"

"Of course," Dani said lightly. *If you don't count the fact that you're distrustful of women in general and emotionally closed off to a clinical degree.* "I think there are a couple of bowl games on. If you want to watch them, I'll read for a while. I grabbed a book when I ran up to the apartment."

"You don't mind?"

"Not at all."

The tension between them was impossible to ignore. Big emotions were at stake, but Nathaniel *wouldn't* talk about them, and Dani couldn't. The result was an uneasy truce.

Peaches woke up after an hour. The atmosphere in the hotel room eased after that. The baby provided not only a center point for conversation, but plenty of hands-on work to keep them busy.

At almost ten, Nathaniel's cell phone dinged. His expression was triumphant as he read the text. He looked up at Dani with a grim smile. "She bought gas and groceries in Decatur."

"That's good, then—right? She's still in town?"

"Unless she's headed north to run away."

"Don't think like that," Dani said. "Being the mother of an infant is stressful and emotionally draining. I'll bet Ophelia had a freak-out moment for some reason, and she brought the baby to you. Once she gets her head on straight, she'll want Peaches back again."

"Let's hope so."

Their little charge went out for the night not long after that. Dani showered and put on the ivory gown and robe. The king-size bed in the center of the room was an invitation for romantic sex, or so it seemed to Dani's heated longings.

As if he had read her mind, Nathaniel crossed the space

separating them and moved behind her, linking his arms around her waist. He rested his chin on top of her head. "I hope you're ready for bed," he said.

"I *am* pretty tired."

He spun her around to face him and bent to stare into her eyes. "Please tell me that was a joke. I should get stars in my crown for keeping my hands off you all day."

"You were too busy with the traffic to notice me."

"Don't fish for compliments, elf. I'm obsessed with you, and it's damned uncomfortable."

Ten

Nathaniel had never meant to be so honest. But his moments with Dani were slipping away. He couldn't afford to waste a single one.

Tonight seemed like an ending—bittersweet and momentous at the same time. He was damned tempted not to let her go. Her openness and caring were the antithesis of the way he lived his life. Keeping her would be not only dangerous, but selfish. He couldn't imagine a future without her, but he *knew* he wasn't equipped to be the man she needed.

He undressed her carefully and then removed the athletic pants he had donned after his shower. They climbed into bed without speaking. He pulled her to the center of the mattress and wrapped his arms around her. "I don't want to hurt you, Dani."

Dani went rigid in his embrace. "I can take care of myself," she said, the words tart. "Maybe you should worry about *me* hurting you."

He smiled in the darkness. She was reminding him that their relationship was a two-way street. What she couldn't know was that he had gone years without letting women get close enough to penetrate the walls around his heart. If anyone had the power, it would have been Dani. But he was in no danger. He held all the cards.

As long as he remained in control, everything would go according to plan. He could assign Dani to a new division and gradually wean himself from her allure.

He hadn't allowed himself to fall in love with her. That was how he knew everything was going to be okay.

For the next hour, he lost himself in the pleasure of her body. The sex was as good as it had ever been, but something was a little off. His Christmas elf wasn't as open with him as before. She held something back. Put up a few no-trespassing signs.

Her reticence might have been infuriating if he hadn't been balls deep in making love to her. Not *loving* her. There was a difference.

Each time he made her come, he was jubilant. She might have other lovers after him, but he was determined she wouldn't be able to erase the memories of tonight.

Beyond that testosterone-fueled goal lingered a strange mixture of elation and terror. His body was sated, lax with bone-deep pleasure. He held Dani close and buried his face in her hair.

It was only sex, he told himself desperately. Only sex…

Morning came far too soon. Peaches had given them a good six-hour stretch, taken a bottle and then gone right back to sleep until almost eight o'clock. Even so, Nathaniel wanted to spend the morning in bed. With Dani.

As they took turns getting ready, his lover was quiet.

It was just as well. He had nothing witty to say, no funny quips about melting snow or holiday blues or poopy diapers.

Dani's mother was preparing Christmas lunch for the midday meal. Dani and Nathaniel were instructed to arrive no later than eleven in order to have time for opening presents and taking official family photos.

The Meadows family owned fifteen acres of land outside of town. Their property ran alongside a rich river bottom and up the side of a small hill. Dani had told him stories about running barefoot through fields of cotton and catching fireflies on hot summer nights.

He was charmed in spite of himself. Such rustic, simple pleasures were a million miles away from his own upbringing. Oftentimes as a kid, he'd spent hours at the kitchen table, figuring out homework on his own and listening to the ticking of the mantel clock as it echoed in their elegant, lonely home.

Shaking off the maudlin thoughts, he concentrated on maneuvering the Hummer around Gainesville. "Nice town," he said.

"It was a fun place to grow up. I love Atlanta, though. I'm a big-city girl at heart. I even thought about moving to New York at one time."

"But?"

"It's expensive. And I would miss my family. Atlanta is home."

At a red light, he braked and glanced in the rearview mirror. "Is she doing okay?"

"Almost asleep. I wish we could drive around long enough for her get a good nap. Mom expects promptness, though. My siblings and I learned that the hard way. If we came in late from a date or a party, we'd be grounded for two weeks. It was effective punishment."

"Don't take this wrong, but it sounds like the Meadowses are a typical American family. It's nice."

Dani shrugged. "You could say that. Still, even typical American families have problems, Nathaniel. Normalcy doesn't exempt anyone from pain and tragedy."

He mulled over her odd answer as they drove ever closer to Dani's childhood home. Was she trying to tell him something, or was he reading too much into her words?

When they finally made it to the other side of town and out into the country, Nathaniel thought they were home free. The sky was gray and the trees bare, but it was warm—fifty degrees already. He hadn't counted on the scenic creek that ran through the Meadowses' property.

To ascend the drive that led to the house, it was necessary to cross the creek on a narrow concrete bridge. Today, the creek was a raging river…and rising rapidly.

Dani's hands gripped the dash and the door, white-knuckle. "I don't like this, Nathaniel."

"Hummers were meant for situations like today," he said. "There's barely any water over the bridge yet, so I'll take it slow and we'll be fine."

They inched their way forward. The water was still rising, but certainly not fast enough to sweep the Hummer off the bridge. For a brief moment, it occurred to him he might be getting stuck with Dani in another weather-related situation, but he ignored the thought. He tightened his grip on the wheel and pressed the gas pedal carefully.

The vehicle kept a gratifying grip on the road surface. "See," he said. "You were worried about nothing."

In the next second, he saw a large section of creek bank in front of them crumble into the muddy water. With a loud, groaning *crack*, a corner of the concrete bridge gave in to forces it was never meant to withstand.

"Hold on," Nathaniel yelled. They were six feet from

safety. More of the concrete could give way at any moment. He gunned the engine, floored the gas pedal and made the unwieldy vehicle lurch forward like an elephant released from a slingshot.

Everything happened in slow motion. Dani screamed. Another chunk of the bridge sheared off. But the Hummer came through for him. They landed on firm ground, inches away from the disaster they had so narrowly missed.

He shifted into Park with a shaky hand and reached for Dani. “God, I’m sorry. Are you okay?” They glanced at the back seat in unison, reassuring themselves that the baby had slept through it all.

Dani nodded, her face milk white. “I’m fine. It wasn’t your fault.”

It was, and he would kick himself for that later, but now all he wanted to do was reassure himself they were alive. He cupped Dani’s head in two hands and turned her face up to his for a frantic kiss. His heart still beat in sickening thuds. “Your parents will shoot me,” he said hoarsely.

Dani’s arms were wrapped so tightly around his neck she threatened to strangle him. It didn’t matter. The fragrance of her skin and the tremors that shook her body were killing him bit by bit with guilt. She might have been hurt. He could have lost her.

“We’re fine,” she insisted, though it was clear she couldn’t stop shaking. “You saved us, Nathaniel. If we’d been on that bridge and it collapsed, we could have ended up nose first in the water. I don’t even want to think about it.”

“Me, either,” he said. He rested his forehead against hers. “Damn it, little elf, I nearly ruined your storybook Christmas.”

She laughed softly, her fingertips caressing the hair at his nape and making him shiver. “There was never anything storybook about this holiday. I suppose today is more of the same. Come on. Let's go get some lunch. Adrenaline makes me hungry."

Dani moved through the next hours in a dream. She'd done her best to reassure Nathaniel that their near disaster wasn't his fault. The experience shook her to the core. Personal danger wasn't at the heart of it. What if Peaches had come to harm? Or Nathaniel?

The terrifying moments on the bridge replayed in slow motion in her brain, even as she greeted her family and introduced Nathaniel and Peaches all around. It had been a long time since the Meadows clan had an infant in the house, so the baby helped defuse any awkwardness about Nathaniel's presence.

Nathaniel himself rolled out a generous helping of charm, complimenting Dani's parents on their home and their view. Lunch was delayed when the men decided they needed to check the status of the rising creek. The four males donned rain boots—some borrowed—and trudged down to the bottom of the hill while Dani and her mom and sister put the finishing touches on the meal.

Dani held the baby and snitched a piece of ham. "This looks amazing, Mom. You must have been up since dawn."

"Angie helped a lot. Why don't we go hang out in the den until the boys get back? No sense standing when we can sit."

Dani knew what was coming next. Jared hadn't brought a date. With only her mother and sister in the room, the confrontation to come was a given.

Angie played leadoff. "So tell me, little sis. Since when are you and the head of NCT so chummy?"

"I explained that already. It was a weird situation. He

was going to drive me to the train station, but the snow got too bad too fast."

"And that's when you found the baby." Angie rolled her eyes. "Give me a break. This sounds like an episode of a really bad soap opera."

Dani's mother intervened. "Don't be rude to your sister, Angie." She pinned Dani with the kind of look parents perfect when their kids are still toddlers. "Are you sleeping with him?"

"Mom!" Mortification flooded Dani's face with heat.

"That's not an answer."

"He's my boss," Dani said, desperately wishing she had never initiated the idea of Nathaniel coming with her. "That would be entirely inappropriate."

"Danielle..." Her mother's voice went up an octave.

Dani clutched Peaches and straightened her spine. "There's nothing going on between us. Nathaniel doesn't trust women. He's a confirmed bachelor."

Angie pointed across the room, sympathy on her face. "Too late, kid. Give it up. Mom was worried about the creek. She and Dad have been scouring the valley all morning."

Dani looked over at the cushioned seat in the bay window. There were the high-end binoculars she had bought her dad last Christmas. For bird-watching. "Oh?"

Her sister put an arm around her waist and leaned in to whisper in her ear. "They saw the kiss, Dani. Every passionate second. You're busted."

"I can explain. We were scared. It was adrenaline."

Her mother frowned. "Is this serious, Dani?"

"No," she cried. "I swear it's not. Please don't make a big deal about nothing."

Fortunately, the men returned before her mother could continue the inquisition. Dani was temporarily saved from further embarrassment. Everyone was hungry, so presents had to wait.

Over lunch, the adults teased each other with old stories about Christmases past. The year Jared opened all his presents in the middle of the night and tried to rewrap them before morning. The time Angie cried when she didn't get a doll she had actually forgotten to ask Santa for. And then Dani's most embarrassing Christmas. The one when her high-school boyfriend gave her a kitten because he didn't know she was allergic.

Jared finished the tale. "Oh, man, Nathaniel, you should have seen Dani. She was covered in red welts from head to toe. It was the quickest breakup in the history of teenage dating."

Nathaniel grinned. "It's hard to imagine. The Dani I know at work never gets flustered by anything."

"Okay," Dani said. "Enough family stories. Pass the sweet potatoes, please. Mom, why don't you and Dad tell Nathaniel about your trip to Hong Kong last summer."

Nathaniel was actually having fun. He had expected to sit back as a spectator while Dani enjoyed holiday rituals with her family. Instead, he had been pulled into the fray with a vengeance. The Meadows clan swapped jokes and debated blockbuster movies and argued politics passionately, including Nathaniel at every turn.

The only subject completely off-limits was Peaches. He knew Dani had explained the bare bones of the situation. Dani's siblings and parents handled the baby's presence with sensitivity. They didn't ignore her, but they also didn't say or do anything to make Nathaniel feel uncomfortable.

In the unlikely situation in which he found himself, his hosts' kindness and generosity were extraordinary. "May I propose a toast?" he asked as Mrs. Meadows brought out a ten-layer apple stack cake and a bowl of freshly whipped cream.

"Of course," Jared said. "But do it quick—before we all fall asleep. The tryptophan in the turkey is doing a number on me."

Nathaniel raised his glass of wine. "To snowstorms and spontaneity and hospitable families. Thanks for including me."

"Hear, hear," Dani's father said. "Now, about that Hummer..."

As Jared and his father argued over who would get first turn behind the wheel, Nathaniel followed Dani into the den where a mound of beautifully wrapped presents was piled beneath a real Fraser fir Christmas tree. The room smelled amazing, a cross between Alpine ski weekends and the comfort of home.

For a moment, Nathaniel felt a keen sense of loss for something he had never known in the first place. Shaking off the odd feeling, he took the baby from Dani. "You've been holding her forever. My turn, I think."

It was eye-opening to watch how the siblings and Dani's parents related to her. At New Century Tech, Nathaniel knew Dani as sharp and capable and goal oriented. In this setting, she was the "baby" of the crew. They petted her and teased her. Perhaps it was so ingrained in the family dynamic they didn't realize how much they underestimated her.

Nathaniel had done nearly the same on a more personal level. At work, he kept such rigid boundaries he never allowed himself to fully appreciate Dani's qualities as a woman, though the physical awareness had been there all along. It had taken a massive snowstorm to make him see what he was missing.

Dani was funny and warm and sexy. Brains and beauty in one appealing package.

Not for the world would he have embarrassed her in front of her family. Despite his hunger to be with her, he kept his distance physically, never touching her arm or tucking her hair behind her ear. He and Dani played the role of business associates perfectly. No one would ever guess they had spent the weekend making love at every turn.

He was touched and surprised to know that Dani's mother had somehow found a couple of things to wrap for *him*. He opened a navy-and-burgundy silk tie and a pair of sterling silver cuff links.

In the midst of the pandemonium of wrapping paper and boxes and bows, Nathaniel found himself trying to imagine what it would be like if he were a real member of this family. Heart pounding in his chest, he looked across the room at Dani and found her gaze on him. Her beautiful blue eyes shone bright with happiness.

The truth hit him without warning. A tsunami of feelings tightened his throat and glazed his eyes with moisture. He loved her. He was in love with his executive assistant.

This was a hell of a time for a personal epiphany. His head spun. The conversation swirled around him. He must have participated in appropriate ways, but he felt clumsy, his faculties impaired.

"Excuse me," he said, when he could form the words. "Peaches wants her bottle. I'll be right back."

He fled the family celebration. In the kitchen, he clutched the baby and searched for the premixed bottles of formula Dani had ordered, the same kind they had used that first night. With shaking hands, he uncapped and heated and tested. The routine was not so intimidating now. Against all odds, he was learning how to deal with a baby.

Once the bottle was ready, he went in search of a quiet bedroom. The house was very nice, but not all that large. Even with the door closed, he could hear echoes of the festivities from down the hall. He sat on the edge of the bed and cradled the little girl in his arms. She smiled up at him as she gripped the bottle.

Damn it. Dani was right. He didn't want the complicated situation, but it was going to break his heart if she weren't his flesh and blood.

Females were trouble. That was the truth. How was he going to let either one of them go?

Immediately after the formula was gone, Peaches fell sound asleep. He tugged the bottle from her hands and set it aside. Carefully, he lifted the small, limp body onto his shoulder.

He wanted to be alone. He needed time and space to process everything that was happening to him. Unfortunately, he was smack-dab in the middle of a good old-fashioned family Christmas.

When he made it back to the den, Jared cornered him. "It's not going to be safe to get across that bridge. At least not until the water goes down and Dad and I can see how much damage was done. There's an alternate route off the back side of the property, but it will add almost an hour to your trip."

Dani's mother joined them. "I know we're crowded, but I would feel better if you stayed the night, Nathaniel. I don't want you taking my daughter and the baby across the bridge today, Hummer or no Hummer. And that other road is terrible. We have all sorts of blankets and sleeping bags, more than enough to make comfy pallets here in front of the fire. I thought about kicking Jared out of his room, but his is a twin bed, so not much help."

Nathaniel swallowed his misgivings. "Dani can have the sofa. I'd be happy to stay, Mrs. Meadows, but I definitely will have to get on the road first thing in the morning to make it back to work."

"Of course," Dani's mother said. She turned around and looked at her daughter. "You don't mind camping out for just one night, do you, sweetheart?"

Dani had a deer-in-the-headlights look. "It's okay with me, Mama, if Nathaniel agrees."

Mrs. Meadows beamed. "Then it's settled."

For Nathaniel, the torture was only beginning. His plan had been to leave around four in the afternoon and hightail it back to Atlanta. He would drop Dani off at her apartment, and he and Peaches would go to his condo to wait for Ophelia.

Now he was going to spend another night with the woman he wanted more than his next breath. In her parents' house. With a baby as chaperone. God help him. It was everything he feared and everything he couldn't have.

The warm, loving family, the precious baby, the woman who tempted him beyond reason. How could he keep a rein on his hunger if the two of them were trapped in this house?

Despite his inner turmoil, the day passed quickly. As Dani had warned, the men were eager to try out the Hummer. Even Angie's husband went along for the excursion across snow-covered fields.

Nathaniel enjoyed the outing far more than he expected. Angie's husband possessed a dry wit. Dani's father turned out to be a good old country boy at heart and Jared was, as Dani had told him, brilliant. The four men took turns behind the wheel, tackling hills and whooping it up when the Hummer conquered all obstacles.

Before returning home, they went as close as they dared to the raging creek and assessed the conditions. According to the National Weather Service, the rising waters had finally peaked. With no rain in the forecast and only the melting snow to feed the torrent, the outlook was good. By morning it was possible that the usually placid brook might be near normal levels.

Back at the house, the women had whipped up another batch of mouthwatering food for dinner. Nathaniel was amazed the whole family managed to stay fit and trim. Maybe they burned it off because no one ever sat still.

The evening was devoted to charades and card games. Nathaniel cleaned up at poker but was lousy at charades. Even Angie's husband, the other outsider, was better at guessing clues than Nathaniel. They all teased him, but it was good-natured.

How could he tell them his focus was shot to hell because he was fixated on the prospect of another night with Dani?

At long last, the day drew to a close. One by one, family members disappeared to shower and get ready for bed. Dani's father dragged out all the extra bedding and helped make a comfortable sleeping spot for Nathaniel and Peaches. Dani tucked a sheet around the sofa cushions and added a blanket.

"We'll be fine, Dad. Thanks for everything."

Nathaniel nodded. "Thank you, sir. It was a great day."

Was it his imagination, or did Dani's father give him the stink eye before walking out of the room? Then it dawned on Nathaniel. The den had no door. A double doorway, yes. But no way to secure privacy with lock and key. *Hell's bells.*

Dani didn't bother with the nightwear he had bought for her. She was wearing borrowed sweatpants from her sister, topped with an Atlanta Braves T-shirt. With her hair up in a ponytail, she could have passed for a teenager.

Nathaniel excused himself for a turn in the bathroom. He opted for soft athletic pants and a thin cotton shirt, leaving it unbuttoned in deference to the fact that the fire made the den *very* toasty. They wouldn't have to worry about Peaches getting cold.

When he returned, Dani had turned out all the lights. She was tucked into her temporary bed on the sofa with the covers pulled up to her chin. She had taken the rubber band out of her hair, and now the thick, caramel tresses fanned out across her pillow in an appealing tumble. Her eyes were closed, but he'd bet a thousand dollars she was wide awake.

Peaches was asleep in her usual position.

He sat down on the end of the sofa and put Dani's feet in his lap.

She opened one eye. "I just got comfortable," she complained. "Shouldn't we get some sleep if we're getting up early?"

"It's ten thirty," he pointed out. "You and I are usually good for another several hours at this point. You know, when things get cranked up."

Her gaze was wild. "Nathaniel! Hush! Are you out of your mind? Somebody could be standing outside in the hall listening to us."

"They're not. I checked." He slipped his hand under the covers and played with her ankle bone. "I've barely touched you all day."

Eleven

Dani moaned. With Nathaniel's thumb pressing into the arch of her foot, her whole body turned to honey. "We can't," she muttered. "Somebody might come in."

"You don't think they'll give us privacy?"

"Yes. No. I don't know." He ran his hand up her calf but stopped at her knee. She wanted him so badly she was shaking. But this situation was fraught with impossibility.

Nathaniel nodded soberly. In the firelight, she could swear his eyes danced with mischief. "I understand. You think this is a bad idea. No worries. I'll read a book on my iPad and let you sleep."

When he started to stand up, Dani grabbed his wrist. "We'll have to be very quiet," she said, caving in to the yearning that made her abandon caution in favor of gratification.

Nathaniel looked shocked. "You're serious? I was kidding, Dani. I assumed fooling around was out of the question. You know, under the circumstances."

She sat up and raked the hair away from her face. "I need you," she said, searching his face to see if he felt even a fraction of the urgency that tore her apart. Need and want and every nuanced shading in between. She loved him. Greedily, she would snatch every possible opportunity to be with him.

"I won't say no to you, elf. How could I?"

He dragged her into his arms and kissed her softly, his fingers winnowing through her tangled hair. His breathing was not quite steady. That reassured Dani on some level. She didn't want to be the only one flying blind—jumping without a net—indulging without weighing the consequences.

Carefully, tenderly, he eased her down onto the carpet and slid both his hands under her shirt. When he cupped her breasts and thumbed her nipples, she had to bite down hard on her lower lip to keep from crying out.

The need for silence was frustrating, but it lent a titillating touch of danger. She cupped his face in her hands. He hadn't shaved. His jaw was covered in masculine stubble. "I'm glad you're here," she whispered.

"Me, too."

After that, there was not much need for words. The fire popped and crackled. Occasionally the baby made tiny noises in her sleep. Nathaniel slid Dani's pants and panties down her legs and removed them. With her shirt rucked up to her armpits, she was essentially naked. He stared her as if he had never seen her before, or maybe he had never seen a *woman* before. That's how wild and reckless and incredulous he seemed.

He freed his sex and found a condom. Seconds later he spread her thighs and thrust roughly, pinning her wrists above her head with one big hand. "I don't know what to do about you, elf. Tell me. Can anything this good last?"

When she didn't answer, his jaw hardened. What did he expect? What did he want from her? It was a rhetorical question as far as Dani could tell.

Nathaniel's big body was warm and hard against hers. He took her forcefully at first and then tauntingly slow in the next minute. Dani unraveled rapidly. With her hands bound, she felt helpless. At his mercy. His masculine scent surrounded her, making her crazy.

"Ah, damn," he groaned. His entire body went rigid. His chest radiated heat. His hips pinned her to the floor. He kissed her with bruising demand.

Rolling onto his side and moving her with him, he took advantage of the new position and touched her sex intimately. Heartbeats later, Dani came.

He covered her mouth with one large hand to smother her cry. Then he shoved her onto her back again and pummeled wildly until he buried his face in her neck and came for long, stormy seconds.

Dani dozed in Nathaniel's embrace until she found the strength to drag herself back to reality. Her body was relaxed and sated, but her heart ached with a throb that frightened her. She didn't want to love Nathaniel like this. She hated feeling so vulnerable. Most of all, she was terrified that sooner rather than later she was going to have to live through the end of whatever this thing was between them.

Affair. Fling. Momentary insanity. Any description she chose sounded temporary and ultimately painful.

Nathaniel roused finally and yawned. "Damn, elf. You're killing me."

She managed a smile. "I don't see you complaining."

"Probably because I'm not an idiot. If a man has to die, there are worse ways to go."

Their lighthearted teasing was a cover for deeper, darker emotions. Nathaniel had to know the end was in sight. She'd told him flat out she wouldn't expect more.

At any point in the past few days he'd had ample opportunity to declare his undying love and beg her to marry him. *That* hadn't happened. He'd done nothing that could be construed as leading her on. Their sexual romp was on her and her alone. She'd made a choice. Now she had to live with the consequences.

"We should get dressed," she said.

"Yeah." His yawn cracked his jaw.

"I hope the creek will be down far enough in the morning. I know you don't want to miss work."

"Doesn't matter," he said. "I called and arranged for a helicopter to pick us up. Jared has offered to return the Hummer to Atlanta for me. If you're afraid to fly, Peaches and I will go without you and you can come with your brother in a day or two."

Was that what he wanted? A clean break?

She swallowed hard. "I don't mind flying. I've never been in a helicopter, though." Men like Nathaniel Winston did things like that. Private jets. Corporate choppers. Once again, the vast gulf between their worlds mocked her.

"You'll like it, I think. Once you catch your breath."

"Sounds fun."

She eluded his embrace and pulled on her clothes. "I need to go to the bathroom."

When she returned, Nathaniel was standing in front of the fire, his back to her. One hand rested on the mantel. The other was shoved in his back pocket. What was he thinking? Poor man. He didn't celebrate Christmas, and yet here he was, neck deep in a Meadows family holiday.

She touched him on the shoulder. "Good night."

He whirled around as if she had startled him, as if

he had been lost in thought. He nodded, his expression hooded. "Sleep well, elf." He kissed her gently on the lips.

Dani held back stupid tears. "You, too."

Surprisingly, the night passed without incident. Peaches didn't wake up at all, perhaps worn out from all the extra attention. When the baby finally roused at seven, Dani and Nathaniel were already dressed.

Her mom and dad were early risers. Angie and her husband were still asleep. Jared wouldn't surface until ten at least. He took his days off seriously. It was only the four other adults in the kitchen drinking coffee as the baby took her bottle.

Dani's mom held out her arms. "May I hold her? It's been far too long since we've had a baby in the house. I thought I would have grandchildren by now."

Nathaniel ignored the verbal bait. Dani flushed. Her father sipped his coffee and smiled placidly.

They dined well on apple cake and hot, crispy bacon with fluffy scrambled eggs. Eventually, Nathaniel dabbed his lips with his napkin and glanced at his watch. "We'd better make sure the bags are ready. Won't be long now. Thank you both, for everything."

Dani's mother smiled. "We're so glad you could visit, Nathaniel. I was very sorry to hear Dani will be leaving NCT. I know she has learned so much from you."

The split second of silence was like the sizzle of ozone in the wake of a lightning strike. Nathaniel flinched, his expression blank with shock.

Perhaps Dani was the only one who noticed. He recovered so rapidly, she was stunned. When he looked at her, his gaze was bleak. "Dani has many talents, Mrs. Meadows. I'm sure she'll land on her feet."

He strode out of the room.

Dani followed on his heels, grabbed his arm in the hallway and tried to halt his progress. She might as well have attempted to hold back the ocean. He jerked free, his big, masculine frame rigid.

"I was going to tell you," she said. The explanation sounded weak even to her own ears. "After the holidays. When things settled down."

He seized her wrist in a bruising grasp and dragged her into the hall bathroom, the only place they could be sure of a private moment. When the door was locked behind them, he dropped her hand abruptly as if he couldn't bear to touch her.

"Tell me now," he said coldly. "Tell me the pay was unfair. Tell me I worked you too hard. Tell me I was a sucky boss."

"That's not why," she said, trying to swallow against the giant lump in her throat. "You know it was none of those things. It was this." She cupped his cheek with her hand. "I couldn't stay, because I knew sooner or later you would realize I wanted you. I never dreamed we would end up in bed together," she whispered, willing him to understand.

He stepped backward, forcing her hand to fall, and wrapped his arms around his chest, staring at her with an inscrutable expression. "Do other people at NCT know?"

"Of course not. I thought about telling you this weekend, but I didn't want to ruin things. It was Christmas, not the time to talk about business."

His tight smile made her stomach hurt. "You forget, Dani. I *am* my business." Then he waved a hand sharply as if consigning her to the trash bin. "No matter. I'll make this easy for you. I accept your resignation. I'll have someone pack up the personal items in your desk and deliver them to you next week."

"Nathaniel." She said his name softly—desperately—

searching for the right words. "I didn't do anything wrong. You're overreacting. I'm sorry I didn't talk to you sooner. But honestly, this was going to happen anyway. You know I can't work for you anymore." She sucked in a ragged breath. "I care about you."

"Do you? Do you really?" His sarcasm was drenched in ice. "Or is this a female ploy to bring me to my knees?"

"That's not fair." Tears clogged her throat.

With a careless grasp, he took her chin and tipped it upward so they were eye to eye. What destroyed her most was the bleak misery beneath his supercilious glare. Against all odds, she had hurt him deeply, it seemed. "Life's not fair, elf. I learned that a long time ago."

She made the mistake of trying one more time. "I'll go back on the chopper with you. We can talk later today. You need my help with the baby, surely."

Every human emotion inside him shut down as if someone had flipped a switch. His smile chilled her. "On the contrary, Dani. I think I can manage just fine on my own."

Stepping around her, he unlocked the door and walked away.

Watching Nathaniel take Peaches and climb into a fragile-looking helicopter was the worst moment of Dani's life. The rotors hummed with a high-pitched shriek. Wild air currents stirred up leaves and other debris. Moments later, the chopper lifted straight into the air and headed south.

Dani couldn't break down. Not in front of her family. "I'm going for a walk," she muttered. "I'll be back for lunch."

Before either of her parents could say a word of protest, she took off for the hill at the back of the house. The chopper had landed on the only flat spot just behind her father's work shed. Now Dani hurtled down the incline, slipping and stumbling, falling to her knees more than once but getting up again and running. Running.

The pain in her chest was unbearable. She couldn't breathe. She couldn't think.

Why hadn't she talked to him about leaving? Surely he would have understood her decision if he hadn't been blindsided. Hell, he probably would have applauded it. Nathaniel Winston didn't want any messy personal situations to derail his perfectly ordered life.

At last, she came to the copse of trees where she'd passed many a childhood afternoon. On balmy summer nights, she and her siblings had occasionally been allowed to sleep out under the stars in rope hammocks—with their father close at hand, of course.

Today, all the tree limbs were barren, the ground below soggy and muddy from the melting snow. Barely conscious of what she was doing, she jumped for a familiar branch and hauled herself up to sit with her legs dangling. Propping her back against the tree trunk, she put her hands to her face and sobbed.

There was no one around to hear. A hawk soared high above on wind currents. The sun's weak rays provided little warmth. She cried forever it seemed, unconsciously scanning the sky between her fingers, hoping to see the helicopter's return.

Everything was ruined. Even if she found the courage now to tell Nathaniel she loved him, he would question her motives. Distrust and cynicism were deeply ingrained in his personality. She understood why, but understanding didn't make it any easier.

Adding to her distress was the knowledge she would never see the baby again, either. She had hoped to be a support for Nathaniel when everything with Ophelia began to shake out. Either way—father or not the father—Nathaniel would need help sorting through his feelings.

Eventually, she became so cold she knew she had to go inside or risk serious consequences. Her fingers were stiff and numb. She lost her grip getting down from the tree and fell on her face, knocking the wind out of her chest and scratching her chin.

Somehow, the pain seemed appropriate.

The uphill return trip to the house was far longer and more difficult than the flight down. With her head bowed and her eyes wet with tears, she concentrated on not throwing up the breakfast she had eaten earlier.

Jared met her halfway back. She never even saw him coming until he was right in front of her.

He took off his coat and wrapped it around her. "You okay, sis?"

She must have looked dreadful, because her brother's gaze was a mix of concern and alarm. "I will be." It was a promise to herself as well as the answer to his question, but a vow she had no idea how to keep.

Jared put an arm around her waist as they climbed. "I'm gonna go out on a limb here and guess that Nathaniel Winston is more than your boss. Am I right?"

She wiped her nose with the back of her hand. "Yes." Then the truth hit her. "No. Not anymore." The tears came again and with them the certainty that she had derailed her life completely. "I didn't want to fall in love with him, so I began sending out résumés, looking for another job. I was going to tell him soon…about the résumés, not the love thing, but then Mom let the cat out of the bag and now he's furious."

Stumbling to a halt, barely able to catch her breath at the crest of the steep incline, she shivered uncontrollably.

Jared took her by the shoulders and gave her a little

shake. "You can't go into the house like this. Mom will freak out. Stay in the shed while I see if the coast is clear."

"Okay."

He was back in under two minutes. "The rest of them are playing cards in the den. If we're quiet, we can slip in the back door and make it to my room. I already grabbed your suitcase."

"Thank you," she whispered.

Jared hesitated. "What are you going to do, Dani?"

She sniffed, wrapping her arms around her waist to keep from flying apart. "I want to go back to Atlanta—right now. I need to talk to him. Will you take me?"

"If we can get the Hummer across the bridge, yes."

"Mom and Dad must be wondering why I didn't get on the helicopter."

"They're smart people. I'm pretty sure they've figured it out by now. Mom feels awful, by the way."

"It wasn't her fault. I never said the job search was a secret."

"Are you positive it wouldn't be better to let this be the end? When only one person is in love, things can get ugly."

"You should know." She managed a teasing tone though she had never felt less like laughing. "Nathaniel doesn't love me. It's true. He won't let himself love anyone. But I *have* been important to him, and I hurt him, I think. I need to apologize. I need closure. So I can move on."

"What if he won't see you?"

She hadn't thought of that. "He will," she said. "I won't give up."

After a restorative hot shower and wearing another set of the clothing Nathaniel had bought for her, Dani found a measure of calm. The conversation with her parents was awkward, but necessary. Though she never mentioned the affair in so many words, it was clear they understood what she had done. They didn't ask questions. It couldn't be easy for a father to think about his daughter having sex.

She spoke with Angie separately and a bit more honestly.

Angie hugged her. "I've had my share of screwups, baby sister. You'll survive this, I swear. Call me day or night. I'll even come to Atlanta if you need me."

"Thank you, Angie. I appreciate it."

After that, it was goodbyes all around, and then time to go. While Dani and Angie were having their heart-to-heart, the men had been down to the creek and decided it was safe to traverse the bridge. Though two small sections of concrete were missing, the rest of the structure was sound.

Dani's mom was worried, but Jared kissed her cheek. "I won't do anything stupid, I swear. We'll be fine."

In the end, crossing the bridge was anticlimactic.

Once they negotiated the streets of Gainesville and made it to the other side of town, Jared turned on the radio. The two of them didn't talk, but the lack of conversation was comfortable. He was her brother. He was on her side.

The trip went smoothly. When Jared finally parked the Hummer in front of the building that housed her apartment, he rested an arm on the steering wheel, and turned to face her. "You want me to come in?"

"Not necessary. Thanks for the ride and thanks for returning the Hummer."

His broad grin was cheeky. "I might take it for a little spin before I swing by the car place."

"Jared," she warned, frowning at him.

"Unlimited mileage. I read the contract. As long as I have it there by five o'clock, it's all good."

"You're impossible."

"But you love me."

"Yes, I do." She leaned over and kissed his cheek. "Thanks for everything."

"Do you mind a word of advice?"

"When has that ever stopped you?" It was a rhetorical question.

Jared grimaced. "I'm a guy, Dani. I know how guys think. Sometimes we have to process things. I think you'd be wise to give Winston a few days to cool off. He'll calm down. He'll realize you weren't keeping him in the dark on purpose. If you try to have a confrontation today, things might get even worse."

"I'll think about it," she promised, jumping down from her seat and retrieving her things. She stood on the sidewalk long enough to watch him drive away. The she picked up her suitcase and trudged up the flagstone path to the house.

Twelve

Nathaniel had woefully underestimated how difficult it was going to be to have Peaches at work with him, even for a little while. To make matters worse, Dani's empty office mocked him at every turn. He'd called a temp agency to hire a nanny for the day, but they had no one available except a college student with no real experience in childcare.

Because he was desperate, he told them to send her over. The girl, Wendy, was fine with the baby, careful and attentive to Nathaniel's instructions, but Wendy was a talker. By midafternoon, Nathaniel's patience was shot.

He desperately needed two files Dani had been working on before the holidays. Both were spreadsheets containing customer information. He found the emails where Dani had sent him an original draft, but the contact info he needed was more recent. Unfortunately, he didn't know the passwords for his executive assistant's computer.

A tension headache wrapped his skull in pain. *Get over*

it, Nathaniel. This is your new reality. No Dani. No smooth days at work. No hot, erotic nights at home. He was alone everywhere he turned.

That was the way he liked it. That was the way he had crafted his life.

At least he had the baby.

Taking Jared's advice was virtually impossible. Dani tried, she really did. She checked off all the items on her vacation-days to-do list one by one. But eventually, her apartment was spotless. Her closets were an efficiency expert's dream, and she had made it through not one but two blockbuster movies at the theater and couldn't have done a recap if she'd been under oath. The hours crawled by.

Friday morning, she caved. With trembling fingers, she picked up her cell phone and called the main line at New Century Tech. When the receptionist answered, Dani cleared her throat. "May I speak to Nathaniel Winston, please?"

The woman's voice was perky. "I'm so sorry, ma'am. Mr. Winston won't be in today. May I give you his voice mail?"

"No, thanks. It will keep till next week."

She hung up and gnawed the edge of her fingernail. Nathaniel Workaholic Winston had taken a day off? It didn't compute. Quickly, she ran through all the scenarios. Maybe he had the flu. Maybe the baby was sick. Maybe Ophelia had eluded investigators.

Or perhaps the baby had been returned to her mother, and Nathaniel was now headed for the Caribbean and a much-needed diving trip to unwind.

In the absence of hard facts, Dani didn't know what to do. In her mind, she had seen herself marching into New Century Tech armed with righteous indignation and confronting the wretched man on familiar ground. She definitely didn't want to go to the one place where she had first been intimate with him.

Memories of Christmas weekend made her shiver with a combination of yearning and dread. For those three days, she had lived in a dream world where Nathaniel needed and wanted her. But it had been a charade. A pleasant fiction.

Today was reality. The only choice left was to venture into enemy territory.

She had laundered the clothes Nathaniel bought for her and tucked them in a corner of her closet where she wouldn't have to think about him. Instead of couture items, today she chose from her own carefully curated wardrobe.

Appearance was important. She wanted to look confidant and poised. If there was any hope of convincing Nathaniel to give their relationship a fair hearing, she had to maintain control of her emotions *and* the confrontation.

He owed her an apology. Beyond that, she desperately hoped he owed her some kind of admission that he wanted more from her. More from them. Despite what he had told her about his childhood and adolescence, she refused to believe his heart was as impenetrable as he pretended.

She had watched him with Peaches. Seen the tenderness. The protectiveness. Nathaniel had a deep capacity for caring, even if he didn't recognize it. There was more to him than the hard-edged businessman who refused to be manipulated.

At least she hoped so. Hope was all she had left at this point.

In the end, she chose a work outfit. Black pencil skirt, royal blue sleeveless silk top and a matching waist-length jacket. The temps had remained balmy since the thaw, so she omitted tights and added her favorite pair of black flats. Her hair was cooperating for once. She brushed it vigorously and left it down.

The snow was completely gone by now, though the ground remained damp and mushy. Spring came early to Atlanta. It wouldn't be many weeks before daffodils began popping up. When she slid behind the wheel of her little car, it was impossible not to compare it to Nathaniel's Mercedes or the Hummer or even the helicopter.

None of those things were requirements for her happiness. As nice as it was to be pampered with fancy clothes and pricey transportation and a luxurious condo, they meant nothing in the end. It was the man she wanted, the man she needed. Even if he lost everything he had built from the ground up, just as his father had, the man at the helm of NCT would be more than enough for Dani.

She found a parking space on the street and fed the meter. Nathaniel's building was not someplace she could simply sashay into and catch a ride upstairs. Fortunately for her, Reggie was on duty.

He gave her a broad smile. "Hey there, Ms. Meadows. How was your holiday with the family?"

"Wonderful. And your clan?"

"Can't complain."

She gave him a conspiratorial smile. "I was hoping to surprise Mr. Winston. Do you mind letting me go up without telling him I'm on the way?"

His smile faded. "Mr. Winston's a tough customer, ma'am. He goes by the book. I can't afford to lose my job."

Squashing her panicky, guilty feelings, she nodded. "I understand. But you have my solemn word that if anything were to happen, I'd vouch for you. I'd tell him I slipped past you when you weren't looking." She stopped and decided to be honest. "We had an argument. A bad one. He's being bullheaded. Please. If he slams the door in my face, I'll leave and won't come back, I swear."

The man shifted from one foot to the other. "Let me call him first."

Damn it. She knew what the answer would be. "Never mind," she said dully. "I'll catch him at work next week." With the one tiny bit of hope she had amassed crushed into nothingness, she turned and headed for the street.

"Wait." Reggie called out to her, but not before her hand was on the glass door.

She turned around. "Yes?"

"I'll do it. I'll let you go up. I've seen how that man looks at you."

"You will? You have?"

The too-overweight-to-run security guard in his navy serge uniform and wrinkled white shirt nodded glumly. "Women. Y'all are pretty to look at, but sometimes you twist a man in knots. No offense, ma'am."

"None taken." She beamed at him. "Thank you. Thank you."

He grimaced. "Don't thank me yet. I've seen that gentleman angry. I hope you know what you're doing."

She didn't. Not at all. In the elevator, she trained her gaze on the neon-lit strip above the doors and watched the numbers increase. At last, the elevator swished to a smooth stop, a distant bell dinged and the doors opened.

Unfortunately, she'd left her stomach behind somewhere, several floors below.

Smoothing her damp palms on her skirt, she hitched the narrow strap of her modest purse higher on her shoulder and said a little prayer. Then she pressed the buzzer and waited.

Long moments later, the door swung open. Nathaniel stood there staring at her with narrowed eyes, naked from the waist up. He wore dress pants and socks and shoes, but his broad, tanned, really spectacular chest was bare.

"What do you want, Dani? I'm busy."

His expression could have frozen the sun.

She refused to take a step backward. "I need to talk to you. It's important."

"I'm not giving you your job back." Now his glare held a lick of heat.

"I'm not here about the job."

A sound from the other room drew his attention. "Fifteen minutes," he said. He strode away, leaving her to follow him in confusion.

In the den, she found Peaches, happily sitting in a wide-based contraption with music knobs and chew toys and other brightly colored amusements. The baby chortled as if she recognized Dani. Dani crouched and tickled the little girl's cheeks. "Hey, honey bunch. Did you miss me?"

Nathaniel stood in silence, frowning, his arms crossed over his chest.

She noticed several things at once—number one, a pale blue dress shirt tossed over the arm of the sofa. It was covered in infant cereal, presumably from the bowl of congealing goo on the coffee table. No fire burned in the grate. The small Christmas tree was gone.

Rising to her feet, she eyed him calmly. "I take it they haven't found Ophelia?"

"That's not really your concern, Dani. Say what you have to say and get out."

He wasn't making this easy. Hostility. Impatience. Barely disguised anger.

When her chin started to tremble, she locked her knees, clasped her hands at her waist and bit down hard on her bottom lip. The pain made her focus. "The reason I was sending out résumés is because I was attracted to you. I knew we couldn't work together under those conditions."

Not by even the flicker of an eyelash did he betray a response.

"Did you hear what I said?"

He shrugged. "It's a nice story."

"You owe me an apology," she said firmly.

Dark eyes glowed with heat. "The hell you say. I wasn't the one sneaking around."

"Don't use that snotty tone with me," she shot back. "You're hardly a saint."

"I'll give you that one. But at least I've been honest with you. Which is more than you can say in return."

She inhaled sharply, taking the biggest gamble of her life. "No," she said bluntly. "You haven't been honest with me at all."

His jaw dropped. "Of course I have."

"You have feelings for me. You might even love me. But you're too scared to let me get close. The reason you freaked out when you heard I was looking for another job was that I hurt your feelings. And maybe you thought I was abandoning you. But I wasn't. I'm not."

"Don't flatter yourself, Dani. Women come and women go. You're no different from the rest."

"Nice speech. Have you been practicing?"

The lightning flash of fury in his gaze told her she might have gone too far.

Peaches played happily between them, her innocent baby noises a bizarre backdrop to the gravity of the moment.

Nathaniel ran a hand through his hair, a gesture indicating he was perhaps no calmer than she was. "Did you know NCT will be having a VP opening in the spring? McCaffrey is moving to the West Coast to care for his ailing parents. I had decided to recommend you for the spot. I'm sure with your new degree and your depth of experience at NCT, the board would have agreed."

"*Had* decided?" she asked faintly.

"Definitely past tense. You're the one who chose to leave." He picked up the baby who had begun to fuss. "It's time for her nap. Feel free to let yourself out."

When he returned several minutes later, Dani glared at him. "You're an ass, you know that?" Frustration clogged her throat.

"And you're an opportunist."

"Let me get this straight," she said tightly. "I produced a blizzard, planted a baby carrier on your car and arranged for myself to become indispensable to you so you would fall for my charms and I wouldn't have to leave?"

"I have no idea what goes through your mind. All I can say for sure is that you tried to manipulate me, but it won't happen. I won't let it, Dani. You can take your stories about *falling in love*—and peddle them elsewhere."

He was goading her. Trying to hurt her. And it was working. But the bitter ridicule was his defense mechanism. No one in his personal life had ever put him first. Through no fault of their own, his parents had abandoned him emotionally. Seeing his father's downfall after cheating with a coworker had cemented the idea that women—and lovers in particular—couldn't be trusted.

And then came Ophelia's manipulations. Poor Nathaniel. Beset at every turn.

Dani refused to back down or look away. In that intense moment, she saw the truth. He *was* feeling something. And it looked a lot like despair and yearning. Could it be true?

Clinging to the hope that what they had shared in this very room was more than lust and opportunity, she went to him and placed both hands, palms flat on his chest. The soft, springy hair beneath her fingertips was like silk. His flesh was hot and smooth.

He sucked in a startled breath when she touched him and then went rigid. "Get out," he said, the words hoarse, barely audible.

Dani shook her head. "I can't," she said softly. "Everything I need is right here. Maybe you don't believe me today. And maybe not tomorrow or the next day or the next. It doesn't matter. I'll keep telling you again and again as long as it takes."

She went up on her tiptoes, cradled his face in her hands and kissed him. "I love you, Nathaniel Winston. You're hard and stubborn and suspicious, but you're also intelligent and decent, and you have a deep capacity for love even if you don't know it. How many men would take in a baby who's probably not even his and care for her despite the havoc she wreaks in his life?"

She kissed him one more time. For a moment, she thought she had won. His hand cupped the back of her head, pulling her close and holding her as he responded to her kiss with bruising desperation.

But it didn't last. He jerked free and wiped his mouth with the back of his hand. "What would you say if I told you Peaches really is mine after all? That her real name is Lila, and that her mother doesn't want her...that Ophelia has signed away her rights because she's leaving the country with a man who doesn't tolerate children. What then, Dani? What if I said I'd marry you, but only with an ironclad prenup that puts everything in trust for the child?"

Stumbling backward in shock, she sank onto the sofa. She looked at the baby and back at Nathaniel. "It's true? She's yours?"

He didn't say a word. He simply stared at her with an expression she couldn't read.

Well, here was her choice. Nathaniel needed a mother for his new daughter. Apparently, he was willing to spin the game to his advantage. Dani swallowed hard. “I’m very happy for you,” she whispered. “I know you’ll be a wonderful father.”

Tears clogged her throat. She couldn’t do it. She couldn’t marry him knowing he didn’t want her the same way she wanted him. It would destroy her.

Before coming here today, she had hoped to look into his eyes and see the truth about what he felt for her. She had told herself even a little flicker of love could grow.

If there was nothing in his feelings for Dani but lust, she was better off without him. She had to clear her throat twice before she could speak. “I’d take that deal in a heartbeat if you loved me. But you don’t, do you?”

She stood on shaky legs and composed her expression. “I won’t bother you again, Nathaniel. I wish you and Peaches all the best.”

Rapidly, she walked out of the room, her heart beating in her chest so wildly she felt sick. Yanking open the door in the foyer that led to the hallway, she wiped her eyes, intending to flee, but Nathaniel was right on her heels.

“That’s it?” he shouted. “You lose your shot at the money, and you’re gone?”

“No,” she said raggedly, turning to face him, tears spilling over and wetting her face. “I didn’t lose. The truth is, I had a narrow escape. I don’t want your money or your sterile condo or your stupidly expensive vehicles. I wanted a man who would love me. That’s all. Now, forgive me for being slow, but I’ve finally figured out that man isn’t you. You’re going to live alone and die alone. I feel sorry for you, actually.”

“I don’t need your pity,” he snarled.

She reached blindly for the doorknob, desperate to escape. A hard masculine hand came down on her shoulder, spinning her around. Nathaniel's face was white, his eyes glittering like coals.

"Let me go," she cried.

He got up in her face, his breath warm on her cheeks, his grip on her shoulders viselike. "What makes you think you can save me from myself?"

And then she saw it. Buried beneath the layers of fury and condemnation was a pained uncertainty. Nathaniel Winston thought he was unlovable.

Her whole body went limp. She could fight his pigheadedness but not such aching vulnerability from a man who prided himself on icy control. She could barely breathe.

"I was hoping we could save each other," she whispered. The time for self-preservation was gone. She would give him complete honesty or nothing at all. "The world is a scary place, Nathaniel. But when I'm with you, everything seems possible. I didn't want to fall in love. That's why I was leaving NCT. But I waited too long and the snow came, and now I can't imagine waking up every morning and not seeing your face."

Thirteen

Nathaniel still reeled from the shock of finding out he was a father, and now Dani expected him to believe the two of them had a chance?

He shoved her away and paced the confines of the foyer, feeling sick. “Love makes a man stupid,” he muttered. “Did you see all that baby stuff I bought? I’m a sucker.”

Dani stood watching him with pity in her eyes, her arms wrapped around her waist. He didn’t need that, not from her. She looked beautiful and professional and exactly like the woman who had worked with him for almost two years. But things had changed.

She lifted her shoulders and let them fall. “You’ll be a better parent than either your father *or* your mother was if you put your mind to it. I’m sorry Ophelia abandoned her daughter.”

Rage filled his chest. “People shouldn’t have babies if they can’t follow through. It’s criminal.”

His ragged shout echoed in the small foyer. Dani stared at him, her blue eyes awash in tears. "I can't make up for what you lost, Nathaniel. I wish to God it was possible. But we could do it right this time. Peaches doesn't have to be the only one. Families are wonderful."

He blinked, not sure what he was hearing. After every cruel, heartless thing he had said to her? He cleared his throat, his head spinning. "Are you offering to give me a baby?"

Her chin wobbled. "No. I'm saying I want to *make* a baby with you. When the time is right." She tried to smile, but the failed attempt broke his heart. "I love you. Even though you're acting like a jackass and trying to shove me out the door, I won't stop loving you. I'll sign a legal document if you need a tangible reason to trust me."

Fear like he had never known clutched him from every angle. Spending time with Dani's parents and siblings had shown him what normal family life could look like. The yearning had hit him hard, reminding of everything his mother's illness had cost him.

"I lied to you, Dani," he muttered, stung by the enormity of his sins.

She frowned. "About what?"

"You asked me if I had ever fantasized about you at the office."

She paled. "You told me you *had*."

"That was an understatement," he said flatly. "The truth was too damning."

"I don't understand."

"Six months after you first started working with me, I began dreaming about you. Every night. In vivid Technicolor."

Her eyes widened. "Oh."

He shrugged. "It scared the hell out of me. I'd watched

my father go down that road and be ripped apart financially and emotionally. For years, I told myself I would never get involved with an employee. But there you were, so bright and funny and damned good at the job. I was stuck. Every day you and I worked together like the proverbial well-oiled machine, and every night I undressed you a thousand times and a thousand ways in my mind."

"So it wasn't just me..." Her eyes were round.

He shuddered, wanting her desperately and yet afraid to touch her. "No."

"Are you in love with me, Nathaniel?"

The words were barely audible. Maybe she was scared, but she didn't show it. The stupid woman didn't know how to protect herself. "Men like fucking," he said. "We don't wrap it up in pretty ribbons."

He was testing her. Pushing her. Trying to drive her away.

Dani inhaled sharply and fell back a step as if his deliberate profanity were a physical blow. "So you would rather have a temporary affair?"

"Are you available?" He stared at his nemesis, stone-faced. Every emotion he felt for her hammered in his chest like a wild swarm of butterflies trying desperately to break free.

In the hushed silence, he witnessed the moment Dani saw past his facade. Her expression softened.

"For one night," she said softly, her face aglow as if she heard something amazing in his crude offer. She was young but wise. Sure of herself and maybe of him, as well. "And the next and the next and all the ones after that."

"Fine," he said. His hands trembled, so he jammed them in his pockets. "Don't most women want a man down on one knee? The pricey ring. The pretty speeches? I'm surprised you're selling yourself short."

"Shut up, Nathaniel." Her wry smile warmed him from the inside out. "Shut up and prove to me I'm not making the biggest mistake of my life." She wrapped her arms around his waist and laid her cheek exactly over the spot where his heart pounded madly.

His hands tangled in her hair. He couldn't stop shaking. It was a mostly unmanly thing to do, but Dani didn't seem to mind. He clutched her tightly. "I don't know how to do forever."

She went up on her tiptoes and pressed her lips to his. "We'll figure it out together," she said. "It won't be so bad, Nathaniel, I promise."

The walls came down, every brick, every fragment of mortar. He inhaled her scent, his mind a blank. "I need you, my sweet Christmas elf."

"I know," Dani whispered. "I know..."

Epilogue

Thirty-six hours later, New Year's Eve

Nathaniel flung open the door to his condo and dropped a pile of packages on the chair in the foyer. "I'm home," he yelled.

Dani appeared, her radiant smile catching him unawares and wiping every coherent thought from his brain. "What took you so long?" she said.

He scooped her up and twirled her in dizzying circles until her hair fanned out from her head and they both laughed breathlessly. "It's not easy finding a Christmas tree on December 31." He released her and grabbed up the largest bag. "What do you think?"

The tree was prelit, but that was its only claim to fame. Twelve inches high and already shedding artificial needles, it was a tree only a mother could love…or a man bent on setting the stage for romance.

"I adore it," Dani said, her eyes dancing with amusement.

"Help me carry everything." he said. He headed straight for the den and began setting out his bounty. Carryout containers from Dani's favorite restaurant. An eighty-dollar bottle of champagne. Tulips and roses from a ridiculously expensive Buckhead florist.

Dani plugged in the tiny tree and set it on the hearth, then stood back and watched, her expression caught somewhere between excitement and apprehension. The two of them had spent the majority of yesterday afternoon and evening making love. Nathaniel had slept the entire night with her in his arms. This morning they had made French toast together.

Now came the hard part.

When he was finished with the accoutrements, he examined his handiwork. He'd never tried to impress a woman before, not really. Tonight, it was vital that Dani understand what was happening.

He took her hand. "We need to talk." Fortunately, Peaches was asleep at the moment.

Dani blinked. "Ouch. Barely a day and a half and we already need to *talk*?"

Drawing her over to the sofa, he sat down and pointed to the opposite end. "You, there," he said. He had important things to say. His self-control was tenuous at best, so he wasn't taking any chances.

She cooperated obediently, leaning back into the corner embrace of his expensive leather sofa and crisscrossing her legs like a child. Her hair was clean and damp and shiny. He knew she had showered while he was gone, because he smelled the soap his housekeeper put in the bathrooms.

They had stopped by Dani's apartment late yesterday, so now she had her own wardrobe to choose from. Tonight she was wearing gray leggings and an off-the-shoulder, cotton-candy-pink sweater. Her feet were bare. There was a good chance she wasn't wearing a bra. He didn't look too closely, because if she weren't, he might forget his speech.

Dani held out her hands, palms up. "The food is getting cold, Nathaniel. Say whatever you have to say."

Her lips smiled, but her gaze was wary. That expression in her eyes crucified him. How long would it take before she ceased expecting the worst from him?

He jumped to his feet and paced. For the past hour, he'd rehearsed what he wanted to say. Now, suddenly, his brain fogged. "You were right to say I owed you an apology. Looking for other employment was a very professional thing for you to do. But the prospect of you not being in the office every day caught me off guard. I never wanted you to resign, not really. I was angry, and I lashed out." His stomach cramped. "You have an incredible brain and the ability to connect with all kinds of people. I would hate to see you leave NCT. You deserve the chance to prove what you can do for the company."

"I see."

"You already said that once," he muttered.

"True." Dani gnawed her bottom lip. "Is what I do at NCT more important to you than talking about us?"

"I didn't say that."

"I'm confused. Now that we're practicing détente, I assumed our personal life was going to take precedence over work."

"It does. It will." He stopped and cleared his throat. "Maybe this will help." He reached inside the pocket of his jacket and pulled out a folded sheaf of papers. "Happy New Year, Dani. I may be the world's most stubborn man, but I believe in second chances, and I hope you do, too. That's not a prenup, by the way," he said hastily.

She unfolded the papers and stared at them, turning one

page at a time slowly. Nathaniel had paid his expensive legal team a fat bonus to put the wheels in motion on his grand gesture before the clock struck midnight.

Dani throat worked. She refolded the document he had worked so hard to procure and handed it back to him. "No. No, Nathaniel. I won't take it."

He had signed over half his company to her. A partnership holding in NCT. It was a small enough price to pay for her willingness to forgive him and promise him a future.

His face heated. "I don't know what you want from me, damn it. How many ways do I have to say it?"

Dani jumped to her feet and scowled. "You haven't even said it once, you big blockhead. I never wanted your life's work. All I want is to hear you tell me the truth."

Ah, hell. The shakes came back. "You know how I feel about you," he said gruffly.

She shook her head slowly. "Not good enough, Winston. Try again."

"Marry me," he blurted.

"Why?"

His throat closed up. Sweat broke out on his forehead. "I can't explain. It won't make sense."

"Try me," she said gently.

He fell to his knees on the thick, plush carpet and wrapped his arms around her hips, resting his cheek against her belly. "I want to feel him here," he said. "Our son, or maybe another daughter, kicking and making herself known. I want her to know she is loved from the moment she takes her first breath."

Dani's hands tangled in his hair. "Is that all?"

He shook his head, his throat tight. "No. I want her to know how much I love her mother."

Dani knelt as well and kissed him softly. "That wasn't so difficult, was it? You're going to have to practice," she whispered, tears streaming down her face. "I'm not going to drag it out of you every time I need to hear it."

He rested his forehead against hers. "I adore you. I want you. I'll love you for a hundred years. I was afraid of this. Afraid of you…"

"And now?"

"Now you're my heart, my home," he said simply. "Everything I ever wanted and more. I'm never letting go…"

* * * * *

Their lips met with an unexpected spark.

She didn't pull away. The old Emma would have. In her mask, she was someone else.

She wrapped her arms around his neck, her lips clinging to his as he probed and explored her with his tongue. It was deliciously naughty. In that moment, Emma wanted it more than anything else in her entire life.

"Come with me," he whispered.

Emma knew what he was offering and every inch of her body urged her to take him up on it. She'd never done anything like this. Ever. And yet there was something about her hero that insisted she go with him.

So she did.

* * *

Little Secrets: Secretly Pregnant
is part of Little Secrets series:
Untamed passion, unexpected pregnancy…

LITTLE SECRETS: SECRETLY PREGNANT

BY
ANDREA LAURENCE

First Published in Great Britain 2017
By Mills & Boon, an imprint of HarperCollins*Publishers*
1 London Bridge Street, London, SE1 9GF

ISBN: 978-0-263-92838-9

51-1017

Our policy is to use papers that are natural, renewable and recyclable products and made from wood grown in sustainable forests. The logging and manufacturing processes conform to the legal environmental regulations of the country of origin.

Printed and bound in Spain
by CPI, Barcelona

Andrea Laurence is an award-winning author of contemporary romances filled with seduction and sass. She has been a lover of reading and writing stories since she was young. A dedicated West Coast girl transplanted into the Deep South, she is thrilled to share her special blend of sensuality and dry, sarcastic humor with readers.

To Dan
Thanks for the inspiration

Prologue

Fat Tuesday

Everyone was dancing and having a good time. Everyone except Emma. That wasn't unusual, though. Emma Dempsey had forgotten how to have fun a long time ago.

After her recent breakup, she was beginning to wonder if something was wrong with her. Her ex, David, had said she was boring both in and out of bed. She made the mistake of telling that to her friend and former sorority sister, Harper Drake, and the next thing she knew, she was at a Mardi Gras party at a loft in Tribeca.

She'd tried. She wore a pretty butterfly mask and a tight skirt, but this just wasn't her cup of tea. Perhaps she should just call a cab and go so she didn't ruin Harper's night. She nibbled absently on a carrot stick as her gaze fell upon a tequila bar that had been set up on the kitchen island beside her. That was always a second option.

Emma knew she had to make a choice. She could either go home and join a local Red Hat Society at the ripe age of twenty-seven or she could take this bull by the horns and have some fun for once.

Feeling brave, she abandoned her plate and moved down the island. There was an assortment of small paper cups, slices of lime, a salt shaker and several bottles of tequila laid out. She prepared a shot and held it there, knowing once she leaped off the cliff, there would be no turning back.

Being with you is like dating my grandma. The memory of David's painful words pushed her over the edge.

Without further hesitation, she licked, drank and sucked the lime furiously to cover the flavor of the liquor. It burned her throat as it went down, splashing in her stomach and sending a scorching sensation almost immediately through her body that a beer couldn't even come close to.

It tasted absolutely terrible, but within seconds, she could feel a pleasant change. Almost as though her spine had loosened. Slinky. Maybe feline. This wasn't bad at all. With a smile of satisfaction, she poured a second shot as someone else came into the kitchen. A quick glance confirmed her worst fears.

"Hey there, beautiful," a creepy guy in a Batman-like mask said, leaning against the counter.

The compliment fell flat considering 75 percent of her face was covered in an ornate Mardi Gras mask. Emma sighed and slammed back the second shot of tequila without salt or lime. She needed it. She started pouring a third, blatantly ignoring him.

"Would you like to dance? I've got some sweet moves."

She doubted it. "I don't dance, sorry."

Batman frowned. "Well, then wanna blow this party off for someplace quiet and dark where we can…talk?"

A shudder ran down Emma's spine. Being alone with him was bad enough. Alone in the dark was downright frightening. "No, I'm here with someone. Sorry."

Batman straightened up, his body language projecting the anger his mask hid away. "Who?"

She opened her mouth to answer him when someone came up behind her and set heavy, warm hands on her shoulders. He leaned in, placing a kiss against her cheek, and Batman finally took a step back.

A deep male voice rumbled near her ear. "Hey, baby, sorry I'm late."

Emma fought the urge to pull away from this second, undesired suitor, but the fingers pressing insistently in her shoulders begged for her cooperation. He wasn't putting the moves on her; he was trying to save her from Batman. Relieved, she turned to face the man and moved without hesitation to say hello.

Whoa. He was taller than she expected, a few inches over six foot, but she couldn't look surprised and convince Batman to bugger off. She strained on tiptoe to reach up and kiss the lips that were the only part of his face visible with a gold-and-green Venetian mask obscuring the rest.

The instant their lips touched, the simple greeting turned into something else. The electricity of the kiss nearly knocked her backward, but his firm, yet gentle grip on her arms wouldn't let her fall away. Her senses were instantly overloaded by the scent of soap and a spicy men's cologne, the soft brush of his lips against hers and the heat of his skin.

Emma wasn't sure if it was the tequila or his kiss, but she was suddenly very aware of her body. The nearness of the man made her skin tingle and her breath quicken. She felt her body leaning into him without her consent. It had to be the tequila. No wonder people got into so much trouble with this stuff.

Regaining some of her senses, she pulled away to break the kiss, but he didn't immediately let go. Batman must still be watching. "I've missed you," she said, snuggling suggestively into him.

His arms wrapped around her and hugged her tightly against the solid wall of his chest. He leaned in, breathing the scent of her hair and whispered, "He left, but he's watching us from the other side of the room. Keep it convincing if you don't want him coming back."

Emma nodded and pulled away. She reached up to affectionately rub a bit of lipstick from her white knight's mouth. The gesture was intimate and quite convincing, she was sure. Once away from him, she had a better view. The mask obscured most of his face, so all she could really decipher was his tall, broad build, tightly fitting jeans and his attractive and bright smile.

"Are we doing tequila shots?" he asked.

"I was, but I think I'm done." She'd had just enough to make this scene authentic, but too much more was trouble for sure.

"Don't be a quitter." He poured himself a shot, and then paused only for a moment to smile wickedly before leaning forward and licking a patch of exposed skin just above her cleavage. Emma sucked a ragged, surprised breath into her chest and held it there. She couldn't respond. Every impulse in her brain was telling her to step back and stop him, but she just stood there, the tequila rendering her mute.

He hesitated, the salt shaker in his hand. His dark blue eyes connected with hers, awaiting her permission. Could she give it? She wanted to. This was what she'd set out for tonight, even if she hadn't known it. Grandmas didn't do body shots with strangers at parties. But the words still escaped her. All she could do was tip her head back to let him sprinkle the salt gently over the swell of her breasts and place the wedge of lime delicately between her lips.

He came closer, shot in hand. Her entire body ached with anticipation as his hot breath hovered over her skin. He licked slowly, taking longer than she ever expected to remove every grain from her chest. Surely Batman wasn't watching that closely. When he tipped the glass back, swallowing the tequila in one sip, she was finally able to release the air she'd held painfully in her lungs. Then he set the cup down.

Emma tensed, not quite sure what to do aside from holding perfectly still as his hand slipped around her neck to cradle her head and tip her mouth up to him. He dipped his head, his lips brushing hers briefly before biting down and sucking the lime juice. A cool, tart stream of it flowed into her own mouth before his teeth tugged the rind away.

When he took a step back, Emma did the same. It had taken everything she had not to moan aloud when he'd touched her this time. The best thing she could do was to get out of this situation before she lost what little control he'd left her with. Never mind that her face had to be flushed with embarrassment and unexpected arousal.

Her hand self-consciously came to her face and

brushed the rough, glittery surface of her mask. She'd forgotten he couldn't see her. Even if she was beet red, he wouldn't know it. She was anonymous tonight. Somehow the knowledge made her bolder and she fought her flight reflex to hold her position by the bar.

He picked up her full paper cup from the counter and held it up in a dangerous and silent offer. It was her turn.

A quick glance confirmed that Batman had disappeared and there was no reason to continue with the show. Aside from her not wanting to stop. "He's gone," she said, giving him the opportunity to stop if this was still just a ruse.

"I know," he said, and handed her the salt shaker.

Given that he was wearing a long-sleeved button-down black shirt, the only real option she had was his neck. She stood on her toes, straining in her heels to reach him. Emma leaned in and left a moist trail from the hollow of his throat to just over his Adam's apple, where her tongue ran across the rough stubble that had grown in since his morning shave. She could feel his pulse quicken as she hovered near to him. This time, she noticed his skin smelled more distinctly male. Salty and slightly musky. She couldn't help lingering to take in a deep breath and commit the scent to memory. Her body's reaction to it was almost primal, parts deep inside of her clenching with a building need.

"Here," he offered as she pulled away to apply the salt. He lowered onto his knees and looked up at her with big blue eyes, his hands resting on the swell of her hips.

Emma could hardly see enough of his face to piece together an expression, but his intense gaze urged her on. As he knelt, it almost felt as though he were worshipping at her feet. She liked it.

She tried to focus on doing the shot properly before his skin dried and the salt wouldn't adhere. She didn't want to give away her inexperience with this. She'd never even dreamed of doing anything as blatantly sexual as body shots. She didn't think she had it in her.

She sprinkled the salt on his throat and positioned the lime between his full, soft lips. Nervously gripping the tequila in one hand, Emma leaned in a second time to lick off the salt. She could feel the vibration of a growl in his throat as her tongue slid across his skin. Pulling away, she quickly threw back the drink and placed her hands on each side of his face. Just before she was able to bite into the fruit, he spat out the lime. Emma didn't have time to stop and their lips met with another unexpected spark.

She didn't pull away. The old Emma would have. In her mask, she was someone else.

The second kiss blew the first out of the water. His fingertips dug into the flesh of her hips as he tugged her close against him. She melted against his mouth, slowly slipping down until she, too, was on her knees in the kitchen. The island shielded them from the crowd only feet away. She wrapped her arms around his neck, her lips clinging to his as he probed and explored her with his tongue.

It was deliciously naughty. In that moment, Emma wanted his kiss more than anything else in her entire life.

Just when she'd convinced herself that the kiss might never end, they parted. His quick breath was hot on the skin of her neck as he pressed his cheek against hers and sat there for a moment to recover. Their arms were still tangled around one another, neither grip loosening. There was an intensity in him that excited and frightened her, but she matched it with her own.

"Come with me," he whispered, then stood and offered his hand.

Emma wasn't ignorant. She knew what he was offering and every inch of her body urged her to take him up on it. She'd never done anything like this. Ever. And yet there was something about her hero that insisted she go with him.

So she did.

One

Three Months Later

"Where the hell is Noah?" Jonah Flynn growled into his telephone and gripped his coffee mug fiercely in his free hand.

"He's…n-not in, sir."

His brother's administrative assistant, Melody, was audibly startled by his tone and he immediately chose to correct it. Jonah didn't raise his voice to his employees, ever. Honestly, the only person he ever shouted at was Noah. And he would direct his anger at his brother if he could find the bastard.

"I'm sorry for yelling, Melody. I didn't think he would be there. He's never in the office. What I really meant was do you know where he's gone to? He isn't answering his home phone and his cell phone goes directly to voice mail like he's got it turned off."

Melody hesitated on the line for a moment. Jonah could hear the clicking of her keyboard as she checked his calendar. "His calendar is wide-open, but he mentioned as he left that he was headed to Bangkok."

Jonah nearly choked on his latte. He swallowed hard and moved the cup out of his reach. "As in Thailand?"

"Yes, sir."

He took a deep breath to swallow his anger. He would not, could not, take this out on Melody. She'd already called him "sir" twice, which just felt wrong. Yes, he was the CEO, but he was also wearing jeans and a Monty Python T-shirt. Everyone just called him Jonah.

"Any idea when he'll be back?"

"No, but he did send me the number of the hotel he's staying at. You could probably reach him there."

"That would be great, thanks, Melody." She read off the number and he quickly scratched it on his desk blotter before hanging up. He dialed it, getting transferred to his brother's suite without much trouble. Of course Noah didn't answer. He was probably frolicking with some exotic beauty. Jonah forced himself to leave a voice mail message that didn't betray the true reason for his call and hung up in disgust.

Thailand.

If he'd had any second thoughts about Noah being involved in his current mess, they immediately dissipated. If the preliminary accounting reports he was looking at were correct, his little brother had just taken off to Southeast Asia with three million dollars that didn't belong to him.

Jonah leaned back in his leather chair and gently rubbed his temples. This was not good.

The timing was never good for embezzlement, really, but his brother had just royally screwed him over in more ways than one. Noah didn't spend much time in the office; his role in the company was to please their mother and nothing else. But Noah knew—he *knew*—that they were close to wrapping up the deal with Game Town. The auditor they'd hired was showing up today. Today!

This could ruin everything. It wasn't a huge amount in terms of the numbers that ran through the company, but his brother wasn't smart and took it in one big chunk, transferring it to some offshore account he had in the Caribbean. Anyone with an interest would run across it eventually. Game Town was hiring FlynnSoft to manage their monthly game subscription service. Who would want the company handling their money to have issues like that? Jonah certainly wouldn't do it if the roles were reversed.

This needed cleaning up and fast. As much as he didn't want to, he could rearrange his assets for some cash and cover the loss. He would take it out of his brother's hide later. Maybe make him sell his overpriced European sports car. Perhaps even make him do some actual work at FlynnSoft for free until he paid off the debt.

But Noah *would* pay for this. By the time Jonah was done with him, his little brother would wish he'd simply called the cops.

But he wouldn't. Not on his brother. And not for any love he had for his useless sibling, but for concern for their mother. Angelica Flynn had a degenerative heart condition and couldn't take much stress. If Noah, the baby and undoubtedly favorite child, ended up in jail, she'd have one hell of an attack. If she found out Noah was turned in by his own brother, he had no doubt she'd drop dead from the strain and embarrassment. In the end, it would all be Jonah's fault and he refused to be the bad guy in this.

He would handle his brother without their mother ever finding out.

Publicly, Jonah could deal with this however he wished. As a privately owned gaming company he had that luxury. Thank heavens he hadn't taken people's advice to go public. The move could make him a fortune overnight, but he'd also have shareholders and a board of directors to answer to. He could even be fired, losing control of the empire he'd started in his college dorm room.

No way. FlynnSoft was his and Jonah didn't answer to anyone, especially some pompous suits who thought they knew better than he did how to run his company. He'd bail FlynnSoft and his brother out one way or another. His employees deserved as much. And they deserved the money this new contract could bring in. *If* Noah hadn't just blown it.

What a mess.

Jonah flopped back into his executive chair and let his gaze drift over to the framed photograph that sat on the edge of his desk. In it, a Blue Morpho butterfly sat sunning itself on a clump of bright yellow flowers.

He'd gotten more than a few odd looks since he'd brought the picture into the office. Jonah wasn't exactly a nature buff. He'd spent his entire adolescence focused on video games and girls, both of which could be enjoyed in the climate-controlled comfort of his bedroom.

Of course, he couldn't tell anyone why it was really there. How do you explain a night like that to people? You just couldn't. They wouldn't believe you. If it wasn't for the proof inked into his skin, he might've believed she was a tequila induced hallucination. His gaze dropped to his right hand and the tattoo etched into the web of skin between his thumb and index finger. His fingertip grazed over the slightly raised design, tracing it as he'd done that night, only then it was across the silky skin of her chest. His half of the heart.

The other half had disappeared with the woman in the butterfly mask. He'd never anticipated a company Mardi Gras party at his loft would turn into an unforgettable night of body shots, anonymous sex and late-night tattoos. But for some reason, she, whoever she was, had gotten under his skin almost instantly. Everything from her soft gasp as he licked the salt from her throat to the way she'd begged for him to take her was etched into his mind.

Even with all the crap going on with Game Town, he couldn't help but let his thoughts drift to her again. She'd asked him for one night. No names, no personal details. Pure fantasy. Her multicolored glitter butterfly mask had obscured everything but her sleek, brunette ponytail, the full pout of her lips and the bewitching emerald green of her eyes.

How, exactly, had he decided that letting her walk out of his life was a good idea?

Jonah had been an idiot. He could see it now. For years, he'd gone through a lineup of women. They were all beautiful. Many were successful or talented in one way or another. They were drawn to his business success and the glamorous lifestyle he could provide. Most men would be content with the kind of woman who would throw herself at them, but he never was. He would inevitably get bored and move on. He'd actually earned a reputation as one of Manhattan's Most Eligible and *Elusive* Bachelors.

But his butterfly had kept his interest. Even three months later, he still found himself thinking about her. Wondering where she was. Who she was. Trying to figure out if the real woman could ever measure up to his memory of her. She'd insisted that the next morning he wouldn't want her anymore, like she would turn into a pumpkin at the stroke of midnight. Was it just the fantasy he craved? If he'd seen her face and known her name, would she have been relegated to the list of women he'd loved and forgotten? He didn't know.

Jonah ran his hand through the long strands of his dark brown hair and gripped the back of his skull. He needed to let this go. Let her go. If he kept looking down the blouse of every woman he met searching for that tattoo, eventually he'd get slapped. Or sued. Maybe arrested.

He simply couldn't help it.

With a sigh, Jonah turned back to his computer. He needed to focus. Noah would eventually come home and suffer mightily, but until then, he needed to clean up the mess. He searched through his contact list for his accountant, Paul. He'd be able to move his assets around and get the cash he needed. He always made sure his money worked as hard for him as he did for it and invested heavily, unlike his brother, who burned through money buying silly toys.

He could get the cash; it just might take a few days for the wheels of finance to turn.

In the meantime, he'd have to find a way to stall the forensic accountant Game Town was sending over. Someone would be showing up this afternoon at two. No one had mentioned the auditor's name, so he had no idea who, or what, to expect. His strategy would rely heavily on who showed up.

If the auditor was male, Jonah would drag his dusty golf clubs from the closet and take the guy out. He hated golf, but found it to be an important social tool in the business world. Few company honchos got together to play *Madden* on their Xbox. It was a pity. Instead, they would play eighteen holes; he'd buy the auditor some drinks. Steaks. Whatever. Perhaps if the guy was hung over enough, the numbers would take longer to crunch.

If the auditor was a woman, there would be a different tactic. The golf clubs would stay in the closet, but the charm would be on in full force. Regardless of whether she had three eyes and a hunchback or looked fresh from the Parisian runways, Jonah's charisma would carry him through. Since the age of fifteen, he'd had a way with women. A gift, he supposed, and one he made good use of. Dinner and drinks would still be involved, but the ambience would improve greatly.

He wouldn't have to lay a hand on her. The last thing he needed was the woman running back to Game Town with that tale. No, Jonah wouldn't go there. The right smile, some intense eye contact and a few compliments would go far, especially with a mousy accountant who wasn't used to the attention. If he planned this right, he'd have her so hot and bothered she wouldn't be able to remember her own name, much less see the problems with the financial reports.

No matter what, Jonah would come out on top. If he had to sit down with Carl Bailey, the CEO of Game Town, and explain what was going on, he would, but if it could be avoided, he'd gladly play eighteen holes or take a lonely accountant to the theater.

He made a note to ask his assistant, Pam, what shows were playing on Broadway at the moment. He wasn't a big fan of musicals, but he found most to be tolerable enough. Except *Cats*. He wasn't making that mistake a second time. That was a phenomenal waste of four hundred dollars, which was saying a lot, given he'd easily spend that much in a week on supplies for the gourmet coffee bar they added on the twenty-third floor.

Speaking of which, he eyed his now-cold coffee with dismay. He'd get a refill and a bagel after he talked to Paul. Picking up the phone, he dialed his accountant and mentally cleared his calendar for the next week. He'd be busy courting the Game Town auditor.

Jonah just prayed it was a woman. He really hated golf.

Surely her boss was a closet sadist. There was no other explanation for why he'd send her to FlynnSoft for two to three weeks. Tim could've sent anyone. Mark. Dee. But no, he had to send Emma. She was the only one who could handle herself in that environment, he said.

Slipping her hand inside the doorway to her closet, she flipped on the light switch and stepped inside. Tim was full of it. He just wanted to see her squirm. She liked to think that she'd been hired for her top grades at Yale and her recommendations from professors, but she had a sneaking suspicion her father had gotten involved and made it happen.

Tim likely resented some rich kid getting dropped into his department against his will and enjoyed making her miserable as a result. It made her more determined than ever not to give him that satisfaction. She was going to do a good job. No—a *great* job. She would not get sucked into FlynnSoft's corporate hippie attitude. She would not fall prey to *Jonah Flynn, Golden God* and his seductive smile.

Not that the notorious CEO would waste any of his smoldering looks on Emma. She wasn't bad to look at, but the last gossip blog she'd seen had him coming out of a restaurant with a model she'd recognized from her lingerie catalog. She simply couldn't compete with abs of steel and breasts of silicone. And she wouldn't even try.

A man like Jonah Flynn was of no interest to her, anyway. He embodied everything her mother, Pauline, had warned her about. *Don't make the same mistakes as Cynthia did*, she'd say. Her older sister hadn't died because of poor choices—a plane crash had done that—but when those choices came to light after her death, the family had been scandalized. Emma had grown up as her sister's polar opposite as a result.

If Tim was being absolutely honest with her, she'd bet that's why she got the job. Dee, although competent, was a tall, thin and attractive woman easily distracted by men. If Flynn even looked at her sideways, she'd be a puddle at his feet. Forensic auditors could not puddle. Emma probably wouldn't earn a second glance.

She eyed the neatly hung rows of clothing in her closet. Although FlynnSoft was a pioneer of the übercasual work environment, there was no way she was walking into that building while wearing jeans and flip-flops. Even if she stuck out like a sore thumb amongst the laid-back software designers, she was wearing one of her suits with high heels. Her sole concession to the casual environment would be leaving off the hosiery. Summer was just around the corner in New York and she preferred staying cooler in the heat.

She pulled a charcoal-gray suit and a light blue top from the rack and smiled in approval. There was just something about the crispness of a freshly starched blouse and a smartly tailored blazer that gave her a much-needed boost of confidence.

It was just the armor she needed to go into battle against Jonah Flynn.

Battle was the wrong word, really. He wasn't the enemy. He was a potential contractor for Game Town. FlynnSoft had managed to build an extremely robust and efficient system for handling subscriptions and other in-game purchases for their addictive online game *Infinity Warriors*. Recently, they'd branched out offering the management of other online game system subscriptions to companies that needed help handling a high number of users or providing additional monetizing options. It allowed small software start-ups to focus on designing the game and let FlynnSoft manage the back end.

Before they went to contract, it was customary for the companies to have a forensic accountant review the vendor's records to ensure everything was shipshape. Carl Bailey, the man who started Game Town twenty years earlier and now headed up the board of directors, hated surprises.

Although FlynnSoft had a sterling reputation, the old man had a general distrust of a company where a suit and tie were not standard issue. Bailey wasn't getting into bed with any company he didn't think was up to snuff, even if paying Flynn was cheaper than developing the capability in-house. She was to go over everything with a fine-tooth comb.

Emma would be welcomed and provided everything she needed to do the job, but at the same time, no one liked an auditor nosing around. She might as well wear a big red button that read I Can Ruin Your Life.

That was a pretty unfair generalization. She could only ruin their lives by calling to light their own misdeeds. If they were good boys and girls, she couldn't get them into trouble.

Her mother had pounded that much into her head as a teenager. *Never say or do anything you wouldn't want printed on the front page of the newspaper*, she was always saying.

Before her sister, Cynthia, died in a plane crash, she'd been engaged to the owner of the *New York Observer*, Will Taylor. He was also the business partner of their father, George. That newspaper was delivered to her childhood home every morning, and to this day, Emma lived in fear that something she did might actually turn up there. The scandals of the remaining socialite daughter of the Dempsey family were news worth printing.

So far, so good.

With a quick glance at the clock, Emma left her closet and started getting ready. She had to be at FlynnSoft at two to meet with Mr. Flynn at his insistence.

Normally, she would've simply worn what she'd put on to go to work that morning, but she came home at lunch to change. It was nerves. Her outfit that morning was more than suitable, but she felt this need to put on something else before she went over there. To get every hair in place.

After thirty minutes of primping, Emma gave herself one last inspection. Her brown hair was twisted into a tight bun. After David moved out, she chopped it off at her shoulders in typical female defiance, but it was still long enough to pull up. Her makeup was flawless—fresh looking, not too heavy. She could still see the faint specks of freckles across her nose, which she hated, but could do nothing about.

The suit was loose because of her recent stress-induced weight loss, allowing it to hide any unfortunate bumps she didn't want to share. The blouse she wore under the coat was a flattering shade of blue and more importantly, the neckline was high enough to hide her tattoo.

The half of a heart that was inked into her chest above the swell of her left breast wasn't the only evidence of the night she'd made the mistake of letting herself go, but at the moment, it was the hardest to hide. That wouldn't be the case much longer.

Like a little devil sitting on her shoulder, Harper told her to have fun that night. And she certainly did. She hadn't intended to take it that far, but there was something about her masked hero that she couldn't resist. Before she knew it, they were having fantastic sex in the laundry room and walking down the streets of New York in the middle of the night in search of adventure.

Every time Emma washed her clothes and felt the cold metal of the washing machine against her skin, a flush of embarrassment would light her cheeks on fire. She had done her best to forget about it and the tequila had done a good job turning the experience into a fuzzy, dream-like memory, but still, it crept into her mind from time to time. If it hadn't been for the bandage on her chest when she awoke the next morning, she might've convinced herself it had never happened.

But it had. She'd allowed herself to do anything and everything she wanted to do. She'd let David's words strike too deeply and questioned everything about her life, when in truth there was nothing wrong with the way she lived. She did everything a proper Upper East Side woman was supposed to do. She was educated, well-spoken, polished and elegant. She took pride in her work as a CPA. It was true that no one would ever describe her as the life of the party, but her escapades would never show up on the front page of the local paper, either.

In retrospect, it took one uninhibited night to prove that she was okay with being that kind of woman. There was no glory in being like her older sister, who followed each pleasurable impulse and left her family mired in scandal after her death. Then again, that one night was enough for the repercussions to echo through her entire life. She could keep it under wraps for now, but eventually everyone would find out.

And of course, the tattoo remained. Emma had considered getting it removed, but it had become her personal reminder of how dangerous the wrong choices could be. Every time she even thought about breaking out of her shell, she could look at her tattoo and remember what a bad idea it was. It was a slippery slope she was determined not to go down again. She would not become her sister and shame her family. It didn't matter how good or right it might feel in the moment.

But in keeping it, she had to work hard to ensure it stayed covered, especially in a professional setting. Or near her mother, who felt tattoos were only for bikers and inmates. Emma had tripled her ownership of high-collared tops the last few weeks. She worried about the challenge of her summer wardrobe as the temperature climbed, but she had to deal with the FlynnSoft job first.

Emma was just thankful she'd gotten hers in a place she could hide easily, unlike her hero with his tattooed hand. There was no way he could disguise his half of the heart, although she wondered how he would explain it. He was at a FlynnSoft party, so he was potentially an employee, like Harper was. She supposed that in the laid-back corporate environment, a tattoo was no big deal. Might even be a requirement.

It was just another reason to be nervous about her assignment.

At any moment, he could appear. An engineer, a programmer, hell, even the janitor. She didn't know a thing about him and had no real way to find him other than the tattoo. She'd shared a few choice details of the night with Harper, and her friend had been on high alert to discover the man's identity since then. She hadn't been as willing to let the romantic fantasy go, especially when Emma confided in her about her predicament.

A few weeks after the party, at the family Easter dinner, Emma took one look at the spiral ham and went running down the hallway to the powder room. After two more weeks of denial and antacids, she realized she had more than a tattoo to show for her wild night—she was having her anonymous hero's baby! And had no way to contact the father and tell him.

In the last three months, there were no tattooed hands to report at FlynnSoft, at least in the marketing or accounting departments, where Harper spent most her time. The odds were that even if the man worked at FlynnSoft last February, he was gone now if Harper hadn't found him. That meant Emma was on her own with this baby, whether she liked it or not. She would tell her family soon. Eventually. When she couldn't hide her belly any longer.

Another glance at the clock proved that she couldn't

delay any longer, as much as she might want to. She brushed her fingers over her hair and grabbed her purse from the table by the front door. With a fleeting look down her blouse, she opted to button her shirt one notch higher.

Just in case.

Two

It was an easy trip down to the FlynnSoft building, as she'd been there several times meeting Harper for a lunch date. They occupied the top five floors of one of the high-rises a few blocks from her apartment. The lobby was like many others with sleek, modern furniture and large LCD screens playing video clips about the company and scenes from the various video games they produced. The only difference, really, was the receptionist, who was wearing khaki shorts and a tank top. Her brown hair was pulled up into a ponytail that highlighted the multiple piercings in her ears.

If this was the first face of the company, she had no doubt things would go downhill from here. After checking her in, the woman gave her a temporary access badge and walked her back to the elevators. She showed her how to wave her badge over the sensor, allowing her to select the twenty-fifth floor, where the executive offices were located.

Emma considered stopping on the twenty-fourth-floor business wing to see Harper, but she didn't have time. They'd see each other plenty over the next few weeks, she was certain. Instead, she pushed the button that read 25 and closed her eyes. As the elevator rose, Emma could feel her anxiety rising, as well. She wished she knew why. She was more than capable of doing this job and being successful. She was an excellent auditor and accountant. Harper had done nothing but praise the company and everyone she worked with. Everything would be fine.

Exiting onto the twenty-fifth and top floor of the building, Emma headed down the hallway to the right as she'd been directed. Pausing in one of the doorways with a placard that read Gaming Lounge, she watched a couple of employees playing foosball. In any other company, the large space would be a conference room, but here, there was a pool table, a *Ms. Pac-Man* machine and some beanbag chairs arranged around a big-screen television.

The players stopped their game to look over at her, staring as though she were wearing a clown suit instead of well-tailored gray separates. Emma quickly started back down the hallway to avoid their gazes. As though they had room to judge with their Converse and baseball caps.

She finally came to a large desk at the end of the hallway. A woman in a spring sundress with reddish-blond hair sat at it, talking into a headset and typing at her computer. She gave a quick glance to Emma and ended her call.

"You must be the auditor sent by Game Town." She stood and grinned, offering her hand over the desk.

Emma accepted it with a self-conscious smile. "Yes, I'm Emma Dempsey. How did you guess?"

The woman laughed, her eyes running over Emma's professional outfit a second time. "I'm Pam, Jonah's assistant. He stepped down the hall, but he should be back any second. Can I get you a drink while you wait? A latte or a soda or something?"

Emma arched a confused eyebrow and shook her head. She didn't want any of the staff going to any trouble on her behalf. Some companies went to great lengths to kiss up to auditors and she didn't want to start out setting that kind of precedent. "No, thank you."

"Okay, but if you change your mind just let me know. We have a coffee bar on the twenty-third floor in addition to a Starbucks on the ground level. I'm sure you'll get the full tour, but while you're here, we hope you'll make use of all our employee amenities. We also have a gym, several game rooms and a pretty decent cafeteria with a salad bar where employees can eat at no charge. All the vending machines are also free to keep our programmers awake and productive."

"Wow." There wasn't really a better word for it. Emma had read in magazines about how Jonah Flynn was some sort of modern business pioneer who was changing everything. That he strived to create a workplace where people wanted to go so that staff would be happier and more productive. A casual work environment was only one piece. Apparently, a foosball table and free caffeinated beverages were another.

"This is a great place to work. Hopefully you'll enjoy your time with us." Pam walked out from behind her station and Emma noticed she was barefoot with sparkly, hot pink nail polish. At this point, that detail was no longer a surprise. Padding softly across the plush carpet, she escorted Emma to a set of double doors a few feet away. She pushed one of the heavy oak panels open, and then stepped back and gestured for her to go inside. "Have a seat and Jonah will be with you shortly."

The door closed silently behind her, and Pam and her toes disappeared, leaving Emma alone in Jonah Flynn's office.

As instructed, she quickly settled into one of the black leather guest chairs, crossing her ankles and holding her portfolio across her lap. She couldn't help but look around as her fingers nervously drummed against the notebook.

The office was massive with impersonal executive-type furniture that was very similar to the decor of the lobby. Glass and chrome, black leather, bookshelves with awards and books he'd probably never read. There was a large conference table that ran along the length of the floor-to-ceiling windows overlooking an amazing view of Manhattan.

She wasn't quite sure what she was expecting to find in the notorious CEO's office—perhaps a stripper pole and a *Donkey Kong* machine—but it all seemed to fit the space in a generic way aside from the giant cardboard cutout of what must be one of his video game characters. Emma was unfamiliar with it, but it looked like some kind of blue troll in battle armor.

There were only a few unexpected details. A photograph of a butterfly on his desk. A world's greatest boss trophy on the shelf behind his chair. A child's crayon drawing addressed to "Mr. Jonah" pinned to his corkboard. She was pretty certain he didn't have children, but she only knew what the gossip bloggers reported, which could be far from the truth.

"Miss Dempsey. Sorry to keep you waiting," a man's voice called out to her from over her shoulder.

With a nervous smile, Emma got up from her chair and turned to face him. He was standing in the doorway, taking up most of the space with his broad shoulders. Shoulders that were covered in a clingy brown T-shirt with what looked like some cartoon knights on the front. He was wearing loose-fitted jeans with a torn-up knee and well-broken-in high-top Converse sneakers. And a Rolex. She could see the large diamonds on the face from across the room as he held his drink.

What a contradiction. Software. Foosball. Jeans. Diamonds. You didn't run into this kind of CEO every day.

As he came closer, she only had a moment to register the face she'd seen in so many magazines: the distinctive dark brown hair with the undercut shaved on the sides, the deep blue eyes that seemed to leap from the glossy pages, the crooked smile that was endearing and arousing all at once. All of it was coming at her, full speed ahead.

Letting her business training kick into gear, she held out her hand. "A pleasure to meet you, Mr. Flynn," she said.

Jonah reached out to her, gripping her with a warm, firm shake. His dark eyes seemed to be appraising her somehow, a faint smile curling the corners of his mouth. If she didn't know better, she'd say he looked pleased about something.

"Call me Jonah. And the pleasure is all mine," he said, his voice as deep and smooth as melted dark chocolate with the hint of a British accent curling his words.

"Emma," she reciprocated, although the word barely made it across her tongue. Emma suddenly felt very aware of herself. Of him. Of the newly uncomfortable temperature of the room that made tiny beads of perspiration gather at the nape of her neck. His cologne tickled her nose, a spicy male scent that was infinitely appealing and somewhat familiar.

She tried to swallow, but a thick lump had formed in her throat. She couldn't even speak while he continued to touch her. Did he have this effect on every woman or was she just that desperate after three months of celibacy and her pregnancy hormones conspiring against her?

Jonah Flynn was everything she expected him to be and then some. The magazines truly hadn't done the man justice. He was handsome without being too pretty, with hard angles and powerful, lean muscles flexing beneath the cotton of his shirt as he reached out to her. His every move was smooth and deliberate, exuding power and confidence even in a T-shirt and jeans. You just couldn't capture that in a picture.

She was blushing; she knew she had to be. How embarrassing. This was not going well at all. She had set out to prove to Tim that she could handle this assignment and here she was, practically mute and drooling after only a few seconds in the CEO's presence. Her clothes should be too big, since she had instantly transformed back into an infatuated twelve-year-old girl.

She needed to pull it together—and now. Emma broke eye contact to collect herself. Casually gazing down, she caught a glimpse of red, then recognized the other half of her tattoo etched into Jonah Flynn's hand.

Emma immediately began to choke.

* * *

Perfect. He'd never get the contract with Game Town if he killed the auditor on the first day.

Jonah quickly escorted the woman to a chair and buzzed Pam to bring her a bottle of water. He wasn't quite sure what just happened. One minute, she was smiling and shaking his hand, the next she was hyperventilating and turning bright red. Maybe it was an allergic reaction. He'd have Pam take the flower arrangement on his conference table to her area just in case. Wasn't there an EpiPen in the kitchen first aid kit? That would be his next move.

She'd calmed down a bit once she sat. Maybe she'd just swallowed her gum. No. She had pearl earrings and crossed ankles despite her inability to breathe. She definitely wasn't the kind of woman who chewed bubble gum at work. If at all.

Pam breezed through the door with the water, which Emma gratefully accepted. Jonah held out his hand for Pam to stand by until he was certain the woman would recover.

Emma took a few breaths, a few sips and closed her eyes. Things were improving. He waved Pam off, but knew she'd be poised and ready if she were needed.

He knelt down in front of Emma, watching with concern as her breathing stabilized and her color began returning to normal. At least, he supposed it was normal. The woman was awfully pale, but his expectations were skewed by spray-tanned celebutantes who usually sported an orange undertone to their skin. No, he decided. Pale was normal.

Once she was no longer deprived of oxygen, he had to admit she was quite pretty. She had silky brown hair that begged to be hanging loose around her shoulders, but she'd forced it into submission in a knot-like bun. She had an interesting face, almost heart shaped, with full lips and creamy skin she didn't hide under a ton of makeup.

From what he could see of her figure beneath that dowdy suit, she had ample curves in all the right places. Although he'd been photographed with the occasional model type, he gravitated toward the lingerie and swimsuit girls because they were equipped with the assets he was looking for.

Completing his inventory, he noticed her nicely manicured nails and naked ring finger. A single woman would be much easier to work his charms on.

This might not be the worst couple of weeks after all. Keeping Emma's mind off the books could turn out to be a pleasurable experience for them both.

"Are you okay?" he asked once she'd drained half the water bottle and he was certain she could speak again.

Emma swallowed hard and nodded, although her eyes were glued to his hand as it rested on her knee. "Yes, I'm sorry about that."

Following her gaze, he immediately removed his hand and stood up, allowing her some personal space. "Don't apologize. Is there anything Pam or I can do? Move the flowers, perhaps?"

"Oh no," she insisted. "I'm fine, really. Please don't worry about me."

She was the kind of woman who didn't like to be fussed over. Jonah made a mental note. "Okay, well, back to business, then." He rounded his desk and sank into the soft leather of his chair. "The Game Town people said it should take you a few weeks to go through everything."

"Yes." She nodded. "Perhaps less if the records are

easily accessible and someone on staff can assist me with questions."

"Of course. I'll alert the finance people to have everything ready for you tomorrow. I'm sure they'll be happy to assist you with anything you need. You have our full cooperation. Everyone is very excited about this potential partnership with Game Town."

"I'm glad to hear it. I'm ready to get started."

Jonah arched an eyebrow, but quickly dropped it back in line. What was the rush? He *would* get an auditor who was hell-bent on getting the job done when it was the last thing he wanted. "How about we go on a tour first?"

"That's not necessary," she said, her answer almost too quick. "I'm sure you have more important things on your agenda. If Pam can point me to my desk, I'm sure I can make do."

If Jonah didn't know better, it sounded like she was trying to dismiss him. Women never dismissed him. He wasn't going to let this one buck the trend. "Nonsense," he insisted, pushing out of his chair to end the argument. "I've got some time and I want to make sure you're settled."

Emma stood, somewhat reluctantly, and walked out of the office ahead of him. Despite her stiff manners, she moved fluidly and gracefully as a woman should. The curves of her rear swayed tantalizingly from left to right as she walked in her high heels to the door. Maybe that suit wasn't so bad after all. It fit nicely, hugging her hips just tight enough. He'd prefer to see her in a pair of clingy jeans and a tight little T-shirt, but the suit was growing on him. As were other things.

He took a deep breath to stifle the thoughts and pulled up alongside her once they started down the hall. "I'm sure you saw our gaming lounge on your way in. Each floor has one." They paused at the doorway and he couldn't help but beam with pride. It was one of his favorite innovations. He probably spent as much time in these rooms as anyone. It was good for the spirit to break away for a while. It was refreshing and gave new enthusiasm to tackle the workload.

"That's very nice." Emma's voice was cold and polite.

She seemed decidedly disinterested and it annoyed him. She should be impressed like everyone else. *Forbes* magazine had done an article on his game lounges and sky-high productivity levels. It was groundbreaking territory. Certainly it should evoke more interest than her watery, patronizing smile suggested. Perhaps if he made it more personal? "What's your favorite video game? We have quite a collection here outside of the ones we produce in-house."

"I'm sorry. I don't play video games."

Jonah tried not to frown. Surely in this day and age everyone had a favorite game. Even his grandmother played bridge on the computer. "Not even *Super Mario Brothers* when you were a kid? *Sonic the Hedgehog*? *Tetris*, even?"

She shook her head, sending a dark strand of hair down along the curve of her cheek. It gave her a softness he found quite a bit more attractive than the uptight accountant thing she had going with that bun. Wearing her hair down around her shoulders would be infinitely more appealing. Seeing the brown waves tousled across one of his pillowcases would be even better. Although that couldn't be a part of his plan while the Game Town deal was pending and she worked under his roof, it didn't mean he couldn't continue to pursue her later.

Emma immediately tucked the rogue strand behind her ear and opened her mouth to ruin the fantasy he'd built in his head. "I was raised not to waste time in idle pursuits."

This time he had to frown. Idle pursuits. *Hmph.* His video game obsession as a child had blossomed into a multimillion-dollar video game empire. Not exactly idle. He wondered what she did with her time that was so superior. She certainly couldn't spend all her weekends feeding the hungry and knitting blankets for the homeless. Sweet ass or no, she was starting to work his nerves. "All work and no play can make for a dull girl."

Emma turned to him with a blankly polite expression. "There's no sin in being dull. Is it better to have scandal chasing your tail?"

"No, but it's certainly more fun." He couldn't help the sarcastic retort. The tone of condescension coming from her full, soft peach lips was a contradiction that set his teeth on edge. It was public knowledge that Jonah had scandal chasing his tail on more than one occasion. If nothing else, it kept a man on his toes.

Emma turned away from the game room and continued down the hall.

This time, watching her walk away was not nearly as enticing, as he'd been dismissed again. Containing his aggravation, he moved quickly to pull alongside her. Taking a breath, he decided to start over. She might be grating his nerves, but Emma was his pet project for the next few weeks.

"You'll be sitting on the twenty-fourth floor with the finance group while you're here. Before we go down there, let's stop by the twenty-third floor and I'll show you the coffee bar. I know I always need something to perk me up midafternoon."

"Mr. Flynn—"

"Jonah," he pressed with the smile that always got him his way where women were concerned.

"*Jonah*, this really isn't necessary. I'm sure someone other than the CEO can show me the coffee bar and the gym and the cafeteria. Right now, I really just want to get out of your hair and start to work."

He mentally amended his prior statement—his smile usually got him his way. Emma seemed immune. He sighed in resignation and held out a hand to escort her to the elevators. How was he supposed to charm this woman when she wouldn't let him? It was downright frustrating. "I'll just show you the area where you'll work, then."

They were silent as they waited for the elevators, which were running slowly just to spite him today. He had to admit he preferred her quiet. When her mouth was closed, she was attractive and graceful with just a touch of mystery in the green eyes that appraised him. When she spoke, it became abundantly clear that they came from two very different schools of thought where business and pleasure were concerned.

Jonah didn't know if it was better or worse that he found her perfume so appealing. Actually, as he anxiously watched the digital numbers of the elevator climb, he began to wonder if it was a perfume at all. The scent was more like a clean, fresh mix of shampoo and a lady's hand cream. It suited her more than the heavy stink of the perfumes that made his nose twinge. Much more delicate. Like the line of her collarbone that was barely visible at the V of her blouse.

The reflex to glance down her top for a tattoo was stifled by the blue dress shirt she wore. One less woman to slap him with a harassment suit, he supposed. Besides, Miss Goody Two-shoes was the least likely candidate to be his butterfly that he'd run across yet.

The doors finally opened and they took the short trip to the twenty-fourth-floor finance department. As they walked, he noticed Emma's gaze didn't wander like so many other visitors. Normally people were interested in the untraditional workings of FlynnSoft. Emma's vision was fixed like a laser in front of her. Her intensity was both intriguing and a touch disconcerting. Would she be this focused on the financial reports?

He stopped at a visitor's office and opened the door. The small L-shaped desk took up much of the space with the computer setup and phone occupying one whole side. There was a corporate lithograph framed on one wall and a ficus shoved in the corner. It wasn't intended for long-term occupancy, but certainly it would be adequate for the short time she required it.

"This will be your home for the next few weeks. The desk is full of supplies, the phone is activated and there's a docking station for your laptop. If you need anything, the finance assistant, Angela, can help you. She's down the hall and to the left."

Emma watched him gesture, then nodded curtly. Another annoyingly dismissive gesture. The woman just couldn't wait for him to go away. What exactly was her problem? She was tight as a drum, every muscle taut, and anxious as though she itched to brush past him into the office and shut the door in his face. Why would such an attractive woman be wound up so damn tightly? She needed a drink. Or a good lay. Both couldn't hurt. He'd be happy to oblige if she'd give him the opportunity.

"Are you all right, Emma?"

Her head snapped toward him, a slight frown puckering the area between her eyebrows. Her green eyes searched his face for a moment before she spoke. "I'm fine."

The hell she was. But pushing her probably wasn't the best tactic this early on, so he let it slide. He didn't have to claim victory on the first day. He'd do it soon enough.

"You just seem a little uncomfortable. I assure you none of us bite." He planted his right hand on the door frame and leaned closer to her to emphasize his words. "You might even find you enjoy your time with us."

Emma's face went pale, her eyes focused on his hand and completely ignoring his persuasive charms. When she turned back to him, she flashed a saccharine smile. Sweetly artificial. "Of course. I'm just anxious to get settled in."

His hand fell heavy at his side. This wasn't going as well as he'd planned. He wasn't sure if she was deliberately being difficult or she was just like this normally. Paul had better be rushing that transaction because his wine-and-dine plan might not pan out the way he hoped. He'd just been assigned the only woman in Manhattan who was immune to him. Possibly even annoyed by him.

Maybe it was just the work environment. It was possible she stuck to strict business protocol and the casual interactions he was used to made her uncomfortable. All the better to get her away from the office, then. Give her the chance to let her hair down, kick off those heels and relax. He'd drop the dinner invitation, then leave her alone for the rest of the afternoon to stew over the possibilities. The anticipation alone would do a great deal of the work for him.

He glanced at his watch to lay it on thick. "I'd love to talk to you some more about your assignment, but I'm afraid I have a meeting in a few minutes. Would you be interested in having dinner with me tomorrow night?"

"No."

Jonah opened his mouth to suggest a restaurant and stopped cold. Had she just said no? That couldn't be right. "What?"

Her pale skin flushed pink and her eyes grew wide for a moment as she seemed to realize her mistake. "I mean no, *thank you*," she corrected, turning on her heel and disappearing into her new office with a swift click of the door.

Three

The following morning, Emma met Harper at the twenty-third-floor coffee bar before work. She'd barely slept the night before and was seriously in need of some caffeine.

"You look like hell," Harper said, always the honest one. When they'd first met at the sorority house, Emma wasn't quite sure what to think of her. Now she'd come to appreciate her candor. Most of the time.

"Thanks. Good morning to you, too."

They got into line and waited to place their orders. "What's wrong?" Harper asked.

"I just didn't sleep well last night."

Harper nodded and took a step forward to call out her customized coffee to the guy at the counter. Emma watched her, her brain trying to decide what she wanted to drink, but it simply refused to function like it should. She hadn't slept. Of course, she hadn't told Harper why.

She'd been in a nervous tizzy. Jonah Flynn. The playboy millionaire of the software world had the matching half to her tattoo. Fate had played a cruel joke. There was not a worse match on the planet for her, much less to father her child. It was just as well she'd kept her identity a secret. He most certainly would've been disappointed to see who she was beyond the tequila and the mask. And fatherhood for the most elusive bachelor in the five boroughs? Yeah, right.

And yet, as she lay in bed that night attempting to sleep, all she could think about was him. How he'd saved her from the creep. How a thrill of excitement had raced through her when he kissed her for the first time. She remembered his hands running over her body as though he couldn't get enough of her. After everything with David, it had felt incredible to be desired like that. It was a feeling that could easily become addictive and that meant it was dangerous.

She'd tried to forget about that night and had been mostly successful, but her body remembered. Being in the same room, touching him and breathing in his familiar scent had brought it all back. With a vengeance. In the dark of her bedroom, she could easily recall the sensations he'd coaxed from her body. Not once, in two years with David, had she ever responded like that. It was something raw, primal.

"Ma'am?"

Emma turned to the man at the counter, who was patiently waiting on her drink order. "Hot tea," she blurted. Although she probably needed the jolt of a black cup of coffee, she knew she wasn't supposed to have too much caffeine. That was a cruel irony for pregnant women everywhere.

The area was as miserably crowded as any Starbucks, so when their drinks were ready, they took them and their pastries, and went on their way back to their offices.

Harper seemed quite pleased with her new work arrangement. "I can get used to having you working here. I'd finally have someone to talk to. Everyone here is pleasant and all, but most of them have their heads in the clouds or their noses in a computer."

Emma had noticed that. Software designers were definitely different than most of the people she'd worked with. They were intensely focused, usually not even making eye contact or saying hello in the hallway. They were all on some mission, be it to fix a software bug or beat their nemesis at some video game. That or perhaps they just didn't know how to speak to women.

"Then why do you stay?" Emma asked. "We both know you don't need to work."

Harper narrowed her gaze at Emma, then shrugged. "I get bored doing nothing."

"You could always help Oliver. He might like having his sister there at the family business."

"Oliver doesn't need my help with anything. Besides, this place is fun. You'll get spoiled quickly. I save so much money with the free food. I was able to drop my gym membership, too, which saved me a bundle. Now I can use that money for Louis Vuitton handbags and trips to Paris, instead. I enjoy having income I earned on my own, not because of my last name. You couldn't get me to leave here and I hope you'll feel the same. We do need to make some adjustments to your wardrobe, though."

Emma looked at Harper's khaki capris and silky, sleeveless top, then down at her conservative suit and frowned. It was her favorite. She'd always thought the dark green had complemented her coloring. "I can't help it if everyone here dresses like college students. I refuse to assimilate. And don't you get your heart set on me being here past a few weeks. The minute I can get out of here, I will."

They paused at the elevator and Harper pushed the button. "Why are you so anxious to go? Is it that bad?"

It wasn't, but staying here a moment longer than she had to was courting disaster. Emma wondered how much she should tell Harper about yesterday. Harper was one of her best friends, but she was lacking in social couth. Anything she told her would instantly be passed along to their friends Violet and Lucy, as well. From there, who knows who would find out. Emma wanted Jonah to stay in the dark about her identity for the time being and the best way to make that happen was to keep her friends out of the loop.

"I'm just not comfortable here."

"You're afraid of running into *him*." The remark hit a little too close to home for her taste. Harper always had a way of seeing too much where Emma was concerned. It made her an excellent friend, but left Emma little privacy, even in her own head.

There was no sense in denying it. "Yes, I'll admit it. It would be awkward, at best, to run into him. And at worst, a conflict of interest if anyone at Game Town found out. My entire report could be compromised if anyone thought I was personally involved with someone here."

"Or it could be the most wonderful thing ever. I thought you wanted to find him. You know, for the sake of the *B-A-B-Y*." She mouthed the last part silently.

Emma didn't respond. Harper was too wrapped up in her romantic ideas to see the situation objectively and there was no sense in explaining herself any further. She just stepped onto the elevator when the doors opened and sipped her hot tea.

"You've already seen him!" Harper accused.

She snapped her head to the side to confirm they were alone in the elevator. "What? No, of course not."

Harper was unconvinced by her response. "Who is it? Is he cute? What department does he work in?"

The doors opened to the twenty-fourth floor and Emma waved at her friend to be discreet as they stepped out. "Would you keep it down? I don't want everyone to know."

"Okay, but you've gotta tell me. I can keep it a secret."

Emma eyed her with dismay. She loved her friend, but honestly… "No, you can't."

Harper frowned and planted a hand defiantly on her hip. "Oh, come on. Why not? I mean, it isn't like it's the CEO or something. Bagging Jonah would be quite gossipworthy, but anyone else is just run-of-the-mill office news. I don't know what the big dea—"

Emma could feel the color drain from her face and there was nothing she could do to stop it. Harper halted in her tracks, forcing Emma to turn and look back at her. Her friend's jaw had dropped open, her perpetual stream of words uncharacteristically on hold.

"Oh my God," she finally managed.

"Shh! Harper, really. It doesn't matter."

"The hell it doesn't!" Her voice dropped to a hushed whisper that was still too loud for Emma's taste. "Jonah Flynn? Seriously?"

Emma nodded. "But he doesn't know who I am or know anything about the baby. And I intend to keep it that way for now. You understand?"

Harper nodded, her mind visibly blown by her friend's news. "Jonah Flynn is the hottest man I've ever seen in real life. He and my brother are friends, and it took everything I had not to throw myself at him every time he came to the house. I can't believe you two… How did you not jump into his lap when you realized who he was?"

"Have we met?"

Harper frowned. "You're right. A damn shame, though. What a prize to land. He was totally smitten with you."

"He's a player. I seriously doubt that."

"If you believe the gossip, then yes, Jonah Flynn is a notorious womanizer. But that's not the guy I've known over the years. And the guy you were with was willing to tattoo himself after one night together on the off chance it might reunite you someday. A playboy wouldn't have an inch of skin unmarked if that was what he did with everyone. You were special to him. Special enough for a guy that goes through women like tissues to take serious notice."

That was true. Emma hadn't spied another tattoo on what she'd seen of his body, then or now. But she refused to believe there was any kind of future with him. Even if he was interested in starting something, he wanted the woman she was that night. Not regular old Emma. And she swore she'd never be that woman again. So what was the point? Telling him who she was would just torture them both and ruin the memory of that night.

And yet she had to. Or did she? Her hand dropped protectively to her belly. If Jonah rejected Emma and their child, it could scar the baby forever knowing its father didn't want him or her. Would it be better to keep quiet? The idea was unsettling to her, but until she decided, not a word could get out. "You have to keep this a secret, Harper. No one can know. Not Violet, not Lucy, not your brother and especially not Jonah."

"Cross my heart." Harper sighed in disgust and Emma could see it was almost physically painful for her to say the words. "You'd better keep that tat of yours under wraps, though."

Emma straightened her collar nervously and started back down the hallway. "I don't make a habit of displaying my décolletage and have every intention of keeping it hidden. I'm here to do my job and get out."

"But what about the baby?" Harper trailed behind her.

"I don't know, Harper. What happened between us is over. Never to be repeated. Ancient history. I don't know that the baby will change that." Emma reached out and opened the door to her office. Sitting on her desk was a large crystal vase filled to overflowing with white lilies in full bloom. The warm scent of them was nearly overwhelming in the small space, making her happy that she was past her morning sickness. She'd never received a more beautiful bouquet of flowers in her life.

She stepped inside and plucked the card from the plastic prong. As she flipped open the envelope, she couldn't decide if she wanted them to be from Jonah or not. His attentions, although flattering, were pointless and even dangerous if he knew who she really was. Yet her impractical, inner girl couldn't help but wish they were from the handsome businessman.

"'To Emma,'" she read, her stomach aflutter with nerves and excitement. "'Welcome to FlynnSoft. I look forward to getting to know you better.' It's signed *Jonah*."

"Ancient history, eh?" Harper said, leaning in to sniff one of the flowers. "Are you so sure about that?"

* * *

Jonah came down the hallway from the elevator, coffee in one hand, bagel in the other, and paused outside his office. There was a large and quite stunning crystal vase of white Casablanca lilies sitting on Pam's desk. He frowned. He'd specifically ordered that type of lily for Emma because he felt they were a reflection of her: elegant, pure and refined. They didn't make any flowers that were stuffy and aggravating.

Plus, he thought she'd see right through roses. Lilies were different, exotic. He'd spent enough on them to catch the attention of even the most difficult to please female.

He would be the first to admit he typically didn't have to work that hard to woo the ladies. He'd been told that with his good looks and irresistible charm, the panties of every woman within a fifty-yard radius simply flew off. It made for an amusing visual, one he'd like to witness really, but he wasn't naive. He figured their interest in him probably had more to do with the fact that he was filthy rich rather than charming. Panties were consistently repelled by obscene displays of money.

But Emma was different. Her iron underwear stayed firmly in place when he was around. And given her stiff, overly polite demeanor and cutting tongue, they were probably chafing.

That was just not acceptable. The one time he needed his way with women to work without fail… The auditor Game Town hired was priority one even if charming her would take everything he had. He was willing to shift his tactics and restrategize his game plan, but in the end, he would be successful.

Even if right now, things didn't appear to be going so

well. Emma had rejected the flowers and in record time. The odds of Pam receiving the same flowers on the same day were slim to none.

"Did Miss Dempsey bring those up here?" he asked.

Pam was beaming with the large bouquet perched on her desk. She seemed to really take pleasure in having them there where everyone who passed by, including her, could see them. Well, at least someone was enjoying them. The money hadn't gone entirely to waste.

"Yes," she said. "She told me she was allergic and I should enjoy them. Aren't they pretty?"

He made a mental note to buy his assistant flowers more often. Make that all the administrative assistants. The occasional flowers probably appealed to them more than the *Ms. Pac-Man* machines, and he probably catered too much to the programmers with his corporate innovations. They couldn't function without the admin staff and something like that would be great for their morale.

"Lovely indeed." He continued past her desk to his office with his breakfast in hand and let the door slam behind him. Allergic, his ass. She swore yesterday that her choking fit had nothing to do with the flowers and he believed her. This was about her being stubborn. Never in his life had he run across a woman so resistant to him. It didn't make any damn sense.

Jonah settled into his chair, set down his food and fired up his computer with a stiff punch of his finger. It almost made him wonder if he'd romanced her before. Or one of her friends. She had the attitude of a woman who'd been loved and left by him or someone like him in the past.

But that couldn't be the case. Despite the lengthy list, Jonah had a great memory for names and faces. He'd never laid eyes on Emma Dempsey before yesterday. If she was bitter about men like him, it wasn't his doing.

But it would be his job to change her outlook. The deal with Game Town was riding on it. Even if he could get his hands on Noah and wring three million dollars from his neck, the transaction would be in the records.

His phone rang, an unknown number lighting up the display. Pam had put the call through, so he figured he wasn't about to be assaulted by a telemarketer.

"Jonah Flynn," he said into the receiver.

"Hey, it's your favorite brother."

Speak of the devil. Jonah took a deep breath before he said anything, choosing each word carefully. "I've told you before that Elijah is my favorite brother, but Noah, you're just the man I was looking for."

His brother chuckled on the line. They both knew the operations of FlynnSoft had nothing to do with Noah. He occupied an office. Drew a paycheck. On a rare occasion when he was bored with his other mysterious pursuits, he helped with charity golf tournaments and presented large, cardboard checks.

"What's so important that it couldn't wait until I came back from this trip? This call is costing me a fortune."

"What?" Jonah asked. "About three million dollars?"

The silence on the end of the line told him everything he needed to know. Noah had taken the money but didn't think anyone would notice it so quickly. Maybe any other time they might not have noticed it before he replaced it. But his timing sucked and Emma would find it, Jonah had no question.

"Listen, I don't care whether you blew it on hookers and fruity drinks or built schools for poor children. It doesn't matter. But I want it back right now."

"Yeah, that's a little iffy at the moment. I don't exactly have it right now. But hopefully I will by the time I come home."

"And when will that be?"

"Two weeks at the most."

"Okay, fine. But if it isn't back in my hands—*in full*—within fifteen minutes of you arriving in the US, I'm going to take every penny out of you with my fist."

"Jonah, I—"

"I don't want to hear your excuses. You come up with three million bucks or I will make you so miserable you'll wish you'd stayed in Thailand. Am I clear?"

This time, Noah didn't try to argue. "Crystal. Have you told Mother?"

Now it was Jonah's turn to laugh. "No. And I have no intention of doing it unless I have to. You and I both know her heart can't take the stress, although it doesn't stop you from pushing the boundaries."

"I would never deliberately hurt Mother," Noah argued.

Jonah shook his head in dismay. "It doesn't matter whether it's deliberate or not, you still do it. You never think of anyone but yourself."

"And you don't think of anyone but your employees and your company," Noah countered. "You practically ignore the whole family. When was the last time you went to the estate to visit her? Or came to my apartment? Or Elijah's place? You accuse me of blowing money on Thai hookers and you spend every bit of time and money you've got on vapid supermodels."

Jonah's jaw grew tighter with every word out of his youngest brother's mouth. If he had the time, he'd fly to Thailand right that instant just so he could punch Noah in the face. His brother seemed to think that this company had appeared out of thin air. That Jonah hadn't had to pour his heart and soul, in addition to all his free time, into building it and making it a success. When he did get to play, he played hard. Yeah, he didn't spend much time with his family, but they all had their own lives, too. None of them had knocked on his door recently, either.

"The company is important to me, yes. It supports a lot of people, including you in case you've forgotten. I have pride in what I've built and I'm not about to lose it because you're a thoughtless little prick. You do know the auditor from the Game Town deal is here, right? That your little stunt may have cost the company a huge, lucrative contract?"

"Oh hell," Noah swore. "I completely forgot about that. I didn't think—"

"No, you didn't think, Noah. You never do."

There was an awkward silence on the line for a few moments while Jonah took another deep breath.

"Do you think they'll find it?" he asked.

"Probably. You did everything short of highlighting the withdrawal with a yellow marker. But I'm trying to clean it up. Paul's moving some money around. Temporarily," he emphasized, "to cover the gap until you pay it back."

"I will pay it back, Jonah."

"Yeah, yeah," he sighed. "Just don't make me regret trusting you."

"I promise you won't."

"I'll see you when you get back," Jonah said, hanging up the phone.

He wanted to believe his brother, but it was hard. He was never a bad kid, just one who was used to getting his way. As the youngest, his pouty lip would melt their mother's heart in an instant, especially after Dad died. When he got older, people seemed to go out of their way to give him whatever he asked them for.

If Jonah was smart, he'd put Noah to work full-time on corporate fund-raisers. His best job fit might be applying that skill to encourage rich people to part with their money. In this economy, FlynnSoft wasn't able to raise as many outside dollars for charity. Noah might make the difference.

That is, if his unorthodox loan didn't cost them a huge contract and put all their donation programs on hold.

Jonah leaned back in his chair and took a bite of his bagel. The day was so complicated already and it wasn't even 9:00 a.m. yet. Two weeks. He had to figure out how to replace or bury the stolen money until Noah came back. And then find some way to put it back in without raising more flags.

Until then, he had to find a way to get around Emma's defenses. The direct approach wasn't working and he didn't want to strong-arm her. He'd never had to beg or coerce a woman to go out with him in his life and he wasn't about to start now. It didn't exactly set the right mood. He wanted her ready and willing, not even more stiff and distant than she already was.

It really was a shame. Emma was a beautiful woman. A sensual woman, although she seemed determined to keep that fully under wraps. He could tell by the luscious sway of her hips and the way her full lips parted slightly when he leaned near to her. She had a reaction to him. Certainly. She just wasn't willing to do anything about it. Yet.

But he could plant the seed. Get under her skin. Whether

or not she agreed to let him wine and dine her, he was going to do everything in his power to make sure she went home every night and thought about him. Whether it was with irritation or suppressed lust, he didn't care. Either would be enough to help her lose focus, and that was the most important part.

It would take Paul a couple more days to get the money. Until then, he had some unofficial FlynnSoft business to tend to.

Popping the last of his bagel in his mouth, Jonah got up from the desk and went in search of his curvy, uptight auditor.

Four

Emma had rarely been as happy to get home as she was tonight. It seemed like no matter where she went or what she was doing, she would run into Jonah. Not like he was following her; he was just always there. She'd look up from the copier and see him down the hall talking to someone. He'd look at her and smile, the charming grin chipping away at her defenses before he turned back to his discussion. He was in the cafeteria, the coffee bar, passing her in the hallway...*constantly*.

And when Jonah wasn't there, she found herself thinking about him anyway with a confusing mix of irritation and, if she was honest with herself, desire.

She didn't want to admit it, but no red-blooded woman could resist Jonah's charms. Emma had tried her best, but he was infuriatingly persistent and wearing her down. Their past didn't help. Knowing what he could coax from her body, knowing what it felt like to cling to him, uninhibited and anonymous, made it that much worse. She couldn't concentrate. The lines of the financial records blurred together, the math not adding up in her head no matter how many times she ran the figures. Her focus was not on the audit and it absolutely had to be—charming, sexy CEO be damned.

It was a relief to get home, the one place where she knew she was safe from Jonah Flynn. There was something about the feminine fabrics, soft throw pillows and cheerful colors that instantly made her entire body and mind relax. She'd decorated her Upper East Side apartment to look like a cozy retreat out of *Country Living* magazine, casual and inviting.

And yet, when she slipped out of her work clothes and into something more comfortable, she realized she wasn't even safe from Jonah here. As she stood in the bathroom, clutching a worn T-shirt to pull over her head, she caught a glimpse of herself in the mirror. There, just above the bare swell of her breast, was the blasted tattoo staring back at her.

She could still see him standing there, his mask obscuring everything but the same boyish grin, sharp jaw and dark blue eyes that seemed to rid her of all her good sense.

"Let's get a tattoo," he'd said.

Emma hadn't realized they'd stopped on the sidewalk outside a tattoo parlor until he said that. It wasn't the kind of place she typically took notice of. Or had any interest in going to.

"Two halves of one heart," he'd lobbied and pressed the palm of his hand against the bare skin of her chest exposed by the low neckline of her top. His fingertips had gently curved around the edge of her breast, sending an unanticipated wave of pleasure through her. He had the uncanny ability to render her brain butter with the simplest touch.

"Right here." He'd traced his skin at the juncture of his thumb and index finger, then across her skin, showing how their touch would make the heart whole. "If we're meant to be together after tonight, I'll find you. And this heart will be how we'll recognize one another."

Emma's heart had swelled in her chest. His suggestion had been romantic and spur-of-the-moment and completely stupid. Not once in her life had she ever considered getting a tattoo, but that night had included a lot of firsts for her. With his hand gently caressing her and those ocean-blue eyes penetrating her soul, she couldn't help but follow him into the shop.

Looking in the mirror now, she let her fingertip trace the heart the way his had done. Just imagining it was his hand instead of her own sent a shiver of longing through her body and her skin drew tight with gooseflesh. He'd been the last man to touch her, three long months ago. Her realization that she was pregnant with the stranger's child had been a big enough disruption, making her physical needs easy to ignore, but now, knowing how close he was, it was as though her libido had flipped a switch.

Flustered by her wanton response to the ghost of a man she couldn't have, she pulled the T-shirt over her head and marched back into the living room to make dinner.

It was Tuesday and if she kept daydreaming, the girls would arrive and she wouldn't be ready.

Every Tuesday, Lucy, Harper and Violet gathered at Emma's apartment for dinner and their favorite television series. They took turns cooking or buying takeout. Tonight, she'd promised Lucy she would make her favorite baked ziti and she hadn't even boiled water yet.

In the kitchen, she busied herself by preheating the oven and gathering the ingredients for the family recipe. The ziti recipe was one of the few valuable things her older sister had taught her before she'd died.

Everything else she'd learned from her sister was more of a cautionary tale. She'd been sixteen when Cynthia died, barely dating herself, and yet the truth of her sister's secret life had scared her parents enough to clamp down on Emma with an iron fist. She was hardly a problem child, but of course, Cynthia had always seemed perfect on the surface, too.

When she was old enough to be in charge of her own life, she'd thought about rebelling. Her hunt for a sorority had been a start, but instead, she went the other direction and chose Pi Beta Phi, the sorority of proper, well-off ladies out to do community service and build sisterhood. She'd seen how her sister's scandal had hurt her parents and she didn't want to be the one responsible for putting that look on their faces ever again. When she finally lost her virginity in college, it was to a well-groomed, polite premed major she'd been dating for nearly six months and had hoped to marry. She pretended to be the proper, sophisticated society darling her parents wanted, and after a while, it just became who she was.

She'd only really, truly let herself go that once. Emma let herself do shots of tequila with a stranger, licking salt from the musky skin of his throat and sucking a lime from his full, soft lips. From there, it was a slippery slope that led to the tattoo on her chest and a positive pregnancy test on the back of the toilet. One night had ruined a decade of good behavior. She had no idea how she was going to tell her parents.

Emma opened the box of pasta and dumped it into a pot of boiling water with an unsatisfying splash. It had been so easy to let herself get carried away that night. Too easy. There was a part of her that understood how her sister could get so wrapped up in a passionate and illicit relationship while she was engaged to someone else. The pleasure and the excitement were enthralling. The other part of her knew there was nothing worth derailing her whole life for.

There was nothing she could do about the choices she'd made in the past, but she certainly wasn't going to make the same mistakes twice. Jonah Flynn was just the kind of man who could make her priorities get all out of whack. That made him dangerous. She would tell him about the baby once the audit was complete and she had done her job. He couldn't know the truth about her identity or the baby before then, which made it imperative that she not let her guard down around him.

"We're here!" Violet called out from the living room.

"I'm in the kitchen," she replied, giving the pasta a stir and setting the timer. Since she'd added the girls to the approved guest list with the doorman, they tended to show up with little warning. "It's nowhere near ready, sorry."

The girls came around the corner with paper sacks and set them on the counter. "We're not in a hurry," Harper insisted. "Anyway, I brought a bottle of chardonnay and Violet picked up some cheese and crackers to keep us busy until dinner is ready. The wine is just for us, of course."

Her best friends unpacked the items from the bags

and set them on the counter. "Oh, and tiramisu," Harper admitted, pulling the seductive dessert from the bag. "I had to."

Emma groaned inwardly. "You said FlynnSoft has a gym, right? After all this I'm going to have to find it or I'll gain fifty pounds with this kid. Now that I've gotten my appetite back, I'm hungry almost all the time."

Harper smiled and nodded. "It's on the ground floor near the rear entrance. You can't miss it. There's usually no one in there after six or so. You can have it all to yourself."

"I don't know what you're complaining about," Lucy said. She reached out and put her hand on Emma's slightly rounded belly. "You look like you had a big lunch, not that you're over three months pregnant. I think you can afford some indulgent carbs."

"I'm glad you think so," Emma quipped. "Now open those crackers. I'm starving."

Violet opened the box of crackers while Lucy pulled wineglasses from the cabinet and the corkscrew from the drawer.

"So how is the FlynnSoft assignment going?" Lucy asked after Harper opened the bottle and poured her glass.

There was something about Lucy's tone that worried Emma. She turned away from the marinara sauce she'd made and frozen to look at Harper and knew instantly that she'd spilled the secret about Jonah to the others. Emma swore under her breath and returned to mixing the cheeses and seasonings into the bowl.

"I'll just presume you all are caught up on who Jonah is—thank you, Harper—and jump right into it. I have never met a man so persistent in my life. You should've seen his face when I told him I wouldn't go to dinner with him. It was as though I was the first woman in his life to ever tell him no."

"You probably were. I sure wouldn't tell him no," Violet spoke up.

"Well, someone needs to," Emma responded. "He's not a god. He can't get his way all the time. That kind of arrogance makes me crazy."

"I've never really thought of him as arrogant in the years I've known him," Harper said, shrugging. "He's confident, sure, very smart, of course. He knows what he wants and he goes after it. I find that attractive. But you're determined not to like him, so he could save puppies from burning buildings and you would find a reason to hate him for it."

Emma opened her mouth to argue, but knew there wasn't much point. It was true. Mostly. She didn't hate him. She couldn't feel that way about the father of her child. But she had to find things wrong with him for her own protection. And if he was perfect, she'd make up lies in her head about all of Jonah's evil doings and pretend they were true. "It's better this way, trust me."

"Why, Em?" Lucy settled into a chair at the kitchen table. "And don't give me some story about your sister. We've all heard it before and know better than anyone that you're not your sister. You certainly aren't going to disappoint your parents with anything you do. You're a better person."

"There's no sense in punishing yourself for sins you've never committed," Lucy said.

Instead of answering right away, Emma drained the pasta and started mixing it with the sauce and cheese to put in the oven. What could she say to that? Was that really what she was doing? "I'm not punishing myself."

"Yes, you are," Harper insisted. "If not for your sister's sins, then for whatever you did at that Mardi Gras party. I think the punishment far outweighs the crime."

"That night was a mistake and I'll never be able to put it behind me. Don't you think getting impregnated out of wedlock by a stranger at a party will disappoint my parents?"

"They might not be thrilled, but grandbabies become a joy no matter what," Violet said.

"I'll remind you of that when you accidentally get pregnant by a man whose name you don't know, Violet."

"Listen, honey," Harper interjected. "I've made plenty of mistakes where men are concerned. But not even one of my best moments were as sexy or romantic as what you told me about your night with him. You jumped in with both feet and scared yourself. Okay, I get it. But that doesn't mean you have to stay out of the pool entirely. If you're not ready for the deep end, at least put your feet in. Test the waters. Letting your hair down every once in a while won't hurt anything. It might be good for you."

Popping the casserole dish in the oven, Emma dusted her hands off on her yoga pants and eyed her friends' wine with a touch of jealousy. If she didn't put an end to this discussion, her friends would continue to badger her and they'd miss the show they'd come over to watch. "That is all well and good, but I'm not getting in a pool of any kind with Jonah Flynn. Not that he'd want to once I'm huge and pregnant anyway."

"With *his* baby!" Lucy pointed out.

"It doesn't matter. Does he look like the paternal type to you? I've told you my reasons for avoiding Jonah, but if nothing else I've said convinces you, know that it's a major conflict of interest. I'm auditing FlynnSoft. If even so much as a whisper of a relationship pops up about Jonah and me, past or present, my credibility is shot. I'd probably lose my job and permanently damage the reputation I've worked so hard to build. No man, not even Jonah Flynn, is worth that. Not to me."

"Well, they're going to find out when the baby is born and everyone figures out what happened between the two of you. There's no avoiding that. Your only option is to tell Tim you can't do it. That would be the most forthright answer," Violet said.

"Technically. But *can't* isn't in my vocabulary. I refuse to back down from this challenge, even if there's a risk."

Harper nodded in resignation and Lucy sighed. Emma hoped her friends would leave it alone, at least for the next two hours.

"Of course," Harper said with a smirk, "if I was going to sully my reputation and ruin my career for a man, it'd be for him."

Jonah was sitting at his desk Wednesday afternoon when his phone rang. He recognized the number as his financial advisor, Paul. Hopefully it was good news.

"Paul," he said. "Tell me what I want to hear."

There was a hesitation on the line that instantly told Jonah he was out of luck. "I'm sorry to tell you, Jonah, but it's going to take me at least two more days to get everything handled. We could look into getting a short-term loan to get you the money, but the banks are really tight on those lately with the market the way it is. I doubt it would come through any faster. Any chance you could borrow it from…um…"

"From my mother?" Jonah asked.

"She does have more liquid assets than you do. That's the only reason I would even suggest it."

Jonah sighed and shook his head. He wanted to keep this situation as close to his vest as he could. "I don't want Mother to know what Noah's done. Ask someone for three million dollars and they'll sure as hell want to know what it's for. At least she'd ask *me*. She'd give it to Noah without blinking."

"Then why didn't he just borrow it from her in the first place?"

Jonah ran his fingers through his messy hair. "I have no idea. The less I know about what he's up to the better. Listen, just move things as quickly as you can and I'll do what I have to on this end."

They wrapped up their conversation and Jonah hung up. He'd given Emma some space this morning, hoping maybe the money would come through and he wouldn't need to continue pursuing a woman who was clearly disinterested in him. It was fun for him, a challenge he'd never had to face before, but he couldn't spend all his time trying to woo the ice princess. He still had a company to run.

Apparently that task was back at the top of his to-do list for the day. He had some time on his calendar, so he slipped out from behind his desk and went in search of his elusive prey.

He spotted her on the twenty-fourth floor down the hall from her office. She was leaning over the copier, pressing buttons and eyeing the pages as they spat out. Jonah was tempted to come up behind her and whisper something in her ear, but nixed the idea. Somehow he thought that might earn him a slap or a knee to the groin.

Instead, he just watched her from a distance, admiring the curve of her calves highlighted by her knee-length skirt and four-inch heels. She held a pen gently to her full, soft lips, the lower one pouting just slightly and urging him to reach out and brush his mouth across hers.

The best thing about watching her from here was that her defenses were down. She was relaxed, a faraway day-dreaming look in her eyes as the constant rhythm of the copier lulled her mind into thoughts about something other than accounting. He didn't know what she was thinking about, but the corner of her mouth curved in a smile. It made her face light up in a way he hadn't seen before. She was always so proper and guarded around him.

It was then that she turned to glance down the hallway and spotted him. Her green gaze ran over the length of his body for just a moment, her tongue darting quickly across her bottom lip. He thought he caught the slightest hint of something other than derision in her eyes, but before he could be certain, she snatched her papers from the copier, turned on her heels and started off in the other direction.

She was avoiding him again. No more avoiding.

Jonah marched up behind her. She was easy to catch with those high heels slowing her escape. He spied one of the janitorial closets just to her right and got a bad idea. Without so much as a hello, he wrapped one arm around her waist and opened the door, tugging her inside.

"What on *Earth*—" she shrieked in surprise, but quickly silenced when the door slammed shut and they were suddenly cloaked in the darkness of the small space.

The room was slightly musty, smelling of industrial cleaner and old cardboard, but the subtle scent of her lotion cut through it all and sent a spike of need down his spine. Memories of the night with his butterfly flooded his mind in an instant. He'd made love to her in the small, private space of his laundry room when no place else was available. If he'd had a second chance with her, he would've made up for it with a bed covered in satin sheets and rose petals. That's what she had deserved.

Again, like the laundry room, the janitorial supply room wasn't the best or most romantic choice, but he would take what he could get. He had no intention of trying to seduce her here, but if this was the only way he had of getting her alone to talk, so be it. He was tired of this game.

He tightened his arms around her waist and tugged her close to him so she couldn't get away. The closet was filled with any number of dangerous things she'd likely hurt herself with if she took a step back from him. She needed to stay right where she was. They were going to talk about what was going on whether she liked it or not.

So far, he was pleased enough with the situation. She was very still and quiet in his arms, albeit a touch stiff. He could hear the soft sound of her breathing, the rise and fall of her chest as she pressed futilely against him with her palms. He liked the feel of her in his arms more than he expected to. It felt natural and familiar somehow.

As his eyes adjusted to the dim light coming under the door, he was able to make out her silhouette and the soft contours of her face. What he could see of her was fighting this tooth and nail. Her eyes were squeezed shut, her lips tightly pressed together. Emma's shoulders were drawn up around her ears. She was strung tight as a drum, the comfortable woman from minutes ago completely forgotten.

"Relax, Emma. I'm not going to bite."

"I need to get back to work," she said, but there was half-heartedness in her voice that betrayed her. There was a part of her that was open to him. He didn't know why she was fighting it so hard. It could be quite an enjoyable experience for them both.

"I want to talk to you first. You've continued to avoid me and have left me with no choice but to abduct you and make you listen to what I have to say."

"I'm not talking to you in a closet with the lights off. It's inappropriate." Emma struggled against him in earnest, gaining little traction and succeeding in doing nothing but rubbing her belly back and forth against his rapidly hardening desire.

Jonah had to swallow a groan as her movements sent a wave of pleasure radiating from his groin. "Stop. Wiggling," he managed through gritted teeth. "I just want to talk. I have no intention of taking advantage of you in here, but if you keep grinding your hips against mine like that, we may have to make some impromptu changes to the agenda." The thought had undeniably crossed his mind, but even *he* had boundaries in the workplace. "I can tell you don't think that highly of me and my reputation with women, but I can assure you that I much prefer the king-size bed in my loft for that kind of thing."

"I don't want to talk. Or to see your king-size bed."

"I hadn't asked you to."

Emma stopped struggling and looked up at him. He could see the dim light reflecting in her eyes as they searched his face for something. Sincerity, maybe. She must've found it because eventually her body relaxed in his arms.

"Then what is it you want, Jonah?"

He couldn't very well tell her that he wanted to distract her until he could clean up his brother's mess. And in that moment, that wasn't his biggest motivation. There was something about the way she said his name that sent a fire raging through his veins and made him want to pull her close and kiss her. It was different from the run-of-the-mill lust most attractive women lured from him. It was more powerful. Potent. And it demanded he take action.

"I just want to get to know you. There's something happening here… I can't explain it, but I want to see where it goes." Jonah released her waist with one hand to reach up and caress her face. He just had to touch her, even if it earned him a slap.

Instead, he heard Emma's sharp intake of breath and decided he wasn't the only one whose plans were crumbling under the strain of their attraction to one another. "Tell me I'm crazy, but I know you feel it, too. You're just determined to fight it. Stop fighting."

"I…" Emma began to protest, but words seemed to escape her in that moment.

They escaped him, too. And words wouldn't fill the need building inside him. Jonah leaned in and pressed his lips against hers. He expected resistance, but he found none. There was only a slight hesitation, then surrender. Maybe it was the safety of the dark, but his uptight auditor melted into him instead, matching the enthusiasm of his touch.

He'd been correct in his assessment of her. Under that straitlaced veneer was a sensual female looking for an outlet. Jonah would gladly provide it.

Deepening the kiss, he let his tongue slide across hers, drinking in the taste of spicy cinnamon. The flavor was sharp, biting him unexpectedly. He liked the surprise contrast. Emma was full of them.

She wrapped her arms around his neck, tugging her body closer to him. The darkness and the familiar feel of her in his arms roused thoughts of his butterfly again. If he didn't know better, he'd swear he was with her, in his laundry room. Without thinking, he let his right hand drift to her chest, stopping short of groping her breast, but aligning his hand where his butterfly's tattoo would be.

She must have misinterpreted his intentions because Emma instantly stiffened in his arms and jerked away from his kiss. "What the hell are we doing?" she whispered.

"Wait," he protested, the distance between them suddenly painful. Jonah let go of her to fumble for the light switch, but the instant he did, he felt her pull away and scramble for the doorknob. The door flew open, flooding the small room with light so he could see her dash away from him and down the hallway to the ladies' room.

Flopping back against the wall, Jonah ran his hand through his hair and wished away his erection. That hadn't exactly gone to plan.

So pulling her into a dark room and pinning her against him might've been the wrong tactic if he'd really just wanted to talk. And he had, at first. His body just had other plans. So had hers, but he went too far, as always. Damn.

He shook his head. Something about her just wasn't quite right. She was nervous around him. Avoided him at all costs. Refused to accept gifts or dinner dates. He'd watched her interact with other employees, and the stiff, overly polite veil dropped. She was still professional, just not militantly so.

Emma was just insistent on keeping the wall up between them. A wall that in the dark, crumbled in an instant. She'd let him in for a brief moment, then regained her senses and ran as fast as she could in the opposite direction.

For some reason, he absolutely repelled her and had since the first moment they met. He didn't understand at all. Yes, he was a force of nature when he wanted something, but he was also friendly, laid-back and fairly easy to get along with. Why would she fight something her body so clearly wanted?

Unless…

Jonah swallowed hard and looked out the door to watch Emma peek out, then dash down the hallway back to her office. Maybe his plan was too little, too late. Perhaps his enterprising accountant had already found the discrepancies in the books. If that was the case, it would explain a lot.

Who would want to date a man they were about to report to Game Town for keeping sketchy books?

Five

Jonah was forced back to his office for a teleconference after the closet incident, but he wasn't about to let that whole thing go. Either she knew about the missing money or she didn't. She liked him or she hated him. But he was going to find out the truth either way.

The next morning, he found her sitting in her temporary office. Jonah watched her silently for a few minutes as she sat hovering over her paperwork, studying it with unmatched intensity. Her nose wrinkled just slightly, a line of concentration settling in between her brows as she scrutinized every number.

Even at her desk and fully immersed in her work, her posture was not slouched over. She sat quite upright, her shoulders back, her breasts pressing insistently against her pink, silk blouse. Her brunette hair was pulled back again, a stray piece framing the curve of her face.

Without looking up, she tucked the strand behind her ear and started to make notes in a spiral notebook. She had some of the neatest penmanship he'd ever seen. Programmers were not known for their handwriting. He typed nearly everything aside from signing his name to contracts and checks. Her handwriting was precise and delicate with full, curling loops and sweeping letters. It suited her, he thought. Rigid and controlled at first glance, but inherently feminine and open if you took the time to study and understand her better.

Audit or no, Jonah was genuinely interested in Emma and it surprised him. She got under his skin and irritated him, but at the same time, she was a fascinating puzzle to try and solve. Yesterday's encounter just made it that much more intriguing. Figuring her out and breaking down her defenses would be an achievement on par with the first time he'd beaten *Legend of Zelda* as a kid.

"What's the matter, Mr. Flynn? Run out of women to abduct so you thought you'd stop by my office and try again?"

The sound of Emma's voice pulled him from his thoughts. She was watching him, but he didn't see the tension in her shoulders that was there before. There was even a touch of amusement in her voice, which surprised him. Giving her some space had been the right thing to do.

"I'm sorry about yesterday. I hadn't intended—"

"That's fine," she interrupted. "It's not a problem. Let's just pretend it never happened."

Jonah didn't expect this. He expected her to be wound tight and ready for a fight, or at least, a harassment suit. Instead, she was insistent on keeping things professional and putting it behind them. Perhaps she hadn't found Noah's indiscretion after all. "Can we talk about it?"

"I'd rather not."

A blush lit her cheeks and Emma let her gaze drop back to her paperwork. She actually looked embarrassed. Jonah had no idea what that was about. It had been virtually impossible to make most of the women he'd dated blush, much less embarrass them with talk of romantic embraces. He wanted to see her porcelain complexion flush pink again, this time after they kissed. Kissing in the dark had robbed him of that tantalizing visual.

"Let me make it up to you."

At that, she rolled her eyes and pushed away from her desk. The sweet blush was gone. "Please…"

"…go to dinner with you? Very well, I accept. How about o ya for sushi? I haven't gotten to try there yet."

Emma stopped in her tracks, seemingly startled by his turn of the conversation. "What? No."

"No sushi? You're right. That's not everyone's cup of tea. How about a steak house?"

"No. I mean, *no*, I don't want to go to dinner." Her face blushed a deeper red this time; she was clearly flustered with irritation. She brushed past him into the hallway. He took a moment to admire the tight fit of her black pants as she sauntered away, then jogged a few steps to catch up to her.

"Why not?" he asked, pulling alongside.

"It would be inappropriate," she said over her shoulder.

"Says who? I'm not your boss. I don't see anything wrong with taking you to dinner as a friendly welcome to my company. I take clients out to eat all the time."

"You haven't built a reputation like yours on simply being *friendly* to women."

Her sharp words jabbed at Jonah. It sounded like her concerns were less about it appearing inappropriate to others and more about her less-than-flattering opinion of his love life. "Ah, so you don't want to be seen in public with a man whore like me, right? Would it damage your sparkling reputation, Emma?"

Emma picked up her pace, quickly turning a corner and heading down an empty hallway, probably to the copier again. "Honestly, yes. I've worked very hard to get where I am. I'm not interested in men like you or the kind of 'friendliness' you offer."

They stopped outside the elevator and she pushed the down button, refusing to look him in the eye. It made him wonder why. Those words didn't jibe with the woman who had kissed him in the dark supply closet. "I don't know..." he teased, letting a sly smile curve his lips. "You might like sullying your reputation a bit with me. It didn't seem to bother you so much yesterday."

Her head snapped around to look at him with a frown pulling down the corners of her pink lips. "Or I might end up in one of those gossip rags and have everyone talking about me."

Jonah hated those publications. Why anyone was interested in his life, he didn't know. "Who cares what other people think about what you and I do?"

The doors opened and Emma rushed inside with Jonah in her wake. "I care. You might be a millionaire playboy, but I'm a professional. Something like that could cost me my job."

"Would your boss really care about the two of us being seen together? Why would you want to work for someone that uptight? Come work here. I could use a new finance officer."

Emma finally looked up at him, her green eyes widening in surprise, but then shook her head. "That's a nice offer, Mr. Flynn, but I don't ever want it to be said that I earned my job on my back."

She'd called him by his formal name again. They were regressing, if that was even possible. "I never said anything about you being on your back, Emma. All I suggested was dinner. You filled in the rest based on your biased presumptions about me."

A chime announced their arrival on the next floor and she shot out the minute she could fit through the doorway. "They aren't presumptions anymore. Now they're from personal experience. Yesterday is all the proof I need to know that even something innocent can go astray when you're involved, Mr. Flynn."

That was three times now. "Please call me Jonah. Mr. Flynn is my father. And he's dead. Besides, I already apologized for that. I told you I didn't know what got into me. I won't do it again unless you ask me to. Just have dinner with me."

Emma turned suddenly and planted her hands on her hips. "Why are you dogging me so hard? Why me? Don't you have some underwear model to keep you entertained?"

Jonah shoved his hands into his pockets in frustration and made a mental note: no more models. They gave him a bad reputation and intimidated other women. He had a universal appreciation of the female body in all its forms. Women rarely understood that, though. They just measured themselves against this perfect ideal and didn't think he could desire them, as well.

"What if I truly, genuinely, was interested in you, Emma? That I thought you were smart and funny and attractive and wanted to see what could happen between us? Is that so bad?"

"In any other time and any other place, maybe not. But as it stands, no dinner. No dates. Just, no thank you." Emma turned and marched into the coffee shop.

It was fairly empty at this hour, so Jonah followed her, refusing to end this conversation until he'd won. "Let me at least buy you coffee."

Emma chuckled and crossed her arms protectively over her chest. "It's free in here."

Jonah arched a brow in amusement. "Not for me, it isn't. I pay for it all. As a matter of fact, I've bought you several meals since you've been here. What's the harm in one more? The only difference is that we eat it at the same time at the same table."

She narrowed her green gaze at him and sighed. "You're not going away until I at least agree to have coffee with you, are you?"

"Coffee is a good start."

"Fine," she said. "I'll have a tall hot tea with two sugars, one cream, and a cinnamon roll. I'll be waiting at a table. And when we're done, I don't want to see you for the rest of the day. Got it?"

Jonah grinned wide, the small victory seeming bigger when Emma was involved. "Absolutely."

He found her seated at a table in the back corner of the coffee shop a few minutes later. Jonah watched silently as she doctored her hot tea and removed the bag. "What got you into accounting?" he asked. This wasn't the time or place for bold moves or hard questions.

"I dislike ambiguity," she responded. "In math, there is no gray area, no questionable decisions. Two plus two equals four. I liked having a career based in something I could depend on. It also seemed to be a respectable profession. My parents were both pleased with my decision."

"And what if you'd wanted to be a fashion model or a rock star?" Jonah asked. "What would they have thought about that?"

Emma only shook her head. "I would never want to do something like that. For one thing, I'm not pretty enough or talented enough. And even if I were, I wouldn't do it. Those kinds of people end up in the magazines right beside you."

Jonah frowned. He didn't like the way she spoke about herself. "It's not so bad," he countered. "People read those magazines because they want to live vicariously through people like me. They want to share in the glamour and excitement."

"My sister was the one destined for the spotlight, not me."

"And what does your sister do?" Jonah asked.

"Nothing. She's dead." Emma put the lid on her cup and picked up her plate. "I'm sorry, Jonah, but I've got to get back to work."

Emma flopped back into her desk chair and buried her face in her hands. This was not going at all to plan. Before she'd come to FlynnSoft, she'd been confident that its handsome CEO wouldn't want anything to do with her. Finding out Jonah was the father of her unborn child made it even more critical that she maintain her distance until her audit was complete. There was tiny, living proof that she'd slept with the FlynnSoft CEO at least once, and that was too much. And yet in the last twenty-four hours, she'd made out with him in a dark closet and agreed to have coffee with him.

What the hell was wrong with her? Kissing Jonah? She wished she could say she lost her mind in that dark room, but what was her excuse today? Chatting with him over breakfast pastry and caffeinated drinks seemed harmless, but they both knew it was anything but. If she gave him an inch, he'd take a mile. There was no such thing as harmless where the two of them were concerned.

Despite her accusations to the contrary, she was fairly certain all Jonah had intended to do yesterday was get her somewhere private and force the conversation she was adamant to avoid. But somewhere things just went wildly off course. Again.

It was just like Mardi Gras all over again. Whatever powerful, magnetic force drew them together and lured them into a night of hedonistic pleasure was still in play. Being pressed against Jonah again, his warm, male scent teasing her brain with arousing memories… It was like the last three months without him never happened.

But they had happened. And for a reason.

The minute his hand came near her chest, the cautionary reminder of her tattoo sent a spike of panic through her. He couldn't see and didn't know he was inches from completing their tattoo, but she knew. And it was far too close for comfort. All she could do was turn and run. Like that night, she couldn't change what she'd just done, but she could put a stop to it and make sure it didn't happen again. He could be a part of her life as the father of her child, but nothing more. And not yet.

This was all her girlfriends' faults. They'd sown the seeds of doubt and discontent in her mind when they came over for dinner. Emma lay awake for hours thinking about the night she'd spent with Jonah and the lonely, miserable ones that had followed since.

She'd convinced herself that a man like Jonah would never be satisfied with a woman like her. The woman who fell into his arms that night didn't really exist. Keeping their romance anonymous was what kept it special, what made it into the fantasy she couldn't forget. It could never be ruined by the reality of who they really were, come daylight. And yet, the child they'd created that night would make destroying that fantasy a necessity.

After the last few days working with Jonah, she was beginning to wonder if ruining the fantasy would matter to him. Inexplicably, there was a draw between them that had nothing to do with masks and secrets. He had no idea who she really was and yet Jonah Flynn seemed genuinely interested in her. He was going out of his way to get her attention and she couldn't understand why. He couldn't possibly want her as she was. She seemed to do nothing but irritate him, based on the crease that was constantly present between his eyebrows.

Was he simply trying to woo his way into a favorable audit finding? It wouldn't be the first time someone had tried to bribe or coerce an auditor. It had never happened to Emma before, so maybe she was being naive about his attentions. Perhaps a man like Jonah preferred the more pleasurable option of seducing them over laying out cash. The spark between them might simply make his job easier.

Of course, if he was going to that much trouble, it meant he had something to hide…

A deep feeling of unease pooled in Emma's stomach. This was a huge and very important contract for FlynnSoft. If he was afraid she might uncover something that could risk it, she had no doubt he'd go out of his way to distract her. He didn't necessarily have to think she was smart or pretty to pull it off. How could he, when he was used to dating fashion models and pop stars? Emma was just the rich daughter of someone far more important than she was. If all he really cared about was nailing the deal with Game Town, he would be willing to do it by any means necessary. Suspecting his motives would make it easier to ignore his advances, right?

At least for now. He'd certainly wanted her back in February when there were no audits, no accounts and no contracts. But then she wasn't herself that night.

Emma tried to push that thought aside and focus on the numbers the rest of the afternoon. While her work might seem boring to some, what she'd said to Jonah about math was true. It never lied. It was a constant, and she found working with numbers to be soothing. She could lose herself for hours in the books, and today was no different. When she looked up, it was after six. Jonah had thankfully kept his promise to stay away for the rest of the day and she'd managed to get a lot done.

She considered packing up and going home, but restlessness still plagued her. She decided she'd been sitting for too long and headed straight down to the FlynnSoft gym. She'd packed a bag of workout clothes and brought them in after the guilty tiramisu consumption.

Tonight wasn't about calories, though. She needed an outlet for the frustration and nervous energy threatening to bubble out of her, and some pounding on the elliptical machine was just the thing since pounding Jonah was not an option. She honestly wasn't sure how much of this she could take. He was relentless, absolutely aggravating and refusing to take no for an answer. Her afternoon of peace would be the exception, not the rule, she was certain. Especially now that he knew he could wear her down after a while and get his way.

It made her wonder if he knew who she really was. Maybe it wasn't about the audit at all. She hadn't found a single questionable thing in the books to warrant a distraction. And yet, it would be impossible for Jonah to recognize her from that night. Not a bit of her tattoo had seen the light of day. Their conversations offered no clues to her identity or their past. And yet he was constantly in pursuit of her.

Before she headed down to the gym, she stopped at the desk of Jonah's assistant, Pam. "Is Mr. Flynn gone for the day?" she asked.

"Yes, he had a five-thirty dinner engagement."

Perfect. "Thank you."

Emma made her way down the hall, thankful that she would be able to work out in peace. In the locker room, Emma changed quickly into her standard gym clothes, which consisted of a tank top over a sports bra and a pair of jogging shorts. The top left the tattoo partially exposed and clung to the barely rounding belly of her pregnancy, making her frown in the mirror. She hadn't thought about that when she packed her bag, but the time of baggy clothes and maternity outfits was right around the corner.

She considered changing back into her regular clothes and just heading home for the night, but she was actually looking forward to the workout. Emma glanced into the still-empty workout room and decided it was safe enough since Jonah wouldn't be around to see it. No one else would understand the significance of either the tattoo or the belly.

The coast was clear. Harper was right. Apparently,

software programmers were more likely to make use of the coffee bar and pinball machine than the exercise facilities. She jumped onto the closest elliptical machine, putting her water bottle into the cup holder and plugging her earbuds into her phone to listen to her favorite workout music.

Emma selected an upbeat seventies playlist and started moving to the disco beat that thrummed through her body. She closed her eyes and gave in to it. The sweat running down her spine and the ache of her muscles were welcome distractions from the confusion and arousal that had been her constant companions the last few days. She hoped that if she worked out long enough, her attraction to Jonah would seep out her pores and she would be better prepared to deal with him.

At least that was the idea.

Emma had always been a fan of exercise. You wouldn't think it to look at her, but she recognized it as an outlet for her body's impulses. The all-girls private school she attended for high school had encouraged them to be as active as possible. The nuns insisted that sweat was purifying and there was no desire that couldn't be suppressed with a good workout.

She had reason to be a believer in its powers and fell back on it instead of eating when stress took over her life. She lost ten pounds after her breakup with David in February. Between him leaving and the fallout of her twenty-four-hour rebellion, she'd clocked in serious overtime at the gym. She'd finally regained those ten pounds due to her blossoming pregnancy, but she continued to work out, nonetheless. She didn't want to get too large and spend valuable time postpartum worrying about extra pounds instead of enjoying precious moments with her newborn.

When her body was about to give out from the strain, Emma slowed her pace to cool down and opened her eyes. She smiled, pleased with her workout stats on the console. She may well have earned herself a treat after dinner. Maybe some nice dark chocolate would provide a pseudosexual chemical release to back her down from the edge.

Emma silenced her music and stepped onto the padded floor with gelatinous kneecaps. Her plan had worked. She was exhausted, sticky and thirsty. Sex with Jonah was the last thing she wanted at the moment. She reached for her water, taking a healthy swig, then began wiping her face with her towel.

The sound of a man's laughter startled her. She yanked the towel from her face, pulled out her earbuds and looked around the gym, but found it to be just as empty as it had been before. Her only guess was that it must've been someone in the hallway walking past the gym. Or maybe her imagination was getting the best of her.

With another quick glance around, she gathered up her things and headed to the locker room just to be safe. Originally, she'd planned to shower and change here, but the unknown man's laughter left her unnerved. What if Jonah had seen her? She had taken a huge risk tonight and she couldn't repeat it. She needed to bring some gym clothes to work that wouldn't leave her so exposed next time. Jonah might be out tonight, but that wouldn't be the case every time she came down here.

Instead, she grabbed her tote bag, slipped a hoodie over her clothes just in case and headed to the exit.

She could bathe in private at home where she didn't have to worry about who might be watching.

Six

Jonah ducked into a corridor and watched Emma as she headed toward the back exit of the building. When his dinner meeting was canceled earlier tonight, he was already at the restaurant waiting. He opted to get a to-go order and take it back to the office. There, he planned to get in some weight training—it was legs day—and eat his dinner as he went over some emails.

The gym was usually empty in the evenings and he enjoyed the solitude. He spent all day in meetings and on phone calls. His time at the gym was an hour out of the day where he could lose himself in some music and let his sore muscles distract him from his worries. He never expected to find Emma there. She seemed like the kind of woman who didn't like to get dirty, much less sweat. Yet there she had been, going to town on one of the machines, music pumping into her ears, her eyes closed.

If he didn't know better, he'd say she was trying to work something out of her system. Perhaps he'd done a better job of sexually frustrating her than he thought. Maybe she only resisted him on the surface.

He'd almost opened his mouth to say as much to her when she suddenly came to a stop and climbed down from the machine. He watched her from the doorway, unnoticed, as she sipped her water and wiped the sweat from her flushed face. It was then that he spied a flash of red peeking out from her black top. He took a few steps farther into the gym and could clearly see half a red heart tattooed on her left breast. Jonah had stopped, looked at the tattoo on his hand, then at her tiny, rounded stomach in disbelief before choking on a nervous laugh and darting out of the gym before she saw him.

Could it be?

Never. Never in a million years would he have pegged Emma as his butterfly. His butterfly had been free, uninhibited, wild. On the surface, Emma appeared to be anything but. She'd told him she was acting out of character that night, but he didn't really believe her. Everyone said something like that when they found themselves in an awkward situation.

She must've been telling the truth. His butterfly had also told him that he wouldn't want her in the morning, like she'd turn into a pumpkin at sunrise. Instead, she turned into an uptight accountant. A beautiful, graceful, aggravating, uptight accountant who looked as though she might be carrying his child.

He was no expert in that department. What he did know was that three months ago, her belly had been flat as a board, trembling as he planted kisses across it. Emma wouldn't show much at three months, but it was hard to hide a belly in workout clothes. Could she really be having his child?

That was something Jonah had never really considered. He wasn't opposed to children as a whole, but he'd not envisioned his life as one where he would settle down and have a family. Maybe one day, but one day always seemed a long way off. It certainly wasn't six months from now.

Jonah let his head roll back against the wall with a dull thud that did little to help the situation. A baby. Was it really possible that Emma was having his child? They'd used protection. He always used protection. He wasn't stupid. There were plenty of women who would be happy to carry his heir to inherit his money along with his blue eyes. Emma didn't seem at all like that kind of woman.

Of course, if you'd asked him an hour ago, he would've told you she was the kind of woman who would tell a man when she was having his baby. And yet she hadn't.

Jonah shook his head and started back down the hallway to his office. He couldn't work out now. His head wasn't in it. Besides, this revelation changed everything.

His pursuit of Emma had been purely business at first. Yes, distracting her would be a pleasurable chore to cover his ass and Noah's until the finances were cleaned up, but still business. When she rebuffed him, it had become a challenge. He always enjoyed conquering impossible tasks.

But now it was a matter of pride. Emma knew who he was. Had known almost from the moment they'd met. She'd seen his hand, seen his tattoo and yet had said nothing despite the fact that she was carrying his child.

Why? The tattoos were supposed to help bring them

together. The only link from the night of fantasy to their reality. Seeing his tattoo should've been a sign to her, a pleasant surprise, especially since she had no other way to contact her baby's father. If he'd found her first, he would've instantly told her who he was. Unless she thought their night together was a mistake. Or that she didn't want him in her or their baby's life now that she knew who he really was.

Impossible! What woman wouldn't be thrilled to find the father of her child was secretly a rich, successful and attractive businessman? There were plenty of outcomes to that scenario that weren't nearly as positive.

Jonah reached his office and spied a copy of a recent entertainment magazine on Pam's desk. It was flipped open to a page that featured a picture of him with a woman he'd only gone out with once or twice. The byline read "Software playboy romances lingerie model." He frowned.

Okay, so maybe his celebrity status wasn't helping his cause. He had a reputation for being a badass and he liked it. Women were just part of the package. Most women didn't mind getting a piece of him, no matter how brief.

Emma was different. He knew that much. She wasn't the type of woman to tolerate that kind of crap from a man. She was an old-fashioned woman who expected the romantic overtures that were practically dead in this day and age. Not flowers and jewelry, but time and attention. The kind of woman who made him cringe. *Needy* and *clingy* were two adjectives that quickly axed a woman from his address book.

And yet she was also the woman who had filled the last three months with erotic fantasies he couldn't shake.

The one who had occupied his thoughts and forced him to compare every other date to the high bar she'd set. So far, no one had measured up.

Pushing the door open and entering his office, he threw his exercise towel over the back of his guest chair. She'd sat in that very chair when she'd had her panic attack.

The attack that had immediately followed their shaking hands. That had to be the moment she realized who he was. Not exactly the romantic response he'd pictured in his mind when they'd sat in that tattoo parlor and held hands while getting inked.

All this time, he'd been worried that her nerves and avoidance of him had been related to the audit. That she'd found out about Noah's indiscretion already. Instead, there had been a bigger issue—she was trying to keep him from uncovering the truth about her. Apparently they both had secrets to hide.

For whatever reason, Emma wasn't interested in Jonah and didn't want him to know who she was. She'd resisted his every advance like no other woman had before, even knowing she was carrying his child. Why would she be so determined to keep that from him? Wasn't he good enough to be her baby's father? Would she prefer some quiet, unassuming banker or insurance broker who would provide stability and no passion?

He didn't believe that for a second. The woman he'd spent Mardi Gras with had been complex, with layers that included passionate minx. Sure, he had a reputation for being wild, too, but he was an adult and knew there was a time and place for everything. Being a responsible father was a duty he wouldn't shirk, no matter how low her opinion of him might be.

Their recent time together proved that she was also a strong-willed, stubborn woman who thought she could outwit him. Emma really thought she could keep this secret from him.

Jonah twisted his lips in thought as he reached for his butterfly photo. He'd imagined the moment he found her would be like taking his first breath, starting his life anew with the amazing woman he'd longed for all this time. Instead, his mystery lover thought he was nothing more than an irritating pebble in her shoe.

But she hadn't seen anything yet.

It wasn't that long ago that he'd coaxed her into a wild night of uninhibited passion and recklessness. Considering the uptight accountant he'd come to know, that was no small feat. Knowing he'd done it once, however, Jonah was confident he could do it again. Before he was done with Emma, she'd be putty in his hands, all too eager to confess her identity and fall into his arms for good.

Until then, the torture would be sweet.

Emma couldn't shake the sensation of being watched. It had been that way since the night before at the gym. Every time she felt the urge to pull her gaze away from her computer screen, she expected to see Jonah loitering in her doorway with his smug, cat-that-ate-the-canary grin. But he wasn't there. In fact, she hadn't seen or heard from him since the coffee shop encounter the day before.

She knew better than to let her guard down, however. She'd made that mistake last night and couldn't do it again.

More importantly, Emma needed to focus on the

books. Something wasn't adding up right and unless she could shut down every part of her brain but the one that dealt with numbers, she'd never be able to determine if this was a real issue or one caused by her own distraction.

The third time she tried running through it and got the same result, she sat back in her chair with a groan. She'd obviously made a mistake a few pages back. A huge chunk of money was missing. "Damn it," she cursed, pushing the unruly strand of hair from her face for the twentieth time today. She needed to buy a barrette.

"What's the matter, Miss Dempsey?"

Startled, Emma sat bolt upright in her seat and clutched her hand to her chest. As she looked over this time, Jonah was loitering in her doorway when she'd least expected him.

"Nothing," she insisted. Even if she had found something of concern in the financials, she wouldn't mention it to anyone until she was absolutely certain. You didn't pull the fire alarm until you saw the flames. Right now, this was just a little smoke. No one was stupid enough to do something that obvious. Smart people took money in small chunks. There had to be an explanation.

She took a deep breath to steady herself and looked back up at Jonah. There was something different about the way he carried himself today. Emma couldn't quite put her finger on it, exactly, but something had changed. Perhaps it was the sly twist of his full lips and the knowing twinkle in his eye. She had no idea what would have pleased him so greatly this afternoon, so she chose to ignore it and the deep-down pangs of desire it caused inside of her.

"Well, I just got off the phone with your boss."

At the mention of her supervisor, the desire immediately melted away like an ice cube dropped into boiling water. "You spoke with Tim? Is there a problem?"

Jonah shook his head. "No, not at all. He was just calling to see if you had settled in okay."

Emma held her breath as she listened to his response. Tim never just called to see if an employee was settled in. He didn't care that much. Knowing him, Tim was calling to see if Emma had fallen for Jonah's charms yet. "And what did you tell him?"

Jonah pursed his lips for a second, drawing out her torture with obvious pleasure. "I told him that you were the most polite and professional worker in the building, myself included. Why? What did you think I would say?"

Emma shrugged. "I don't know," she admitted. "Hopefully nothing related to the supply closet."

At that, he chuckled and gripped the door frame of her office, flashing his tattoo at her. "I didn't build a successful company by being a fool, Emma. And despite what you seem to think, I'm not out to put your job in jeopardy."

She expelled a sigh of relief that was premature.

"It did occur to me," he continued, "that your boss seemed like a bit of a hard-ass. I get why you're so concerned about appearances. And that's why I'm offering you a compromise."

Emma tried not to frown. There was nothing to compromise over.

"You don't want to be seen with me because it's inappropriate. I get that. But I am going to take you to dinner one way or another. So I can either find a way to blackmail you into having dinner with me here in town, or you can accept my offer of having dinner with me out of town, where no one will find out."

Blackmail? Emma leaped up from her chair. "I don't know what the hell you're playing at, Jonah, but there's nothing to blackmail me with."

He didn't seem fazed by her sudden bravado. "So you say. And maybe that's true. But there's nothing stopping me from telling Tim some fabricated misdeed. He'll believe me over you, don't you think?"

Emma's jaw dropped. "You wouldn't. Why would you even consider such a thing?"

Jonah crossed his arms over his chest, wrinkling the fabric of his flannel shirt. "Because I get what I want, Emma. And I want you to have dinner with me. If I thought for one second that you weren't sincerely interested, I would let it drop. But you can't fool me with your tight hair buns and your formal demeanor. The woman that was in the supply closet with me wants to have dinner. And who am I to deny her?"

"You don't know anything about me, in or out of a closet, Jonah."

"Don't I?"

His blue eyes challenged her, and that made her instantly nervous. She self-consciously reached for the collar of her blouse and pulled it tighter to ensure she hadn't given away her identity.

"I certainly don't want to take it this far, which is why I'm offering you an alternative that will make everyone happy. Tomorrow night, meet me at the Wall Street Heliport at six sharp. From there, I will whisk you away to a location where we won't run into anyone we know. We can have a nice, private dinner without you needing to worry about your job. You can just relax for once and enjoy your time with me."

It wasn't an ideal scenario, but it was certainly better than losing her job over a lie. She couldn't believe a man that high profile could just disappear like that, though. "And what about your little paparazzi friends?"

Jonah shrugged. "They only take pictures when I allow them to know where I am. When I want privacy I'm more than capable of arranging it. I assure you that no one will know where we're going tomorrow night, even you."

That was one less concern, but it still left several on the table she wasn't ready to discuss with him. Like how being alone with him turned her knees to butter and how if she fell prey to his charms, she'd run the risk of him finding out all her secrets. It was too soon for that. But did she really have a choice? "And if I go to dinner with you…just dinner…you'll leave me alone?"

"If at the end of the evening that's what you want, then yes."

Emma would make sure that was how the evening ended, even if she regretted every word out of her mouth. While she didn't anticipate much to come out of her attraction to the infamous CEO, she didn't want even a whisper of it to happen before her job here was completed.

"Okay, fine," she said in a huge rush of breath before she could change her mind. "What shall I wear?"

Jonah grinned wide with unmasked pleasure. "Excellent. Now you might be surprised to hear this, but I plan to take you somewhere that requires a jacket and maybe even a tie on my part."

Emma's eyebrows shot up in surprise. "You mean you own a suit?"

"I own several. I'm not antisuit under the right circumstances, despite what my mother would say if she were asked. I just don't need them to feel important or in control like some people do. I like to be comfortable and a T-shirt with a video game reference on it is far more representative of my personality than a boring old pin-striped tie."

Emma tried not to get excited by the idea of seeing Jonah in a suit. He obviously underestimated what a sharp suit on the right man could do to a woman's resolve. "Then I'll meet you at the heliport tomorrow at six."

Jonah gave her a curt nod and disappeared from her office. Once he was gone, Emma was finally able to take a deep breath and realized what she'd just agreed to. She peeked out around her door, and when he was nowhere in sight, dashed down the hallway to Harper's cubicle.

"Help!" she said as she rounded the corner.

Harper looked up with wide, surprised eyes. "What's the matter?"

"I've got a date tomorrow. With *him*."

"Him?" Harper leaped up from her chair. "I thought you refused to go out with him right now."

"I know, but he shot down every excuse I could think of. I agreed to it this time on the condition that he would leave me alone after that if I asked him to."

Harper just shook her head. "How could you ever ask a man like him to leave you alone?"

"Well," Emma sighed, "at the moment, I have bigger problems than that."

"Like what?"

"Like I have no idea what I'm going to wear. Most

of my clothes are somewhere between business casual and business professional. I need date clothes. You're the fashion diva. I need you to go through my closet and tell me what to wear."

"I doubt there's much in there we can use," Harper said with obvious dismay. "Especially with junior playing havoc with your waistline. I think we need to go shopping."

Emma frowned. "I don't think I have time to—"

"Right now," Harper interrupted. She reached into her desk drawer and pulled out her Kate Spade purse. "Get your things. We're going shopping right now."

Emma let Harper shove her down the hallway as she protested. "It's three in the afternoon."

"You need all the help you can get."

Emma couldn't argue with that. The next thing she knew they were in a cab and on their way to Fifth Avenue. As they strolled along the sidewalk, Harper had her gaze narrowed at every window scanning for just the right thing. They had stepped into about seven or eight stores, but left with nothing. Harper was searching for something special—a standout look—she said.

Emma was happy to hang back and let Harper decide what was best. After all, that was what Harper lived for—designer clothes, cute shoes, a fabulous handbag—she didn't need much else in life. Her apartment was paid for, so Emma was pretty sure that her entire paycheck from FlynnSoft went directly to Neiman Marcus or Saks Fifth Avenue. Thankfully, she was raised by a father with more money than he, or she, could ever spend.

And that was coming from Emma's point of view—a girl who'd never wanted for a thing in her life.

"That!" Harper came to a sudden stop and pointed at

a mannequin in the window. "That's what you're wearing." She snatched Emma's hand and pulled her into the boutique before she had really even gotten a good look at the dress. All she saw was a blur of blue.

When they stopped at the rack inside the store, Emma realized it wasn't even a dress. It was a jumpsuit. "Are you serious?"

"Absolutely. Jumpsuits are very in right now. Any woman he's dated could wear some slinky little dress to dinner. That's what he expects. Blow him out of the water with this instead."

Harper held up the royal blue silk jumpsuit and Emma's eyes got big. It was sleeveless with wide straps that went over the shoulders and a neckline that dipped down to her sternum. She'd need a specialty bra to pull this outfit off, for sure.

"What about my tattoo?" Emma whispered.

"It will cover it. The wide straps are perfect."

That was one concern dealt with. "And where's the back of it?" she asked.

"The fabric crisscrosses in the back and leaves the rest bare. Just enough skin to be sexy, but not overtly so. Pair it with some silver heels and a silver chain belt and you're going to look fabulous. Ooh...maybe even a chunky bracelet."

Emma frowned at the dress—*er*—jumpsuit. She wasn't ready to talk about accessories yet. She'd never even worn a jumpsuit before. She wasn't entirely sure she could pull it off. Then again, it would make it easier to get in and out of the helicopter if she wasn't worried about her dress blowing up over her head. She could appreciate the practicality of that.

"So what do you think?" Harper pressed.

It was also the same blue as his eyes. She could almost feel his warm hand brushing against the bare small of her back as he escorted her into a restaurant. It sent a chill through her whole body and she finally came to appreciate Harper's genius.

"I think we need to try it on."

Seven

Emma anxiously stepped out of her cab outside the Wall Street Heliport. Before she headed inside, she made certain to adjust her jumpsuit and ensure everything was in place. It was all fine. She looked amazing in the jumpsuit, something she never would've believed until she looked in the mirror at the store and noticed her jaw had dropped along with Harper's.

She took a deep breath, swung her uncharacteristically loose brunette waves over her shoulder and headed inside. Looking around the small waiting room, she didn't see Jonah anywhere at first. Only a few of the seats were taken, mostly with families awaiting helicopter tours around Manhattan. Then she noticed a tall, slim man in a dark gray suit at the window with his back to her. Could it be?

As though he sensed her arrival, the man turned

around to look at her, and she was surprised to see it *was* Jonah standing there. He was wearing a royal blue dress shirt, almost the same shade as her jumpsuit, but it was unbuttoned at the collar, with no tie in sight. Even then, the effect was amazing. The suit coat highlighted his broad shoulders and the narrow hips she remembered cradling between her thighs. The blue of the shirt made his eyes an even deeper shade, like the darkest waters of the ocean.

Standing there with his hands casually stuffed into his pants pockets, he looked every inch the powerful CEO of a software empire. And yet, he had been right about it being an unnecessary accessory. He didn't need an expensive suit to command the attention of every person in the room. The crisp lines and exquisite tailoring on his body were just the delicious icing on the man cake that made her heart race in her chest and her resolve weaken.

Emma had to remind herself that although this felt like a date, it wasn't really. He didn't know who she was and she couldn't be certain of his motives for asking her out. Besides, being blackmailed into dinner was not a date. And yet she couldn't help preening as he took his turn looking her over from head to toe. She went with it, ignoring everyone else in the waiting area and giving him a little spin to showcase the bare back and the fit that clung to her curves. If he was a little uncomfortable all night, all the better.

His pleased smirk convinced her it was the right choice of outfit for the evening. When he was finished admiring her, she approached the window and closed the gap between them. "Good evening, Mr. Flynn."

"Tonight, of all nights," he insisted, "it's Jonah. You can call me Mr. Flynn at work tomorrow if you insist."

"I suppose that depends on how tonight goes," she added with a smile, and then turned to look at the helicopters waiting just outside. "So when will our ride be ready?"

"It's ready now." Jonah turned to the desk and gestured to the man at the counter. The attendant buzzed them out and Jonah pushed open the door that led to the helipad. "Just waiting on you."

Stepping outside, she was glad it was a calm day, not too windy. Emma had been in a helicopter twice with her parents. Sometimes her father needed to be able to get back from the Hamptons for a work emergency faster than a car or train would allow. It had never been her favorite mode of travel, but the unsteady movement didn't bother her, thankfully. Even so, she was sucking on a ginger candy to soothe her stomach just in case. She would not be remembered by Jonah as the woman who puked in the helicopter.

As they approached the sleek black helicopter, the pilot waved to them. He and Jonah helped her up inside and once she was buckled in, Jonah climbed in beside her and shut the door.

"Where are we going to dinner?" she asked as the blades started to spin overhead.

"It's a surprise."

"Of course it is," Emma muttered, but her voice was drowned out by the sound of the helicopter.

Jonah offered her a headset to wear and she accepted it. It muffled the engine sounds and allowed her to speak to the others without shouting. She didn't have much to say at first. It was a clear day and she was too busy admiring her city. New York by helicopter was a truly amazing sight. You could get up close to the architectural wonders, unlike taking a plane, and without getting bogged down by the traffic and the noise of being on the ground.

She thought they might be heading toward Long Island, but then the helicopter turned and headed farther north. They could be heading to Boston, perhaps. Or Martha's Vineyard. It was high season there.

"Stop trying to guess," Jonah said to her through the headsets. "I can see it all over your face. You're not going to be right and it will make you crazy trying to figure it out. Just relax and enjoy the flight."

Emma smirked and flopped back against her seat. She supposed he was right. Instead of looking for clues, she glanced out the window to take in the view. When she turned back to Jonah a few minutes later, she noticed he was intently watching her instead of the landscape speeding by.

"I suppose the view bores you when you've seen it repeatedly."

"Not at all," he said. "I've just got something more intriguing to look at this time."

Emma gasped softly, but didn't know what to say. Instinctively, she held her breath as he leaned close to her and put his arm around her shoulder. She started to worry that he would be able to see down her top from this angle, but it was hard to focus on that when she could smell his cologne and feel the warm press of his leg against hers.

"Thank you for agreeing to have dinner with me."

"You didn't really give me a choice," she replied, mostly in jest.

Jonah only shrugged. "I know. And I apologize for that. I guess I just wasn't sure what to do when you kept turning me down."

"Taking the hint was always an option."

"Yes." He laughed. "And I would have if your eyes were sending the same message as your mouth. But I could see you were conflicted, so I thought I'd give you a little push in the right direction."

"Threatening to get me fired is not a little push. That's blackmail."

Jonah winced. "Agreed. It was a drastic step on my part. But I wouldn't have called your boss, for the record. I was bluffing."

Emma crossed her arms over her chest, realizing too late that it gave him a tantalizing view of her cleavage. His blue eyes flickered down for only a moment before returning to hers. She was surprised by his restraint.

"Even if you're mad at me, by the end of the night, we will have kissed and made up," he said confidently.

Emma couldn't help but arch an eyebrow at him. "You're just used to getting your way, aren't you?"

"Usually."

She eyed the full swell of his bottom lip as he spoke, remembering those lips as they sucked salt and lime juice from her body at the Mardi Gras party. The memory sent a flush of heat to her cheeks that she was certain he could see. She turned away from him, looking out as the sun started to set and lights began twinkling in the distance.

"Perhaps not this time," she said, both hoping she was right and knowing she was wrong. Every minute she spent with Jonah, the more convinced she was that she wouldn't be able to resist him much longer.

"Mr. Flynn, we're about five minutes from landing."

Jonah smiled and pulled away from her. "Excellent. See, now it didn't take very long to get here, did it?"

Emma glanced at her phone in her purse. It had been a little over forty minutes. Not far enough for Boston. Too far for the Hamptons. She didn't recognize the skyline, but it was a smaller town on the water. She could see the shore. Within minutes, they came to a gentle, bouncing landing on top of a bank building.

"We're going to a bank?"

"Very funny. I'm actually friends with the president of this bank. He's the only one that uses the helipad and said we were welcome to make use of it tonight. It's that or fly all the way to the outskirts of town to the airport and charter a car to drive us right back here. This way we're only a block from the restaurant."

They slipped off their headsets and unfastened their seat belts. The pilot opened the door of the cabin and they stepped out onto the tarmac. "I'll be waiting on you, sir," he said.

"Thank you," Jonah replied before taking Emma's hand and leading her to the rooftop door. They took the elevator down to the lobby and exited onto a quiet street in a quaint-looking seaside village she didn't recognize.

They walked about a block before she saw a taxi go by advertising a place that claimed to have the finest seafood in Newport. Newport, Rhode Island? She'd never been there before, although she knew it had once been a very popular summer retreat for the wealthy of New England. It was famous for its huge mansions only blocks from the sea.

Emma kept her suspicions to herself until they reached a building just off the harbor that looked like an old Georgian-style inn with white siding, dormer windows and the charm of an old-fashioned seaport village. The sign hanging overhead read Restaurant Bouchard & Inn.

"Here we are," Jonah announced as they climbed the

short staircase that led inside. "The best French restaurant I've found on this side of the Atlantic."

The maître d' greeted them, noted their arrival in his book and escorted them to a table beside one of the large bay windows. Once they were alone with their menus of the day, Jonah leaned across the table. "Anything you order here will be amazingly delicious and beautiful. Their chef makes food into art. Tasty art at that."

Emma scanned the menu, desperately hoping her three years of high school French would assist her in not sounding foolish tonight when she ordered. Madame Colette would be so disappointed in her for mangling such a beautiful language. She had finally decided on a ratatouille ravioli starter and the rosemary lamb chops when the sommelier arrived at the table.

"Wine?" Jonah asked with a pointed look.

Emma was about to request a dry red to go with the lamb when she realized she wasn't allowed to drink. The last week of her life had been so different it was easy to forget about her situation. "None for me, please. I'd just like some seltzer with a twist of lime."

Jonah ordered a single glass of cabernet for himself. When the waiter came to take their order a few minutes later, she made her selections and he opted for the stuffed lobster starter and the sautéed duck breast with brandied balsamic glaze.

Emma was surprised by his flawless French accent as he ordered. As the waiter stepped away, Jonah turned to her with a mildly amused expression on his face. "What? Do you think that just because I wear jeans every day and play video games for a living that I wasn't properly educated in expensive British preparatory schools like most ridiculously rich kids?"

Emma frowned and looked down at the glass of seltzer in front of her. She was bad at making presumptions where he was concerned. He was just so different from what she was used to. It made her wish she did have wine to drown her embarrassment. "No, I'm just a little surprised—and jealous—of how flawless your accent is."

"You should hear my Japanese."

She looked back up, truly stunned this time. "You speak Japanese?"

"If you want to be successful in the Japanese video game market, you have to. I also speak Spanish and I'm learning Mandarin as we expand further into the Asian markets. I'm an accomplished pianist and was the captain of my rowing team at Harvard, although that was just to appease my parents. I would've much rather been indoors playing games or romancing the ladies. As you can see, there's a lot more to me than meets the eye, Emma. The same could be said of you."

"What do you mean?" she asked, feeling suddenly anxious at the turn of their discussion. "I'm just boring, uptight Emma the accountant."

"You're selling yourself short. For starters, you're great at keeping secrets."

Emma stiffened in her seat and swallowed hard. "Secrets? I don't—"

Jonah raised his hand to silence her protests. "Now that we're away from New York and the prying eyes of anyone that might care besides the two of us, I can say as much. And you can finally be truthful with me. Because you've known. All this time, you've known who I was and you didn't say anything to me about it."

The steely edge in Jonah's voice sent her spine straight in a defensive posture. When she looked into his eyes, however, she didn't see the anger she expected. Just hurt. The jovial, carefree CEO had a tender spot and she'd managed to find it without trying.

"We had something special and you don't seem to care about it at all. Why didn't you tell me the moment you realized who I was?" He slipped his hand, palm down, across the white linen tablecloth to expose his half of the tattoo, then wrapped his fingers around her hand.

It was happening. The moment she'd been dreading since he walked into his office and turned her world upside down. "I couldn't," she said in a hushed whisper.

"You absolutely could! You've had dozens of opportunities to speak up."

"No." Emma pulled her hand away into her lap and sat back to regain some of her personal space. "Up until this moment, we weren't just Emma and Jonah, we were the Game Town auditor and the CEO of FlynnSoft. Yes, I knew the moment I shook your hand, but I wasn't sure what to do. I know it's hard for you to understand, but I wanted to do my job first. I've been doing my damnedest to finish this audit, despite your constant distractions, so I could put it behind me and finally come to you and tell you the truth about everything."

Jonah nodded, acknowledging her struggle. "You mean about the baby."

Emma's green eyes widened in panic and Jonah felt his own pulse speed up in his throat. She wasn't expecting him to say that at all. He'd uncovered all her secrets, it seemed.

"How did you…?" She shook her head in denial.

"I saw you in the gym the other night after work."

She continued to shake her head, letting her gaze drop

to her lap. "I knew I heard someone as I was leaving. It was stupid of me to wear that outfit, but I didn't even think about it as I packed it. No one was around and I've really just started to show recently, so I didn't think anyone would notice. Especially you. You were supposed to be out at dinner." She glanced up with an accusing look in her eye.

Jonah felt his chest tighten more and more the longer she spoke. Not because of her pointed look, but because up until this moment, the baby had been a suspicion, not a fact. Yes, she skipped the wine, but she could just not like it. Yes, she had a little tummy, but she could've overindulged. He was no expert where pregnant women were concerned.

Now it was confirmed.

He was going to be a father. *A father.* He'd taken every precaution, and yet fate had laughed in his face and put him in this position anyway. He reached out to brace his hand on the edge of the table and squeezed his eyes shut. "My dinner meeting got canceled, so I came back to lift some weights. I'm usually alone in there. And yes, I sure as hell noticed. I noticed the tattoo and I noticed the… stomach. I wasn't sure until now, but I noticed."

Emma slumped back against her seat and dropped her face into her hand. "This wasn't how I wanted you to find out, Jonah. I'm sorry. I wasn't keeping it from you forever. I was going to tell you."

Jonah's head snapped up and his gaze pinned hers. "Were you?" He wasn't so sure. Sometimes she looked at him as though he were something stuck to her shoe, not the father of her child.

"I swear I was. Like I said, I wanted to finish the audit, do my job without any whispers of impropriety, but then yes, I was going to tell you who I am and that I'm pregnant. If I'd known how to contact you two months ago, I would've done it then, but by the time I figured it out, I was already involved in the audit. That said, I've been scared to death to tell you the truth."

Jonah swallowed hard and furrowed his brow. He was far from a hulking, intimidating person that people were scared of. He picked up his glass of wine and took a large sip to slow his spinning brain. "Why?"

Emma pulled her gaze from his and crossed her arms protectively over her chest. "It's like I told you that night—I'm not the woman you think I am. I knew that you wanted *her*, the wild and passionate anonymous stranger, not me. I couldn't bear to see the look on your face when you realized that I was that girl and the fantasy was shattered forever. I'm just boring old, stick-in-the-mud Emma. And to make matters worse, then I'd have to tell you that we were stuck together for the sake of our baby."

"Stuck together?" Jonah flinched at her choice of words. Is that how she saw her situation? She was *stuck* with him because they screwed up and she got pregnant?

The waiter returned with imperfect timing, placing each of their appetizers in front of them and disappearing silently when he sensed the tension between them.

"You know what I mean!" Emma leaned in and whispered harshly across the table at him. "Even if you were disappointed beyond belief to find out it was me, even if you never wanted to lay another hand on me again, I'm having your child, Jonah. I would hope that you would want to be a part of his or her life, even if I'm just on the periphery."

Jonah didn't know what to say. He honestly didn't

know how he wanted to move forward where Emma and the baby were concerned. His thoughts were spinning too quickly to light on one in particular. His strict upbringing nagged at him to marry her on the spot. Mother would insist when she found out. Noah could embezzle three million dollars, but it would be Jonah's scandal of an out-of-wedlock child that would be the biggest family disgrace in her eyes. Emma wasn't the only one constantly worried about gossip.

At the same time, his rebellious nature insisted that people didn't get married in this day and age just because they were having a baby. He and Emma hardly knew each other, much less loved each other. Coparenting was a more popular thing for people who didn't want to make the previous generations' mistakes and stick out a miserable marriage for the sake of the children.

What did he want? Jonah had no idea. He'd barely become accustomed to the concept of fatherhood, but he certainly never imagined that Emma would just be on the periphery, no matter the scenario.

"Emma…to start off, you're not a disappointment. Look at me," he demanded, and then reached across the table and took her hand, gripping tightly so she couldn't pull away from him again. Once she reluctantly met his gaze with her own, he continued. "I mean it. While this is all a surprise, I can assure you that disappointment has never crossed my mind."

She studied his face with disbelief lining her weary eyes. How had he not noticed how tired she looked? He'd been blinded tonight by flawless makeup and the silky jumpsuit he wanted to run his hands over. Now that he was really looking, he could see the sense of overwhelming stress and exhaustion in her eyes. She was working too much, and too hard, in her condition. They'd discuss that before long.

"But I'm not the woman you wanted, Jonah. I'm not wild and sexually adventurous. I'd never done body shots or had a one-night stand before. I'd certainly never have a tattoo if it weren't for that night. Everything you saw and liked about me was out of character. I mean, I...I don't even know what I'm doing here. Coming with you tonight was a mistake."

Emma moved fast, slipping out of the booth and taking the nearest door out to the back patio that overlooked the water.

"Emma?" Jonah rushed after her, catching her wrist as she leaned over the railing seemingly looking for an escape. What was she going to do? Swim away from him? All the way back to New York?

"Emma! Would you just stop and listen to me?" he demanded as she tugged at his grip. She finally turned around to face him, leaning her back against the railing. He instinctively wrapped his arms around her waist. He knew immediately that pressing against each other like this wasn't the best idea to keep his focus, but at the very least, he could convince her that he was attracted to her.

"Jonah, I want to go home."

"If that's what you want, I will, but not until you hear me out. I sat there and listened to all your excuses for lying to me. You owe me the opportunity to tell you how I feel, whether you believe me or not."

Emma finally stilled in his arms, although her gaze was fixed on the buttons of his shirt. He breathed a sigh of relief that he could finally focus his thoughts on telling her how he felt. This was important.

"I want you to know that you're totally and completely wrong." Jonah pulled aside the blue silk strap of her jumpsuit to expose her shoulder and upper chest. He placed his hand over the curve of her breast as he'd done that first night. Their tattoos aligned, creating one heart again at last. Emma looked down at the heart with tears shimmering in her eyes, but she didn't say anything.

"These tattoos weren't just something I suggested on a whim, Emma. They were supposed to be instruments of fate. This heart becoming whole again would only happen if it was meant to. Yes, we don't know much about each other, but now is our second chance to make that happen. Not just because of the baby, but because we've been brought together again to do just that."

"Jonah..." she started to argue.

"No," he silenced her. "From the moment I saw you sitting in my office, I've had this pull towards you that I couldn't explain. It was the same feeling that led me to rescue a pretty stranger from a creep at a party. I didn't know why then and I don't know why now, but I know I'm not letting this second chance slip between our fingers. I don't know how it's going to end. No one ever does. This might not be forever. It might not turn into the love affair of the century. But we owe it to ourselves, and to our child, to at least try and see where it can take us."

She sighed and relaxed into his touch. "And what if my company finds out? I'll lose my job. They'll never believe that I can be impartial. I have a vested interest in the successful business dealings of my baby's father."

Her mention of the audit was enough to remind Jonah of why he started romancing his auditor to begin with. Yes, he'd been drawn to her, but he'd stuck it out to cover Noah's ass and keep from botching the Game Town deal. He hadn't heard from his accountant in days, and that wasn't good. Sooner or later, she was going to find the discrepancy. If he couldn't keep it from her, there was a part of him that hoped maybe she wouldn't mention it in her report as a favor to him. That he could explain it away somehow.

"Can you be impartial, Emma?" he asked.

Her green eyes met his with a hard glint shining in them. Her spine straightened and her pointed chin thrust forward in the defiant response he seemed to coax out of her so easily. "Yes. Despite what Tim thinks, I'm first and foremost a professional and I will do my job."

Jonah didn't doubt that at all. That's exactly what he was afraid of. But for now, he needed to salvage tonight and worry about Noah's mess tomorrow. "Then there's nothing your boss could say or do to prove otherwise. Now come back inside and eat that amazing-looking dinner with me."

Emma sighed and nodded. She slipped the strap of her jumpsuit back over her shoulder, hiding away the tattoo and removing the temptation of her bare skin.

They went back inside, crisis averted, and yet Jonah couldn't help but feel a new sense of worry. The audit for Game Town was at risk and it had nothing to do with Emma and everything to do with Jonah.

Eight

Thankfully, the rest of the dinner went well. Jonah had been worried that the whole evening would be ruined, but the opposite turned out to be true. Uptight Emma seemed to finally, truly relax. All her secrets were out in the open and lifting that burden had an almost-physical impact on her. She smiled more, flirted happily through dinner by sharing bites of her food and making eyes at him, and didn't once refer to him as Mr. Flynn.

All their issues weren't behind them, but they were able to at least focus on enjoying each other's company tonight and worrying about the rest tomorrow. With that thought in mind, Jonah directed the pilot to land on his building's rooftop instead of returning them to the heliport.

When they touched down, Emma frowned out the window. "Where are we?"

"My place." He opened the helicopter door and offered his hand to help her.

Suspicion wrinkled her nose, but she still accepted his hand and stepped out onto his rooftop with him. They hustled away from the helicopter and over to the door. He led her down a set of stairs and out onto the landing where the entrance to his penthouse loft was located.

"Wait a minute," Emma said as she stared at the door.

"What?"

"This was your place? Where the Mardi Gras party was held?"

"Yes," he replied as he reached out to unlock the door. Jonah didn't hold many parties at his loft in Tribeca, but the Mardi Gras shindig had been one of them. "You don't think I'm tacky enough to seduce a woman in someone else's laundry room, do you?"

Emma's cheeks flushed bright red at the mention of their impulsive encounter. "I didn't really think about it. Although now that you mention it, I think Harper did say that party was at her boss's place. I assumed she meant the head of finance, not the CEO's apartment."

"I was right under your nose the whole time," Jonah said. He pushed open the door and gestured her in ahead of him. He followed behind, watching her as she studied the open, industrial space he'd fallen in love with the first time he toured it.

"It looks different without a hundred people crammed in here. It's huge."

"It takes up the whole top floor," Jonah explained. "Originally, I think this building was some sort of textile factory. When I bought it ten years ago, part of it had been converted to offices and shops and the top two floors were a storage warehouse. I ended up turning the whole thing into loft apartments with shared common areas on the ground floor."

Emma stopped and turned to face him. “You own the whole building?”

Jonah nodded and slipped out of the suit coat that had been irritating him all evening. He was hot-blooded and the suit on top of the long-sleeved shirt and glasses of wine had him almost at the point of sweating.

“If I listened to nothing else my mother, the great Angelica Flynn, told me, I did learn to diversify my investments.” He tossed the jacket over the back of a dining room chair and spread his arms out. “This was my foray into the real estate market. She thought I was crazy, of course. She prefers stuffy uptown mansions with marble and gold inlay. I like exposed brick and ductwork. Fortunately, I’m not the only one. The other lofts were rented with an extensive waiting list within weeks of being on the market.”

Emma set her purse on the concrete countertop of his kitchen and ran her fingers across the slightly roughened surface. “It’s definitely a different style. Not my style, but I know plenty of people who would like it.”

He followed behind her as she strolled through the living room and dining area, nearing the door that led into the infamous laundry room. As a true loft, there were only three doors in the whole space. One for the laundry and utility room, and the others for the guest and master bathrooms. Even if he’d wanted to take her to his bed that night, he wouldn’t have been able to. The space was wide-open to the party. It wasn’t ideal but the laundry room had been his only real option.

Emma hesitated for a moment, then reached out and turned the knob of the door. Was she really heading straight for the scene of the crime? He’d brought her back to his place with the intention of tasting every inch of her skin, but he'd anticipated using the bed this time.

She went straight to the washing machine, running her hand over the same top that he'd lifted her onto. Emma turned and pressed her back against the machine, then looked up at him with a sly smile curling her lips. "That night was..."

Mind-blowing? Crazy? Amazing? Passionate? Life changing?

"...unforgettable."

Jonah took a step closer, narrowing the gap between them. "That it was. Every minute I spent with you was seared into my brain. Every soft moan and cry permanently etched into my memory."

Emma made a familiar sound, barely louder than an intake of breath. He remembered that gasp. She'd made that same sound of surprise when he pushed up her skirt and pressed his fingertips into the flesh of her upper thighs.

He moved closer with that thought in mind. His every nerve tingled in anticipation as they remembered that moment. His blood rushed through his veins as his heart pounded loudly in his ears. "Over these last few months, I've thought of little else but having my butterfly back in my arms again."

Emma looked up at him as he came near enough to slip his arms around her waist. For once, she didn't fight or squirm. Instead, she pressed into him and clutched at the fabric of his dress shirt. "I've thought about that night a lot, too. I've wondered what I would do if I were given a second chance to be with my hero."

"Any ideas?" Jonah asked with a wicked grin. He leaned into her, pressing her back against the washing machine and imprinting his desire for her against her stomach.

"I have a few." Emma laced her fingers behind his neck and pulled his mouth down to hers.

As their lips made contact, Jonah realized this was the first time that he'd kissed Emma knowing who she really was. The kiss they'd shared before, aside from being slightly antagonistic, was just a kiss from the uptight Game Town auditor. There were no real expectations there, unlike a kiss from his butterfly.

He worried that this moment might be tainted by shaded memories of that night that no mortal woman could ever live up to. The minute they touched, however, it was no longer a concern. Her scent, her taste, the feel of her in his arms—it all combined in a familiar tidal wave that washed over him all at once. Before, there had been things about her that seemed familiar, but it had been like a déjà vu moment with one piece missing, the piece to tie it all together.

Now he had the tattoo to bring it all into focus and suddenly everything was right in the world.

He pulled her tight against him, loving the feel of her silken tongue as it glided along his own. Her touches weren't as bold as they had been that night, but tequila did that to a person. Yes, it made her wild and uninhibited, but with her in his arms again, he realized that wasn't the part of her that he craved. Emma was wrong to think that he wouldn't want her the way she was. Who she was, was the core of what he was after. The inner woman; the one who felt free to be herself for the first time in her life.

Jonah's hands spanned her hips and he slid one up the soft fabric of her jumpsuit to caress her breast. He took advantage of the low neckline to slip his hand beneath the cups of her strapless bra and happily mold her flesh in his palm until the peaks of her nipples dug into him.

He'd never gotten to see what her breasts looked like. If he had one regret about the night they'd spent together, it was that he'd had to rush things. It wasn't the time or the place for a leisurely exploration of a woman's body. Most of their clothes stayed on in the process.

That was not going to be the case tonight.

Taking a step back, he drew in a lungful of cool air. He braced his hands on the washing machine, trapping her there while he took a moment to collect himself.

"What's the matter?" she asked softly.

"Not a damn thing." And it was true.

"Then why—"

Jonah shook his head, interrupting her question. When he looked in her eyes, he saw confusion and disappointment mixed into the emerald green. Did she honestly think he was pulling away because he didn't want her? Nothing was further from the truth.

"Emma, I am not about to take you on this washing machine a second time. Tonight, I'm going to take my time and do it properly. I'm going to strip you naked from head to toe and press my mouth against every inch of your skin. I plan to make your body quiver and your throat go raw. So, nothing is the matter. I'm just taking a moment to keep myself from ruining my plans for tonight."

"They're good plans," she replied, and let her pink tongue snake across her bottom lip. Easing up from the washing machine, she laced her fingers behind his neck and pulled him close to her again. "You should show me where your bed is so we can implement them immediately."

* * *

Any anxiety Emma felt about this moment with Jonah vanished when he looked at her like that. He gazed at her so intently she couldn't help but believe he would do everything he promised, and then some. That was the look of a man who kept his word, and she couldn't wait.

He'd taken her hand and led her out of the laundry room and back into the main part of the loft. There, to her right, she saw the bed. Without all the party guests to block the view, it was easy to see the massive king-size bed along the far back wall of the loft.

It was placed in a niche between the bathroom and the closet to give it a little privacy despite it being out in the open. The plush, black velvet headboard rested against a wall of exposed, worn red brick. The comforter, like so much else in the loft, was a soft, steely gray that almost looked like liquid mercury pouring across the bed.

She couldn't take her eyes off their final destination. This was the moment she'd fantasized about, feared and longed for. How could it ever live up to either of their memories of that night they shared? David had told her she was a wet noodle in bed. She didn't want to be that for Jonah. She wanted to be the wild, passionate woman she'd been for him once. But how long could she maintain that facade? Was it better that she not try so hard and let him see the real Emma?

Jonah stopped in front of the bed and wrapped his arms around her waist. "Stop it," he chastised.

That snapped Emma out of her worried fog. "Stop what?"

"Stop overthinking it. Maybe that's all the tequila accomplished for you. It kept you out of your head, allowing you to just feel and go with the moment."

That may have been true. Emma found herself almost too nervous to move the more she thought about being with Jonah. She wasn't about to make love to a mysterious, heroic stranger. This was millionaire playboy Jonah Flynn. He was a man who'd romanced some of the most beautiful women in the world. She couldn't wrap her head around why he would want her. How could he not be disappointed with plain, boring old Emma? The thought was paralyzing.

Jonah seemed to notice the hesitation in her and compensated for it. His hands sought out the zipper on the side of her jumpsuit and pulled the tab to the end at her hip. "I guess I'll just have to overwhelm you with pleasure so you have no choice but to stop thinking."

His words coincided with his fingertips brushing along the sensitive bare skin of her side, making Emma gasp. He gripped the fabric at her shoulders and pulled it down. The silky material slipped over her arms, exposing her satin strapless bra, and then the slightly rounding curve of her pregnant stomach.

Emma instantly felt self-conscious about it. She had always been relatively slim, but never had the hard abs of someone who worked out at the gym doing core exercises. Jonah had seen her stomach when he was spying on her at the gym, but this was different.

He seemed to realize it, too. When he pushed the fabric of the jumpsuit over the curve of her hips, his eyes seemed fixated on her midsection. Jonah dropped down onto one knee, helping her step out of the outfit and slip out of her heels. Even then his eyes never flicked away.

When she was wearing nothing more than the bra and matching satin thong that wouldn't show through her jumpsuit, Jonah gripped her hips and pulled her to him. It reminded her of that first night where he'd done the same thing in his kitchen, looking up at her through his mask.

This time, as he leaned in to unfasten her bra and cast it to the floor, he pressed a kiss against the swell of her stomach. The gesture was simple and sweet, so unlike the man she envisioned from the newspapers. Emma closed her eyes to hide the glimmer of tears that started to gather there. Despite her worries and fears of Jonah rejecting his child along with her, it seemed as though she'd judged him too harshly. He would be a good father. That was all she dared ask of him for now.

She felt her panties slide down her legs and was too anxious to open her eyes again. There she was, completely naked in a well-lit room for his inspection. Jonah didn't seem to mind what he saw. He continued with his work, letting his hands and lips roam from her inner ankles up to her thighs. He stopped when he reached the exposed skin where her panties had once been. With a gentle nudge, he knocked Emma off balance and she sprawled back onto the bed with a shout of surprise.

Emma's eyes flew open in time to see the exposed beams and ductwork overhead. Before she could sit up and yell at Jonah, she realized he was kneeling between her spread thighs. She bit anxiously at her bottom lip as she felt his hot breath against her exposed center.

"I never got to taste you," he said. "Do you know how much I've regretted that?"

She covered her face with her hands to keep him from seeing her bright red cheeks. A moment later she felt one hand close around her wrists, pulling them away. He pinned them to the bed and when she finally opened her eyes, he was hovering over her. His shirt was unbuttoned now, showing off his lean, muscled torso.

"Does it embarrass you when I say things like that?" he asked.

Emma could only nod. How else could she explain that she was twenty-seven but about as comfortable with sexual topics as a twelve-year-old? She liked sex. And she'd had a good bit of it. But talking about it so blatantly? She just couldn't take it.

"Well, then I'll stop *talking* about it," he said, releasing her hands.

Before she could breathe a sigh of relief, she realized what he meant by that. He slipped down off the edge of the bed and pressed his palms against the inside of her knees to spread her legs wider.

The first touch was light, like a flicker over her skin that set off sparks under her eyelids. Every muscle in her body tensed in anticipation of the second contact. This time, his tongue lingered, moving slowly across her skin and making Emma squirm. After that, she lost count. Her hands gripped at the comforter as his lips, teeth and tongue feasted on her without showing signs of letting up.

Emma had done this before, and yet, she felt as though this were a totally new experience. Nothing any man had ever done to her had felt this amazing. She couldn't think, not really. Not when the waves of pleasure were coming at her from all sides. The only clear realization she had was that perhaps her lack of enthusiasm in bed with other partners was more of a reflection on them than on her.

It was as though a burden was lifted from her shoulders. Yes, perhaps David was just crappy in the sack and she accepted that because he was the kind of man she should want on paper. Successful, respectable, boring... The fears of becoming her sister had sent her on a path of living half a life. What else had she missed out on?

Emma looked up at Jonah and realized that he could definitely be the one to show her what was missing from her life. It might not ever be love or marriage or romance, but it would certainly be something more exciting than what she'd had. With a baby on the way, she had years of 2:00 a.m. feedings and runny noses in her future. She was excited to start that new part of her life, but there was no reason why she couldn't relish every second with Jonah now.

The thought released the last of the barricades she'd put up in her mind and she finally was able to relax and thoroughly enjoy the pleasure Jonah was giving her. She'd been holding tight to the release that was building up, somehow afraid to give in to it until now. When he slipped a finger inside of her and flicked his tongue over her swollen flesh, she couldn't hold back any longer.

Arching her back, Emma cried out. Her whole body convulsed against her will as the pulsating pleasure radiated through her. She clutched hopelessly at the blankets as Jonah continued his assault on her body, but there was nothing to hold her down.

This wasn't a release like she'd had before. Not even like the one he'd coaxed out of her the night of the Mardi Gras party. This blew them all out of the water and she found she couldn't control her body while it was happening. Only once the sensations finally faded away was she able to take a deep breath and lick her parched lips. She drew her legs together and melted into the bed like butter on a warm biscuit.

"That's my butterfly," he soothed as he stood up with a pleased smile curling his lips.

Emma could only watch him, the energy completely drained from her body, as he slipped out of his shirt, then went to work removing the rest of his clothes. Watching him was enough for now. There was so much of him she hadn't seen. He was lean and hard with the build of a marathon runner. Were there more tattoos he kept hidden beneath his clothes? In addition to their shared tattoo, she'd seen one peeking out from the sleeve of his T-shirts, but nothing she'd been able to study closely. Even now, she didn't really have the mental capacity to focus too much. Her body and her mind were gelatin.

"You seemed to enjoy that," he said. Completely nude, he offered his hand to help her sit up on the edge of the bed. "I'm anxious to hear you make those sounds again."

"Again?" she said, bewildered. She pushed herself back until she was centered, closer to the headboard.

Jonah crawled across the mattress until his body was covering hers. "Maybe even three times," he teased, pressing a kiss to her lips.

Emma couldn't imagine, but she wasn't about to argue with him while he was hovering between her thighs. With his lips still locked on hers, he pressed his hips forward, slipping inside of her with little resistance.

Now this, Emma remembered. She could hardly forget. He had been the perfect size for her, filling and stretching her body without being overwhelming. She drew her legs up to wrap around his hips and give him a better angle to go even deeper. The movement forced Jonah to pull away from her lips and curse softly with his cheek against hers. After a moment, he pushed up onto his arms with tightly closed eyes and a clenched jaw to maintain control.

"I don't know how you do this to me," he said as he withdrew and surged forward a second time. "It's like your body was just made for me. Everything about you…

your scent, your taste, the way you feel wrapped around me…I've been obsessed with experiencing this moment again. I can't believe I finally found you."

Emma couldn't believe they found each other, either. Or that despite everything, they'd ended up back in this place. She wanted to savor every moment they spent together so later she could use these memories to keep her warm on lonely nights. She reached up and cupped his face in her hands. The stubble of his beard was rough against her palms. She looked into his eyes, those blue, mesmerizing eyes, and drew his face down to hers so she could kiss him again.

"Stop talking and make love to me," she whispered against his lips.

Jonah grinned and kissed her full and hard before focusing on the task at hand. Adjusting his positioning, he settled into a slow, steady pace guaranteed to make them both crazy before too long. Resting on his elbow, he was able to dip his head down to nibble at her throat and taste her breasts, drawing hard on them until she arched her back and cried out.

He quickly adjusted his pace after that. They both knew that neither of them were patient enough to drag this pleasure on for too long. Jonah lifted her leg and hooked her knee over his shoulder. As he increased his speed and depth, Emma could only press her hands against the headboard to keep steady. That only made the thrusts more intense.

She couldn't imagine she could come again after the orgasm he'd just given her, but she felt the buildup start in her belly. She tensed her muscles and bit at her bottom lip as the pressure increased. She whispered soft encouragements between harsh gasps and groans as she got closer and closer.

"Oh Emma," he growled, planting a rough kiss against her inner knee.

Hearing her name on his lips was enough for her. She wasn't his butterfly, or his anonymous lover anymore. She was Emma. The one he wanted. And she came undone with her name on his lips.

As Emma cried and bucked her hips beneath him, Jonah finally gave in to his own pleasure. With a loud groan, he thrust hard and poured into her.

With his arms quivering, he kissed her, and then rolled to her side and collapsed back against the mattress. There was a long period of silence filled by ragged breathing and the occasional sigh of contentment.

Emma was wondering if he'd expect her to make her exit soon, when he rolled onto his side and tugged her body against him. She snuggled into the comfortable nook he created for her and felt herself start to drift off to sleep.

When she was on the edge of unconsciousness, she heard Jonah's voice whisper into her ear.

"I know you think that we're not good together and can't be a family. I'm here to tell you, Emma, that I worked too hard to find you and get you back in my bed again. I may not be willing to let you go this time."

Nine

Jonah was awakened the next morning by his cell phone ringing. He untangled from his grip on Emma's naked body and rolled over to grab his phone from the nightstand. It was Paul, his financial advisor. With everything else going on in his life lately, it was easy to ignore the fact that he was trying to cover up his brother's embezzlement.

"Hello?"

"It's done!" Paul said, triumphantly. "The money is in your accounts so you can move it wherever you need to."

Perfect. Of course, now he had to do that with Emma's eagle eyes watching the books, but what was done, was done. If he had to explain it to her, he would. He just didn't want to until the money was back where it belonged.

"Thanks, Paul. How much did it cost me to liquidate that quickly?"

"Er..." Paul stalled. "Perhaps a conversation better suited to a weekday at my office where we can look at all the figures."

That meant he'd taken a huge loss. "I'll be sure to take it, plus interest, out of Noah's hide."

"And we can hopefully make some of it back when we reinvest the funds."

Ever the optimist. "Okay. Thanks again, Paul." Jonah hung up the phone and scowled at the black screen. His advisor was working under the presumption that Noah was going to pay him back. He didn't have as much faith in his brother. Their mother would argue that he always treated Noah unfairly. Jonah would say the same of her. She coddled him, turning him into the monster that the rest of the family had to cope with.

"Is everything okay?"

Emma's voice drew him back to the here and now. "Yes, that was nothing. Just business."

"It's awful early on a Sunday morning for business." Emma yawned and curled into a ball against his chest.

Jonah wrapped his arms around her and clenched his jaw to hold in the angry words that had nothing to do with her. "Luckily we can go back to sleep," he said instead.

At first, his worry had been that Noah would screw up the Game Town deal. Covering up the stolen money had been at the forefront of his mind until he realized who Emma was. Then he'd nearly forgotten about why he was pursuing her in the first place. Now everything was different. Emma was more than an auditor; she was the mother of his child. She was the one who had held his interest, the one he couldn't forget about, the one who could make his blood race with a simple touch. It was possible that she could be The One.

How would she feel about what was going on with Noah? If she uncovered the truth, would she question every moment they'd spent together? Could she trust Jonah knowing he had been lying to her about this the whole time?

Jonah might very well lose the Game Town deal because of Noah, but if he lost Emma… He would never forgive his brother for screwing this up for him. This was the closest thing to love he'd ever experienced before and he didn't want it ruined by another one of Noah's wild ideas before it even had a chance.

"What are you thinking about?" she asked softly.

"Nothing important. Why?"

She placed her palm against his bare chest. "Your heart is pounding like mad. I was thinking you were upset about something."

He wasn't going to ruin this moment with Noah's nonsense. If he had to tell her, he would do it later. "Did it ever occur to you," he said, tugging her tight to his chest, "that I just woke up to a beautiful naked woman curled against me? That can make a man's heart pound pretty hard. As well as other things."

Emma's eyes widened, teasing him. "You mean you want to do it again?"

Was it teasing? He wasn't so sure now. "Emma, I would make love to you ten times a day if you could take it and we could get anything else done. Does that surprise you? I don't know how it could."

She pulled out of his grasp and sat up in bed, tugging the sheets to her chest. "A little. I mean…this is going to sound ridiculous. I'm just not used to all that. I went to Catholic school and got my sex education from nuns. I was raised to be more conservative. Not so conservative as to wait for marriage, obviously, but I've never really had the wild kind of nights you're probably used to."

"Were all the guys you dated just that boring?"

Emma frowned, a crease forming between her eyebrows. "Yes, in a way. But I suppose that was what I was looking for."

Now it was Jonah's turn to sit up. "You were looking for someone boring?" He couldn't imagine someone like Emma wasting her life with someone like that.

"Not *boring*. More like…responsible. Respectable. The kind of man you'd be happy to take home to your parents."

"You mean the opposite of me?"

"No!" she insisted. "Well…not exactly."

Jonah tried not to be offended. He knew he wasn't the clean-cut lawyer or investment banker some parents wanted for their daughter. "Do your parents know you're having my baby?"

Emma shook her head. "They don't even know I'm pregnant yet."

"Emma! How could you keep that a secret?"

"Easy. I assure you that it was far simpler to avoid my parents than to tell them I'm pregnant but don't know who the father is. And I didn't until a week ago. Listen, my parents are very overprotective of me. My sister ended up being an embarrassment to the family. I was just a teenager when she died and my mother was constantly on me not to make the same mistakes Cynthia made. So I guess I've been more worried about pleasing them than pleasing myself. It wasn't until my ex said those horrible things that I gave myself permission to rebel for just one night."

"And look what happened!" Jonah said jokingly, but he could instantly tell by the pained expression on Emma's face that she felt exactly that way. He was used to scandal, but he sensed that Emma was out of her element with this entire situation. He opted to change his tactic. "Listen, I'm sorry about all this, Emma. I certainly didn't expect you to suffer permanent consequences from our night together. At least outside of the tattoo. I know how you feel—"

"How could you possibly?" she interrupted.

"Well, you might be surprised to know that my parents were very conservative and very strict. I wasn't allowed to do anything. Me and my younger brothers got sent to a boarding school in England when my father died. I only had a year or so left, then I returned for college. There, I realized that I could live my life the way I wanted to, and everything changed for me. I think my professional success is due in part to my rebellious management style. It doesn't work for everyone, but it really worked out for me."

"And what does your mother say about how you live your life?"

"She said plenty at first, when she thought I still cared. Then she realized I was a grown man, a CEO of my own company, and she finally let it go. At least until Thanksgiving rolls around. It wouldn't be a family holiday without Angelica Flynn putting her two cents in."

"I don't know that it will ever be that easy with my parents. Once they lost Cynthia, I was all they had left. I've never wanted to disappoint them."

Jonah put his arm around Emma's shoulders. "I don't know how you could possibly disappoint anyone."

Emma brought her hand to her stomach and rubbed the small bulge there unconsciously as she stared off across the expanse of his loft. "They won't be happy about the baby. My mother has been waiting years to put together a huge society wedding for me. Cynthia died before she could get married, so I'm her only chance to be the mother of the bride at an outrageous affair at The Plaza Hotel. You don't have a big affair like that when the bride is obviously pregnant. And there's no hope of a wedding at The Plaza, or otherwise, when the baby is the result of a one-night stand and they have no intention of marrying."

There were a lot of things about Emma's pregnancy that he really hadn't taken into consideration until now. He'd only thought about how fatherhood would affect his life, not hers. Not really, and that was stupid and selfish of him. "Will your parents insist you get married?"

Emma shrugged. "They can try, but they can't force you into it. My father doesn't own a shotgun, so you're safe there. I'm certainly not going to force you into it. The pregnancy was a mistake. I'm not going to compound it by demanding that we add a marriage into the mix."

The last few days with Emma had changed a lot of the ways Jonah looked at the world. Once, long before she walked through the doors of FlynnSoft, Jonah told himself that if he ever found his butterfly, he wouldn't let her go. That hadn't entirely changed when he realized Emma was his fantasy woman. When he saw her, he saw a future without a line of women outside his door. Yes, he would absolutely stand up and be a father to their child, but for the first time in his life, Emma made him consider more—more than this cold, empty loft, trysts with random actresses and lonely nights working late at the office.

The idea of coming home after work to a nice, comfortable apartment and spending time with his very own family was suddenly more appealing than it had ever been. Having a family was something he'd never put much thought into, perhaps just because at heart he was still a teenager rebelling against his parents at every turn. As a grown man with a child on the way, things were different.

But it didn't sound like a future together held the same appeal for Emma. "You don't want to marry me?" he asked.

She turned to look at him with wide green eyes. "No, I don't."

Jonah had never asked a woman if she wanted to marry him before, and although it wasn't really a proposal, he was a little hurt by her blunt rejection. "Why? Am I not good enough to be your husband?"

"Of course you're good enough," she chided. "It has nothing to do with that. Despite the fact that we're having a child together, we hardly know each other, Jonah. *That's* why. We agreed to give the relationship time to develop and see what—if anything—happened, and I'm fine with that. If one day, you decide you're truly in love with me and want to marry me that will be completely different. But I'm not going to rush things because of an artificial ticking time bomb that ends with this kid entering the world. My mother and her dreams of a big Plaza wedding will have to just be dreams."

Emma had hoped that the weekend would clear her mind and she could return to work Monday ready to wrap up this project at FlynnSoft. Instead she found herself just as baffled by the discrepancy in the financials as she was the week before. If her calculations were correct, and she'd checked them three times, someone had taken out three million dollars without logging the expense properly. The money had been transferred to an offshore account she couldn't find any record of, nor did it have any relation to the corporation that she could find. It looked very fishy. And yet who would be foolish enough to steal such a large amount? Someone was bound to notice it.

This was the part of Emma's job that she didn't like. She had to tell the CEO that someone was stealing from him. Then she had to hope the finger didn't point back at Jonah himself. He had that right, she supposed—it was his company, after all—but it wouldn't look good. Then, worst of all, she had to report it back to Game Town, where the stodgy owner would likely pass on the contract. This wasn't going to end well for anyone but the creep who made off with three million.

With a heavy sigh, Emma picked up her phone to call Mark, one of her coworkers at the firm. She needed some advice on how to handle this so she could make certain she wasn't letting her relationship with Jonah cloud the issue. Mark had been doing this job for twenty years and had seen it all. He would know what to do.

"Hey there, Emma," Mark said as he answered. "How're the crazy kids over there at FlynnSoft?"

"It's definitely a different kind of company," Emma admitted. "Listen, I'm about to wrap up but I've come across something questionable that I wanted to run by you." She went through everything she found as briefly as she could. "Do you think I should speak to the CEO before I make my report?" she asked when she was done.

"You can. And I would. It's possible he can find an explanation and documentation for it that you haven't thought of. But if there's the slightest whisper of funds mismanagement, you need to report it back to Game Town. It's not your job to protect FlynnSoft from themselves."

Emma's stomach sank. "Of course. I just wanted a second opinion. Thanks for your time, Mark."

She hung up the phone and gathered some of her papers to take upstairs to Jonah's office. She hadn't seen him yet this morning. She tried not to think about what that meant. He'd said a lot about a potential future for the two of them, but she didn't believe it. Not really. It sounded good; it was the right thing to say, but would he follow through? Or would he chase the next shiny thing that caught his eye?

His secretary, Pam, wasn't at her desk when she came upstairs, so Emma went ahead and knocked on his door.

"Come in," she heard him yell from inside.

Emma pushed the heavy door open and slipped into his office. The moment he laid eyes on her, his eyes brightened and he smiled. Jonah leaped up from his seat behind his desk and rushed over to her. Before she could stop him, he swept her up in his arms and pulled her into a passionate good-morning kiss.

Emma tried to untangle herself as delicately as she could. "Jonah, please," she fussed, straightening up her paperwork and taking a step back.

"No one can see into my office, butterfly."

"Don't call me that at work, Jonah. And someone could walk in and catch us together at any time."

Jonah frowned and leaned back against his desk. "I guess. But what if you worked here?" he asked. "Would you still worry all the time?"

"What do you mean?" she asked.

"Well," he explained, "I told you before that I need a new financial director. From everything I've seen of your work thus far, I think you'd be great for the job. And besides that, if you worked for me instead of this pesky third party, you wouldn't have to worry about the impropriety of it all."

It was a little more complicated than just that. She'd thought he was only joking when he'd mentioned the job last week. "No, I'd only have to worry about people saying I slept with the boss instead."

"Well, to be fair you did sleep with the boss," Jonah said with an impish grin. He leaned in and whispered "multiple times," like he was sharing a secret.

Emma shook her head. It seemed like everything was a joke to Jonah sometimes. "I'm serious."

"So am I," he countered. "I need a finance director and I want you to take the job."

"I'm not taking the job, Jonah. I don't like the way it would look."

"My brother works here. He collects a paycheck and doesn't do a damn thing. Everyone knows that and no one cares. Nepotism is alive and well in the corporate world."

"Yes, but if we continue to date, if everyone finds out I'm having your baby… I just don't like it. You know how I feel about that sort of thing. Reputations are important to me."

Jonah sighed. "Okay, fine. You won't kiss me. You don't want to work for me. I suppose that means you won't give yourself to me on the conference room table. So tell me what it is that brings you here today, Miss Dempsey."

Emma ignored his sexual comments and tried not to bristle at his sudden use of her formal name. A week ago she would've preferred it, but now things were different. Now she knew he was only doing it to get a rise out of her because he was irritated.

She clutched the paperwork tight to her chest and tried

to focus on what she needed to say instead of the dark blue eyes that were watching her curiously. "I'm finished with my audit."

"Oh, excellent. You're very efficient, considering how much I distracted you. Does that mean you'll be free to be seen with me in public? Or do we have to wait for the Game Town deal to go through?"

"Well, the Game Town deal is what I came to talk to you about. I've found a significant discrepancy in the books."

The curiosity on his face instantly faded. His brow drew together with a serious expression of concern that seemed out of place on his face. "What did you find?"

Emma took the pages over to him where she'd highlighted the withdrawal. "Exactly three million has been taken out and wired to this offshore account in the Caymans. I haven't been able to figure out who it belongs to, but I can't make any connection to a legitimate business expense or account."

Jonah nodded, his face unusually blank of its usual emotion or amusement. His gaze simply flicked over the pages as she spoke without really seeming to take in the data. She wasn't sure what to think, so she continued to nervously prattle on.

"Do you know anything about this? I was hoping you might have some kind of insight that would keep it from looking as bad as it does right now."

Jonah turned his gaze to her and he nodded curtly. "I do have some insight, but unfortunately, it won't improve the circumstances. Please have a seat."

He returned to his desk chair and Emma lowered slowly into the guest seat where she'd first met the infamous Jonah Flynn a week ago. So much had changed and yet she was just as anxious talking to him now as she was then. "Am I missing something?" she asked. "Is this some kind of third world charity outreach in the Caribbean?"

Jonah shook his head. "I'm pretty sure we document our charity funds appropriately. You haven't missed anything, and I didn't think you would. The truth of the matter is that my younger brother Noah is a vice president here, as I mentioned earlier. He transferred the money out to one of his private accounts—an unauthorized loan of sorts. A member of the finance department brought it to my attention the day you arrived to conduct the audit. Had I known about it earlier, I would've disclosed the issue, but instead, I hoped that perhaps I could resolve it. I spoke with Noah last week and confirmed my suspicions."

Emma's stomach felt like the baby was flittering around with butterflies. Unauthorized loan? That was a nice way to say stealing. She'd never even met Jonah's brothers and now she was learning that one of them was a thief. Her *baby's uncle* was a thief. As though her parents weren't already going to have a meltdown over this.

"And?" she pressed.

"And, he's returning it all. I can't tell you what he needed the money for—I didn't ask—but he swore he would return it when he got back into the States. At the moment, he's in Southeast Asia. In the meantime, I have deposited enough money to cover the withdrawal. The accounts should register it as of this morning. Since this is a privately owned company with no board of directors to answer to, I've covered the loss and opted not to publicize the theft outside of the company."

"You still have the president of Game Town to answer to," Emma pointed out. "When I disclose this, I'm pretty sure Carl Bailey is going to back out of the partnership deal with FlynnSoft. He was suspicious enough of your company and its unorthodox methods going into it. I don't see him as the kind of man that would want to do business with a company that could potentially lose money it's handling on his behalf."

"We won't lose Game Town's money. I guarantee it."

"How can you do that?" she asked. Was he willing to use his own money to replace every dime his brother or anyone else decided they could take?

"I can guarantee it because I intend to make my brother's life so miserable he'd sooner stab himself in the eye with a butter knife than touch a penny of this company's funds again. When I'm done making an example of him, neither he, nor anyone else in this company, would even consider it."

"Well, hopefully when you meet with Game Town, you can convince Carl of that. I'm not the one you need to sell it to."

"That's where you're wrong. I need you to understand that this is really a private matter between my brother and I, and I would like to keep it that way. I covered the loss and would do so again if necessary."

The unease returned. It all sounded very nice and good, but Emma couldn't shake the feeling that this was bad news. She believed Jonah and what he said about the money, but the implication was clear. "Are you asking me to leave the stolen money out of the report?"

Jonah looked her in the eye for a moment, as though he were silently pleading with her. But he didn't say the words. "I can show you the records of the deposits, Emma. Would that make you feel better?"

It would. To a point. "I would like to see those records.

Then I can and will include in my report that the funds have been reinstated. But I won't be a party to covering this up. If someone were to find out, I would lose all credibility. I would be fired. I wouldn't be able to get a job anywhere in my field." Emma placed a hand protectively over her stomach, which seemed to grow a tiny bit every day now. "As it is, my impartiality will be questioned when the truth about the baby comes out. If anyone were to uncover that I knew about the theft and hid it…"

"You know you don't need to work, Emma. I can take care of you and our baby."

Emma shook her head adamantly. "Support your child because you want to and it's the right thing to do. I don't want it to feel like a kickback. Please don't ask me to do something that compromises my integrity, Jonah."

With a sigh, Jonah set aside the financial paperwork and walked over to her. She reluctantly let him wrap his arms around her and pull her into his protective embrace. "I won't. Report what you need to report, butterfly. FlynnSoft will recover, no matter what happens with the Game Town deal."

Emma eased back to look him in the eye and see that he really meant what he said. "You're okay with this?"

He nodded with a soft, reassuring smile. "I'm okay with this. In the end, it is what it is, right? You have to tell the truth and I have to be willing to stand in front of Carl and explain to him why he can still trust us to do a good job, despite it."

A sense of relief washed over her. She didn't like what she'd found, and she didn't like that Jonah and his employees might be punished for someone else's actions, but thankfully it would be out of her hands. "Thank you."

"When you get done typing that report up, I insist you

let me take you out to dinner tonight. Anyplace on the island you want."

"I'm still not comfortable with us being seen together. It's not over until my report is filed, I'm back at my old office and the deal is done, Jonah."

"Okay, fine," he relented. "How about some very privately consumed takeout at your place, then?"

"Perfect," she agreed, letting him pull her tight against him again. Even now, when it felt like things were unraveling, she was okay as long as she was in his arms. Hopefully she'd be able to stay there and weather the upcoming storms.

Ten

Jonah wasn't sure what to expect from Emma's apartment, but it wasn't what he got. Her work persona was so strait-laced and uptight, he anticipated her home would be boring, neat, with a place for everything and everything in its place. But the large and spacious apartment was flooded with daylight through large picture windows and the decor was relaxed, comfortable and filled with personality.

He followed her inside clutching a bag of Thai food from the restaurant up the block. Once he made it in far enough, he closed the door behind him and just stopped to take it all in. The fabrics on the curtains and the furniture were soft and romantic with florals and lace. The furniture itself looked comfortable like you would want to settle in and read for hours. It was soft, feminine with a touch of rustic country charm, telling him more about the real Emma than he expected to uncover.

"What's the matter?" Emma asked.

"Your apartment. It just wasn't what I was expecting." He followed her into the kitchen with its white Shaker cabinetry and gray-washed wood floors. A vase of multicolored zinnias sat in the middle of the kitchen table, likely from the flower shop on the corner.

"Not enough chrome and glass for your taste?" she asked. "Industrial chic isn't exactly my thing. I get enough concrete and steel walking around Manhattan every day. When I got my own place after college, I decided that I wanted something softer and more comforting to come home to."

"It's nice. Certainly more inviting than my place, but I'm more about function than anything. Here, I keep expecting a chicken to run across the hallway."

"You quit it," she chided, taking the bag away from him and unpacking cartons of Thai food onto the butcher-block countertop. "I don't have any pets, and that includes chickens. I think that's against the co-op restrictions," Emma added with a chuckle. "This is still the Upper East Side, you know."

They both made plates and bypassed the dining table to sit together in the living room on the couch. As they finished their food, Jonah found himself more curious about Emma's personal hideaway. He wanted to see it all and gain more insight into her.

"May I have the rest of the tour?" he asked as she set her mostly empty plate on the coffee table.

Emma shrugged. "If you want. There isn't much left to see. Two bedrooms, one bath." She got up and he followed her down a little hallway where she pointed out the black-and-white retro bathroom. "This," she said as she opened the opposite door, "used to be my office. I've cleared all that out to uh...for the nursery."

That was right. This wasn't just a cute bachelorette pad any longer. This was where she intended to raise their child. They stepped inside the room together. There wasn't anything in it yet.

"I thought it was too early to buy much. I had the walls painted a soft gray. I thought that was neutral enough for whatever I...*we* end up having."

"It's a pretty small room, Emma. The baby is going to outgrow it fairly quickly."

"I know," she said with a sigh. "I didn't buy this place expecting to raise a child in it. When the baby needs more space, I'll look at something larger. I want to save money while I can. If my parents haven't disowned me, perhaps they can help with a down payment."

It baffled Jonah how she continued to talk about the baby as though she was having to do this entirely on her own. "Or I could."

"Well...yes, maybe. I'm just not used to thinking about it that way. Up until a week ago, the baby's father was not in the picture. I had no idea how to find you, so I was having to make plans to do this all on my own."

"I may need a new place, too," Jonah said, thinking aloud. His loft didn't have any walls. How was a baby supposed to sleep without walls to block out noise? "Perhaps...perhaps we could look at getting something together."

Emma froze on her way out of the nursery. She looked at Jonah with wide eyes. "You want to move in together?"

"Uh..." When she said it that way, it was a little terrifying, but still accurate. "Yes. If we both need a bigger place, we could look into something large enough to accommodate all of us. Then the baby doesn't have to move back and forth between us. We could even look for something where you could have your own room, if that would make you more comfortable."

She took a ragged breath before pushing past him into the hallway. "That's something we could talk about," she said in a noncommittal tone he'd gotten used to with her. It was better than a complete dismissal. "We have time."

"Do you have a due date?"

"The doctor told me it would be November twenty-first."

With every detail, the baby became more and more real in his mind. Now he knew when to expect his life to change forever—before the holidays rolled around again. "A Thanksgiving baby?"

Emma nodded. "Seems like a long time from now, but it will probably be here before we know it." She continued down the hallway to the last door. "This is my bedroom."

They stepped into a room that was much larger than the nursery. A queen-size bed sat along one wall with a white wooden headboard that was worn and gouged to reveal the darker color of the wood beneath the paint. The bed had an eyelet coverlet and easily a dozen pillows, all different. An antique oval mirror, a dresser and an old cedar chest at the foot of the bed finished it off.

The place was nice, but the addition of a baby, plus a stroller, high chair, bassinet, toys and all the other accessories a child came with, would eat up the space she had left. It was a lovely, spacious apartment for a single woman, but that wasn't what she was anymore.

"We need to get a new place. This just seals the deal. Your apartment is too small and mine is too impractical. I'm going to call a Realtor next week to have him start looking for apartments. How do you feel about the Village?"

Emma turned around to face him and placed a cautionary hand on his chest. "Slow down. I'm not ready yet, Jonah."

"Not ready to get an apartment or not ready for everyone to know we're together?" He asked the question knowing the answer. Emma and her blasted reputation. "When?" he pressed.

"Once the FlynnSoft deal is done. And we tell our parents. Then, if they haven't killed us, it should be okay to let others know about us and about the baby."

"It can't happen soon enough. I don't like hiding. I'm used to living my life out in the open. I can't wait until I can touch you whenever I want to. Kiss you whenever I want to."

Emma turned to him with a sigh. "It won't be too much longer. Until then, you'll just have to take advantage of your opportunities when they arise."

Jonah sat down on the edge of the bed and looked at her. He had an opportunity right now he wasn't going to pass up. "Come here."

Emma took a few steps toward him, stopping when she was standing just between his knees. She placed her hands on his shoulders and looked down at him.

God, she was beautiful. The fact that she didn't think so just made her that much more attractive. Even when the mask had hidden most of her face, there was a beauty that shone out of her from the inside. Perhaps that was what he'd been drawn to all this time. No mask, no boxy suit, no stuffy demeanor could suppress it.

Jonah ran his palms along the outside of her legs, down and back up to her hips. There, he pulled her dress shirt out from where she'd tucked it into her waistband. He immediately sought out the silk of her skin beneath it, stroking her elegantly arched back and sides that seemed to quiver at his touch. She was content to let him explore, closing her eyes and just feeling him.

He unfastened her dress pants, sliding them over her hips to the floor. Once she'd stepped out of them, Jonah hooked his hand behind her knee and pulled her toward him. With little resistance, she crawled into his lap, straddling him on the bed. He ran his hands over her smooth thighs and hips before turning his attention to her blouse. One by one, he slipped the pearl buttons through the holes until Emma was astride him in little more than a lacy peach-colored bra and panties.

Emma reached up and pulled a few pins from her hair. With a shake of her head, the dark brown waves broke free of their restraints and tumbled down around her shoulders. The scent of her shampoo swirled around him. Jonah could only wrap his arms around her waist to hold her securely in his lap as he leaned in and buried his face in her creamy, lace-clad breasts.

She gasped and wove her fingers into his hair, pulling him closer as he teased and tasted her sensitive skin. His tongue rubbed across the rough lace that kept her nipples confined, over and over until the fabric was damp. Frustrated by the impediment, he tugged the straps down her shoulders until her breasts were exposed. He kissed the inside of each one, then placed a kiss on the ridge of her sternum between them.

"Why are you wearing so much clothing while I'm wearing so little?" Emma asked. "I feel like I'm at a distinct disadvantage here."

"You're prettier naked than I am," Jonah replied with

a grin. He immediately followed his words with action, tugging his shirt up and over his head. He wanted as much of his skin to touch hers as possible. He wrapped his arms around her and pressed his bare chest against hers before meeting her lips with a searing kiss.

He couldn't get enough of her. Not then and not now. She was unlike any other woman he'd ever known. She was his and he was hers in more ways than he could even describe. His butterfly had changed everything. And even if the thing with Game Town ended badly, he knew that if he made it out of this situation with Emma still in his arms, everything would be okay. She was his anchor, holding him steady so he wouldn't drift out to sea. He couldn't lose her.

Emma pulled away from his kiss, shifting in his lap and grinding against his erection with a wicked grin lighting her face. "Now," she pouted.

He wasn't about to deny her. Emma rose up onto her knees while he scrambled out of his jeans and kicked them away. And then, she slowly lowered herself back down, taking in every inch of him at a deliciously slow pace.

"Oh Emma," he groaned into her hair, pulling her close as her heat enveloped him. "I'm never letting you go. Never."

She didn't want him to let go. She was content to stay right where she was forever. Emma had never felt so close, so connected to a man before. As she raised her hips and lowered them, rocking back and forth in his lap, the delicious friction her movement generated hit in all the right places.

A heat that started in her belly seemed to spread

through her whole self. As her temperature shot up, the close proximity of their bodies made her skin break out in a thin sheen of perspiration. Each time Emma moved, her moist skin glided across his. Jonah only clutched her tighter as the sensations they were each experiencing grew more and more intense.

Emma wanted to find her release like this. She wanted to come apart wrapped in his arms. She wanted him to feel every tremble, every aftershock, and then she wanted to experience the same thing for him. This closeness was what she truly craved with Jonah. Here, in this moment, she could truly believe that they were supposed to be together. She could open her heart enough to let him in, if just for a moment.

She was roused from her thoughts by Jonah's encouraging whispers in her ear. "Ahh, yeah. That's my beautiful butterfly. Come apart for me, baby."

The low rumble of his voice against her ear and neck sent goose bumps through her body. She moved faster, rocking her hips hard until her muscles ached and her knees burned. It was when she almost had nothing more to give that she reached her goal. As suddenly as a snapping of fingers, her body gave in and the pleasurable sensations rushed through her.

Jonah held her tight, continuing to whisper to her as her body shuddered and spasmed in his arms. When the rush subsided and she barely had the energy to hold on to him, he thrust hard from beneath her until with a final groan, lost himself in her. Jonah collapsed back onto the bed, taking Emma with him. After a moment, she rolled off and flattened into her mattress, drawing in a lungful of cooler air. They shifted around until Jonah could pull the covers up over them both and they snuggled together in the plush softness of her bed.

Lying there, looking up at her ceiling and listening to Jonah's heartbeat pound in his chest, she wondered if this could really be what her life would be like now. With the audit behind her, she would soon be free to be with Jonah. She wasn't sure how things would turn out, but even if they didn't marry, surely her parents would be happier about the pregnancy if they were together. If they *loved* each other.

Did she love him?

She had questioned her feelings for Jonah repeatedly over the last few days. Now, lying in his arms, making love to him again, it was easy to admit to herself that she did. She had loved him since that first night. She'd just been afraid to acknowledge the truth, even to herself. Love was a scary proposition, and love with a man like Jonah could be downright terrifying.

He was everything she thought she shouldn't want. Exciting, spontaneous, rebellious, passionate… For some reason, she'd lumped all those qualities in with irresponsible and dangerous, when that was hardly the case. She didn't need a man to be boring. She just needed him to be there for her. Jonah might very well be that man.

Emma was so content in his arms and so deep in thought that when her cell phone rang, she was tempted not to answer. And she wouldn't have except for the fact that it was her work ringtone. It was awfully late to be fielding calls from the office. Then again, they wouldn't call her if it wasn't necessary.

She answered the phone, seeing her boss's name on the screen. "Hello?"

"Emma. We have a problem," Tim said.

Her stomach instantly felt as though it had twisted into a knot. How could they have a problem? She hadn't even filed the report yet. And she'd disclosed everything. She sat up in bed and grabbed her robe off the hook. "What's wrong?" she asked as she nervously walked out of the bedroom and tied her belt. She needed to focus and couldn't with Jonah's nude body sprawled on her bed.

"I spoke with Mark not too long ago. He told me about the conversation you had with him today. I really don't appreciate being left out of the loop on something so important. You should've come to me with this issue first."

Emma's free hand curled into a fist at her side. She went to her coworker for support and he'd ratted her out before she'd had a chance to do what she needed to do. "He gave me some advice and I'm following it. I'll have my report to you first thing in the morning. I wanted to read over it again before I submitted it."

"And what will the report say?"

"It will say that I discussed the issue with Jo—*Mr. Flynn* and he provided an explanation. Both the discrepancy and how FlynnSoft handled the issue will be included in the report for Mr. Bailey to handle as he pleases."

There was a long pause on the phone that Emma didn't like. When Tim was quiet, he was preparing his words, and they usually weren't good. "So you're on a first name basis with *Jonah*, are you, Emma?"

She swallowed hard, measuring her words carefully and trying to ignore the heat of Jonah's naked body that still warmed her. "The environment at FlynnSoft is very casual, sir. You know that as well as anyone."

"You know, Emma, I sent you because I thought you

had some sense. More than Dee. I should've sent Mark, though. I underestimated Mr. Flynn's allure. I see that now."

Emma's mouth dropped open. "Sir, are you accusing me of some kind of wrongdoing? I assure you that my report is as accurate and impartial as Mark's would have been."

"So you're willing to sit there and deny any type of personal relationship with Mr. Flynn?"

Could she lie? No, she couldn't. But could she convince him it wouldn't matter? "No, I can't do that, sir. But I can say with complete confidence that I did my job as well as anyone."

Tim groaned loudly over the phone line. "Can't you see that he just used you, Emma? I'm willing to bet that he turned on the charm the minute you walked in the door. Did he offer to give you a personal tour of the building? Did he take you out to dinner and welcome you to the company? Just to be friendly, of course? He dates models and actresses, Emma. You're a pretty girl, but do you really think a man like him would be interested in a woman like you if he didn't want something from you? I'm pretty sure his entire plan from the beginning was to distract you from your work so you wouldn't find the problem in the books. Or if you did, to convince you not to disclose it. Now that it's done, he's going to drop you like a bad habit."

His sharp words hit their target, bruising her ego, but she wouldn't back down on her report. "But I *did* disclose it," she insisted. "I don't understand why you're saying all this when I haven't even submitted my report yet."

"Yes, you disclosed the problem, but then you followed it up with the recommendation that the deal still go through because Jonah had handled it in a fiscally responsible manner."

"How...?" She hadn't submitted her report yet, and he'd just quoted her own words back to her.

"I pulled it off our server and read your draft when I got off the phone with Mark. I couldn't believe what I was reading. Would you have made that recommendation with anyone else, Emma? Tell me the truth."

Emma couldn't answer. She didn't know. Perhaps she wasn't as impartial as she thought. Perhaps Jonah had managed to get his way in the end without her even realizing he was doing it.

"You've lost your objectivity because you've gotten romantically involved with him, just as he'd planned. If I can't count on you to do your job, Emma, I have no choice but to let you go. Come in tomorrow and pack up your office."

She couldn't believe what she was hearing. It was everything she'd feared and dreaded since the moment she laid eyes on Jonah. She thought she'd been so cautious, so careful, and yet it was all falling down around her. "Are you serious? You're firing me?"

She heard the bed squeak and Jonah's heavy footsteps coming down the hallway. He must've heard her say she was fired. Panic started to close her throat. She couldn't deal with Tim and Jonah at the same time.

"I am," Tim said. "I'm sorry, Emma."

The line disconnected, leaving her dumbstruck. The phone slipped from her hand to the living room floor, where she left it.

Jonah appeared in the room wearing nothing but his boxers and jeans. "He fired you?" he asked, but she didn't answer.

She couldn't. Tim's words were swirling in her head and muffling Jonah's voice. She was pregnant and unemployed. She'd just lost her medical insurance. What was she going to do? Turn to her baby's father? The same man who may have very well used her to close the deal with Game Town?

That was the part that really ate at her insides. She wasn't the kind of woman Jonah was known to date. He'd pursued Emma from the moment he walked into his office and first laid eyes on her. Well before he knew who she really was, he was asking her to dinner, to coffee, buying her expensive flowers and pouring on the charm layers thick. Maybe Tim was right. All of this was just his way of securing the contract by any means necessary.

"Emma, what did he say? What's happened? Did he find out about us? We were so careful."

"Jonah, please," she said, holding out her hand to silence him. "Just answer one question for me. That's all I want to hear right now."

Jonah's jaw flexed as he held in his own questions and nodded. "Okay. What do you want to know?"

"Before you knew who I really was, why were you pursuing me so doggedly? The truth. Were you only feigning an interest in me in an attempt to distract me and keep me from finding that Noah stole all that money from the company?"

"Is that what Tim told you?" he asked.

"Just answer the question, please."

Jonah's blue eyes focused on her for a second before they dropped to the floor. "Yes," he said after a prolonged and uncomfortable silence.

"Oh my God," she said, tears rushing to her eyes.

"Emma, no. Listen to me. Yes, that was my original

intention, okay. I wanted to charm you a little to see if it would help things. I don't want to lie to you about that. But once I knew who you were, I was nothing but sincere. You're my butterfly. I—"

He reached out to her, but Emma dodged him. "Don't. Just don't. I can't have you touching me and calling me pet names when I'm trying to come to terms with the fact that you were just using me."

"Emma, please. You've got to listen to me."

"No, I don't. The only thing I have to do is pack my office tomorrow and update my résumé. I need medical insurance and a way to support my baby."

"Our baby," he corrected.

Emma only ignored him. She couldn't think about that right now. A future of dealing with him as her baby's father was too painful a thought. "I need you to get your things and go home, Jonah."

He took a step toward her, but she backed away and he stopped short. "I told you I'd never let you go and I meant it, Emma."

His eyes pleaded with her, the deep blue tugging at her heartstrings, but she didn't dare back down. He'd used her to get what he'd wanted and she couldn't forget that. He'd destroyed her career and her reputation just to save his own ass. "I'm not giving you the choice, Jonah. I need you to leave. Right now." Her voice was as stone cold and unemotional as she could make it with her feelings threatening to explode out of her.

This time, he didn't bother to argue. He returned to the bedroom, gathered up the rest of his clothes and pulled them on without another word. Emma followed him to the front door, fighting to hold in her tears until he was gone.

"I didn't mean to hurt you, Emma," he said before stepping out the front door.

She closed and locked it behind him, and rested her forehead against the cold wood. The tears started flowing freely then.

"Well, you did," she whispered.

Eleven

"Someone is looking awfully grumpy this morning."

Jonah looked up from his desk to see his brother Noah standing in the doorway. Just the sight of him was enough to send his blood pressure rocketing.

His brother had chosen the wrong day to come strolling into his office with that smug grin on his face. He hadn't slept for days after the fight with Emma. He couldn't eat. The worst part was that he knew he'd handled the situation with her all wrong. He didn't know how he would fix things, if he even could. But he could get some justice by making the culprit that put him in that position pay.

Without responding, Jonah slowly stood up from his desk with his hands curled into fists at his sides. He had no doubt the waves of anger were rolling off him with the way the perpetual smirk on Noah's face faded.

Jonah stalked his brother around the room like a panther toying with his cornered prey. Slowly. Deliberately. Silently. He would savor this punishment. Weeks of frustration, heartache, not to mention millions of dollars—all because of his reckless, stupid younger brother.

"Jonah…" Noah held his hands up and backed away toward the conference room table. "Let me explain first, please."

"Oh, you're going to explain," Jonah said. "But you're going to do it with a split lip and a bloody nose."

"Oh, come on, Jonah. Physical violence? What would Mother say? I'm going to see her tonight. Do you want me to look like I've been in a fight?"

Normally, the mention of the grand dame would've given him pause, but not today. "Nope," he replied. "I want you to look like you've lost a fight."

Now Noah looked worried. He moved until the conference table was between them. "Why are you so angry? Did the Game Town deal fall through?"

"Did the Game Town deal fall through?" Jonah said with a near-hysterical edge to his voice. He had no idea. He hadn't heard a word on the deal since he left Emma's apartment Monday night. He laughed and continued to circle the table. "That's the least of my worries at the moment, Noah."

That puzzled his younger brother. "Well, wait. Really. What has happened? Because I spoke with the Game Town CEO yesterday and he sounded like he understood and everything would go through just fine."

Jonah froze. He hadn't. Noah hadn't gone to their potential partner and spoken with him without even telling Jonah he was back in the country. He wouldn't. "You what?"

"I'll tell you everything if you sit down and promise

not to hit me. That's why I came here after all. I'm not stupid."

Jonah sincerely doubted that, but he was more curious about his brother's story at the moment. He couldn't fathom a scenario where he could explain the theft to Carl and have everything be okay. "Fine. But I still might hit you."

"Fine," Noah agreed. "Please sit down and let me finish first."

Jonah returned to his desk, his eyes never leaving his younger brother as he crossed the room and sat in his chair. Noah took a seat in the guest chair, perching on the edge as though he were preparing to make a quick getaway.

"Talk," Jonah demanded.

"I got back from Thailand two days ago," Noah explained. "The jet lag is unbelievable, really. I spent the first day in bed, and the next day Melody called me and told me there were whispers in the halls that the Game Town deal might not go through because of me and the money. I felt bad about the whole thing, so I went to Game Town and talked to the CEO myself."

Noah Flynn was not known for his initiative, so Jonah refrained from interrupting him to see exactly what his angle was with all of this. There had to be an angle. Had to. Noah always had an angle.

"I explained to him what the money was for and that it was extenuating circumstances that would never happen again."

Every word out of his brother's mouth made Jonah angrier. "And what, exactly, was the money for, Noah?"

"Ransom."

Well, that was certainly not what he was expecting. Was he serious? "Ransom for whom?"

"For my son."

Jonah didn't think his younger brother could shock him any more than he already had, but Noah was always full of surprises. "What son? You don't have a son."

Noah sighed. "So, about a year and a half ago, I met this doctor named Reagan Hardy at a charity event. We spent a week or so together, but not long after that, she took her next Doctors Without Borders assignment in Southeast Asia. She found out she was pregnant after she left and never told me. Her high-profile work in the community made her a target of the *chao pho*, the Thai mafia. They kidnapped Kai from the clinic where she was working. I didn't know he even existed until she called and asked for help. They demanded three million dollars in seven days or they would kill Kai. If Reagan contacted the police or told anyone, they would kill Kai. I had to act quickly, so I took the money and got on a plane. I'm sorry it caused you trouble, but I'd do it again in a heartbeat."

Somehow, the knowledge that his infant nephew had been in the hands of dangerous criminals made everything else seem trivial. "What happened?"

"I paid the ransom, and they returned him unharmed. The cops picked the kidnappers up the next day and we recovered most of the money, so I have it to pay back, as I promised. When I told Carl about it, he was understanding. It's not the kind of thing that happens very often. He said that he wouldn't hold that against you under the circumstances. Did he change his mind?"

Jonah shook his head. "I don't know. I haven't heard from Game Town. And at this point, I don't really care."

Noah studied Jonah for a moment with a curious look on his face. "The guy that nearly pummeled me a few minutes ago cared quite a bit. If you're not angry about the Game Town deal, what is it?"

Jonah didn't even know where to begin. How could he explain what he'd had with Emma and how he'd lost it?

"A woman has gotten to you," Noah stated.

Was it that obvious? "It hardly matters anymore, Noah. She was the auditor involved in this whole mess and she lost her job because of me."

"I'm sure you could help her find a new job. Hell, just hire her to work here."

Jonah shook his head. He knew Emma would say no, even now. Especially now. Everything blowing up in her face was just proof that she was right all along. "She wouldn't accept my help—I know it. Her reputation was the most important thing to her and I ended up ruining everything. Not just her job, but I screwed up us. She was the one, Noah. I love her. She's having my baby. And what did I do? I lied to her, trying to cover up the missing money and save our asses. It all blew up in my face."

"Is this the same woman from the Mardi Gras party? The one with the tattoo?"

Jonah could only nod. Just the mention of that night made the whole thing that much worse.

"Well, then you've got to fix it."

Jonah frowned. Things were always so simple to Noah for some reason. Even a harrowing kidnapping seemed to go smoothly for him. "How? I don't even know where to begin. I don't think she wants anything to do with me anymore."

"Probably not, but that doesn't mean it can't change. You said the most important thing to her was her reputation. So step up. Talk to her boss, tell them it wasn't her fault and get her job back. Taking the blame and making things right for her again is something you can offer her."

That all sounded good, but was it really enough? "What if she doesn't forgive me? Or does, but doesn't want me back?"

"Then you'll have to be content knowing you did the right thing."

For once, Jonah had to admit that Noah's idea was a good one. He might never win back her trust or her love, but he could make things right for her reputation and her career.

"Unless, of course, you're ready to make your big move."

Jonah's brows went up. "My big move?"

Noah held up his left hand and waggled his ring finger. "Give her everything she could possibly want from you in a two-pronged approach—restore her job and her reputation at work, and then restore her personal reputation and faith in you by declaring your love for her and asking for her hand in marriage. If she's that concerned about what people think of her at work, how does she feel about the fact that she's having your baby out of wedlock?"

"I already asked her to marry me. She said no."

"Well, ask again. And not because of the baby, but because you love her and you want to spend the rest of your life with her."

Once again, Noah was right. Jonah wouldn't say it out loud, though. Instead, he turned to his computer and looked up a few numbers. He had quite a few calls to make to put all this to rights.

"Who are you calling?" Noah asked as Jonah picked up his office phone.

"Everyone."

* * *

Emma was moping and she knew it. It had been a week since she'd been fired. At least she thought it was. She'd honestly lost track of time spent wallowing. She was pretty certain she'd worn the same cartoon-clad pajama pants three days in a row and hadn't washed her hair. She couldn't work up the enthusiasm to care. What did it matter? She had nowhere to go. No one to see. She was unemployed, single, pregnant and miserable.

Her phone rang just then, but she ignored it. She knew who it was just by the ringtone. Harper, Lucy and Violet all seemed to be taking turns checking in on her unsuccessfully. This time it happened to be Lucy calling. Emma had no doubt that before too long, they would show up at the door. They were on the visitor list and Violet had a key, so there would be no putting them off in that scenario.

It didn't matter. It felt almost as though little did. At least for now. After a few more days, she'd have no choice but to pick herself up, dust herself off and move on with life. There were bills to pay and soon, a baby to feed. She could borrow money from her parents, she supposed, but that would require her to confess what a mess her life had become lately. She wasn't ready for that yet.

That meant she had to work.

Emma had been looking at jobs online. Her only hope was that perhaps she could find another position before word got out about why she'd left her last one. They would eventually call a reference and her company would disclose that she was terminated and ineligible for rehire—she couldn't help that—but that would be better than the rumors that would build as they circulated. Especially once she could no longer hide her baby bump.

So far, she hadn't run across much of interest. There was a financial analyst position at Sandlin-Kline. That was probably a demotion, but she'd take it if they offered because they were a big firm where she could grow. They even had a day care for employees, which she would need before too long. There was also a CPA position at a large tax firm, which she could do, but it was a last resort. Taxes were not her favorite.

The only other job that had piqued her interest was the finance director at FlynnSoft. She'd giggled with hysteria when she saw the posting. Obviously she was a masochist for that to catch her eye. There was no other excuse as working with Jonah on a daily basis would be pure torture.

As it was, she would have to deal with him where the baby was concerned. Seeing him day in and day out, having him as her actual boss this time… That was out of the question. She was qualified for the position, and he'd already offered her the job twice, but that door had closed for them both when he lied to her. She would bag groceries at the corner market before she'd go crawling back to him for a job.

George and Pauline Dempsey would have a stroke if they caught their pregnant, single daughter bagging fruits and vegetables. But she'd do it, because if nothing else, she still had her pride and she would work to support her child. At least once she got out of this funk and moved on.

Emma was pondering eating ice cream for dinner when her phone rang again. This time it was Tim's number. She frowned as she picked it up and studied the screen. Why would Tim be calling? Her last check was coming via direct deposit. She'd already cleaned out everything from the office. If he thought she'd be willing to answer questions about her accounts after he fired her, he would be sadly mistaken.

Unable to resist finding out what was behind the call, she broke down and answered. “Hello.” She tried to hide the displeasure in her voice, but failed.

“Emma! Hey, this is Tim.”

“I know.”

“Do you have a second to chat?”

Emma sighed. “Not really, Tim. I’ve got an interview with Sandlin-Kline Financials first thing in the morning. I’ve got to pick up my suits from the cleaners before they close,” she lied. She hadn’t even submitted her résumé anywhere yet. She wasn’t about to let Tim know that, though.

“Well, then I’ll be brief, Emma. The truth of the matter is that I think I acted prematurely the other day in firing you. I was upset about being left out of the loop and I came down too hard. I shouldn’t have let you go for that.”

Emma slowly lowered herself down onto her living room sofa. Was Tim apologizing? Tim never apologized. There was something fishy about this. “I’m glad you recognize that,” she said. She wasn’t about to read any more into it, though. She hadn’t known of a single person cut from the company that ever returned.

“Things have been pretty chaotic the last few days. I think I underestimated how much work you actually managed here. There’s no way we can handle this workload without you. I know I’ve made a terrible mistake. I’d like you to come back, Emma.”

Her jaw dropped silently as she tried to absorb the information. He was giving her the chance to come back. “Are you serious?”

“I am. I really shouldn’t have blamed you for Flynn’s

actions. There's no way you could've known what he was doing. He's a very charismatic and persuasive man. You did everything I'd asked you to do."

Emma paused. This didn't sound like the manager she knew. "Tim, did Jonah talk you into giving me my job back?"

There was a long silence on the line.

"Tim," she pressed. "Did Jonah Flynn call you and tell you to give me my job back?"

Tim sighed heavily. "He did. He came into the office in person this morning. He explained about the kidnapping and how the management at Game Town wasn't holding FlynnSoft accountable."

"Kidnapping?" Emma was suddenly very lost. "What kidnapping?"

"Flynn's nephew. That's what the three million was for. Did he not tell you that? Anyway, he said the whole situation was entirely his fault, that he pressured you into going along with it and that I was a damn fool if I let you go."

"A damn fool?" All she could do was repeat what Tim was saying because she couldn't grasp the conversation at all. Jonah's nephew was kidnapped? What nephew?

"Yes, that's a direct quote. And since I am not a damn fool, I decided I needed to call and ask you to come back. What do you say, Emma?"

She didn't know what to say. The fact that Jonah had gone to Tim and stood up for her was amazing. And unexpected. She hadn't heard a word from him since he left her apartment. After throwing him out like that she didn't really expect to hear from him until it was time for the baby to be born. He hadn't had to do this for her. And yet he had.

Perhaps he'd meant what he said that day.

Emma had been too upset in the moment to really listen to his protests. As far as she was concerned it was all just excuses to cover up the fact that he'd been caught. But if he'd really been sincere once he knew who she really was… If he really truly cared about her and their baby… He probably thought she wouldn't believe him, so he did what he could to at least undo the damage he'd caused.

Jonah knew this was important to her. But the job and her reputation suddenly weren't as important as they used to be. In that moment, they shifted to a distant second to the future of her family. Her future with Jonah.

"Emma?"

"What?" She realized she wasn't listening to her phone conversation like she should.

"Will you come back?" Tim repeated.

Emma thought about it for a few moments, but she already knew her answer. "No thank you, Tim. I appreciate the offer, but I think it's time for me to move on to other things. Good luck to you. Goodbye."

She hit the button, disconnecting the call before she could lose her nerve. And she did almost instantly. The second she dropped the phone on the couch beside her, she felt the panic well up inside of her. She'd just turned down her job. It frustrated her, but it was a good job. It paid well. What the hell was she thinking?

Was she thinking she didn't need it because Jonah loved her and wanted her back? If that was the case, she'd just taken a huge gamble. He may have only been trying to be nice. Or to put things to rights. And she'd tossed that gift back in his face. Now what was she going to do?

The chime of her doorbell drew her attention from her

worries. What was the point of being in a building with a doorman when people could just trot up to her apartment unannounced? Who could it be, now? People just seemed unwilling to take the hint. She approached the door cautiously and peered out the peephole.

It was Lucy and Harper. As expected.

"What do you want?" Emma shouted through the closed door.

"What do we want?" Harper repeated. "It's Tuesday at seven, Em. What do you think we want?"

"I've called three times today, Emma," Lucy chimed in. "If you'd answer your phone this wouldn't be a surprise. It's girls' night!"

Shoot. Emma had totally and completely forgotten about girls' night. With a groan, she unlocked the door and pulled it open. "I'm sorry," she said. "I've lost track of the days, apparently."

Harper's appraising gaze ran over Emma's sloppy bun, oversize T-shirt and Eeyore pajama pants. "I can see that. Lucky for you, Lucy picked up everything for dinner tonight, so we won't starve."

Emma stepped back to let them in the apartment. "I don't know if I feel up to this tonight, you guys."

"Well, too bad," Lucy quipped. "Alice refuses to pay for cable despite her millions in the bank, so I don't get this channel at my place. I need to know what happens this week on our show. So I'm not leaving."

Lucy and Harper pushed past her and started setting up in her kitchen. Apparently this was happening whether she wanted it to or not.

"I'll go clean up a bit while you guys are getting dinner ready." Emma cruised through the living room, quickly snatching up tearstained tissues and empty snack cartons, and tossing them in the trash before she headed to the bathroom. She opted for a quick shower. By the time she emerged about fifteen minutes later, she felt a little more human and dinner was ready.

They gathered in the living room as they always did. This time, they each had plates of Greek food from a restaurant down the block from Lucy's place. Emma took a few big bites, savoring the first real food she'd eaten in days. It was so good it took her a moment to notice the other girls were looking at her with expectation on their faces.

"Where is Violet?" Emma asked, hoping to shift the discussion away from her for the moment.

"She's been MIA the last couple of days," Harper explained.

"I think she and Beau had another blowup," Lucy added. Violet had been dating an investment banker named Beau on and off for the last three years. "Who knows with those two? What's more important is what's going on with you and Jonah?" Lucy asked.

Emma told them about the phone call and how she'd just turned down the job offer from Tim. Lucy looked as stunned as Emma felt, but Harper seemed pleased by her reckless decision.

"Good girl," Harper said. "Tim deserves to suffer for turning on you like that. I bet he's up to his ears in your work right now."

Emma wasn't quite as convinced. "You think it was the right thing to do? I wish I was that certain. I mean, what the hell am I going to do now? I've got to work."

Harper nodded with a wicked glint in her eyes that made Emma uneasy. "Of course you have to work. And I have the perfect job in mind for you."

Twelve

Jonah eyed the tiny Tiffany blue box on his desk. Today was the day. He'd made things right with Tim and hopefully Emma had gotten her job back. He'd talked to Carl Bailey at Game Town and Noah had been right—things were smoothed out there. All the broken pieces from the last week had been glued back together except for one.

Tonight, when Emma got home from work, he was going to her apartment. He would beg her forgiveness, swear his love for her and their baby, and then present her with the shiny two-and-a-half-karat Soleste emerald cut ring set in platinum that he'd picked up on Fifth Avenue yesterday evening. He would ask her to marry him—the Big Move as Noah had suggested—and hopefully, the last piece would fall into place.

Hell, he'd even worn a suit and a tie for the occasion. A classic, black Armani suit with a green silk tie that reminded him of her eyes. Every employee he passed in the hallway made a joke about him having a job interview somewhere today, as though he didn't own the place.

A soft knock at the door caught his attention. Jonah snapped the box closed and scooped it off the desk and into his pocket. "Come in," he replied.

Pam stuck her head into the room. "I've got the stack of résumés for your interviews today."

Jonah had forgotten about that. He'd agreed to interview a few candidates for the financial director position. His human resources team had already narrowed it down to the top three candidates for him to talk to today. Fine. Whatever. If they could keep his brother from stealing from him again, they were hired.

Pam carried the papers into his office and set them down on the blotter. "Today is the big day, isn't it?"

Jonah nodded. Pam always knew his business because she made his business possible. She'd called Tiffany's and set up a private, after-hours appointment to select a ring. She'd made sure a car picked him up on time so he didn't miss it. She was the one who saw to it that his suit went to the cleaners so he'd have it to wear today. She was pleased as punch to be part of such a big moment for her boss.

"She's going to love it," Pam insisted. "Don't be nervous."

"I'm not nervous," Jonah said with a smile, but Pam didn't seem to buy it.

"Of course you're not. You've just got to keep it together through a couple of interviews and you'll be fine. The first candidate should be here at ten."

Jonah looked down at his watch. He had about ten minutes. Just enough time to scan the résumé, finish his coffee and think up a couple of intelligent-sounding questions for the interview. He hated doing this kind of stuff. Hiring smart, capable people was his goal. It was also his goal to do so well at that, that the smart, capable people could handle hiring more smart, capable people without him.

This was a director-level position, though. After the minor scandal with Noah, he needed to be really cautious about who he chose to head up the finance department. He needed Carl and any other CEO who might want to work with FlynnSoft to be completely confident in their decision.

With a sigh of resignation, Jonah took a big sip of his coffee and picked up the first résumé. As his eyes scanned the top, the coffee spewed from his mouth, coating the paper in mocha speckles.

Emma Dempsey.

Jonah reached for a napkin and wiped up the coffee, dabbing her résumé carefully so he could still read it. Never in a million years did he expect her to actually apply for this job. He'd offered it to her more than once and she'd turned him down. Of course, now the Game Town audit was over, maybe she felt freer to make that decision.

He tried to scan over her qualifications and education, but the only thought that kept running through his mind was that Emma was going to be here. In his office. In five minutes. He had her engagement ring in his pocket. Could he hold on to it for the entire interview and not give it to her? Play it cool?

Yeah, no. He was pretty certain he wouldn't make it through the meeting playing the coy interviewer and interviewee.

How was it that no one mentioned Emma applying before now? Someone had to have known. At the very least, Pam. Perhaps that was behind the twinkle in her eye earlier. He'd thought she was just excited about colluding over the engagement, but perhaps she knew something he didn't.

Another knock sounded at the door. It was exactly 10:00 a.m. and that meant she was here. "Come in," he repeated, and stood up at his desk.

Pam pushed the door open with a devious grin and behind her was Emma. At least it looked a bit like Emma, but not in any way he'd ever seen her at the office before. The stuffy suit and severe hair bun were gone. Her hair was down in loose brown waves around her face like it had been on their date. She was wearing a pair of dark denim skinny jeans with comfy-looking ballet flats and a T-shirt with a navy corduroy blazer over it.

It was the perfect mix of dress and casual, as though Emma had merged her style with his and finally found her niche here at FlynnSoft.

It looked good on her. Amazing. It made him want to reach out and stroke the waves of her hair between his fingertips. But he knew better. First and foremost, this was an interview and even if she had forgiven him, Emma would want to keep things professional.

"Jonah, this is your first applicant, Emma Dempsey." Pam grinned and disappeared from the office as quickly as she could manage.

He smiled and reached out his hand to greet her properly. "Hello, Miss Dempsey."

"Call me Emma, please," she said with a soft, knowing smile as she shook his hand.

It took everything he had for Jonah to let her go, but

he had to. "Please have a seat," he said, indicating the guest chair she'd sat in many times before.

Once they were settled, Jonah picked up her résumé and tried to think of something intelligent to say. He decided to continue as though they'd never met before and start with his basic opening question for any interview. "So. Emma, please tell me a little about why you want to work here at FlynnSoft."

Normally, this question would help him pinpoint whether or not the applicant had the same core values as most FlynnSoft employees. A love of gaming and graphic design, joy for their work, hell, even an interest in free coffee was worth a mention. People who appreciated his workplace innovations before they even started would be much happier and more productive employees later on.

"Well," Emma began, "I recently had an opportunity to work with some of the FlynnSoft family as part of an audit I conducted for my previous position. It was not at all what I was used to in a corporate environment, but after I adjusted, I really learned to appreciate what FlynnSoft offers their employees."

"And what is that?"

"Freedom to work at their own pace on projects that excite them. All the tools they need—traditional or otherwise—to get their jobs done. Time and amenities to recharge and maintain their enthusiasm for their work. Also, an owner and CEO that truly cares for his staff. At first I thought he was all about the money, but I realized that so much of what motivated him was the success of his company for the benefit of the employees that depended on him."

"So you understand that despite how things might look, he was just trying to protect them?" he asked.

Emma nodded.

"And you realize that he would never deliberately hurt one of his employees, even if they were just on a temporary assignment?"

Emma looked at him with her big green eyes and he was happy to see no hurt hiding there. "Yes. I can see that now. At first, it was hard to believe, but I've had a little time to think about it and I've really come to appreciate what he was willing to do."

She understood why he did what he did. Jonah wanted to sigh loudly in relief and thank his lucky stars, but he wouldn't. Not yet. "Okay, great answer. Now, what skills and experience do you have that would be an asset to FlynnSoft if we were to bring you on board?"

At this question, Emma grinned. "Well, I am very structured and organized. I like to keep things professional in the workplace, but I also know when to let my hair down. I think that with my experience, I am the perfect candidate to keep not only the FlynnSoft financial department in line, but to keep the CEO himself in line, as well."

"Oh really?" Jonah's brows rose in curiosity. Now things were getting interesting.

"Yes. He has some weaknesses that I can exploit when necessary to keep things on track."

"What kind of weaknesses?" Jonah asked.

Emma's soft pink lips curled into a smile. "Me, for one thing. I happen to know that the CEO has a soft spot where I'm concerned."

Jonah leaned forward onto his elbows, getting as close to her as he could with the massive furniture between them. "That's true. You could probably negotiate an amazing benefits package with that kind of leverage."

"I'm mostly interested in maternity leave," Emma responded. "Flexible schedules and telecommuting are always good with little ones, as well. If my office was big enough, I would also like to be able to bring my daughter in to work with me."

Jonah opened his mouth to respond, but found there were no words. He had been following along until suddenly—*wham*! Did she just say *daughter*? They were having a girl? How could she know so soon?

Emma reached into her portfolio and slid a grainy black-and-white photo across the desk to him. He'd seen normal ultrasound pictures before, but this one had amazing detail.

"I had a 3-D ultrasound done yesterday. Fourteen weeks is still a little early to be absolutely sure, but the technician was very confident that I, we, are having a little girl."

Emma was fairly certain the interview was over. Jonah had managed to maintain as professional a face as he'd ever had, but the minute she slid the photo of his daughter across the desk to him, it was done.

Sitting there, she had the rare opportunity to actually watch a man fall in love with his child. It was something she thought she might never see before now, and she was so relieved she could almost cry. But she wouldn't. She could already see the sheen of tears in Jonah's eyes and the whole meeting would devolve into sobbing if she started.

Jonah stared at the picture for a few minutes before gently wiping at his eyes and setting it back down on his desk. "I am fairly certain we can accommodate whatever needs you may have to bring our daughter into the office.

I'll kick Noah out of his office and turn it into a nursery if you want me to."

He smiled and stood up, walking slowly around his desk to her. He stopped just short of touching her, sitting down in the other guest chair beside her so they were at eye level. "I love you, Emma," he said without the slightest hesitation. "I love you and I've missed you so badly. I'm so sorry that I hurt you. I never meant to do that."

Emma reached out and covered his hand with her own. She gave it a gentle squeeze, reveling in the touch of his skin against hers once again. "I know. I love you, too. And I'm sorry, as well."

Jonah frowned at her. "Sorry for what? You didn't do anything wrong."

"Yes, I did," she insisted. Emma had put a lot of thought into this the last few days and she wanted to make sure he knew how she felt now. "I let my worries about what other people think of me interfere with living my life and loving you the way I wanted to. I've spent my whole life more concerned with what other people thought than what I thought of myself. I didn't like the uptight, boring woman I'd become, but I thought that's who I should be.

"You loved the parts of me that I was ashamed of, and it helped me to realize that what other people think of me is none of my business. All that really matters is that I'm happy and living my life the way I want to live it. And I want to live it with you. I want to make a family with you, Jonah, however we decide to have it."

Emma didn't care if they got married with a big Plaza wedding, eloped at the courthouse or didn't get married at all. The big wedding was her mother's dream anyway, not hers. A wedding and a marriage was only important if they put importance on it. All Emma wanted was Jonah in her life, and in her baby's life, every day. She wanted to love him and be with him. That was what would make her happy.

Jonah looked at her for a moment and she could swear there was a flicker of nervousness across his face. Before she could say anything else, he reached into his coat pocket and slipped out of his chair onto one knee.

He kept a tight grip on her left hand as he moved, so Emma had to clutch the arm of the chair with her right. Her entire body tensed up as she watched him and realized what he was doing. "Jonah..." she gasped, but he ignored her.

In his left hand, he held a Tiffany blue jewelry box. Before he opened it, he looked at her and said, "I know you said you didn't want to marry me the last time I mentioned it. You said we hardly knew each other and that if, given time, I fell in love with you and wanted to get married, you would reconsider." His thumb anxiously stroked the back of her hand as he spoke, making it hard for her to focus on his words.

Finally, he let go long enough to pull the black jewelry box out of its bright blue container and pry open the lid. He held the ring up for her to see it. Nestled in the velvet was the ring of her dreams. Emerald cut, surrounded in tiny diamonds and with a delicate band inset with even more. It picked up the morning sunlight in Jonah's office, displaying a dazzling show of rainbow colors. It was simply breathtaking.

"I'm hoping that you've reconsidered, Emma. I know that not much time has really passed, but this week without you has felt like a lifetime. I couldn't let another day, much less another week, go by without telling you how much I love you. And that I want to make you my wife." Jonah paused for a second to look her in the eye and swallow hard. "Will you marry me, Emma?"

How had she gotten to this point in her life? From her lowest moment before that Mardi Gras party, to the thrill of romance with a stranger, to the crushing loss of everything she held dear… And now love. Marriage. A family.

"I will. Of course I will, Jonah," Emma managed with tears filling her eyes.

With a cheer of satisfaction, Jonah leaned in and gave her a firm, soft kiss. Emma held his scruffy face with both hands to keep him close for as long as possible, but eventually he pulled away. Taking her hand in his, he plucked the ring out of its velvet bed and slid it onto her finger. It was perhaps half a size too big, but with her blooming pregnancy, she had no doubt it would be snug before too long.

Emma admired the glittering stone on her finger, then turned her attention back to her fiancé. "Thank you, Jonah," she said. "You're amazing and I'm so lucky to have found you."

Jonah stood up and shook his head. He pulled Emma to her feet, then wrapped his arms around her waist. "I'm the lucky one, butterfly."

They would have to agree to disagree. Emma put an end to the discussion by pressing her lips to his and losing herself in his kiss. Somehow, despite the odds being against her, everything had come together and she couldn't be happier. Sometimes the scary decisions in life reaped the greatest rewards, and today, her reward was marrying the most amazing man she'd ever met.

A chime sounded over their shoulder from Jonah's

computer. "Crap," he groaned as he broke away from her kiss and looked down at his watch.

Emma frowned at Jonah. "What's the matter?"

"Well, to be honest," he said with a sigh, "none of this was supposed to happen until tonight at your apartment. I wasn't expecting to see you this morning until I saw your résumé."

Emma wouldn't tell him that she'd sworn everyone, from HR to Pam, to absolute secrecy about the interview. "So?"

"So, you were my first interview of the day. I've got two more lined up after this. Why didn't they schedule you last? I want to take you home and make love to my fiancée."

Emma laughed, pulling back from his snug grip on her body. "Well, that's not going to happen right now, so you'd better get prepared, Mr. Flynn. Even if you marry me, you'll still need a financial director."

Jonah narrowed his blue gaze at her in surprise. "You mean you don't want the job?"

"Of course I want the job!" Emma said. "But I want it fair and square. I told you before, I'm not letting anyone say I earned it on my back."

At that, Jonah laughed. "You're seriously going to make me interview all those people even though I have every intention of hiring you in the end?"

"Yes. I'm pretty sure your HR director would say the same thing. And if you hire me," she said, poking him in the chest with her finger, "it better be because I'm the most qualified." She might be marrying the boss, but Emma still had her pride. She'd worked hard to achieve a director-level position and she wanted it on merit alone.

Jonah studied her face for a moment and nodded. He took a step back and sucked in a deep lungful of air. Then he held his hand out to Emma. “Well, thank you for coming in today, Emma. Pam will see you back down to Human Resources. I’m sure they have some paperwork for you to fill out and they can answer any questions you have about the company and our total compensation package.”

Emma grinned as she shook his hand and picked up her leather portfolio. “Thank you for your time, Mr. Flynn. When should I expect to hear back from you about the position?”

With her hand still in his, he leaned in and whispered into her ear. “I’ll be at your place by six.”

* * * * *

If you liked this story of pregnancy and passion, pick up these other novels from Andrea Laurence!

MORE THAN HE EXPECTED
HIS LOVER'S LITTLE SECRET
THIRTY DAYS TO WIN HIS WIFE
THE CEO'S UNEXPECTED CHILD
THE PREGNANCY PROPOSITION

Available now from Mills & Boon Desire!

***

And don't miss the next LITTLE SECRETS *story.*
LITTLE SECRETS: HOLIDAY BABY BOMBSHELL
by Karen Booth.
Available November 2017!